Madame Bovary

Madame Bovary

PATTERNS OF PROVINCIAL LIFE

by Gustave Flaubert

TRANSLATED BY
FRANCIS STEEGMULLER

THE MODERN LIBRARY • New York

Translator's Introduction

SCHOLARS WITH A CALENDRICAL TURN OF MIND HAVE COMPUTED that the first scene of *Madame Bovary* — Charles's entry into the classroom — takes place in October, 1827, and the last scene — Charles's death — in August, 1846. The married life of Charles and Emma extends over a period of nine years, beginning in 1837.

In French history, this was the heyday of the "July Monarchy" — the reign of King Louis-Philippe, who was brought to power by the Revolution of 1830 and ousted by the Revolution of 1848. Louis-Philippe was known as the "Citizen King" — also as "The Pear," from the unfortunate resemblance of the shape of his head to the fruit whose name is sometimes used in France to denote a dull fellow.

Member of the Orléans family though Louis-Philippe was, his regime was blatantly, almost aggressively, middle-class. His advice to his subjects was: "Get rich!" He strolled about Paris carrying an umbrella, like a bourgeois. In dress, furniture, architecture and decoration the style associated with his name connotes everything graceless, pretentious and unimaginative. The French bourgeoisie—heirs of the victors of the first French Revolution of 1789—were solidly in the saddle.

Characteristics of life under the July Monarchy, and events of the regime, are thickly mirrored in *Madame Bovary*. The novelist's smallest touch is apt to be a political or social echo, employed to "situate" his story. When Emma burns incense that she had "bought at an Algerian shop in Rouen," it is a reminder that Algerian products were in fashion during the French conquest of Algeria in the 1840's. Her surprise, at the chateau of La Vaubyessard, at seeing that "several of the ladies had failed to put their gloves in their wineglasses," points up a difference between social classes. Provincial *bourgeoises* of that time, brought up in a spirit of genteel puritanism, considered it ladylike to eschew wine at dinner parties; they proclaimed their intention by filling their wineglasses with their flimsy evening gloves or with a lace handkerchief. Ladies of the old aristocracy were freer in their behavior.

In laying his novel in the July Monarchy, Flaubert was writing of the period of his own youth. He was born in 1821; and he witnessed, in his twenty-seventh year, some of the Paris street-fighting that marked the end of the regime that he had always considered frustrating to noble aspirations. In the autumn of 1849 he set out with a friend for an eighteen-month tour of the Near East to get a "bellyful of color." So far he had produced some turgid, "escapist" writing, but had published nothing. Now on his return to France he sat down almost immediately to write the novel that marked his break with the romanticism of his early days. His declared aim was to paint a mercilessly accurate picture of lower middle-class provincial life in all its stifling dreariness. His method was to contrast it with the fantasies of his heroine, whose romantic yearnings reflect both the futility and the persistent attraction of older ways of life.

The composition took him five years. *Madame Bovary* was first published serially in a magazine, the *Revue de Paris*. The editors, fearing censorship, attempted to bowdlerize it by cutting; but even so Flaubert was summoned before the public prosecutor for "offenses against morality and religion." After a sensational trial, marked by fiery exchanges of French eloquence between the state and the defense lawyers, he was acquitted; and the publication of the novel in book form, under the title *Madame Bovary, Moeurs de Province*, was announced on April 18, 1857. Its popularity was immediate. Superficially it seemed a *succès de scandale*, but the best French critics and artists knew that this was no ordinary best seller, and that for once public acclaim and true merit coincided.*

The poet Baudelaire, who had himself recently been fined by a court for the "immorality" of his volume *Les Fleurs du Mal*, was among those who sensed the epoch-making significance of *Madame Bovary*. Since Balzac, he said in his review, the art of the novel had been stagnant in France, and despite various attempts to renovate it, general interest had not been captured. Now Flaubert had come and opened a new horizon. Analyzing Flaubert's

---

* The story of Flaubert's youth, his Near Eastern tour, and his emergence as a writer, the story of the composition and reception of *Madame Bovary*, can be read in the translator's *Flaubert and Madame Bovary* (Farrar, Straus and Company, 1950; Knopf, Vintage Books, 1957). Flaubert described his own literary birth-pangs in incomparable letters: see *The Selected Letters of Flaubert* (Farrar, Straus and Young, 1953; Knopf, Vintage Books, 1957).

achievement in detail, Baudelaire showed that every element of *Madame Bovary*, whether of form or content, was
perfectly designed to break the public's apathy and to give
society and literature the needed sting of the gadfly.

Indeed, the translator who seeks to do justice to the
original of *Madame Bovary*, and who by the very nature of
his effort becomes more intimate with the text than any
reader no matter how critical, soon realizes that nothing
in this novel has been left to chance, that nothing is
arbitrary. Everything flows from the central conception,
as by a natural law. The plot, the psychology of the pro-
tagonists, the tragic end, the triumph of that epitome of
bourgeois banality, Monsieur Homais, are all of a piece. This
extraordinary coherence is reflected in the masterly and
subtle construction, full of foreshadowings and echoes,
points and counterpoints, intricate cross-references.

Exactness of time-portrayal had to be matched by place-
description of the utmost precision. Flaubert chose a setting which he knew intimately. He was born in the city
of Rouen, a river port on the right bank of the lower Seine.
Before the French Revolution, Rouen had been the capital
of the province of Normandy; and with the redivision of
France into departments it was made the prefecture of
the department of the Seine-Inférieure (rebaptized Seine-
Maritime in 1955), whose sub-prefectures are the Channel
ports of Le Havre and Dieppe. The action of the book
takes place partly in Rouen, partly in the countryside lying between Rouen and those two sub-prefectures—a countryside known as the *pays de Caux* (probably from the
Latin *calx*, chalk, referring to the quality of the soil). The
inhabitants are called *cauchois* (male) and *cauchoises* (female); and *Madame Bovary* abounds in references to their
local customs and costumes. It also contains a certain
amount of the rural dialect and habits of speech—peasant
and near-peasant words and characteristic turns of phrase.

Certain earlier translators, Englishmen or persons living in England, have attempted to reproduce the flavor of this popular language by making some of the "lower-class" characters—Emma Bovary's father, for example, and Madame Lefrançois the hotel-keeper—sound like a cross between present-day British rustics and Shakespearean clowns. In the present translation no attempt has been made to transform *cauchois* country speech into a New England twang or a Texas drawl. Incidentally, not all of Flaubert's rural references are clear even to French readers of the present day. Most of them have to be told, for example, that the maggoty moles which Monsieur Rouault saw hanging on tree branches had been put there by peasants in the belief that they would frighten away live moles.

Flaubert was the son of a surgeon. His father—the model, supposedly, for the Doctor Larivière who comes galloping to Emma Bovary's deathbed—was for many years head of the Hôtel-Dieu (public hospital) of Rouen. The family lived in a wing of the building, and from his earliest youth Flaubert was accustomed to the sight of illness, death, operations and dissections. This medical background was undoubtedly decisive in his making Emma Bovary's husband a medical man. And since Charles Bovary was to be depicted as a creature in many ways inferior, his creator made him an *officier de santé*—a licensed medical man without an M.D. degree. Such a practitioner could treat patients only in the department of France in which he had passed his examination, and could perform important surgical operations only when an M.D. was present. The category of *officiers de santé* (which existed under other names in Germany, Russia and elsewhere) was originally created to assure medical service in French country districts. It was abolished in 1892. Not everyone holding the inferior rank of *officier de santé* was a poor physician. Flaubert himself, when he lived in the country, often consulted a "*simple officier de santé*" named Fortin, whom he greatly respected. In the present translation the term has been kept in French, since the rank it designates does not exist in American life and a literal rendering ("health officer") would only mislead. On the other hand, Charles Bovary is referred to in these pages as a "doctor" whenever Flaubert calls him a "*médecin*"—a term which in France is also applied to real M.D.'s.

Depending on how well acquainted, and how sympathetic, one is with the ardors of novel writing, the five years that Flaubert spent on *Madame Bovary* will seem very long indeed, or a normal amount of time, or perhaps even somewhat short. Flaubert's letters are full of laments about the time and effort his task required. Still in existence are numbers of his preliminary drafts and rewritings: many a passage was slowly and painfully composed, slowly and painfully recast in a dozen or more different versions, only finally to be discarded entirely. Very occasionally the multiplicity of his different versions was a source of error for the author. For example, Flaubert originally made Charles's fee for the setting of Monsieur Rouault's fracture one hundred francs; later he reduced it to seventy-five; but he forgetfully left the rest of the sentence unchanged. The resulting impossibility—"seventy-five francs in two-franc pieces"—is Flaubert's most famous nod. Attentive readers will also note that the façade of the Yonville town hall has three columns on one page and four on another, that Yonvillians turn sometimes right, sometimes left, to reach the cemetery from the town square, and that Emma's financial transactions are somewhat mixed up mathematically. Slips of this kind have been left untouched. In one or two instances of a different kind, however, the translator has presumed to emend. At La Vaubyessard, the travel snobs chattering about Italy speak (in the French original) of *"les Cassines"*—a mysterious reference: surely Flaubert meant the Cascine, the public park in Florence, at that time a particularly fashionable spot for afternoon drives. In the Hotel de Boulogne, where we are told that Emma "even said 'our slippers,' meaning a pair that Léon had given her," all the French texts (both manuscript and printed) read "my slippers." The word "my" in this place seems merely an inadvertence: to retain it would render meaningless a particularly keen bit of observation.

Quite distinct from those rare slips is another type of departure from exactitude. Famous though he is for precision of detail, Flaubert felt free to neglect it when such a course was justified artistically. Painstaking scholars have been able to show, for instance, that Emma could not have spent as much time with Léon in Rouen on Thursdays as she did, if the time schedule of the Hirondelle and the duration of the Yonville-Rouen run were as Flaubert describes them elsewhere in the book. Her rendezvous with Rodolphe, both at his chateau and in her garden, do not invite too-close chronological and topographical scrutiny. In the present translation, no attempt has been made to eliminate such discrepancies: they will disturb only those who confuse artistic realism with mechanical faithfulness to detail, regardless of its significance. On the other hand, a few minor imprecisions, apparently resulting from merely mechanical causes—for instance, illogical sequence of verbs describing an action—have not been preserved in translation.

One of Flaubert's great concerns during the years of writing *Madame Bovary* was for the rhythm and assonance of his prose. He had a specific artistic idea in mind, which required the transformation of even the most sordid subject matter by the magic of style. Typically eloquent of his effort is a passage from a letter to his friend Louis

Bouilhet about Emma Bovary's financial difficulties: "Speaking of money, I'm tangled up in explanations of promissory notes, discounts, etc., that I don't understand too well myself. I'm arranging all this in rhythmical dialogue, God help me!" Only a Flaubert among translators could do full justice to Flaubert the novelist in this respect. It is of course impossible to retain in translation the precise rhythm of each of Flaubert's carefully polished sentences; nor would an attempt to reproduce the general characteristic cadence of his prose in a foreign tongue lead to anything but disaster. But there must be an English equivalent of the French music. Without it, the idea of what *Madame Bovary* "is like" in the original could not begin to be conveyed. An over-all rhythmic flow is inseparable from the novel's total coherence.

A work as "realistic" as this, filled with concrete details, many of them belonging to another age, constantly defies any translator to accomplish even his most basic task—accurate rendering of individual terms. In *Madame Bovary*, children walking through the fields don't merely pull the flowers from the oats; they "pull the bell-shaped flowers from the oat stalks." The various versions of the novel already existing in English are strewn with unintentional comedy. Emma's cousin, the fish peddler, who brings "a pair of soles" (fish native to the English Channel) as a wedding present, turns up in one translation as a cobbler who brings a pair of (shoe) soles. In another, Emma doesn't wear "a cocked hat over one ear" at the mi-carême ball as she should: rather, as she dances she has "a Chinese lantern dangling from one ear"—a merry picture indeed. And Charles, the medical student, instead of singing songs at student gatherings, (*"aux bienvenues"*), is made to sing them to "women who were always welcome." But even apart from trying to avoid such howlers as those, the translator has often to cope with other, subtler puzzles.

What sound did Flaubert have in mind, exactly, when he wrote that the strings of Emma's old piano *"frisaient"* as she pounded? What is a *"cliquetis des capucines,"* which at a present-arms makes a noise "like a copper cauldron rolling down a flight of stairs"? When bourgeois in the streets stand *"au coin des bornes,"* what is the picture? To find out, one exhausts dictionaries, encyclopedias and reference librarians; one telephones to friends, acquaintances and strangers; one consults practitioners of various trades, both at home and abroad. An occasional word one decides to leave in French. *"Huissier,"* for example: "bailiff," the usual rendering, does not evoke anything specific in the American reader's mind, whereas "sheriff" is too full of Western connotations.

Madame Bovary was not only the most "realistic" novel of its age. It was also the most "psychological." More than any of his predecessors or contemporaries among fiction writers, Flaubert probes his characters' minds, trying to account fully for their actions and emotions. He excels at showing the unconscious mind at work: were it not for the vocabulary, it would be easy to forget that Freud was less than a year old when *Madame Bovary* was published. Often the translator has to resist the temptation to interpret Flaubert's words in the light of present-day theories. When Emma, consumed by her repressed early passion for Léon, finds her husband exasperating, Flaubert says that she *"s'étonnait parfois des conjectures atroces qui lui arrivaient à la pensée"*—"sometimes she was surprised by the horrible possibilities that she imagined." Does Flaubert imply, here, that Emma feared accidents happening to her husband, and that these fears reflected wishful thinking? Plausible as such an interpretation would be, the translator regretfully decides to confine himself to translation. In other cases, however, detailed and precise passages of psychological analysis must be almost paraphrased to make their rich allusions as intelligible and as telling in English as they are in the original.

A whole body of critical literature has grown up around *Madame Bovary*, which makes the most of all possible symbolic implications of individual words and phrases. Some critics point exclusively to the many biological metaphors denoting fading and decay; others tell us that the *leitmotiv* is physical, namely, the motions of slipping and falling; and the novel has even been described mathematically, as a "circular" concept. It is not the translator's role to judge these various theories, but he cannot help noticing that occasionally their authors resort to arguments based on obvious, if minor, mistranslation. For example, when Doctor Larivière, at Emma's deathbed, says, "*C'est bien, c'est bien,*" he is merely murmuring the equivalent of "Yes, yes"—expressing more or less polite impatience with Doctor Canivet, whose circumstantial narration of the case is pointless now that Emma is beyond help. On the basis of an inaccurate rendering ("Good, good"), Doctor Larivière's words have been interpreted as expressing his satisfaction in Emma's imminent death, a satisfaction reflecting Flaubert's supposed conception of his heroine as a character too sublime for this world.

On the other hand, a perfectly "correct" translation of a phrase can be inadequate, in that it fails to render an essential symbolic meaning. On the last page of the book Flaubert proclaims Homais' growing prosperity by saying "*Il fait une clientèle d'enfer*"—which appears in various English versions as "His practise grows like wildfire," or "He is doing extremely well," or "He has a terrific practise." All these are faithful to the French idiom. And yet, surely, the word "*enfer*" ("hell") isn't present in the original for nothing. The mere use of the term suggests at once that Homais, prince of the bourgeois, is an earthly counterpart of the prince of darkness.

The foregoing notes make it apparent, perhaps, that to translate a masterpiece with any justice requires an effort which parallels the author's own labor in translating his idea into adequate words. Problems of language, transition, rhythm, symbolism, and secret relationships that make up texture—all these have to be solved anew, in a new medium. The great difference is, of course, that the translator does not work in the dark. Even though the trail he follows has to be followed in a vehicle which it was not meant to accommodate, there *is* a trail. The author has blazed it in his lonely and perilous earlier journey, leaving behind him the certainty that the terrain is not impassable. The translator of *Madame Bovary* knows that all these ideas, all these emotions, all these subtleties and shadings have been expressed in French. And he takes it for granted, as a kind of postulate, that they can all be re-expressed in English. His faith in his own language is such that he will never be tempted to excuse inadequacies by pointing to its inherent limitations; he will blame only his own human fallibility.

Francis Steegmuller

PART ONE

I

WE WERE IN STUDY-HALL WHEN THE HEADMASTER ENTERED, followed by a new boy not yet in school uniform and by the handyman carrying a large desk. Their arrival disturbed the slumbers of some of us, but we all stood up in our places as though rising from our work.

The headmaster motioned us to be seated; then, turning to the teacher:

"Monsieur Roger," he said in an undertone, "here's a pupil I'd like you to keep your eye on. I'm putting him in the last year of the lower school. If he does good work and behaves himself we'll move him up to where he ought to be at his age."

The newcomer, who was hanging back in the corner so

that the door half hid him from view, was a country lad of about fifteen, taller than any of us. He had his hair cut in bangs like a cantor in a village church, and he had a gentle, timid look. He wasn't broad in the shoulders, but his green jacket with its black buttons seemed tight under the arms; and through the vents of his cuffs we could see red wrists that were clearly unaccustomed to being covered. His yellowish breeches were hiked up by his suspenders, and from them emerged a pair of blue-stockinged legs. He wore heavy shoes, hobnailed and badly shined.

We began to recite our lessons. He listened avidly, as though to a sermon—he didn't dare even cross his legs or lean on his elbows; and at two o'clock, when the bell rang for the next class, the teacher had to tell him to line up with the rest of us.

We always flung our caps on the floor when entering a classroom, to free our hands; we hurled them under the seats from the doorway itself, in such a way that they struck the wall and raised a cloud of dust: that was "how it was done."

But whether he had failed to notice this ritual or hadn't dared join in observance of it, his cap was still in his lap when we'd finished reciting our prayer. It was a headgear of composite order, containing elements of an ordinary hat, a hussar's busby, a lancer's cap, a sealskin cap and a nightcap: one of those wretched things whose mute hideousness suggests unplumbed depths, like an idiot's face. Ovoid and stiffened with whalebone, it began with three convex strips; then followed alternating lozenges of velvet and rabbit's fur, separated by a red band; then came a kind of bag, terminating in a cardboard-lined polygon intricately decorated with braid. From this hung a long, excessively thin cord ending in a kind of tassel of gold netting. The cap was new; its peak was shiny.

"Stand up," said the teacher.

He rose. His cap dropped to the floor. Everyone began to laugh.

He bent over for it. A boy beside him sent it down again with his elbow. Once again he picked it up.

"How about getting rid of your helmet?" suggested the teacher, who was something of a wit.

Another loud laugh from the students confused the poor fellow. He didn't know whether to keep the cap in his hand, drop it on the floor, or put it on his head. He sat down again and placed it in his lap.

"Stand up," repeated the professor, "and tell me your name."

The new boy mumbled a name that was unintelligible.

"Say it again!"

The same jumble of syllables came out, drowned in the jeers of the class.

"Louder!" cried the teacher. "Louder!"

With desperate resolve the new boy opened a mouth that seemed enormous, and as though calling someone he cried at the top of his lungs the word "Charbovari!"

This touched off a roar that rose *crescendo*, punctuated with shrill screams. There was a shrieking, a banging of desks as everyone yelled, "Charbovari! Charbovari!" Then the din broke up into isolated cries that slowly diminished, occasionally starting up again along a line of desks where a stifled laugh would burst out here and there like a half-spent firecracker.

But a shower of penalties gradually restored order; and the teacher, finally grasping the name Charles Bovary after it had been several times spelled out and repeated and he had read it aloud himself, at once commanded the poor devil to sit in the dunce's seat, at the foot of the platform. He began to move toward it, then hesitated.

"What are you looking for?" the teacher demanded.

"My c—" the new boy said timidly, casting an uneasy glance around him.

"Everybody will stay and write five hundred lines!"

Like Neptune's "*Quos ego*," those words, furiously uttered, cut short the threat of a new storm. "Quiet!" the indignant teacher continued, mopping his forehead with a handkerchief he took from his toque. "As for you," he said to the new boy, "you'll copy out for me twenty times all the tenses of *ridiculus sum*."

Then, more gently: "You'll find your cap. No one has stolen it."

All was calm again. Heads bent over copybooks, and for the next two hours the new boy's conduct was exemplary, even though an occasional spitball, sent from the nib of a pen, struck him wetly in the face. He wiped himself each time with his hand, and otherwise sat there motionless, his eyes lowered.

That evening, in study period, he took his sleeveguards from his desk, arranged his meager equipment, and carefully ruled his paper. We saw him working conscientiously, looking up every word in the dictionary, taking great pains. It was doubtless thanks to this display of effort that he was not demoted to a lower form. For while he had a fair knowledge of grammatical rules, his translations lacked elegance. He had begun his Latin with his village priest: his thrifty parents had sent him away to school as late as possible.

His father, Monsieur Charles-Denis-Bartholomé Bovary, had been an army surgeon's aide, forced to leave the service about 1812 as a result of involvement in a conscription scandal. He had then turned his personal charms to advantage, picking up a dowry of 60,000 francs brought to him by a knit-goods dealer's daughter who had fallen in love with his appearance. He was a handsome man, much given to bragging and clanking his spurs. His side whiskers merged with his mustache, his fingers were always loaded with rings, his clothes were flashy: he had the look of a bully and the easy cajoling ways of a traveling salesman. Once married, he lived off his wife's money for two or three years. He ate well, rose late, smoked big porcelain pipes, stayed out every night to see a show, spent much of his time in cafés. His father-in-law died and left very little; this made him indignant, and he "went into textiles" and lost some money. Then he retired to the country, with the intention of "making things pay." But he knew as little about crops as he did about calico; and since he rode his horses instead of working them in the fields, drank his cider bottled instead of selling it by the barrel, ate his best poultry, and greased his hunting boots with the fat from his pigs, he soon realized that he had better give up all idea of profit-making.

So for two hundred francs a year he rented, in a village on the border of Normandy and Picardy, a dwelling that was half farm, half gentleman's residence; and there, surly, eaten by discontent, cursing heaven, envying everyone, he shut himself up at the age of forty-five, disgusted with mankind, he said, and resolved to live in peace.

His wife had been mad about him at the beginning; in her love she had tendered him a thousand servilities that had alienated him all the more. Once sprightly, all outgoing and affectionate, with age she had grown touchy, nagging and nervous, like stale wine turning to vinegar. At first she had suffered uncomplainingly, watching him chase after every trollop in the village and having him come back to her at night from any one of twenty disgusting places surfeited and stinking of drink. Then her pride rebelled. She withdrew into her shell; and swallowing her rage she bore up stoically until her death. She was always busy, always doing things. She was constantly running to lawyers, to the judge, remembering when notes fell due and obtaining renewals; and at home she was forever ironing, sewing, washing, keeping an eye on the hired men, figuring their wages. Monsieur, meanwhile, never lifted a finger. He sat smoking in the chimney corner and spitting into the ashes, continually falling into a grumpy doze and waking to utter uncomplimentary remarks.

When she had a child it had to be placed out with a wet nurse. And then later, when the little boy was back with its parents, he was pampered like a prince. His mother stuffed him with jams and jellies; his father let him run barefoot, and fancied himself a disciple of Rousseau to the point of saying he'd be quite willing to have the boy go naked like a young animal. To counter his wife's maternal tendencies he tried to form his son according to a certain virile ideal of childhood and to harden his constitution by subjecting him to strict discipline, Spartan-style. He sent him to bed without a fire, taught him to take great swigs of rum and to ridicule religious processions. But the child was pacific by nature, and such training had little effect. His mother kept him tied to her apron-strings: she made him paper cutouts, told him stories, and conversed with him in endless bitter-sweet monologues full of coaxing chatter. In the isolation of her life she transferred to her baby all her own poor frustrated ambitions. She dreamed of glamorous careers: she saw him tall, handsome, witty, successful—a bridge builder or a judge. She taught him to read, and even, on an old piano she had, to sing two or three sentimental little songs. But from Monsieur Bovary, who cared little for culture, all this brought merely the comment that it was "useless." Could they ever afford to give him an education, to buy him a practice or a business? Besides, "with enough nerve a man could always get ahead in the world." Madame Bovary pursed her lips, and the boy ran wild in the village.

He followed the hired men and chased crows, pelting them with clods of earth until they flew off. He ate the wild blackberries that grew along the ditches, looked after the turkeys with a long stick, pitched hay, roamed the woods, played hopscotch in the shelter of the church porch when it rained, and on important feast-days begged the sexton to let him toll the bells so that he could hang with his full weight from the heavy rope and feel it sweep him off his feet as it swung in its arc.

He throve like an oak. His hands grew strong and his complexion ruddy.

When he was twelve, his mother had her way: he began his studies. The priest was asked to tutor him. But the lessons were so short and irregular that they served little purpose. They took place at odd hurried moments—in the sacristy between a baptism and a funeral; or else the priest would send for him after the Angelus, when his parish business was over for the day. They would go up to his bedroom and begin, midges and moths fluttering around the candle. There in the warmth the child would fall asleep; and the old man, too, would soon be dozing and snoring, his hands folded over his stomach and his mouth open. Other times, as Monsieur le curé was returning from a sickbed with the holy oils, he would catch sight of Charles scampering in the fields, and would call him over and lecture him for a few minutes, taking advantage of the occasion to make him conjugate a verb right there, under a tree. Rain would interrupt them, or some passer-by whom they knew. However, he was always satisfied with him, and even said that "the young fellow had a good memory."

Things weren't allowed to stop there. Madame was persistent. Shamed into consent—or, rather, his resistance worn down—Monsieur gave in without further struggle. They waited a year, until the boy had made his First Communion, then six months more; and finally Charles was sent to the lycée in Rouen. His father delivered him himself, toward the end of October, during the fortnight of the Saint-Romain fair.

It would be very difficult today for any of us to say what he was like. There was nothing striking about him: he played during recess, worked in study-hall, paid attention in class, slept soundly in the dormitory, ate heartily in the refectory. His local guardian was a wholesale hardware dealer in the rue Ganterie, who called for him one Sunday a month after early closing, sent him for a walk along the riverfront to look at the boats, then brought him back to school by seven, in time for supper. Every Thursday night Charles wrote a long letter to his mother, using red ink and three seals; then he looked over his history notes, or leafed through an old volume of *Anacharsis* that lay around the study-hall. When his class went for outings he talked with the school servant who accompanied them, a countryman like himself.

By working hard he managed to stay about in the middle of the class; once he even got an honorable mention in natural history. But before he finished upper school his parents took him out of the lycée entirely and sent him to study medicine, confident that he could get his baccalaureate degree anyway by making up the intervening years on his own.

His mother chose a room for him, four flights up overlooking the stream called the Eau-de-Robec, in the house of a dyer she knew. She arranged for his board, got him a table and two chairs, and sent home for an old cherry bed; and to keep her darling warm she bought him a small cast-iron stove and a load of wood. Then after a week she went back to her village, urging him a thousand times over to behave himself now that he was on his own.

The curriculum that he read on the bulletin board staggered him. Courses in anatomy, pathology, pharmacy, chemistry, botany, clinical practice, therapeutics, to say nothing of hygiene and materia medica—names of unfamiliar etymology that were like so many doors leading to solemn shadowy sanctuaries.

He understood absolutely nothing of any of it. He listened in vain: he could not grasp it. Even so, he worked. He filled his notebooks, attended every lecture, never missed hospital rounds. In the performance of his daily task he was like a mill-horse that treads blindfolded in a circle, utterly ignorant of what he is grinding.

To save him money, his mother sent him a roast of veal each week by the stagecoach, and off this he lunched when he came in from the hospital, warming his feet by beating them against the wall. Then he had to hurry off to lectures, to the amphitheatre, to another hospital, crossing the entire city again when he returned. At night, after eating the meager dinner his landlord provided, he climbed back up to his room, back to work. Steam rose from his damp clothes as he sat beside the red-hot stove.

On fine summer evenings, at the hour when the warm streets are empty and servant girls play at shuttlecock in front of the houses, he would open his window and lean out. The stream, which makes this part of Rouen a kind of squalid little Venice, flowed just below, stained yellow, purple or blue between its bridges and railings. Workmen from the dye plants, crouching on the bank, washed their arms in the water. Above him, on poles projecting from attics, skeins of cotton were drying in the open. And beyond the roof-tops stretched the sky, vast and pure, with the red sun setting. How good it must be in the country! How cool in the beech grove! And he opened his nostrils wide, longing for a whiff of the fresh and fragrant air, but none was ever wafted to where he was.

He grew thinner and taller, and his face took on a kind of plaintive expression that almost made it interesting.

The fecklessness that was part of his nature soon led him to break all his good resolutions. One day he skipped rounds; the next, a lecture; idleness, he found, was to his taste, and gradually he stayed away entirely.

He began to go to cafés. Soon he was crazy about dominoes. To spend his evenings shut up in a dirty public room, clinking black-dotted pieces of sheep's bone on a marble table, seemed to him a marvelous assertion of his freedom that raised him in his own esteem. It was like an initiation into the world, admission to a realm of forbidden delights; and every time he entered the café the feel of the doorknob in his hand gave him a pleasure that was almost sensual. Now many things pent up within him burst their bonds; he learned verses by heart and sang them at student gatherings, developed an enthusiasm for Béranger, learned to make punch, and knew, at long last, the joys of love.

Thanks to that kind of preparation he failed completely the examination that would have entitled him to practice medicine as an *officier de santé*. And his parents were waiting for him at home that very night to celebrate his success!

He set out on foot; at the outskirts of the village he stopped, sent someone for his mother, and told her all. She forgave him, laying his downfall to the unfairness of the examiners, and steadied him by promising to make all explanations. (It was five years before Monsieur Bovary learned the truth: by that time it was an old story and he could accept it, especially since he couldn't conceive of his own offspring as being stupid.)

Charles set to work again and crammed ceaselessly, memorizing everything on which he could possibly be questioned. He passed with a fairly good grade. What a wonderful day for his mother! Everyone was asked to dinner.

Where should he practice? At Tostes. In that town there was only one elderly doctor, whose death Madame

Bovary had long been waiting for; and the old man hadn't yet breathed his last when Charles moved in across the road as his successor.

But it wasn't enough to have raised her son, sent him into medicine, and discovered Tostes for him to practice in: he had to have a wife. She found him one: a *huissier's* widow in Dieppe, forty-five years old, with twelve hundred francs a year.

Ugly though she was, and thin as a lath, with a face as spotted as a meadow in springtime, Madame Dubuc unquestionably had plenty of suitors to choose from. To gain her ends Madame Bovary had to get rid of all the rivals, and her outwitting of one of them, a butcher whose candidacy was favored by the local clergy, was nothing short of masterly.

Charles had envisaged marriage as the beginning of a better time, thinking that he would have greater freedom and be able to do as he liked with himself and his money. But it was his wife who ruled: in front of company he had to say certain things and not others, he had to eat fish on Friday, dress the way she wanted, obey her when she ordered him to dun nonpaying patients. She opened his mail, watched his every move, and listened through the thinness of the wall when there were women in his office.

She had to have her cup of chocolate every morning: there was no end to the attentions she required. She complained incessantly of her nerves, of pains in her chest, of depressions and faintnesses. The sound of anyone moving about near her made her ill; when people left her she couldn't bear her loneliness; when they came to see her it was, of course, "to watch her die." When Charles came home in the evening she would bring her long thin arms out from under her bedclothes, twine them around his neck, draw him down beside her on the edge of the bed, and launch into the tale of her woes: he was forgetting her, he was in love with someone else! How right people had been, to warn her that he'd make her unhappy! And she always ended by asking him to give her a new tonic and a little more love.

II

ONE NIGHT ABOUT ELEVEN O'CLOCK THEY WERE AWAKENED BY a noise: a horse had stopped just at their door. The maid opened the attic window and parleyed for some time with a man who stood in the street below. He had been sent to fetch the doctor; he had a letter. Nastasie came downstairs, shivering, turned the key in the lock and pushed back the bolts one by one. The man left his horse, followed the maid, and entered the bedroom at her heels. Out of his gray-tasseled woolen cap he drew a letter wrapped in a piece of cloth, and with a careful gesture handed it to Charles, who raised himself on his pillow to read it. Nastasie stood close to the bed, holding the light. Madame had modestly turned her back and lay facing the wall.

This letter, sealed with a small blue wax seal, begged Monsieur Bovary to come immediately to a farm called Les Bertaux, to set a broken leg. Now, from Tostes to Les Bertaux is at least fifteen miles, going by way of Longueville and Saint-Victor. It was a pitch-black night. Madame Bovary was fearful lest her husband meet with an accident. So it was decided that the stable hand who had brought the letter should start out ahead, and that Charles should follow three hours later: by that time there would be a moon. A boy would be sent out to meet him, to show him the way to the farm and open the field gates.

About four o'clock in the morning Charles set out for Les Bertaux, wrapped in a heavy coat. He was still drowsy from his warm sleep, and the peaceful trot of his mare lulled him like the rocking of a cradle. Whenever she stopped of her own accord in front of one of those spike-edged holes that farmers dig along the roadside to protect their crops, he would wake up with a start, quickly remember the broken leg, and try to recall all the fractures he had ever seen. The rain had stopped; day was breaking, and on the leafless branches of the apple trees birds were perched motionless, ruffling up their little feathers in the cold morning wind. The countryside stretched flat as far as eye could see; and the tufts of trees clustered around the farmhouses were widely spaced dark purple stains on the vast gray surface that merged at the horizon into the dull tone of the sky. From time to time Charles would open his eyes; and then, his senses dimmed by a return of sleep, he would fall again into a drowsiness in which recent sensations became confused with older memories to give him double visions of himself: as husband and as student—lying in bed as he had been only an hour or so before, and walking through a surgical ward as in the past. In his mind the hot smell of poultices mingled with the fresh smell of the dew; he heard at once the rattle of the curtain rings on hospital beds, and the sound of his wife's breathing as she lay asleep. At Vassonville he saw a little boy sitting in the grass beside a ditch.

"Are you the doctor?" the child asked.

And when Charles answered, he took his wooden shoes in his hands and began to run in front of him.

As they continued on their way, the *officier de santé* gathered from what his guide told him that Monsieur Rouault must be a very well-to-do farmer indeed. He had broken his leg the previous evening, on his way back from celebrating Twelfth Night at the home of a neighbor.

His wife had been dead for two years. He had with him only his "demoiselle"—his daughter—who kept house for him.

Now the road was more deeply rutted: they were approaching Les Bertaux. The boy slipped through an opening in a hedge, disappeared, then reappeared ahead, opening a farmyard gate from within. The horse was slipping on the wet grass; Charles had to bend low to escape overhanging branches. Kenneled watchdogs were barking, pulling at their chains. As he passed through the gate of Les Bertaux, his horse took fright and shied wildly.

It was a prosperous-looking farm. Through the open upper-halves of the stable doors great plough-horses could be seen placidly feeding from new racks. Next to the outbuildings stood a big manure pile, and in among the chickens and turkeys pecking at its steaming surface were five or six peacocks—favorite show pieces of *cauchois* farmyards. The sheepfold was long, the barn lofty, its walls as smooth as your hand. In the shed were two large carts and four ploughs complete with whips, horse collars and full trappings, the blue wool pads gray under the fine dust that sifted down from the lofts. The farmyard sloped upwards, planted with symmetrically spaced trees, and from near the pond came the merry sound of a flock of geese.

A young woman wearing a blue merino dress with three flounces came to the door of the house to greet Monsieur Bovary, and she ushered him into the kitchen, where a big open fire was blazing. Around its edges the farm hands' breakfast was bubbling in small pots of assorted sizes. Damp clothes were drying inside the vast chimney-opening. The fire shovel, the tongs, and the nose of the bellows, all of colossal proportions, shone like polished steel; and along the walls hung a lavish array of kitchen utensils, glimmering in the bright light of the fire and in the first rays of the sun that were now beginning to come in through the window-panes.

Charles went upstairs to see the patient. He found him in bed, sweating under blankets, his nightcap lying where he had flung it. He was a stocky little man of fifty, fair-skinned, blue-eyed, bald in front and wearing earrings. On a chair beside him was a big decanter of brandy: he had been pouring himself drinks to keep up his courage. But as soon as he saw the doctor he dropped his bluster, and instead of cursing as he had been doing for the past twelve hours he began to groan weakly.

The fracture was a simple one, without complications of any kind. Charles couldn't have wished for anything eas-ier. Then he recalled his teachers' bedside manner in acci-dent cases, and proceeded to cheer up his patient with all kinds of facetious remarks—a truly surgical attention, like the oiling of a scalpel. For splints, they sent someone to bring a bundle of laths from the carriage shed. Charles se-lected one, cut it into lengths and smoothed it down with a piece of broken window glass, while the maidservant tore sheets for bandages and Mademoiselle Emma tried to sew some pads. She was a long time finding her workbox, and her father showed his impatience. She made no reply; but as she sewed she kept pricking her fingers and raising them to her mouth to suck.

Charles was surprised by the whiteness of her fingernails. They were almond-shaped, tapering, as polished and shining as Dieppe ivories. Her hands, however, were not pretty—not pale enough, perhaps, a little rough at the knuckles; and they were too long, without softness of line. The fin-est thing about her was her eyes. They were brown, but seemed black under the long eyelashes; and she had an open gaze that met yours with fearless candor.

When the binding was done, the doctor was invited by

Monsieur Rouault himself to "have something" before he left.

Charles went down to the parlor on the ground floor. At the foot of a great canopied bed, its calico hangings printed with a design of people in Turkish dress, there stood a little table on which places had been laid for two, a silver mug beside each plate. From a tall oaken cupboard facing the window came an odor of orris root and damp sheets. In corners stood rows of grain sacks—the overflow from the granary, which was just adjoining, approached by three stone steps. The room's only decoration, hanging from a nail in the center of the flaking green-painted wall, was a black pencil drawing of a head of Minerva framed in gold and inscribed at the bottom in Gothic letters "To my dear Papa."

They spoke about the patient first, and then about the weather, about the bitter cold, about the wolves that roamed the fields at night. Mademoiselle Rouault didn't enjoy country life, especially now, with almost the full responsibility of the farm on her shoulders. The room was chilly, and she shivered as she ate. Charles noticed that her lips were full, and that she had the habit of biting them in moments of silence.

Her neck rose out of the low fold of a white collar. The two black sweeps of her hair, pulled down from a fine center part that followed the curve of her skull, were so sleek that each seemed to be one piece. Covering all but the very tips of her ears, it was gathered at the back into a large chignon, and toward the temples it waved a bit—a detail that the country doctor now observed for the first time in his life. Her skin was rosy over her cheekbones. A pair of shell-rimmed eyeglasses, like a man's, was tucked between two buttons of her bodice.

When Charles came back downstairs after going up to take leave of Monsieur Rouault, he found her standing with her forehead pressed against the windowpane, looking out at the garden, where the beanpoles had been thrown down by the wind. She turned around.

"Are you looking for something?" she asked.

"For my riding crop," he said.

And he began to rummage on the bed, behind doors, under chairs. It had fallen on the floor between the grainbags and the wall. Mademoiselle Emma caught sight of it and reached for it, bending down across the sacks. Charles hurried over politely, and as he, too, stretched out his arm he felt his body in slight contact with the girl's back, bent there beneath him. She stood up, blushing crimson, and glanced at him over her shoulder as she handed him his crop.

Instead of returning to Les Bertaux three days later, as he had promised, he went back the very next day, then twice a week regularly, not to mention unscheduled calls he made from time to time, as though by chance.

Everything went well; the bone knit according to the rules; and after forty-six days, when Monsieur Rouault was seen trying to get around his farmyard by himself, everyone began to think of Monsieur Bovary as a man of great competence. Monsieur Rouault said he wouldn't have been better mended by the biggest doctors of Yvetot or even Rouen.

As for Charles, he didn't ask himself why he enjoyed going to Les Bertaux. Had he thought of it, he would doubtless have attributed his zeal to the seriousness of the case, or perhaps to the fee he hoped to earn. Still, was that really why his visits to the farm formed so charming a contrast to the drabness of the rest of his life? On such days he would rise early, set off at a gallop, urge his horse; and when he was almost there he would dismount to dust his shoes on the grass, and put on his black gloves. He enjoyed the moment of arrival, the feel of the gate as it yielded against his shoulder; he enjoyed the rooster crowing on the wall, the farm boys coming to greet him. He enjoyed the barn and the stables; he enjoyed Monsieur Rouault, who would clap him in the palm of the hand and call him his "savior"; he enjoyed hearing Mademoiselle Emma's little sabots on the newly washed flagstones of the kitchen floor. With their high heels they made her a little taller; and when she walked in them ahead of him their wooden soles kept coming up with a quick, sharp, tapping sound against the leather of her shoes.

She always accompanied him to the foot of the steps outside the door. If his horse hadn't been brought around she would wait there with him. At such moments they had already said good-bye, and stood there silent; the breeze eddied around her, swirling the stray wisps of hair at her neck, or sending her apron strings flying like streamers around her waist. Once she was standing there on a day of thaw, when the bark of the trees in the farmyard was oozing sap and the snow was melting on the roofs. She went inside for her parasol, and opened it. The parasol was of rosy iridescent silk, and the sun pouring through it painted the white skin of her face with flickering patches of light. Beneath it she smiled at the springlike warmth; and drops of water could be heard falling one by one on the taut moiré.

During the first period of Charles's visits to Les Bertaux, Madame Bovary never failed to ask about the patient's progress; and in her double-entry ledger she had given Monsieur Rouault a fine new page to himself. But when she heard that he had a daughter she began to make inquiries; and she learned that Mademoiselle Rouault had had her schooling in a convent, with the Ursuline nuns—had received, as the saying went, a "fine education," in the course of which she had been taught dancing, geography, drawing, needlework and a little piano. Think of that!

"So that's why he brightens up when he goes there!

That's why he wears his new waistcoat, even in the rain! Ah! So she's at the bottom of it!"

Instinctively she hated her. At first she relieved her feelings by making insinuations. Charles didn't get them. Then she let fall parenthetical remarks which he left unanswered out of fear of a storm; and finally she was driven to point-blank reproaches which he didn't know how to answer. Why was it that he kept going back to Les Bertaux, now that Monsieur Rouault was completely mended and hadn't even paid his bill? Ah! Because there was *a certain person* there. Somebody who knew how to talk. Somebody who did embroidery. Somebody clever. That's what he enjoyed: he had to have city girls! And she went on:

"Rouault's daughter, a city girl! Don't make me laugh! The grandfather was a shepherd, and there's a cousin who barely escaped sentence for assault and battery. Scarcely good reasons for giving herself airs, for wearing silk dresses to church like a countess! Besides—her father, poor fellow: if it hadn't been for last year's colza crop he'd have been hard put to it to pay his debts."

For the sake of peace, Charles stopped going to Les Bertaux. Heloise had made him swear—his hand on his prayer book—that he would never go back there again: she had accomplished it after much sobbing and kissing, in the midst of a great amorous explosion. He yielded; but the strength of his desire kept protesting against the servility of his behavior, and with a naïve sort of hypocrisy he told himself that this very prohibition against seeing her implicitly allowed him to love her. And then the widow he was married to was skinny; she was long in the tooth; all year round she wore a little black shawl with a corner hanging down between her shoulder blades; her rigid form was always sheathed in dresses that were like scabbards; they were always too short; they showed her ankles, her big shoes, and her shoelaces crisscrossing their way up her gray stockings.

Charles's mother came to see them from time to time; but after a few days she invariably took on her daughter-in-law's sharpness against her son, and like a pair of knives they kept scarifying him with their comments and criticisms. He oughtn't to eat so much! Why always offer a drink to everyone who called? So pigheaded not to wear flannel underwear!

Early in the spring it happened that a notary in Ingouville, custodian of the Widow Dubuc's capital, sailed away one fine day, taking with him all his clients' money. To be sure, Heloise still owned her house in the rue Saint-François in Dieppe, as well as a six-thousand-franc interest in a certain ship; nevertheless, of the great fortune she'd always talked so much about, nothing except a few bits of furniture and some clothes had ever been seen in the household. Now, inevitably, everything came under investigation. The house in Dieppe, it turned out, was mortgaged up to its eaves; what she had placed with the notary, God only knew; and her share in the boat didn't amount to more than three thousand. So she'd been lying—lying all along, the dear, good lady! In his rage the older Monsieur Bovary dashed a chair to pieces on the floor and accused his wife of ruining their son's life by yoking him to such an ancient nag, whose harness was worth even less than her carcass. They came to Tostes. The four of them had it out. There were scenes. The weeping Heloise threw herself into her husband's arms and appealed to him to defend her against his parents. Charles began to take her part. The others flew into a rage and left.

But—"the fatal blow had been struck." A week later she was hanging out washing in her yard when suddenly she began to spit blood; and the next day, while Charles was looking the other way, drawing the window curtain, she gave a cry, then a sigh, and fainted. She was dead! Who would have believed it?

When everything was over at the cemetery, Charles returned to the house. There was no one downstairs, and he went up to the bedroom. One of her dresses was still hanging in the alcove. He stayed there until dark, leaning against the writing desk, his mind full of sad thoughts. Poor thing! She had loved him, after all.

III

ONE MORNING MONSIEUR ROUAULT CAME TO PAY CHARLES FOR setting his leg—seventy-five francs in two-franc pieces, with a turkey thrown in for good measure. He had heard of his bereavement, and offered him what consolation he could.

"I know what it is," he said, patting him on the shoulder. "I've been through just what you're going through. When I lost my wife I went out into the fields to be by myself. I lay down under a tree and cried. I talked to God, told him all kinds of crazy things. I wished I were dead, like the maggoty moles I saw hanging on the branches. And when I thought of how other men were holding their wives in their arms at that very moment, I began to pound my stick on the ground. I was almost out of my mind. I couldn't eat: the very thought of going to a café made me sick—you'd never believe it. Well, you know, what with one day gradually nosing out another, and spring coming on top of winter and then fall after the summer—it passed bit by bit, drop by drop. It just went away; it disappeared; I mean it grew less and less—there's always part of it you never get rid of entirely; you always feel something here." And he put his hand on his chest. "But it happens to us all, and you mustn't let yourself go, you mustn't want to die just because other people are dead. You must brace up, Monsieur Bovary: things will get better. Come and see us. My daughter talks about you every once in a while; she says you've probably forgotten her. Spring will soon be here: you and I'll go out after a rabbit—it will take your mind off things."

Charles took his advice. He went back to Les Bertaux; he found it unchanged since yesterday—since five months before, that is. The pear trees were already in flower; and the sight of Monsieur Rouault coming and going normally around the place made everything livelier.

The farmer seemed to think that the doctor's grief-stricken condition called for a special show of consideration, and he urged him to keep his hat on, addressed him in a low voice as though he were ill, and even pretended to be angry that no one had thought to cook him something special and light, like custard or stewed pears. He told him funny stories. Charles found himself laughing, but then the thought of his wife returned to sober him. By the end of the meal he had forgotten her again.

He thought of her less and less as he grew used to living alone. The novelty and pleasure of being independent soon made solitude more bearable. Now he could change his meal hours at will, come and go without explanation, stretch out across the bed if he was particularly tired. So he pampered and coddled himself and accepted all the comforting everyone offered. Besides, his wife's death had helped him quite a bit professionally: for a month or so everyone had kept saying, "Poor young man! What a tragedy!" His reputation grew; more and more patients came. Now he went to Les Bertaux whenever he pleased. He was aware of a feeling of hope—nothing very specific, a vague happiness: he thought himself better-looking when he stood at the mirror to brush his whiskers.

One day he arrived about three o'clock. Everyone was in the fields. He went into the kitchen, and at first didn't see Emma. The shutters were closed; the sun, streaming in between the slats, patterned the floor with long thin stripes that broke off at the corners of the furniture and quivered on the ceiling. On the table, flies were climbing up the sides of glasses that had recently been used, and buzzing as they struggled to keep from drowning in the cider at the bottom. The light coming down the chimney turned the soot on the fireback to velvet and gave a bluish cast to the cold ashes. Between the window and the hearth Emma sat sewing; her shoulders were bare, beaded with little drops of sweat.

Country-style, she offered him something to drink. He refused, she insisted, and finally suggested with a laugh that he take a liqueur with her. She brought a bottle of curaçao from the cupboard, reached to a high shelf for two liqueur glasses, filled one to the brim and poured a few drops in the other. She touched her glass to his and raised it to her mouth. Because it was almost empty she had to bend backwards to be able to drink; and with her head tilted back, her neck and her lips outstretched, she began to laugh at tasting nothing; and then the tip of her tongue came out from between her small teeth and began daintily to lick the bottom of the glass.

She sat down again and resumed her work—she was darning a white cotton stocking. She sewed with her head bowed, and she did not speak: nor did Charles. A draft was coming in under the door and blowing a little dust across the stone floor; he watched it drift, and was aware of a pulsating sound inside his head—that, and the clucking of a laying hen outside in the yard. From time to time Emma cooled her cheeks with the palms of her hands, and then cooled her hands against the iron knobs of the tall andirons.

She complained that the heat had been giving her dizzy spells, and asked whether sea bathing would help; then she began to talk about her convent school and Charles about his lycée: words came to them both. They went upstairs to her room. She showed him her old music exercise books, and the little volumes and the oak-leaf wreaths—the latter now lying abandoned in the bottom of a cupboard—that she had won as prizes. Then she spoke of her mother, and the cemetery, and took him out to the garden to see the bed where she picked flowers the first Friday of every month to put on her grave. But their gardener had no understanding of such things: farm help was so trying! She would love, if only for the winter, to live in the city—though she had to say that it was really in summer, with the days so long, that the country was most boring of all. Depending on what she talked about, her voice was clear, or shrill, or would grow suddenly languorous and trail off almost into a murmur, as though she were speaking to herself. One moment she would be gay and wide-eyed; the next, she would half shut her eyelids and seem to be drowned in boredom, her thoughts miles away.

That evening, on his homeward ride, Charles went over one by one the things she had said, trying to remember her exact words and sense their implications, in an effort to picture what her life had been like before their meeting. But in his thoughts he could never see her any differently from the way she had been when he had seen her the first time, or as she had been just now, when he left her. Then he wondered what would become of her, whether she would marry, and whom. Alas! Monsieur Rouault was very rich, and she . . . so beautiful! But Emma's face appeared constantly before his eyes, and in his ears there was a monotonous throbbing, like the humming of a top: "But why don't *you* get married! Why don't *you* get married!"

That night he didn't sleep, his throat was tight, he was thirsty; he got up to drink from his water jug and opened the window; the sky was covered with stars, a hot wind was blowing, dogs were barking in the distance. He stared out in the direction of Les Bertaux.

After all, he thought, nothing would be lost by trying; and he resolved to ask his question when the occasion presented itself; but each time it did, the fear of not finding the proper words paralyzed his lips.

Actually, Rouault wouldn't have been a bit displeased to have someone take his daughter off his hands. She was of no use to him on the farm. He didn't really hold it against her, being of the opinion that she was too clever to have anything to do with farming—that accursed occupation that had never yet made a man a millionaire. Far from having grown rich at it, the poor fellow was losing money every year: he more than held his own in the market place, where he relished all the tricks of the trade, but no one was less suited than he to the actual growing of crops and the managing of a farm. He never lifted a finger if he could help it, and never spared any expense in matters of daily living: he insisted on good food, a good fire, and a good bed. He liked his cider hard, his leg of mutton rare, his coffee well laced with brandy. He took his meals in the kitchen, alone, facing the fire, at a little table that was brought in to him already set, like on the stage.

So when he noticed that Charles tended to be flushed in his daughter's presence—meaning that one of these days he would ask for her hand—he pondered every aspect of the question well in advance. Charles was a bit namby-pamby, not his dream of a son-in-law; but he was said to be reliable, thrifty, very well educated; and he probably wouldn't haggle too much over the dowry. Moreover, Rouault was soon going to have to sell twenty-two of his acres: he owed considerable to the mason and considerable to the harness-maker, and the cider press needed a new shaft. "If he asks me for her," he said to himself, "I won't refuse."

Toward the beginning of October, Charles spent three days at Les Bertaux. The last day had slipped by like the others, with the big step put off from one minute to the next. Rouault was escorting him on the first lap of his homeward journey; they were walking along a sunken road; they were just about to part—the moment had come. Charles gave himself to the corner of the hedge; and finally, when they had passed it: "Monsieur Rouault," he murmured, "there's something I'd like to say to you."

They stopped. Charles fell silent.

"Well, tell me what's on your mind! I know it already anyway!" Rouault said with a gentle laugh.

"Monsieur Rouault . . . Monsieur Rouault . . ." Charles stammered.

"Personally I wouldn't like anything better," continued the farmer. "I imagine the child agrees with me, but we'd better ask her. I'll leave you here now, and go back to the house. If it's 'Yes'—now listen to what I'm saying—you won't have to come in: there are too many people around, and besides she'd be too upset. But to take you off the anxious seat I'll slam a shutter against the wall: you can look back and see, if you lean over the hedge."

And he went off.

Charles tied his horse to a tree. He hastily stationed himself on the path and waited. Half an hour went by; then he counted nineteen minutes by his watch. Suddenly there was a noise against the wall: the shutter had swung back; the catch was still quivering.

The next morning he was at the farm by nine. Emma blushed when he entered, laughing a little in an attempt to be casual. Rouault embraced his future son-in-law. They postponed all talk of financial arrangements: there was plenty of time, since the wedding couldn't decently take place before the end of Charles's mourning—that is, toward the spring of the next year.

It was a winter of waiting. Mademoiselle Rouault busied herself with her trousseau. Part of it was ordered in Rouen, and she made her slips and nightcaps herself, copying fashion drawings that she borrowed. Whenever Charles visited the farm they spoke about preparations for the wedding, discussing which room the dinner should be served in, wondering how many courses to have and what the entrees should be.

Emma herself would have liked to be married at midnight, by torchlight; but Rouault wouldn't listen to the idea. So there was the usual kind of wedding, with forty-three guests, and everybody was sixteen hours at table, and the festivities began all over again the next day and even carried over a little into the days following.

IV

THE INVITED GUESTS ARRIVED EARLY IN A VARIETY OF VEHICLES —one-horse shays, two-wheeled charabancs, old gigs without tops, vans with leather curtains; and the young men from the nearest villages came in farm-carts, standing one behind the other along the sides and grasping the rails to keep from being thrown, for the horses trotted briskly and the roads were rough. They came from as far as twenty-five miles away, from Goderville, from Normanville, from Cany. All the relations of both families had been asked, old quarrels had been patched up, letters sent to acquaintances long lost sight of.

From time to time the crack of a whip would be heard behind the hedge, then after a moment the gate would open and a cart would roll in; it would come at a gallop as far as the doorstep, then stop with a lurch, and out would pour its passengers, rubbing their knees and stretching their arms. The ladies wore country-style headdresses and city-style gowns, with gold watch chains, tippets (the ends crossed and tucked into their belts), or small colored fichus attached at the back with pins and leaving the neck bare. The boys, attired exactly like their papas, looked ill at ease in their new clothes (and indeed many of them were wearing leather shoes that day for the first time in their lives); and next to them would be some speech-less, gangling girl of fourteen or sixteen, probably their cousin or their older sister, flushed and awkward in her white First Communion dress let down for the occasion, her hair sticky with scented pomade, terribly worried lest she dirty her gloves. Since there weren't enough stable hands to unharness all the carriages, the men rolled up their sleeves and went to it themselves. According to their so-cial status, they wore tail coats, frock coats, long jackets or short jackets. The tail coats were worthy garments, each of them a prized family possession taken out of the closet only on great occasions; the frock coats had great flaring skirts that billowed in the wind, cylindrical collars, and pockets as capacious as bags; the long jackets were double-breasted, of coarse wool, and usually worn with a cap of some kind, its peak trimmed with brass; and the short jack-ets were very short indeed, with two back buttons set close together like a pair of eyes, and stiff tails that looked as though a carpenter had hacked them with his axe out of a single block of wood. A few guests (these, of course, would sit at the foot of the table) wore dress smocks— that is, smocks with turned-down collars, fine pleating at the back, and stitched belts low on the hips.

And the shirts! They bulged like breastplates. Every man was freshly shorn; ears stood out from heads; faces were of a holiday smoothness. Some of the guests from farthest away, who had got up before dawn and had to shave in the dark, had slanting gashes under their noses, or patches of skin the size of a three-franc piece peeled from their jaws. During the journey their wounds had been inflamed by the wind, and as a result red blotches adorned many a big beaming white face.

Since the mayor's office was scarcely more than a mile from the farm, the wedding party went there on foot and came back the same way after the church ceremony. The procession was compact at first, like a bright sash festooning the countryside as it followed the narrow path winding between the green grain fields; but soon it lengthened out and broke up into different groups, which lingered to gossip along the way. The fiddler went first, the scroll of his violin gay with ribbons; then came the bridal pair; then their families; then their friends in no particular order; and last of all the children, having a good time pulling the bell-shaped flowers from the oat stalks or playing among themselves out of sight of their elders. Emma's gown was too long, and trailed a little; from time to time she stopped to pull it up; and at such moments she would carefully pick off the coarse grasses and thistle spikes with her gloved fingers, as Charles waited empty-handed beside her. Rouault, in a new silk hat, the cuffs of his black tail coat coming down over his hands as far as his fingertips, had given his arm to the older Madame Bovary. The older Monsieur Bovary, who looked on all these people with contempt, and had come wearing simply a single-breasted overcoat of military cut, was acting the barroom gallant with a blonde young peasant girl. She bobbed and blushed, tongue-tied and confused. The other members of the wedding party discussed matters of business, or played tricks behind each other's backs, their spirits already soaring in anticipation of the fun. If they listened, they could hear the steady scraping of the fiddle in the fields. When the fiddler realized that he had left everyone far behind, he stopped for breath, carefully rubbed his bow with rosin to make his strings squeak all the better, and then set off again on his course, raising and lowering the neck of his violin to keep time. The sound of the instrument frightened away all the birds for a long distance ahead.

The table was set up in the carriage shed. On it were four roasts of beef, six fricassees of chicken, a veal casserole, three legs of mutton, and in the center a charming little suckling pig flanked by four *andouilles à l'oseille*—pork sausages flavored with sorrel. At the corners stood decanters of brandy. The sweet cider foamed up around its corks, and before anyone was seated, every glass had been filled to the brim with wine. Great dishes of yellow custard, their smooth surfaces decorated with the newlyweds' initials in candy-dot arabesques, were set trembling whenever the table was given the slightest knock. The pies and cakes had been ordered from a caterer in Yvetot. Since he was just starting up in the district, he had gone to considerable pains; and when dessert time came he himself brought to the table a wedding cake that drew exclamations from all. Its base was a square of blue cardboard representing a temple with porticos and colonnades and adorned on all sides with stucco statuettes standing in niches spangled with gold-paper stars. The second tier was a mediaeval castle in *gateau de Savoie*, surrounded by miniature fortifications of angelica, almonds, raisins, and orange sections. And finally, on the topmost layer—which was a green meadow, with rocks, jelly lakes, and boats of hazelnut shells —a little Cupid was swinging in a chocolate swing. The tips of the two uprights, the highest points of the whole, were two real rosebuds.

The banquet went on till nightfall. Those who grew tired of sitting took a stroll in the yard or played a kind of shuffleboard in the barn; then they returned to table. A few, toward the end, fell asleep and snored. But everything came to life again with the coffee: there were songs, displays of strength. The men lifted weights, played the game of passing their heads under their arms while holding one thumb on the table, tried to raise carts to their shoulders. Dirty jokes were in order; the ladies were kissed. In the evening, when it came time to go, the horses, stuffed with oats to the bursting point, could scarcely be forced between the shafts; they kicked and reared, broke their harness, brought curses or laughs from their masters. And all night long, under the light of the moon on the country roads, runaway carts were bouncing along ditches at a gallop, leaping over gravel piles and crashing into banks, with women leaning out trying desperately to seize the reins.

Those who stayed at Les Bertaux spent the night drinking in the kitchen. The children fell asleep on the floor.

The bride had begged her father that she be spared the usual pranks. However, a fishmonger cousin (who had actually brought a pair of soles as a wedding present) was just beginning to spurt water from his mouth through the keyhole when Rouault came along and stopped him, explaining that the importance of his son-in-law's position didn't permit such unseemliness. The cousin complied very grudgingly. In his heart he accused Rouault of being a snob, and he joined a group of four or five other guests, who had happened several times in succession to be given inferior cuts of meat at table and so considered that they, too, had been badly treated. The whole group sat there whispering derogatory things about their host, and in veiled language expressed hopes for his downfall.

The older Madame Bovary hadn't opened her mouth all day. No one had consulted her about her daughter-in-law's bridal dress, or the arrangements for the party: she went up to bed early. Her husband didn't accompany her; instead, he sent to Saint-Victor for cigars and sat up till dawn smoking and drinking kirsch and hot water. This variety of grog was new to his fellow guests, and made him feel that their respect for him rose all the higher.

Charles was far from being a wag. He had been dull throughout the festivities, responding but feebly to the witticisms, puns, *doubles-entendres*, teasings and dubious jokes that everyone had felt obliged to toss at him from the moment they had sat down to the soup.

The next day, however, he seemed a different man. It was he who gave the impression of having lost his virginity overnight: the bride made not the slightest sign that could be taken to betray anything at all. Even the shrewdest were nonplused, and stared at her with the most intense curiosity whenever she came near. But Charles hid nothing. He addressed her as *"ma femme,"* using the intimate *"tu,"* kept asking everyone where she was and looking for her everywhere, and often took her out into the yard, where he could be glimpsed through the trees with his arm around her waist, leaning over her as they walked, his head rumpling the yoke of her bodice.

Two days after the wedding the bridal pair left: because of his patients Charles could stay away no longer. Rouault had them driven to Tostes in his cart, going with them himself as far as Vassonville. There he kissed his daughter a last time, got out, and retraced his way. When he had walked about a hundred yards he stopped; and the sight of the cart disappearing in the distance, its wheels spinning in the dust, made him utter a deep sigh. He remembered his own wedding, his own earlier days, his wife's first pregnancy. He, too, had been very happy, the day he had taken her from her father's house to his own. She had ridden pillion behind him as their horse trotted over the snow, for it had been close to Christmas and the fields were white; she had clutched him with one arm, her basket hooked over the other; the wind was whipping the long lace streamers of her *coiffure cauchoise* so that at times they blew across his mouth; and by turning his head he could see her rosy little face close behind his shoulder, smiling silently at him under the gold buckle of her bonnet. From time to time she would warm her fingers by sliding them inside his coat. How long ago it all was! Their boy would be thirty if he were alive today! Then he looked back again, and there was nothing to be seen on the road. He felt dismal, like a stripped and empty house; and as tender memories and black thoughts mingled in his brain, dulled by the vapors of the feast, he considered for a moment turning his steps toward the church. But he was afraid that the sight of it might make him even sadder, so he went straight home.

Monsieur and Madame Charles reached Tostes about six o'clock. The neighbors came to their windows to see their doctor's new wife.

The elderly maidservant appeared, greeted them, apologized for not having dinner ready, and suggested that Madame, in the meantime, might like to make a tour of inspection of her house.

V

THE BRICK HOUSE-FRONT WAS EXACTLY FLUSH WITH THE street, or rather the road. Behind the door hung a coat with a short cape, a bridle, and a black leather cap; and on the floor in a corner lay a pair of gaiters still caked with mud. To the right was the parlor, which served as both dining and sitting room. A canary-yellow wallpaper, set off at the top by a border of pale flowers, rippled everywhere on its loose canvas lining; white calico curtains edged with red braid hung crosswise down the length of the windows; and on the narrow mantelpiece a clock ornamented with a head of Hippocrates stood proudly between two silver-plated candlesticks under oval glass domes. Across the hall was Charles's small consulting room, about eighteen feet wide, with a table, three straight chairs and an office arm-chair. There was a fir bookcase with six shelves, occupied almost exclusively by a set of the *Dictionary of the Medical Sciences*, its pages uncut but its binding battered by a long succession of owners. Cooking smells seeped through the wall during office hours, and the patients' coughs and confidences were quite audible in the kitchen. In the rear, opening directly into the yard (which contained the stables), was a big ramshackle room with an oven, now serving as woodshed, wine bin and store room; it was filled with old junk, empty barrels, broken tools, and a quantity of other objects all dusty and nondescript.

The long narrow garden ran back between two clay walls covered with espaliered apricot trees to the thorn hedge that marked it off from the fields. In the middle was a slate sundial on a stone pedestal. Four beds of scrawny rose bushes were arranged symmetrically around a square plot given over to vegetables. At the far end, under some spruces, a plaster priest stood reading his breviary.

Emma went up to the bedrooms. The first was empty; in the second, the conjugal chamber, a mahogany bed stood in an alcove hung with red draperies. A box made of sea-shells adorned the chest of drawers; and on the desk near the window, standing in a decanter and tied with white satin ribbon, was a bouquet of orange blossoms—a bride's bouquet: the *other* bride's bouquet! She stared at it. Charles noticed, picked it up, and took it to the attic; and as her boxes and bags were brought up and placed around her, she sat in an armchair and thought of her own bridal bouquet, which was packed in one of those very boxes, wondering what would be done with it if she were to die.

She spent the first few days planning changes in the house. She took the domes off the candlesticks, had the parlor repapered, the stairs painted, and seats made to go around the sundial in the garden. She even made inquiries as to the best way of installing a fountain and a fish pond. And her husband, knowing that she liked to go for drives, bought a secondhand two-wheeled buggy. With new lamps and quilted leather mudguards it looked almost like a tilbury.

He was happy now, without a care in the world. A meal alone with her, a stroll along the highway in the evening, the way she touched her hand to her hair, the sight of her straw hat hanging from a window hasp, and many other things in which it had never occurred to him to look for pleasure—such now formed the steady current of his happiness. In bed in the morning, his head beside hers on the pillow, he would watch the sunlight on the downy gold of her cheeks, half covered by the scalloped tabs of her nightcap. Seen from so close, her eyes appeared larger than life, especially when she opened and shut her eyelids several times on awakening: black when looked at in shadow, dark blue in bright light, they seemed to contain layer upon layer of color, thicker and cloudier beneath, lighter and more transparent toward the lustrous surface. As his own eyes plunged into those depths, he saw himself reflected there in miniature down to his shoulders—his foulard on his head, his nightshirt open. After he had dressed she would go to the window and watch him leave for his rounds; she would lean out between two pots of geraniums, her elbows on the sill, her dressing gown loose around her. In the street, Charles would strap on his spurs at the mounting-block; and she would continue to talk to him from above, blowing down to him some bit of flower or leaf she had bitten off in her teeth. It would flutter down hesitantly, weaving semicircles in the air like a bird, and before reaching the ground it would catch in the tangled mane of the old white mare standing motionless at the door. From the saddle Charles would send her a kiss; she would respond with a wave; then she would close the window, and he was off. And on the endless dusty ribbon of the highway, on sunken roads vaulted over by branches, on paths between stands of grain that rose to his knees—the sun on his shoulders and the morning air in his nostrils, his heart full of the night's bliss, his spirit at peace and his flesh content—he would ride on his way ruminating his happiness, like someone who keeps savoring, hours later, the fragrance of the truffles he has eaten for dinner.

Up until now, had there ever been a happy time in his life? His years at the lycée, where he had lived shut in behind high walls, lonely among richer, cleverer schoolmates who laughed at his country accent and made fun of his clothes and whose mothers brought them cookies in their muffs on visiting days? Or later, when he was studying medicine and hadn't enough in his purse to go dancing with some little working girl who might have become his mistress? After that he had lived fourteen months with the widow, whose feet in bed had been like icicles. But now he possessed, and for always, this pretty wife whom he so loved. The universe, for him, went not beyond the silken circuit of her petticoat; and he would reproach himself for not showing her his love, and yearn to be back with her. He would gallop home, rush upstairs, his heart pounding. Emma would be at her dressing table; he would creep up silently behind her and kiss her; she would cry out in surprise.

He couldn't keep from constantly touching her comb, her rings, everything she wore; sometimes he gave her great full-lipped kisses on the cheek, or a whole series of tiny kisses up her bare arm, from her fingertips to her shoulder; and half amused, half annoyed, she would push him away as one does an importunate child.

Before her marriage she had thought that she had love within her grasp; but since the happiness which she had expected this love to bring her hadn't come, she supposed she must have been mistaken. And Emma tried to imagine just what was meant, in life, by the words "bliss," "passion," and "rapture"—words that had seemed so beautiful to her in books.

VI

SHE HAD READ *Paul and Virginia*, AND HAD DREAMED OF THE bamboo cabin, of the Negro Domingo and the dog Fidèle; and especially she dreamed that she, too, had a sweet little brother for a devoted friend, and that he climbed trees as tall as church steeples to pluck her their crimson fruit, and came running barefoot over the sand to bring her a bird's nest.

When she was thirteen, her father took her to the city to enter her as a boarder in the convent. They stayed at a hotel near Saint-Gervais, where their supper plates were decorated with scenes from the life of Mademoiselle de La Vallière. The explanatory captions, slashed here and there by knife scratches, were all in praise of piety, the sensibilities of the heart, and the splendors of the court.

Far from being unhappy in the convent, at first, she enjoyed the company of the nuns: it was fun when they took her to the chapel, down a long corridor from the refectory. She rarely played during recess, and she was very quick at catechism: it was always Mademoiselle Rouault who answered Monsieur le vicaire's hardest questions. As she continued to live uninterruptedly in the insipid atmosphere of the classrooms, among the white-faced women with their brass crucifixes dangling from their rosaries, she gently succumbed to the mystical languor induced by the perfumes of the altar, the coolness of the holy-water fonts, the gleaming of the candles. Instead of following the Mass she kept her prayer book open at the holy pictures with their sky-blue borders; and she loved the Good Shepherd, the Sacred Heart pierced by sharp arrows, and poor Jesus stumbling and falling under his cross. To mortify herself she tried to go a whole day without eating. She looked for some vow that she might accomplish.

When she went to confession she invented small sins in order to linger on her knees there in the darkness, her hands joined, her face at the grille, the priest whispering just above her. The metaphors constantly used in sermons —"betrothed," "spouse," "heavenly lover," "mystical marriage"—excited her in a thrilling new way.

Every evening before prayers a piece of religious writing was read aloud in study hall. During the week it would be some digest of Biblical history or the Abbé Frayssinous' lectures; on Sunday it was always a passage from the *Génie du Christianisme*, offered as entertainment. How intently she listened, the first times, to the ringing lamentations of that romantic melancholy, echoed and re-echoed by all the voices of earth and heaven! Had her childhood been spent in cramped quarters behind some city shop, she might have been open to the lyric appeal of nature—which usually reaches us only by way of literary interpretations.

But she knew too much about country life: she was well acquainted with lowing herds, with dairy maids and ploughs. From such familiar, peaceful aspects, she turned to the picturesque. She loved the sea for its storms alone, cared for vegetation only when it grew here and there among ruins. She had to extract a kind of personal advantage from things; and she rejected as useless everything that promised no immediate gratification—for her temperament was more sentimental than artistic, and what she was looking for was emotions, not scenery.

At the convent there was an old spinster who came for a week every month to look after the linen. As a member of an ancient noble family ruined by the Revolution she was a protégée of the archdiocese; and she ate at the nuns' table in the refectory and always stayed for a chat with them before returning upstairs to her work. The girls often slipped out of study-hall to pay her a visit. She had a repertoire of eighteenth-century love songs, and sang them in a low voice as she sewed. She told stories, kept the girls abreast of the news, did errands for them in the city, and to the older ones would surreptitiously lend one of the novels she always carried in her apron pocket—novels of which the good spinster herself was accustomed to devour long chapters in the intervals of her task. They were invariably about love affairs, lovers, mistresses, harassed ladies swooning in remote pavilions. Couriers were killed at every relay, horses ridden to death on every page; there were gloomy forests, broken hearts, vows, sobs, tears and kisses, skiffs in the moonlight, nightingales in thickets; the noblemen were all brave as lions, gentle as lambs, incredibly virtuous, always beautifully dressed, and wept copiously on every occasion. For six months, when she was fifteen, Emma begrimed her hands with this dust from old lending libraries. Later, reading Walter Scott, she became infatuated with everything historical and dreamed about oaken chests and guardrooms and troubadours. She would have liked to live in some old manor, like those long-waisted chatelaines who spent their days leaning out of fretted Gothic casements, elbow on parapet and chin in hand, watching a white-plumed knight come galloping out of the distance on a black horse. At that time she worshipped Mary Queen of Scots, and venerated women illustrious or ill-starred. In her mind Joan of Arc, Héloïse, Agnès Sorel, La Belle Ferronière and Clémence Isaure stood out like comets on the shadowy immensity of history; and here and there (though less clearly outlined than the others against the dim background, and quite unrelated among themselves) were visible also St. Louis and his oak, the dying Bayard, certain atrocities of Louis XI, bits of the Massacre of St. Bartholomew, the plumed crest of Henri IV, and, always, the memory of the hotel plates glorifying Louis XIV.

The sentimental songs she sang in music class were all about little angels with golden wings, madonnas, lagoons, gondoliers—mawkish compositions that allowed her to glimpse, through the silliness of the words and the indiscretions of the music, the alluring, phantasmagoric realm of genuine feeling. Some of her schoolmates brought to the convent the keepsake albums they had received as New Year's gifts. They had to hide them—it was very exciting; they could be read only at night, in the dormitory. Careful not to harm the lovely satin bindings, Emma stared bedazzled at the names of the unknown authors—counts or viscounts, most of them—who had written their signatures under their contributions.

She quivered as she blew back the tissue paper from each engraving: it would curl up into the air, then sink gently down against the page. Behind a balcony railing a young man in a short cloak clasped in his arms a girl in a white dress, a chatelaine bag fastened to her belt; or there were portraits of unidentified aristocratic English beauties with blond curls, staring out at you with their wide light-colored eyes from under great straw hats. Some were shown lolling in carriages, gliding through parks; their greyhound ran ahead, and two little grooms in white knee breeches drove the trotting horses. Others, dreaming on sofas, an opened letter lying beside them, gazed at the moon through a window that was half open, half draped with a black curtain. Coy maidens with tears on their cheeks kissed turtledoves through the bars of Gothic bird cages; or, smiling, their cheeks practically touching their own shoulders, they pulled the petals from daisies with pointed fingers that curved up at the ends like Eastern slippers. Then there were sultans with long pipes swooning under arbors in the arms of dancing girls; there were Giaours, Turkish sabres, fezzes. And invariably there were blotchy, pale landscapes of fantastic countries: pines and palms growing together, tigers on the right, a lion on the left, Tartar minarets on the horizon, Roman ruins in the foreground, a few kneeling camels—all of it set in a very neat and orderly virgin forest, with a great perpendicular sunbeam quivering in the water; and standing out on the water's surface—scratched in white on the steel-gray background—a few widely spaced floating swans.

The bracket lamp above Emma's head shone down on those pictures of every corner of the world as she turned them over one by one in the silence of the dormitory, the only sound, coming from the distance, that of some belated cab on the boulevards.

When her mother died, she wept profusely for several days. She had a memorial picture made for herself from the dead woman's hair; and in a letter filled with sorrowful reflections on life that she sent to Les Bertaux, she begged to be buried, when her time came, in the same grave. Her father thought she must be ill, and went to see her. Emma was privately pleased to feel that she had so very quickly attained this ideal of ethereal languor, inaccessible to mediocre spirits. So she let herself meander along Lamartinian paths, listening to the throbbing of harps on lakes, to all the songs of dying swans, to the falling of every leaf, to the flight of pure virgins ascending to heaven, and to the voice of the Eternal speaking in the valleys. Gradually these things began to bore her, but she refused to admit it and continued as before, first out of habit, then out of vanity; until one day she discovered with surprise that the whole mood had evaporated, leaving her heart as free of melancholy as her brow was free of wrinkles.

The good nuns, who had been taking her vocation quite for granted, were greatly surprised to find that Mademoiselle Rouault was apparently slipping out of their control. And indeed they had so deluged her with prayers, retreats, novenas and sermons, preached so constantly the respect due the saints and the martyrs, and given her so much good advice about modest behavior and the saving of her soul, that she reacted like a horse too tightly reined: she balked, and the bit fell from her teeth. In her enthusiasms she had always looked for something tangible: she had loved the church for its flowers, music for its romantic words, literature for its power to stir the passions; and she rebelled before the mysteries of faith just as she grew ever more restive under discipline, which was antipathetic to her nature. When her father took her out of school no one was sorry to see her go. The Mother Superior, indeed, remarked that she had lately been displaying a certain lack of reverence toward the community.

Back at home, Emma at first enjoyed giving orders to the servants, then grew sick of country life and longed to be back in the convent. By the time Charles first appeared at Les Bertaux she thought that she was cured of illusions—that she had nothing more to learn, and no great emotions to look forward to.

But in her eagerness for a change, or perhaps overstimulated by this man's presence, she easily persuaded herself that love, that marvelous thing which had hitherto been like a great rosy-plumaged bird soaring in the splendors of poetic skies, was at last within her grasp. And now she could not bring herself to believe that the uneventful life she was leading was the happiness of which she had dreamed.

VII

SHE REFLECTED OCCASIONALLY THAT THESE WERE, NEVERTHE-less, the most beautiful days of her life—the honeymoon days, as people called them. To be sure, their sweetness would be best enjoyed far off, in one of those lands with exciting names where the first weeks of marriage can be savored so much more deliciously and languidly! The post-chaise with its blue silk curtains would have climbed slowly up the mountain roads, and the postilion's song would have re-echoed among the cliffs, mingling with the tinkling of goat bells and the dull roar of waterfalls. They would have breathed the fragrance of lemon trees at sunset by the shore of some bay; and at night, alone on the terrace of a villa, their fingers intertwined, they would have gazed at the stars and planned their lives. It seemed to her that certain portions of the earth must produce happiness—as though it were a plant native only to those soils and doomed to languish elsewhere. Why couldn't she be leaning over the balcony of some Swiss chalet? Or nursing her melancholy in a cottage in Scotland, with a husband clad in a long black velvet coat and wearing soft leather shoes, a high-crowned hat and fancy cuffs?

She might have been glad to confide all these things to someone. But how speak about so elusive a malaise, one that keeps changing its shape like the clouds and its direction like the winds? She could find no words; and hence neither occasion nor courage came to hand.

Still, if Charles had made the slightest effort, if he had had the slightest inkling, if his glance had a single time divined her thought, it seemed to her that her heart would have been relieved of its fullness as quickly and easily as a tree drops its ripe fruit at the touch of a hand. But even as they were brought closer together by the details of daily life, she was separated from him by a growing sense of inward detachment.

Charles's conversation was flat as a sidewalk, a place of passage for the ideas of everyman; they wore drab everyday clothes, and they inspired neither laughter nor dreams. When he had lived in Rouen, he said, he had never had any interest in going to the theatre to see the Parisian company that was acting there. He couldn't swim or fence or fire a pistol; one day he couldn't tell her the meaning of a riding term she had come upon in a novel.

Wasn't it a man's role, though, to know everything? Shouldn't he be expert at all kinds of things, able to initiate you into the intensities of passion, the refinements of life, all the mysteries? *This* man could teach you nothing; he knew nothing, he wished for nothing. He took it for granted that she was content; and she resented his settled calm, his serene dullness, the very happiness she herself brought him.

She drew occasionally; and Charles enjoyed nothing more than standing beside her watching her bent over her sketchbook, half shutting his eyes the better to see her work, or rolling her bread-crumb erasers between his thumb and finger. As for the piano, the faster her fingers flew the more he marveled. She played with dash, swooping up and down the keyboard without a break. The strings of the old instrument jangled as she pounded, and when the window was open it could be heard to the end of the village. The *huissier*'s clerk often stopped to listen as he passed on the road—bareheaded, shuffling along in slippers, holding in his hand the notice he was about to post.

Moreover, Emma knew how to run her house. She let Charles's patients know how much they owed him, writing them nicely phrased letters that didn't sound like bills. When a neighbor came to Sunday dinner she always managed to think up some attractive dish. She would arrange greengages in a pyramid on a bed of vine leaves; she served her jellies not in their jars but neatly turned out on a plate; she spoke of buying finger bowls for dessert. All this redounded greatly to Bovary's credit.

He came to esteem himself the higher for having such a wife. He had two of her pencil sketches framed in wide frames, and hung them proudly in the parlor, at the end of long green cords. Citizens returning from Mass saw him standing on his doorstep, wearing a splendid pair of carpet slippers.

He came home from his rounds late—ten o'clock, sometimes midnight. He was hungry at that hour, and since the servant had gone to bed it was Emma who served him. He would take off his coat to be more comfortable at table, tell her every person he had seen, every village he had been to, every prescription he had written; and he would complacently eat what was left of the stew, pare his cheese, munch an apple, pour himself the last drop of wine. Then he would go up to bed, fall asleep the minute he was stretched on his back, and begin to snore.

He had so long been used to wearing cotton nightcaps that he couldn't get his foulard to stay on his head, and in the morning his hair was all over his face and white with down—the strings of his pillowcase often came undone during the night. He always wore heavy boots, with deep creases slanting from instep to ankle and the rest of the uppers so stiff that they seemed to be made of wood. He said that they were "plenty good enough for the country."

His mother approved his thriftiness. As in the past, she came to visit him whenever there was a particularly violent crisis in her own home; and yet she seemed to be prejudiced against her new daughter-in-law. She considered her "too grand in her tastes for the kind of people they were": the younger Bovarys ran through wood, sugar and candles at the rate of some great establishment; and the amount of charcoal they used would have done the cooking for twenty-five. She rearranged Emma's linen in the closets and taught her to check on the butcher when he delivered the meat. Emma listened to these lectures; Madame Bovary did not stint herself; and all day there would be a tremulous-lipped exchange of "*ma fille*" and "*ma mère*," each of the ladies uttering the sugary words in a voice that quivered with rage.

In Madame Dubuc's day the older woman had known herself to be the favorite; but now Charles's love for Emma seemed to her a desertion, an invasion of her own right; and she looked on sadly at Charles's happiness, like a ruined man staring through a window at revelers in a house that was once his own. Using the device of "Do you remember?" she reminded him of everything she had suffered and sacrificed for his sake; and contrasting all this with Emma's careless ways she pointed out how wrong he was to adore his wife to the exclusion of herself.

Charles didn't know what to answer. He respected his mother, and his love for his wife was boundless; he considered the former's opinions infallible, and yet Emma seemed to him perfect. After the older Madame Bovary's departure he made a fainthearted attempt to repeat one or two of the milder things he had heard her say, using her own phraseology; but with a word or two Emma convinced him he was wrong, and sent him back to his patients.

Throughout all this, following formulas she believed efficacious, she kept trying to experience love. Under the moonlight in the garden she would recite to Charles all the amorous verses she knew by heart, and sing him soulful sighing songs; but it all left her as unruffled as before, and Charles, too, seemed as little lovesick, as little stirred, as ever.

Having thus failed to produce the slightest spark of love in herself, and since she was incapable of understanding what she didn't experience, or of recognizing anything that wasn't expressed in conventional terms, she reached the conclusion that Charles's desire for her was nothing very extraordinary. His transports had become regularized; he embraced her only at certain times. This had now become a habit like any other—like a dessert that could be counted on to end a monotonous meal.

A gamekeeper whom Monsieur had cured of pneumonia made Madame a present of a little Italian greyhound bitch, and she took her with her whenever she went for a stroll: she did this every now and then, for the sake of a moment's solitude, a momentary relief from the everlasting sight of the back garden and the dusty road.

She would walk to the avenue of beeches at Banneville, near the abandoned pavilion at the corner of the wall along the fields. Rushes grow in the ditch there, tall and sharp-edged among the grass.

Once arrived she would look around her, to see whether anything had changed since the last time she had come. The foxgloves and the wallflowers were where they had been; clumps of nettles were still growing around the stones; patches of lichen still clung along the three windows, whose perennially closed shutters were rotting away from their rusty iron bars. Her thoughts would be vague at first, straying like her dog, who would be running circles, barking at yellow butterflies, chasing field mice, nibbling poppies at the edge of a wheatfield. Then her ideas would gradually focus; and sitting on the grass, jabbing it with little pokes of her parasol, Emma would ask herself again and again: "Why—*why*—did I ever marry?"

She wondered whether some different set of circumstances might not have resulted in her meeting some different man; and she tried to picture those imaginary circumstances, the life they would have brought her, the unknown other husband. However she imagined him, he wasn't a bit like Charles. He might have been handsome, witty, distinguished, magnetic—the kind of man her convent schoolmates had doubtless married. What kind of lives were they leading now? Cities, busy streets, buzzing theatres, brilliant balls—such surroundings afforded them unlimited opportunities for deep emotions and exciting sensations. But *her* life was as cold as an attic facing north; and boredom, like a silent spider, was weaving its web in the shadows, in every corner of her heart. She remembered Prize Days, when she had gone up onto the stage to receive her little wreaths. She had been charming, with her braids, her white dress, her prunella-cloth slippers. Gentlemen had leaned over, when she was back in her seat, and paid her compliments; the courtyard had been full of carriages; guests called good-bye to her as they rolled away; the music teacher with his violin case bowed to her as he passed. How far away it all was! How far!

She would call Djali, take her between her knees, stroke her long delicate head. "Kiss your mistress," she would say, "you happy, carefree thing." The slender Djali would yawn slowly, as a dog does; and the melancholy look in her eyes would touch Emma, and she would liken her to herself, talking to her aloud as though comforting someone in distress.

Sometimes squalls blew up, winds that suddenly swept in from the sea over the plateau of the *pays de Caux* and filled the countryside with fresh, salt-smelling air. The whistling wind would flatten the reeds and rustle the trembling beech leaves, while the tops of the trees swayed and murmured. Emma would pull her shawl close about her shoulders and get up.

Under the double row of trees a green light filtered down through the leaves onto the velvety moss that crunched softly beneath her feet. The sun was setting; the sky showed red between the branches; and the identical trunks of the straight line of trees were like a row of brown columns against a golden backdrop; a terror would seize her, she would call Djali and walk quickly back to Tostes along the highway. There she would sink into an armchair, and sit silent all evening.

Then, late in September, something exceptional happened: she was invited to La Vaubyessard, home of the marquis d'Andervilliers.

The marquis had been a member of the cabinet under the Restoration; and now, hoping to re-enter political life, he was paving the way for his candidature to the Chamber of Deputies. He made generous distributions of firewood among the poor in the winter, and in sessions of the departmental council he was always eloquent in demanding better roads for his district. During the hot weather he had had a mouth abscess, which Charles had relieved—miraculously, it seemed—by a timely nick of the scalpel. His steward, sent to Tostes to pay the bill for the operation, reported that evening that he had seen some superb cherries in the doctor's little garden. The cherry trees at La Vaubyessard weren't doing well; Monsieur le marquis asked Charles for a few grafts, made a point of going to thank him personally, saw Emma, and noticed that she had a pretty figure and didn't curtsy like a peasant. So at the chateau it was decided that the doctor and his young wife could be invited without any transgression of the limits of condescension, and at the same time could be counted on to behave with decorum among their betters.

One Wednesday at three in the afternoon, therefore, Monsieur and Madame Bovary set out in their buggy for La Vaubyessard, a large trunk tied on behind and a hatbox in front. Charles had another box between his legs.

They arrived at nightfall, just as lanterns were being lit in the grounds to illuminate the driveway.

VIII

THE CHATEAU, A MODERN BUILDING IN THE ITALIAN STYLE, with two projecting wings and three entrances along the front, stretched across the far end of a vast expanse of turf where cows grazed in the open spaces between groups of tall trees. Tufts of shrubbery—rhododendrons, syringas and snowballs—made a variegated border along the curving line of the graveled drive. A stream flowed under a bridge; through the evening haze the thatched farm buildings could be seen scattered over a meadow shut in by two gently rising wooded ridges; and at the rear, in among thick plantings of trees, were the two parallel lines of the coach houses and the stables—remains of the original, ancient chateau that had been torn down.

Charles's buggy drew up before the middle door; servants appeared, then the marquis, who gave the doctor's wife his arm and led her into the entrance hall.

This had a marble floor and a high ceiling; footsteps and voices echoed as in a church. From the far side rose a straight staircase; and to the left a gallery giving on the garden led to the billiard room: the sound of clicking ivory balls could be heard ahead. As she passed through on her way to the drawing room Emma noticed the men around the table: dignified-looking, with cravats reaching up to their chins and decorations on their chests, they smiled silently as they made their shots. On the dark wall-paneling hung great gilded frames, inscribed at the base with names in black letters. "Jean-Antoine d'Andervilliers d'Yverbonville, comte de la Vaubyessard and baron de la Fresnaye, killed at the battle of Coutras, October 20, 1587." Or: "Jean-Antoine-Henry-Guy d'Andervilliers de la Vaubyessard, admiral of the fleet and knight of the order of St. Michael, wounded in the battle of La Hogue, May 29, 1692, died at La Vaubyessard January 23, 1693." The rest were barely visible, for the lamplight was directed down on the green felt of the tables, and much of the room was in shadow. This darkened the row of pictures: only the crackle of their varnish caught an occasional broken gleam, and here and there some detail of painting lighter than the rest stood out from one of the dim, gold-framed rectangles: a pale forehead, two staring eyes, powdered wigs cascading onto red-coated shoulders, a garter buckle high up on a fleshy calf.

The marquis opened the drawing-room door, and one of the ladies rose. It was the marquise, and she came over to Emma, greeted her, drew her down beside her on a settee and talked to her as easily as though they were old acquaintances. She was a woman of forty or so, with fine shoulders, a hooked nose and a drawling voice; on her auburn hair she was wearing a simple bit of lace, the points falling down behind. Close beside her sat a blonde young woman in a high-backed chair; and around the fireplace gentlemen with flowers in their buttonholes were chatting with the ladies.

Dinner was served at seven. The men, more numerous than the ladies, were put at a table in the entrance hall; the ladies sat down in the dining room, with the marquis and the marquise.

Here the air was warm and fragrant; the scent of flowers and fine linen mingled with the odor of cooked meats and truffles. Candle flames cast long gleams on rounded silver dish-covers; the clouded facets of the cut glass shone palely; there was a row of bouquets all down the table; and on the wide-bordered plates the napkins stood like bishops' mitres, each with an oval-shaped roll between its folds. Red lobster claws protruded from platters; oversized fruit was piled up on moss in openwork baskets; quail were served in their plumage; steam rose from open dishes; and the platters of carved meat were brought round by the maître d'hotel himself, grave as a judge in silk stockings, knee breeches, white neckcloth and jabot. He reached them down between the guests, and with a flick of his spoon transferred to each plate the piece desired. Atop the high copper-banded porcelain stove the statue of a woman swathed to the chin in drapery stared down motionless at the company.

Madame Bovary was surprised to notice that several of the ladies had failed to put their gloves in their wine glasses.

At the head of the table, alone among ladies, was an old man. His napkin was tied around his neck like a child's, and he sat hunched over his heaped plate, gravy dribbling from his mouth. The underlids of his eyes hung down and showed red inside, and he wore his hair in a little pigtail wound with black ribbon. This was the marquis' father-in-law, the old duc de Laverdière, favorite of the duc d'Artois in the days of the marquis de Conflans' hunting parties at

Le Vaudreuil: he was said to have been Marie-Antoinette's lover between Monsieur de Coigny and Monsieur de Lauzun. He had led a wild, dissipated life, filled with duels, wagers and abductions; he had gone through his money and been the terror of his family. Now, muttering unintelligibly, he pointed his finger at one dish after another, and a servant standing behind his chair shouted their names in his ear. Emma's eyes kept coming back to this pendulous-lipped old man as though he were someone extraordinary, someone august. He had lived at court! He had slept with a queen!

Iced champagne was served, and the feel of the cold wine in her mouth gave Emma a shiver that ran over her from head to toe. She had never seen pomegranates or eaten pineapple. Even the powdered sugar seemed to her whiter and finer than elsewhere.

Then the ladies went up to their rooms to dress for the ball.

Emma devoted herself to her toilette with the meticulous care of an actress the night of her debut. She did her hair as the hairdresser advised, and slipped into her gauzy *barège* gown, which had been laid out for her on the bed.

Charles's trousers were too tight at the waist. And then, "The shoestraps will interfere with my dancing," he said.

"You? Dance?" Emma cried.

"Of course!"

"But you're crazy! Everybody would laugh. You mustn't. It's not suitable for a doctor, anyway," she added.

Charles said no more. He walked up and down waiting for Emma to be ready.

He saw her from behind in a mirror, between two sconces. Her dark eyes seemed darker than ever. Her hair, drawn down smoothly on both sides and slightly fluffed out over the ears, shone with a blue luster; in her chignon a rose quivered on its flexible stem, with artificial dewdrops at the leaf-tips. Her gown was pale saffron, trimmed with three bunches of pompon roses and green sprays.

Charles came up to kiss her on the shoulder. "Don't!" she cried. "You're rumpling me."

The strains of a violin floated up the stairs; a horn joined in. As Emma went down she had to restrain herself from running.

The quadrilles had begun. More and more guests were arriving; there was something of a crush. Emma stayed near the door on a settee.

When the music stopped, the dance floor was left to the men, who stood there talking in groups, and to the liveried servants, who crossed it with their heavy trays. Along the line of seated women there was a flutter of painted fans; smiles were half hidden behind bouquets; gold-stoppered scent bottles twisted and turned in white-gloved hands, the tight silk binding the wrists and showing the form of the nails. There was a froth of lace around décolletages, a flashing of diamonds at throats; bracelets dangling medals and coins tinkled on bare arms. Hair was sleek and shining in front, twisted and knotted behind; and every coiffure had its wreath or bunch or sprig—of forget-me-nots, jasmine, pomegranate blossoms, wheat-sprays, cornflowers. The dowagers, sitting calm and formidable, wore red headdresses like turbans.

Emma's heart pounded a bit as her partner led her out by the fingertips and she waited in line for the starting signal on the violin. But her nervousness soon wore off, and swaying and nodding in time with the orchestra, she glided forward. She responded with a smile to the violinist's flourishes as he continued to play solo when the other instruments stopped; at such moments the chink of gold pieces came clearly from the gaming tables in the next room; then everything was in full swing again: the cornet blared, once again feet tramped in rhythm, skirts

ballooned and brushed together, hands joined and separated; eyes lowered one moment looked intently into yours
the next.

Scattered among the dancers or talking in doorways
were a number of men—a dozen or so, aged from twenty-
five to forty—who were clearly distinguishable from the
rest by a certain look of overbreeding common to them all
despite differences of age, dress, or feature.

Their coats were better cut, and seemed to be of finer
cloth; their hair, brought forward in ringlets over the
temples, seemed to glisten with more expensive pomades.
Their complexion bespoke wealth: they had the pale, very
white skin that goes so well with the diaphanous tints of
porcelain, the luster of satin, the patina of old wood, and
is kept flawless by simple, exquisite fare. These men moved
their heads unconstrainedly above low cravats; their long
side whiskers drooped onto turned-down collars; they
wiped their lips with handkerchiefs that were deliciously
scented and monogrammed with huge initials. Those who
were beginning to age preserved a youthful look, while the
faces of the young had a touch of ripeness. There was an air
of indifference about them, a calm produced by the gratification of every passion; and though their manners were
suave, one could sense beneath them that special brutality
which comes from the habit of breaking down half-
hearted resistances that keep one fit and tickle one's vanity—the handling of blooded horses, the pursuit of loose
women.

A few steps from Emma a blue-coated gentleman was
deep in Italy with a pale young woman in pearls. They were
gushing about the massiveness of the piers in St. Peter's,
about Tivoli, Vesuvius, Castellamare and the Cascine, the
roses in Genoa, the Colosseum by moonlight. And the
conversation heard with her other ear was full of words
she didn't understand: it was coming from a circle that

had formed around a very young man who only the week before had "beaten Miss Arabella and Romulus" and seemed to have won two thousand louis d'or by jumping a certain ditch in England. One of the speakers was complaining that his racers were putting on weight, another that misprints had made the name of his horse unrecognizable in the newspapers.

The air in the ballroom had grown heavy; the lamps were beginning to dim; a number of the men disappeared in the direction of the billiard room. A servant climbed on a chair and broke two panes in a window; at the sound of the smash Madame Bovary turned her head and saw peasants peering in from the garden, their faces pressed against the glass. She thought of Les Bertaux: she saw the farm, the muddy pond, her father in a smock under the apple trees; and she saw herself as she had been there, skimming cream with her finger from the milk jars in the dairy. But amid the splendors of this night her past life, hitherto so vividly present, was vanishing utterly; indeed she was beginning almost to doubt that she had lived it. She was here: and around the brilliant ball was a shadow that veiled all else. She was eating a maraschino ice, at that precise moment, from a gilded silver scallop-shell that she was holding in her left hand; the spoon was between her teeth, her eyes were half shut.

A lady near her dropped her fan just as a gentleman was passing. "Would you be good enough to pick up my fan, Monsieur?" she asked him. "It's there behind the sofa."

The gentleman bowed, and as he stretched out his arm Emma saw the lady toss something into his hat, something white, folded in the shape of a triangle. The gentleman recovered the fan and handed it to the lady respectfully; she thanked him with a nod and began to sniff at her bouquet.

For supper there was an array of Spanish wines and Rhine

wines, bisque soup and cream of almond soup, Trafalgar pudding, and platters of all kinds of cold meat in trembling aspic; and after it the carriages began gradually to leave. Drawing back a corner of a muslin curtain, Emma could see their lamps slipping away into the darkness. The settees emptied; some of the card players stayed on; the musicians cooled the tips of their fingers on their tongues; Charles was half asleep, propped up against a door.

At three in the morning the closing cotillion began. Emma had never waltzed. Everyone else was waltzing, including Mademoiselle d'Andervilliers and the marquise; by this time only the hosts and the house guests remained, about a dozen in all. One of the waltzers, whom everyone called simply "Vicomte," and whose very low-cut waistcoat seemed to be molded on his torso, came up to Madame Bovary and for the second time asked her to be his partner. He would lead her, he urged; she'd do very well.

They started out slowly, then quickened their step. They whirled: or, rather, everything—lamps, furniture, walls, floor—whirled around them, like a disc on a spindle. As they passed close to a door the hem of Emma's gown caught on her partner's trousers, and for a moment their legs were all but intertwined; he looked down at her, she up at him; a paralyzing numbness came over her, and she stopped. Then they resumed; and spinning more quickly the vicomte swept her off until they were alone at the very end of the gallery; there, out of breath, she almost fell, and for an instant leaned her head against his chest. Then, still circling, but more slowly, he returned her to her seat. She sank back with her head against the wall, and put her hand over her eyes.

When she opened them, a lady was sitting on a low stool in the middle of the salon, three waltzers on their knees before her. The lady chose the vicomte, and the violin struck up again.

Everyone watched them as they went round and round. She held her body rigid, her head inclined; he maintained the same posture as before, very erect, elbow curved, chin forward. This time he had a partner worthy of him! They danced on and on, long after all the others had dropped out exhausted.

Hosts and guests chatted a few minutes longer; and then, bidding each other good night, or rather good morning, they all went up to bed.

Charles dragged himself up the stairs by the handrail; his legs, he said, were "ready to drop off." He had spent five solid hours on his feet by the card tables watching people play whist, unable to make head or tail of it. So he gave a great sigh of relief when he pulled his shoes off at last.

Emma slipped a shawl over her shoulders, opened the window and leaned out.

The night was very dark. A few drops of rain were falling. She breathed the moist wind, so cooling to her eyelids. The music was still throbbing in her ears, and she forced herself to stay awake in order to prolong the illusion of this luxurious life she would so soon have to be leaving.

The sky began to lighten. Her glance lingered on the windows of the various rooms as she tried to imagine which of them were occupied by the people she had seen the night before. She longed to know all about their lives, to penetrate into them, to be part of them.

But she was shivering with cold. She undressed and crept into bed beside the sleeping Charles.

Everyone came downstairs for breakfast. The meal lasted ten minutes; to the doctor's surprise, no liqueurs were served. Mademoiselle d'Andervilliers gathered up the remains of the brioches in a basket to feed the swans in the lake; and everyone went for a stroll in the greenhouse, where strange hairy plants were displayed on pyramidal stands, and hanging jars that looked like nests crawling with snakes dripped long, dangling, intertwined green tendrils. From the orangery at the end of the greenhouse a roofed passage led to the outbuildings. To please the young woman the marquis took her to see the stables. Above the basket-shaped racks were porcelain name plates with the horses' names in black letters. Each horse moved restlessly in his stall at the approach of the visitors and the coaxing, clicking sounds they made with their tongues. The boards of the harness-room floor shone like the parquet floor of a drawing room. The carriage harness hung in the middle, on two revolving posts; and the bits, whips, stirrups and curbs were on a line of hooks along the wall.

Charles, meanwhile, had gone to ask a groom to harness his buggy. It was brought round to the front door, and when all the bundles were stowed away, the Bovarys said their thank-yous to the marquis and the marquise and set out for home.

Emma sat silent, watching the turning wheels. Charles drove perched on the edge of the seat, arms wide apart; and the little horse went along at an ambling trot between the overwide shafts. The slack reins slapped against his rump and grew wet with lather; and the case tied on behind thumped heavily and regularly against the body of the buggy.

They were climbing one of the rises near Thibourville when just ahead of them, coming from the opposite direction, there appeared a group of riders, who passed by laughing and smoking cigars. Emma thought she recognized the vicomte; she turned and stared; but all she saw was the bobbing heads of trotting or galloping riders silhouetted against the sky.

Half a mile further along they had to stop: the breeching broke, and Charles mended it with rope. As he was checking his harness he saw something on the ground between the horse's feet, and he picked up a cigar case trimmed with green silk and bearing a crest in the center like a carriage door.

"A couple of cigars in it, too," he said. "I'll smoke them after dinner."

"You've taken up smoking?" Emma demanded.

"Once in a while, when I get the chance."

He put his find in his pocket and gave the pony a flick of the whip.

When they reached home dinner was far from ready. Madame lost her temper. Nastasie talked back.

"It's too much!" Emma cried. "I've had enough of your insolence!" And she gave her notice on the spot.

For dinner there was onion soup and veal with sorrel. Charles, sitting opposite Emma, rubbed his hands with satisfaction: "How good to be home!"

They could hear Nastasie weeping. Charles had an affection for the poor thing. She had kept him company on many an idle evening during his widowerhood. She had been his first patient, his first acquaintance in the village.

"Are you really letting her go?" he finally asked.

"Yes—what's to stop me?"

Then they warmed themselves in the kitchen while their room was made ready. Charles proceeded to smoke. He curled and pursed his lips around the cigar, spat every other minute, shrank back from every puff.

"You're going to make yourself sick," she said scornfully.

He put down his cigar and rushed to the pump for a drink of cold water. Emma snatched the cigar case and quickly flung it to the back of the closet.

The next day was endless. She walked in her garden, up and down the same paths over and over again, stopping to look at the flower beds, the fruit trees, the plaster priest, staring with a kind of amazement at all these things from her past life, things once so familiar. How remote the ball already was! What was it that made tonight seem so very far removed from the day before yesterday? Her visit to La Vaubyessard had opened a breach in her life, like one of those great crevasses that a storm can tear across the face of a mountain in the course of a single night. But there was nothing to do about it. She put her beautiful ball costume reverently away in a drawer—even to her satin slippers, whose soles were yellow from the slippery wax of the dance floor. Her heart was like them: contact with luxury had left an indelible mark on it.

The memory of the ball would not leave her. Every Wednesday she told herself as she woke: "Ah! One week ago . . . two weeks ago . . . three weeks ago, I was there!" Little by little the faces grew confused in her mind; she forgot the tune of the quadrille; the liveries and the splendid rooms became blurred. Some of the details departed—but the yearning remained.

IX

OFTEN WHEN CHARLES WAS OUT SHE WENT TO THE CLOSET AND took the green silk cigar case from among the piles of linen where she kept it.

She would look at it, open it, even sniff its lining, fragrant with verbena and tobacco. Whose was it? The vicomte's. A present from his mistress, perhaps. It had been embroidered on some rosewood frame, a charming little piece of furniture kept hidden from prying eyes, over which a pensive girl had bent for hours and hours, her soft curls brushing its surface. Love had breathed through the mesh of the canvas; every stroke of the needle had recorded a hope or a memory; and all these intertwined silken threads bespoke one constant, silent passion. And then one morning the vicomte had taken it away with him. What words had they exchanged as he stood leaning his elbow on one of those elaborate mantelpieces decked with vases of flowers and rococo clocks? She was in Tostes. Whereas he, now, was in Paris—in Paris! What was it like, Paris? The very name had such a vastness about it! She repeated it to herself under her breath with a thrill of pleasure; it sounded in her ears like the great bell of a cathedral; it blazed before her eyes everywhere, glamorous even on the labels of her jars of pomade.

At night when the fishmongers passed below her window in their carts, singing *La Marjolaine*, she would awaken; and listening to the sound of the iron-rimmed wheels on the pavement, and then the quick change in the sound as they reached the unpaved road at the end of the village, she would tell herself: "They'll be there tomorrow!"

And she followed them in thought, up and down hills, through villages, along the highway by the light of the stars. Then, somewhere along the way, her dream always petered out.

She bought a map of Paris, and with her fingertip she went for walks. She followed the boulevards, stopping at every corner, between the lines indicating the streets, in front of the white squares that were the houses. Then, closing her tired eyes, she would have a shadowy vision of gas lamps flickering in the wind and carriage steps clattering open in front of theatres.

She subscribed to a women's magazine called *La Corbeille*, and to *Le Sylphe des salons*. She devoured every word of every account of a first night, a horse race, a soirée; she was fascinated by the debut of every new singer, the opening of every new shop. She knew the latest fashions, the addresses of the best tailors, the proper days to go to the Bois and the opera. She pored over the interior decorating details in the novels of Eugène Sue; she read Balzac and George Sand, seeking in their pages vicarious satisfactions for her own desires. She brought her book with her even to meals, and turned the leaves while Charles ate and talked to her. Her readings always brought the vicomte back to her mind: she continually found similarities between him and the fictitious characters. But the circle whose center he was gradually widened; and the halo she had given him spread beyond his image; gilding other dreams.

Paris, city vaster than the ocean, glittered before Emma's eyes in a rosy light. But the teeming life of the tumultuous place was divided into compartments, separated into distinct scenes. Emma was aware of only two or three, which shut out the sight of the others and stood for all of mankind. In drawing rooms with mirrored walls and gleaming floors, around oval tables covered with gold-fringed velvet, moved the world of the ambassadors. It was full of trailing gowns, deep secrets, and unbearable tensions concealed beneath smiles. Then came the circle of the duchesses: here everyone was pale and lay in bed till four; the women—poor darlings!—wore English lace on their petticoat hems; and the men, their true worth unsuspected under their frivolous exteriors, rode horses to death for the fun of it, spent their summers at Baden-Baden, and eventually, when they were about forty, married heiresses. After midnight, the gay, motley world of writers and actresses congregated at candlelit suppers in the private rooms of restaurants. They were profligate as kings, full of idealistic ambitions and fantastic frenzies. They lived on a higher plane than other people, somewhere sublime between heaven and earth, up among the storm clouds. As for the rest of the world, it was in some indeterminate place beyond the pale; it could scarcely be said to exist. Indeed the closer to her things were, the further away from them her thoughts turned. Everything immediately surrounding her—boring countryside, inane petty bourgeois, the mediocrity of daily life—seemed to her the exception rather than the rule. She had been caught in it all by some accident: out beyond, there stretched as far as eye could see the immense territory of rapture and passions. In her longing she made no difference between the pleasures of luxury and the joys of the heart, between elegant living and sensitive feeling. Didn't love, like Indian plants, require rich soils, special temperatures? Sighs in the moonlight, long embraces, hands bathed in lovers' tears—all the fevers of the flesh and the languors of love—were inseparable from the balconies of great idle-houred castles, from a silk-curtained, thick-carpeted, beflowered boudoir with its bed on a dais, from the sparkle of precious stones and the swank of liveries.

The hired boy at the relay post across the road, who came in every morning to rub down the mare, walked through the hall in his heavy wooden shoes; his smock was in holes, his feet were innocent of stockings. Such was the groom in knee breeches she had to content herself with! When his work was done he left for the day: Charles stabled his horse himself when he returned from his rounds—took off the saddle and attached the halter; and the maid brought a truss of straw and tossed it as best she could into the manger.

To replace Nastasie (who finally departed from Tostes in a torrent of tears) Emma hired a sweet-faced orphan girl of fourteen. She forbade her to wear a cotton nightcap during the day, taught her to address her superiors in the third person, to hand a glass of water on a tray, to knock on doors before entering, and to iron, to starch, to help her dress—tried to turn her into a lady's maid. The girl obeyed without a murmur because she was afraid of losing her place; and since Madame usually left the key in the sideboard, Félicité took a little sugar upstairs with her every night, and ate it by herself in bed after saying her prayers.

Afternoons she sometimes crossed the road for a chat with the postilions while Madame was up in her room.

There Emma wore a shawl-collared dressing gown, open very low over a pleated dicky with three gold buttons. Her belt was a cord with large tassels, and her little garnet-colored slippers had rosettes of wide ribbons at the instep. Though she had no one to write to, she had bought herself a blotter, a writing case, a pen and envelopes; she would dust off her whatnot, look at herself in the mirror, take up a book, and then begin to daydream and let it fall to her lap.

She longed to travel; she longed to go back and live in the convent. She wanted to die. And she wanted to live in Paris.

Charles jogged back and forth across the countryside under snow and rain. He ate omelettes at farmhouse tables, thrust his arm into damp beds, had his face spattered with jets of warm blood at bleedings; he listened to death rattles, examined the contents of basins, handled a lot of soiled underclothing. But every night he came home to a blazing fire, a well-set table, a comfortable chair, and a dainty, prettily dressed wife smelling so sweet that he never quite knew where the scent came from, and half wondered whether it wasn't her skin that was perfuming her slip.

She delighted him by countless little niceties: a new way of making sconces out of paper to catch the wax under candles, a flounce that she changed on her dress, or the fancy name of some very plain dish that the maid hadn't got right but that Charles enjoyed eating every bit of. In Rouen she saw ladies with charms dangling from their watch fobs; she bought some charms. She took a fancy to a pair of large blue glass vases for her mantelpiece, and a little later to an ivory workbox with a silver-gilt thimble. The less Charles understood these refinements, the more alluring he found them. They added something to the pleasure of his senses and the charm of his home. They were like a trickle of golden dust along the petty pathway of his life.

His health was good, his appearance hearty; his reputation was secure. The country people liked him because he gave himself no airs. He always fondled the children and never went to a café; moreover, his morals inspired confidence. He was especially successful in treating catarrhs and chest ailments. Actually, Charles had such a dread of killing his patients that he seldom prescribed anything but sedatives—once in a while an emetic or a foot-bath or leeches. Not that surgery held any terrors for him: when he bled a patient he bled him hard, like a horse; and he was famous for his iron grip as a tooth-puller.

Eventually, "to keep himself up to date," he took out a subscription to the *La Ruche médicale*, a new publication whose prospectus had been sent him. He read a little in it after his dinner, but the heat of the room plus digestion resulted in his falling asleep at the end of five minutes; and he sat there under the lamp with his chin in his hands and his hair falling forward like a mane. Emma looked at him and shrugged her shoulders. Why didn't she at least have for a husband one of those silent, dedicated men who spend their nights immersed in books and who by the time they're sixty and rheumatic have acquired a row of decorations to wear on their ill-fitting black coats? She would have liked the name Bovary—her name—to be famous, on display in all the bookshops, constantly mentioned in the newspapers, known all over France. But Charles had no ambition! A doctor from Yvetot with whom he had recently held a consultation had humiliated him right at the sickbed, in front of the assembled relatives. When Charles told her the story that evening, Emma burst out furiously against the other doctor. Charles was so moved that he shed a tear and kissed her on the forehead. But it was shame that had exasperated her: she wanted to strike him. She went into the hall, opened the window and took a breath of fresh air to calm herself.

"It's pathetic!" she whispered to herself, despair in her heart. "What a booby!"

And indeed he got on her nerves more and more. As he grew older he grew coarser: at the end of a meal he whittled the cork of the wine bottle with his dessert knife and cleaned his teeth with his tongue; he made a gulping noise every time he took a mouthful of soup; and as he put on weight his eyes, small to begin with, seemed to be pushed toward his temples by the puffing of his cheeks.

Emma sometimes tucked the red edge of his sweater up under his vest, or straightened his tie, or threw away a pair of faded old gloves he was about to put on; and it was never, as he believed, for his sake that she did it, but for her own, out of exasperated vanity. And sometimes she told him about things she had read—a passage in a novel or a new play, some high-life anecdote recounted in a gossip column, for Charles was a presence, at least, an ear that was always open, a sure source of approval. She confided many a secret to her dog, after all! She could almost have opened her heart to the logs in the fireplace and the pendulum of the clock.

Deep down, all the while, she was waiting for something to happen. Like a sailor in distress, she kept casting desperate glances over the solitary waste of her life, seeking some white sail in the distant mists of the horizon. She had no idea by what wind it would reach her, toward what shore it would bear her, or what kind of craft it would be—tiny boat or towering vessel, laden with heartbreaks or filled to the gunwales with rapture. But every morning when she awoke she hoped that today would be the day; she listened for every sound, gave sudden starts, was surprised when nothing happened; and then, sadder with each succeeding sunset, she longed for tomorrow.

Spring came again. She found it hard to breathe, the first warm days, when the pear trees were bursting into bloom.

From early in July she began to count on her fingers how many weeks there were till October, thinking that the marquis d'Andervilliers might give another ball at La Vaubyessard. But September passed without letters or visitors.

After the pain of this disappointment had gone, her heart stood empty once more; and then the series of identical days began all over again.

So from now on they were going to continue one after the other like this, always the same, innumerable, bringing nothing! Other people's lives, drab though they might be, held at least the possibility of an event. One unexpected happening often set in motion a whole chain of change: the entire setting of one's life could be transformed. But to her nothing happened. It was God's will. The future was a pitch-black tunnel, ending in a locked door.

She gave up her music: why should she play? Who was there to listen? There wasn't a chance of her ever giving a concert in a short-sleeved velvet gown, skimming butterfly fingers over the ivory keys of a grand piano, feeling the public's ecstatic murmur flow round her like a breeze —so why go through the tedium of practicing? She left her drawing books and her embroidery in a closet. What was the use of anything? What was the use? She loathed sewing.

"I've read everything there is to read," she told herself.

And so she sat—holding the fire tongs in the fire till they glowed red, or watching the falling of the rain.

How depressed she was on Sundays, when the churchbell tolled for vespers! With a dull awareness she listened to the cracked sound as it rang out again and again. Sometimes a cat walking slowly along one of the roofs outside her window arched its back against the pale rays of the sun. The wind blew trails of dust on the highway. Far off somewhere a dog was howling. And the bell would keep on giving its regular, monotonous peals that died away over the countryside.

People came out of church. Women with their wooden shoes polished, peasant men in new smocks, little children skipping bareheaded in front of them—all moved toward home. And until dark five or six men, always the same ones, stayed playing their shuffleboard game before the main entrance of the inn.

The winter was a cold one. Every morning the windowpanes were frosted over, and the whitish light that came through—as though filtered through ground glass—sometimes didn't vary all day. By four o'clock it was time to light the lamps.

On sunny days she went out into the garden. The dew had garnished the cabbages with silvery lace, and joined head to head with long shining filaments. There was no sound of birds; everything seemed to be sleeping—the espaliered trees under their straw, the vine like a great sick snake under the wall coping, where she could see many-legged wood lice crawling as she came near. In among the spruces near the hedge the priest in a tricorn reading his breviary had lost his right foot, and the scaling of the plaster in the frost had left a white scurf on his face.

Then she would return upstairs, close her door, poke the coals; and languid in the heat of the fire she would feel boredom descend again, heavier than before. She would have liked to go down for a chat with the maid, but self-respect held her back.

Every day at the same time the schoolmaster in his black silk skullcap opened the shutters of his house; every day at the same time the village policeman passed, his sword buckled around his smock. Morning and evening the post horses crossed the road in threes to drink at the pond. Now and again the bell of a café door would tinkle as it opened; and when there was a wind she could hear the little copper basins that formed the barber's shop-sign creaking on their two rods. His window display consisted of an old fashion plate stuck on one of the panes, and a wax bust of a woman with yellow hair. The barber, too, was accustomed to bewail the waste of his talents, his ruined career; and dreaming of a shop in a large city—in Rouen, perhaps, on the river front, or near the theatre—he paced back and forth all day between the mayor's office and the church, gloomily waiting for customers. When Madame Bovary raised her eyes she always saw him there with his cap over one ear, and his short work jacket, like a sentry on duty.

In the afternoon, sometimes, a man's face appeared outside the parlor windows, a swarthy face with black side whiskers and a slow, wide, gentle smile that showed very white teeth. Then would come the strain of a waltz; and in a miniature drawing room on top of the hurdy-gurdy a set of tiny dancers would begin to revolve. Women in pink turbans, Tyrolians in jackets, monkeys in black tailcoats, gentlemen in knee breeches—they all spun around among the armchairs, sofas and tables, and were reflected in bits of mirror glass joined together at the edges by strips of gold paper. As he turned his crank the man would glance to his right, to his left, and toward the windows. Now and then he would let out a spurt of brown saliva against the curb and raise his knee to lift the instrument and ease the

heavy shoulder strap; and the music, now doleful and dragging, now merry and quick, came out of the box through a
pink taffeta curtain under a fancy brasswork grill. The
tunes it played were tunes that were being heard in
other places—in theatres, in drawing rooms, under the
lighted chandeliers of ballrooms: echoes from the world
that reached Emma this way. Sarabands ran on endlessly in
her head; and her thoughts, like dancing girls on some
flowery carpet, leapt with the notes from dream to dream,
from sorrow to sorrow. Then, when the man had caught in
his cap the coin she threw him, he would pull down an old
blue wool cover, hoist his organ onto his back, and move
heavily off. She always watched him till he disappeared.

But it was above all at mealtime that she could bear it
no longer—in that small ground-floor room with its smoking stove, its squeaking door, its sweating walls and its
damp floor tiles. All the bitterness of life seemed to be
served up to her on her plate; and the steam rising from the
boiled meat brought gusts of revulsion from the depths
of her soul. Charles was a slow eater; she would nibble a few
hazelnuts, or lean on her elbow and draw lines on the
oilcloth with the point of her table knife.

Now she let everything in the house go, and the older
Madame Bovary was amazed by the change she found when
she came to spend part of Lent in Tostes. Emma, once so
careful and dainty, now went whole days without putting
on a dress; she wore gray cotton stockings, lit the house
with cheap tallow candles. She kept saying that they had
to be careful, since they weren't rich; and she always went
on to add that she was very contented, very happy, that
she liked Tostes very much; and she made other surprising
statements that shut up her mother-in-law. However,
she seemed no more inclined than ever to follow her advice.
Once, indeed, when Madame Bovary took it into her head
to suggest that employers should keep an eye on their

servants' religious life, Emma replied with such a terrible look and such a freezing smile that the dear woman henceforth kept her fingers out of things.

Emma was becoming capricious, hard to please. She would order special dishes for herself and then not touch them; one day she would drink nothing but fresh milk; the next, cups of tea by the dozen. Often she refused absolutely to go out; then she would feel stifled, open the windows, change to a light dress. She would give the maid a tongue-lashing and then turn around and give her presents, or time off to visit the neighbors, just as occasionally she would give a beggar all the silver she had in her purse, though she was anything but tenderhearted or sympathetic to other people's troubles. (In this she was like most sons and daughters of country folk: their souls always keep some of the horniness of their fathers' hands.)

Toward the end of February, Monsieur Rouault celebrated the anniversary of his recovery by bringing his son-in-law a magnificent turkey, and he stayed on at Tostes for three days. Charles was out most of the time with his patients, and it was Emma who kept her father company. He smoked in her bedroom, spit on the andirons, talked about crops, calves, cows, chickens and the village council; when he finally left and she had shut the door behind him, her feeling of relief surprised even herself. But then she no longer hid her scorn for anything or anyone; and she was beginning now and then to express peculiar opinions, condemning what everyone else approved and approving things that were perverse or immoral—a way of talking that made her husband stare at her wide-eyed.

Would this wretchedness last forever? Was there no way out? And yet she was every bit as good as all the other women, who lived in contentment! She had seen duchesses at La Vaubyessard who were dumpier and more common than she, and she cursed God for his injustice. She leaned her head against the wall and wept. She thought with envy of riotous living, of nights spent at masked balls, of shameless revels and all the mysterious raptures they must bring in their train.

She grew pale and developed palpitations. Charles gave her valerian drops and camphor baths. Everything he tried seemed to exacerbate her the more.

Some days she chattered endlessly, almost feverishly; and such a period of overexcitement would suddenly be followed by a torpor in which she neither spoke nor moved. At such times she would revive herself with eau de Cologne, pouring a bottle of it over her arms.

Since she continually complained about Tostes, Charles supposed that the cause of her illness must have something to do with the town's situation; and struck by this idea he thought seriously of settling somewhere else.

As soon as she knew this she began to drink vinegar to lose weight, acquired a little dry cough, and lost her appetite completely.

It was a wrench for Charles to leave Tostes, after living there four years and just when he was beginning to be really established. Still, if it had to be— He took her to Rouen, to see one of his old teachers. The diagnosis was that she was suffering from a nervous illness: a change of air was indicated.

After looking here and there, Charles learned that in the district of Neufchâtel there was a good-sized market town named Yonville-l'Abbaye, whose doctor, a Polish refugee, had decamped just the week before. So he wrote to the local pharmacist and inquired about the population, the distance to the nearest doctor, how much his predecessor had earned a year, etc.; and when the answers were satisfactory he decided to move by spring if Emma's health didn't improve.

One day when she was going through a drawer in preparation for moving, something pricked her finger. It was the wire around her bridal bouquet. The orange-blossom buds were yellow with dust, and the silver-edged satin ribbons were frayed. She tossed it into the fire. It blazed up quicker than dry straw. Then it lay like a red bush on the ashes, slowly consuming itself. She watched it burn. The pasteboard berries burst open, the brass wire curled, the braid melted; and the shriveled paper petals hovered along the fireback like black butterflies and finally flew away up the chimney.

When they left Tostes in March, Madame Bovary was pregnant.

PART TWO

I

YONVILLE-L'ABBAYE (EVEN THE RUINS OF THE ANCIENT CAPU-
chin friary from which it derives its name are no longer
there) is a market town twenty miles from Rouen, between the highways to Abbeville and Beauvais in the
valley of the Rieule. This is a small tributary of the
Andelle: it turns the wheels of three mills before joining
the larger stream, and contains some trout that boys like
to fish for on Sundays.

Branching off from the highway at La Boissière, the
road to Yonville continues level until it climbs the hill at
Les Leux; and from there it commands a view of the valley.
This is divided by the Rieule into two contrasting bits of
countryside: everything to the left is grazing land, every-

thing to the right is ploughed field. The pastures extend along the base of a chain of low hills and merge at the far end with the meadows of Bray; while eastward the plain rises gently and grows steadily wider, flaunting its golden grainfields as far as eye can see. The stream, flowing along the edge of the grass, is a white line dividing the color of the meadows from that of the ploughed earth: the country thus resembles a great spread-out cloak, its green velvet collar edged with silver braid.

On the horizon beyond Yonville loom the oaks of the Argueil forest and the escarpments of the bluffs of Saint-Jean, the latter streaked from top to bottom with long, irregular lines of red: these are marks left by rain, and their brickish color, standing out so sharply against the gray rock of the hill, comes from the iron content of the many springs in the country just beyond.

This is where Normandy, Picardy and the Ile-de-France come together, a mongrel region where the speech of the natives is as colorless as the landscape is lacking in character. Here they make the worst Neufchâtel cheeses in the entire district; and here farming calls for considerable investment: great quantities of manure are needed to fertilize the friable, sandy, stony soil.

Up until 1835 no road was kept open to Yonville, but about that time the cross-cut was made that links the Abbeville and Amiens highways and is sometimes used by carters traveling from Rouen to Flanders. Nevertheless, despite its "new avenues for trade," Yonville-l'Abbaye has stood still. Instead of adopting improved methods of farming, the natives stick to their pastures, worn-out though they are; and the lazy town, spurning the farmland, has continued its spontaneous growth in the direction of the river. The sight of it from a distance, stretched out along the bank, brings to mind a cowherd taking a noonday nap beside the stream.

At the foot of the hill the road crosses the Rieule on a bridge, and then, becoming an avenue planted with young aspens, leads in a straight line to the first outlying houses. These are surrounded by hedges, and their yards are full of scattered outbuildings—cider presses, carriage houses and distilling sheds standing here and there under thick trees with ladders and poles leaning against their trunks and scythes hooked over their branches. The thatched roofs hide the top third or so of the low windows like fur caps pulled down over eyes, and each windowpane, thick and convex, has a bull's-eye in its center like the bottom of a bottle. Some of the plastered house walls with their diagonal black timbers are the background for scraggly espaliered pear trees; and the house doors have little swinging gates to keep out the baby chicks, who come to the sill to peck at brown-bread crumbs soaked in cider. Gradually the yards become narrower, houses are closer together, the hedges disappear; occasionally a fern broom put out to dry is seen hanging from a window; there is a blacksmith shop, a cart-maker's with two or three new carts outside half blocking the roadway. Then comes a white house behind an iron fence, its circular lawn adorned by a cupid holding finger to lips. Two cast-iron urns stand at either end of the entrance terrace; brass plates gleam brightly at the door: this is the notary's house, the finest in town.

The church is across the street, twenty yards further on, at the corner of the main square. The little graveyard surrounding it, enclosed by an elbow-high wall, is so full of graves that the old tombstones, lying flat on the ground, form a continuous pavement divided into rectangular blocks by the grass that pushes up between. The church was remodeled during the last years of the reign of Charles X. The wooden vaulting is beginning to rot at the top: black cavities are appearing here and there in the blue paint. Above the door, in the place usually occupied by an organ, is a gallery for the men, reached by a spiral staircase that echoes loudly under the tread of wooden shoes.

Daylight, coming through the windows of plain glass, falls obliquely on the pews; and here and there on the wall from which they jut out at right angles is tacked a bit of straw matting, with the name of the pew-holder in large letters below. Beyond, where the nave narrows, stands the confessional, and opposite it a statuette of the Virgin: she is dressed in a satin gown and a tulle veil spangled with silver stars, and her cheeks are daubed red like some idol from the Sandwich Islands. A painting by a copyist, inscribed "Holy Family: Presented by the Minister of the Interior," hangs over the main altar; and there, flanked by four candlesticks, it closes the vista. The cheap fir choir stalls have never been painted.

The market—that is, a tile roof supported by about twenty pillars—takes up approximately half the main square of Yonville. The town hall, designed, as everyone will tell you, "by a Paris architect," is a kind of Greek temple forming one corner of the square, next door to the pharmacy. Its lower story has three Ionic columns; above is a row of arched windows; and the culminating pediment is filled with a figure of the Gallic cock, one of its claws resting on the Constitution and the other holding the scales of justice.

But what catches the eye the most is across the square from the Lion d'Or hotel: Monsieur Homais' pharmacy! Especially at night, when his lamp is lit, and the red and green glass jars decorating his window cast the glow of their two colors far out across the roadway! Peering through it, as through the glare of Bengal lights, one can catch a glimpse, at that hour, of the dim figure of the pharmacist himself, bent over his desk. The entire façade of his establishment is plastered from top to bottom with inscriptions—in running script, in round hand, in block capitals: "Vichy, Seltzer and Barèges Waters; Depurative Fruit Essences; Raspail's Remedy; Arabian Racahout; Darcet's Pastilles; Regnault's Ointment; Bandages, Baths, Laxative Chocolates, etc." And the shop-sign, as wide as the shop itself, proclaims in gold letters: "Homais Pharmacy." At the rear of the shop, behind the great scales fastened to the counter, the word "Laboratory" is inscribed above a glass door; and this door itself, halfway up, bears once again the name "Homais," in gold letters on a black ground.

That is as much as there is to see in Yonville. The street (the only street), long as a rifle-shot and lined with a few shops, abruptly ceases to be a street at a turn of the road. If you leave it on the right and follow the base of the bluffs of Saint-Jean, you soon reach the cemetery.

This was enlarged the year of the cholera—one wall was torn down and three adjoining acres were added; but all this new portion is almost uninhabited, and new graves continue as in the past to be dug in the crowded area near the gate. The caretaker, who is also gravedigger and sexton at the church (thus profiting doubly ·from the parish corpses), has taken advantage of the empty land to plant potatoes. Nevertheless, his little field grows smaller every year, and when there is an epidemic he doesn't know whether to rejoice in the deaths or lament the space taken by the new graves.

"You are feeding on the dead, Lestiboudois!" Monsieur le curé told him, one day.

The somber words gave him pause, and for a time he desisted; but today he continues to plant his tubers, coolly telling everyone that they come up by themselves.

Since the events which we are about to relate, absolutely nothing has changed in Yonville. To this day the tin tricolor still turns atop the church tower; the two calico streamers outside the dry-goods shop still blow in the wind; the spongy foetuses in the pharmacy window continue to disintegrate in their cloudy alcohol; and over the main entrance of the hotel the old golden lion, much discolored by the rains, stares down like a curly-headed poodle on passers-by.

The evening the Bovarys were expected at Yonville, Madame Lefrançois, the widow who owned this hotel, was so frantically busy with her saucepans that large beads of sweat stood out on her face. Tomorrow was market-day, and she had to get everything ready in advance—cut the meat, clean the chickens, make soup, roast and grind the coffee. In addition, she had tonight's dinner to get for her regular boarders and for the new doctor and his wife and their maid. Bursts of laughter came from the billiard room; in the small dining room three millers were calling for brandy; logs were blazing, charcoal was crackling, and on the long table in the kitchen, in among the quarters of raw mutton, stood high piles of plates that shook with the chopping of the spinach on the chopping-block. From the yard came the squawking of the chickens that the kitchen maid was chasing with murderous intent.

Warming his back at the fire was a man in green leather slippers, wearing a velvet skullcap with a gold tassel. His face, slightly pitted by smallpox, expressed nothing but self-satisfaction, and he seemed as contented with life as the goldfinch in a wicker cage hanging above his head. This was the pharmacist.

"Artémise!" cried the mistress of the inn. "Chop some kindling, fill the decanters, bring some brandy—hurry up! Lord! If I only knew what dessert to offer these people you're waiting for! Listen to their moving-men starting up that racket in the billiard room again! They've left their van in the driveway, too: the Hirondelle will probably crash into it. Call 'Polyte and tell him to put it in the shed! Would you believe it, Monsieur Homais—since this morning they've played at least fifteen games and drunk eight pots of cider! But they're going to ruin my table," she said, staring over at them across the room, her skimming-spoon in her hand.

"That wouldn't be much of a loss," replied Monsieur Homais. "You'd buy another one."

"Another billiard table!" cried the widow.

"But this one's falling apart, Madame Lefrançois! I tell you again; it's shortsighted of you not to invest in a new one! Very shortsighted! Players today want narrow pockets and heavy cues, you know. They don't play billiards the way they used to. Everything's changed. We must keep up with the times! Just look at Tellier . . ."

The hostess flushed with anger.

"Say what you like," the pharmacist went on, "his billiard table is nicer than yours. And if a patriotic tournament were to be got up, for Polish independence or Lyons flood relief . . ."

"We're not afraid of fly-by-nights like Tellier," the hostess interrupted, shrugging her heavy shoulders. "Don't worry, Monsieur Homais. As long as the Lion d'Or exists we'll keep our customers. We're a well-established house. But the Café Français . . . One of these mornings you'll find it sealed up, with a nice big notice on the window blinds. A new billiard table?" she went on, talking as though to herself. "But this one's so handy to stack the washing on! And in the hunting season it's slept as many as six! . . . But what's keeping that slowpoke Hivert?"

"You'll wait till he arrives, to give your gentlemen their dinner?" the pharmacist asked.

"Wait? And what about Monsieur Binet? You'll see him come in on the stroke of six: he's the most punctual man in the world. He always has to sit at the same place in the little room: he'd die rather than eat his dinner anywhere else. And finicky! So particular about his cider! Not like Monsieur Léon! Monsieur Léon sometimes doesn't come in till seven, or even half-past, and half the time he doesn't even know what he's eating. What a nice young man! So polite! So soft-spoken!"

"Ah, Madame! There's a great difference, you know, between someone who's been properly brought up and a tax collector who got his only schooling in the army."

The clock struck six. Binet entered.

He was clad in a blue frock coat that hung straight down all around his skinny body; and the raised peak of his leather cap, its earflaps pulled up and fastened at the top, displayed a bald, squashed-looking forehead, deformed by long pressure of a helmet. He was wearing a coarse wool vest, a crinoline collar, gray trousers, and—as he did in every season—well-shined shoes that bulged in two parallel lines over the rising of his two big toes. Not a hair was out of place in the blond chin whisker outlining his jaw: it was like the edging of a flower bed around his long, dreary face with its small eyes and hooked nose. He was a clever card player, a good hunter, and wrote a fine hand. His hobby was making napkin rings on his own lathe: jealous as an artist and stingy as a bourgeois, he cluttered up his house with his handiwork.

He headed for the small room, but the three millers had to be got out before he would go in. While his table was being set he stood next to the stove without saying a word; then he closed the door and took off his cap as usual.

"He won't wear out his tongue with civilities," the pharmacist remarked, as soon as he was alone with the hostess.

"He never talks a bit more than that," she answered. "Last week I had two cloth salesmen here—two of the funniest fellows you ever listened to. They told me stories that made me laugh till I cried. Would you believe it? He sat there like a clam—didn't open his mouth."

"No imagination," pronounced the pharmacist. "Not a hint of a spark! No manners whatever!"

"And yet they say he has something to him," objected the hostess.

"Something to him?" cried Monsieur Homais. "That man? Something to him? Still, in his own line I suppose he may have," he conceded.

And he went on: "Ah! A business man with vast connections, a lawyer, a doctor, a pharmacist—I can understand it if they get so engrossed in their affairs that they become eccentric, even surly: history is full of such examples. But at least they have important affairs to be engrossed in! Take me, for instance: how often I've turned my desk upside down looking for my pen to write some labels, only to find I'd stuck it behind my ear!"

Meanwhile Madame Lefrançois had approached the door to see whether the Hirondelle wasn't in sight, and she started as a black-clad man that moment entered the kitchen. In the last faint light of dusk it was just possible to make out his florid face and athletic figure.

"What can I offer you, Monsieur le curé?" she asked, reaching down a brass candlestick from a row that stood all ready and complete with candles on the mantelpiece. "A drop of cassis? A glass of wine?"

The priest very politely declined. He had come to fetch his umbrella, he said: he had left it at the convent in Ernemont the other day, and had supposed the Hirondelle would have delivered it by now. He asked Madame Lefrançois to have it brought to him at the rectory during the evening, and then left for the church, where the bell was tolling the Angelus.

When the sound of his footsteps in the square had died away, the pharmacist declared that in his opinion the priest's behavior had been most improper. His refusal to take a glass of something was the most revolting kind of hypocrisy: all priests were secret tipplers, he said, and they were all doing their best to bring back the days of the tithe.

The hostess said some words in the curé's defense. "Besides," she went on, "he could take on four like you. Last year he helped our men get in the straw: he carried as many as six bundles at a time—that shows you how strong he is."

"Bravo!" cried the pharmacist. "Go ahead! Keep sending your daughters to confession to strapping fellows like that! But if I were the government I'd have every priest bled once a month. Yes, a fine generous phlebotomy every month, Madame, in the interests of morals and decency."

"That's enough, Monsieur Homais! You've no respect for religion!"

"On the contrary. I'm a very religious man, in my own way, far more so than all these people with their mummeries and their tricks. I worship God, I assure you! I believe in a Supreme Being, a Creator. Whoever he is—and what difference does it make?—he put us here on earth to fulfill our duties as citizens and parents. But I don't have to go into church and kiss silver platters and hand over my money to fatten up a lot of rascals that eat better than you and I! To him, one can do full honor in a forest, a field—or merely by gazing up at the ethereal vault, like the ancients. My God is the God of Socrates, of Franklin, of Voltaire, of Béranger! My credo is the credo of Rousseau! I adhere to the immortal principles of '89! I have no use for the kind of God who goes walking in his garden with a stick, sends his friends to live in the bellies of whales, gives up the ghost with a groan and then comes back to life three days later! Those things aren't only absurd in themselves, Madame—they're completely opposed to all physical laws. It goes to prove, by the way, that priests have always wallowed in squalid ignorance and have wanted nothing better than to drag the entire world down to their own level."

As he ended, he glanced about in search of an audience: for a moment, during his outburst, he had had the illusion that he was addressing the village council. But the mistress of the inn was no longer listening to him: her ears had caught a distant sound of wheels. There was the rattle of a coach, the pounding of loose horseshoes on the road; and the Hirondelle drew up before the door at last.

It was a yellow box-shaped affair mounted on two large wheels that came up as high as the top, blocking the passengers' view and spattering their shoulders. When the carriage was closed the tiny panes of its narrow windows rattled in their frames, and there were mud stains here and there on the ancient coating of dust that even heavy rainstorms never washed off completely. It was drawn by three horses, one ahead and two abreast. Its under side bumped against the ground on down grades.

A number of the local inhabitants made their appearance in the square, and all speaking at once they asked for news, for explanations of the delay, for their packages. Hivert didn't know whom to answer first. It was he who attended to things in the city for the Yonvillians. He shopped for them, brought back rolls of leather for the shoemaker, scrap iron for the blacksmith, a keg of herrings for Madame Lefrançois his employer, ladies' bonnets from the milliner, wigs from the hairdresser; and all along the road on the way back he distributed his packages, standing up on his seat and hurling them over the farmyard fences with a shout as his horses kept galloping ahead.

An accident had delayed him: Madame Bovary's greyhound had run away—disappeared across the fields. They had whistled for her a good fifteen minutes. Hivert had even turned his coach around and gone back over the road for more than a mile, expecting to come upon her any minute; but they'd had to go on without her. Emma had wept and made a scene, blaming it all on Charles. Monsieur Lheureux, the Yonville dry-goods dealer, who was also in the carriage, had tried to comfort her by citing numerous examples of lost dogs' recognizing their masters many years later. There was a famous one, he said, that had returned to Paris all the way from Constantinople. Another had traveled one hundred twenty-five miles in a straight line, swimming four rivers. And his own father had had a poodle who after being gone for twelve years had suddenly jumped up on his back one night in the street, as he was on his way to a friend's house for dinner.

II

EMMA STEPPED OUT FIRST, FOLLOWED BY FÉLICITÉ, MONSIEUR Lheureux, and a wet nurse; and Charles had to be shaken awake in his corner, where he had dozed off as soon as darkness had fallen.

Homais introduced himself: he paid his compliments to Madame and spoke politely to Monsieur, said he was delighted to have been of service to them, and cordially added that he had taken the liberty of inviting himself to share their dinner, his wife being for the moment out of town.

In the kitchen, Madame Bovary crossed to the fireplace. Reaching halfway down her skirt, she grasped it with the tips of two of her fingers, raised it to her ankles, and stretched out a black-shod foot toward the flame, over the leg of mutton that was turning on the spit. She was standing in the full light of the fire, and by its harsh glare one could see the weave of her dress, the pores of her white skin, even her eyelids when she briefly shut her eyes. Now and again she was flooded by a great glow of red, as a gust of wind blew into the fire from the half-open kitchen door.

From the other side of the fireplace a fair-haired young man was silently watching her.

This was Monsieur Léon Dupuis, the second of the Lion d'Or's regular diners, clerk to Maître Guillaumin the notary. Finding Yonville very dull, he dined as late as possible, in the hope that some traveler might turn up at the inn with whom he could have an evening's conversation. On days when there was no work to detain him at the office, he had no way of filling the interval, and ended up arriving on time and enduring a tête-à-tête with Binet straight through from soup to cheese. So it was with pleasure that he accepted the hostess' suggestion that he dine with the new arrivals, and they all went into the large dining room, where their four places had been set: Madame Lefrançois was making an occasion of it.

Homais asked permission to keep his cap on; he had a dread of head colds. Then, turning to his neighbor: "Madame is a bit tired, I presume? Our old Hirondelle does such a frightful lot of bumping and shaking!"

"It does," Emma answered. "But I always love traveling anyway. I enjoy a change of scene."

The clerk sighed. "It's so boring to be always stuck in the same place!"

"If you were like me," said Charles, "always having to be on horseback . . ."

"But there's nothing more charming than riding, I think," said the clerk, addressing Madame Bovary. "If you have the opportunity, of course."

"As a matter of fact," said the apothecary, "the practice

of medicine isn't particularly arduous in this part of the world. The condition of our roads makes it possible to use a gig, and, generally speaking, payment is good—the farmers are well off. Aside from the usual cases of enteritis, bronchitis, liver complaint, etc., our roster of illnesses includes an occasional intermittent fever at harvest time, but on the whole very little that's serious except for a good deal of scrofula, probably the result of the deplorable hygienic conditions in our countryside. Ah! You'll have to fight many a prejudice, Monsieur Bovary; every day your scientific efforts will be thwarted by the peasant's stubborn adherence to his old ways. Plenty of our people still have recourse to novenas and relics and the priest, instead of doing the natural thing and coming to the doctor or the pharmacist. To tell the truth, however, the climate isn't at all bad: we even have a few nonagenarians. The thermometer—this I can tell you from personal observation—goes down in winter to four degrees, and in the hottest season touches twenty-five or thirty degrees Centigrade at the most—that is, twenty-four degrees Réaumur at a maximum, or, in other words, fifty-four degrees Fahrenheit, to use the English scale—not more! You see, we're sheltered from the north winds by the Argueil forest on the one side and from the west winds by the bluffs of Saint-Jean on the other. However, this warmth, which because of the dampness given off by the river and the number of cattle in the pastures, which themselves exhale, as you know, a great deal of ammonia, that is nitrogen, hydrogen, and oxygen (no, just nitrogen and hydrogen), and which, sucking up the humus from the soil, mixing all these different emanations together—making a package of them, so to speak—and combining also with the electricity in the atmosphere when there is any, could in the long run result in noxious miasmas, as in tropical countries; this warmth, I was saying, is actually moderated from the direction from which it comes, or rather the direction from which it could come, namely, from the south, by southeast winds, which being of course cool themselves as a result of crossing the Seine sometimes burst on us all of a sudden like arctic air from Russia!"

"Are there some nice walks in the neighborhood, at least?" Madame Bovary asked, speaking to the young man.

"Oh, hardly any," he answered. "There's one place, called the Pasture, on top of the bluffs at the edge of the woods. I go there Sundays sometimes with a book and watch the sunset."

"There's nothing I love as much as sunsets," she said. "But my favorite place for them is the seashore."

"Oh, I adore the sea," said Monsieur Léon.

"Don't you have the feeling," asked Madame Bovary, "that something happens to free your spirit in the presence of all that vastness? It raises up my soul to look at it, somehow. It makes me think of the infinite, and all kinds of wonderful things."

"Mountain scenery does the same," said Léon. "A cousin of mine traveled in Switzerland last year, and he told me that no one who hasn't been there can imagine the poetry and charm of the lakes and waterfalls and the majesty of the glaciers. You can look across the rivers there and see pine trees so high you can't believe your eyes. They build their chalets right on the edge of precipices. If you look down you can see whole valleys a thousand feet below you through openings in the clouds. Think what it must do to you to see things like that! I'd fall on my knees, I think. I'd want to pray. I can well understand the famous composer who used to play the piano in such places, to get inspiration."

"Are you a musician?" she asked.

"No, but I love music," he answered.

"Ah, don't listen to him, Madame Bovary," interrupted

Homais, leaning across his plate. "He's just being modest. What about the other day, my friend? You were singing *L'Ange gardien* in your room—it was delightful. I heard you from the laboratory; you rendered it like a real actor."

Léon lived at the pharmacist's, in a small third-floor room looking out on the square. He blushed at his landlord's compliment. But the latter had already turned back to the doctor and was briefing him on the leading citizens of Yonville. He told stories about them and gave vital statistics. No one knew for sure how well off the notary was; and then there was the Tuvache family, all of them hard to get on with.

Emma went on: "What is your favorite kind of music?"

"Oh, German music. It's the most inspiring."

"Do you know Italian opera?"

"Not yet—but I'll hear some next year when I go to Paris to finish law school."

"As I was just telling your husband," the pharmacist said, "speaking of our poor runaway friend Yanoda, thanks to his extravagance you're going to enjoy one of the most comfortable houses in Yonville. What's especially convenient about it for a doctor is that it has a door opening on the lane, so that people can come and go without being seen. Besides, it has everything a housekeeper needs: laundry, kitchen and pantry, sitting room, fruit closet, etc. Yanoda didn't care how he spent his money! He built an arbor alongside the river at the foot of the garden, just to drink beer in during the summer! If Madame likes gardening, she'll be able to . . ."

"My wife never gardens," said Charles. "She's been advised to take exercise, but even so she'd much rather stay in her room and read."

"So would I," said Léon. "What's more delightful than an evening beside the fire with a nice bright lamp and a book, listening to the wind beating against the windows . . . ?"

"How true!" she said, her great dark eyes fixed widely on him.

"I'm absolutely removed from the world at such times," he said. "The hours go by without my knowing it. Sitting there I'm wandering in countries I can see every detail of —I'm playing a role in the story I'm reading. I actually feel I'm the characters—I live and breathe with them."

"I know!" she said. "I feel the same!"

"Have you ever had the experience," Léon went on, "of running across in a book some vague idea you've had, some image that you realize has been lurking all the time in the back of your mind and now seems to express absolutely your most subtle feelings?"

"Indeed I have," she answered.

"That's why I'm especially fond of poetry," he said. "I find it much more affecting than prose. It's much more apt to make me cry."

"Still, it's tiresome in the long run," Emma replied. "Nowadays I'm crazy about a different kind of thing— stories full of suspense, stories that frighten you. I hate to read about low-class heroes and their down-to-earth concerns, the sort of thing the real world's full of."

"You're quite right," the clerk approved. "Writing like that doesn't move you: it seems to me to miss the whole true aim of art. Noble characters and pure affections and happy scenes are very comforting things. They're a refuge from life's disillusionments. As for me, they're my *only* means of relief, living here as I do, cut off from the world. Yonville has so little to offer!"

"It's like Tostes, I suppose," Emma said. "That's why I always subscribed to a lending library."

"If Madame would do me the honor of using it," said

the pharmacist, who had heard her last words, "I can offer her a library composed of the best authors—Voltaire, Rousseau, Delille, Walter Scott, the *Echo des Feuilletons.* I subscribe to a number of periodicals, too. The *Fanal de Rouen* comes every day: as a matter of fact I happen to be its local correspondent for Buchy, Forges, Neufchâtel, Yonville and all this vicinity."

They had been at table two hours and a half. Artémise was a wretched waitress: she dragged her cloth slippers over the tile floor, brought plates one by one, forgot everything, paid no attention to what was told her, and constantly left the door of the billiard room ajar so that the latch kept banging against the wall.

As he talked, Léon had unconsciously rested his foot on one of the rungs of Madame Bovary's chair. She was wearing a little blue silk scarf that held her pleated batiste collar stiff as a ruff; and as she moved her head the lower part of her face buried itself in the folds or gently rose out of them. Sitting thus side by side while Charles and the pharmacist chatted, they entered into one of those vague conversations in which every new subject that comes up proves to be one more aspect of a core of shared feelings. The names of plays running in Paris, the titles of novels, new dance tunes, the inaccessible great world, Tostes where she had just come from, Yonville where they both were now—all this they went into and talked about until dinner was over.

When coffee was brought in, Félicité went off to prepare the bedroom in the new house, and soon they all got up from the table. Madame Lefrançois was asleep beside her smoldering fire, and the stable-boy, lantern in hand, was waiting to light Monsieur and Madame Bovary home. There were wisps of straw in his red hair, and his left leg was lame. He took Monsieur le curé's umbrella in his other hand, and the company set out.

The town was asleep. The pillars of the market cast long shadows, and the pallor of the road in the moonlight gave the effect of a summer night.

But the doctor's house was only fifty yards from the inn, and almost at once it was time to say good night and they went their separate ways.

The moment she stepped inside the entrance hall Emma felt the chill from the plaster walls fall on her shoulders, like the touch of a damp cloth. The walls were new and the wooden stairs creaked. Upstairs in the bedroom a whitish light came through the uncurtained windows. She could glimpse the tops of trees, and, beyond them, meadows half drowned in the mist that rose up in the moonlight along the river. In the middle of the room was a heap of bureau drawers, bottles, metal and wooden curtain rods; mattresses lying on chairs, basins strewn over the floor—everything had been left there in disorder by the two moving-men.

It was the fourth time that she had gone to bed in a strange place. The first was the day she entered the convent, the second the day she arrived in Tostes, the third at La Vaubyessard, and now the fourth: each time it had been like the opening of a new phase of her life. She refused to believe that things could be the same in different places; and since what had gone before was so bad, what was to come must certainly be better.

III

THE NEXT MORNING SHE WAS BARELY UP WHEN SHE SAW THE clerk in the square. She was in her dressing gown. He caught sight of her and bowed. She responded with a brief nod and closed the window.

Léon waited all day for six o'clock to come, but when he entered the inn he found only Monsieur Binet, already at table.

The dinner of the previous evening had been a notable event for him: never before had he spoken for two consecutive hours with a "lady." How did it happen that he had been able to tell her so many things, in words that previously he wouldn't have thought of? He was ordinarily timid, with a reticence that was part modesty, part dissimulation. In Yonville he was thought to have very gentlemanly manners. He listened respectfully to his elders, and seemed not to get excited about politics—a remarkable trait in a young man. Besides, he was talented. He painted in water colors, could read the key of G, and when he didn't play cards after dinner he often took up a book. Monsieur Homais esteemed him because he was educated; Madame Homais liked him because he was helpful: he often spent some time with her children in the garden. They were brats, the Homais children, always dirty, wretchedly brought up, sluggish like their mother. Besides the maid, they were looked after by the pharmacist's apprentice, Justin, a distant cousin of Monsieur Homais, who had been taken in out of charity and was exploited as a servant.

The apothecary proved the best of neighbors. He advised Madame Bovary about tradesmen, had his cider dealer make a special delivery, tasted the brew himself, and saw to it that the barrel was properly installed in the cellar. He told her how to buy butter most advantageously, and made an arrangement for her with Lestiboudois the sacristan, who in addition to his ecclesiastical and funerary functions tended the principal gardens in Yonville by the hour or by the year, depending on the owners' preference.

It wasn't mere kindness that prompted the pharmacist to such obsequious cordiality: there was a scheme behind it.

He had violated the law of 19th Ventose, Year XI, Article I, which forbids anyone not holding a diploma to practice medicine; and in consequence had been denounced by anonymous informants and summoned to Rouen to the private chambers of the royal prosecutor. The magistrate had received him standing, clad in his robe of office banded at the shoulders with ermine and wearing his high official toque. It was in the morning, before the opening of court. Homais could hear the heavy tread of policemen in the corridor, and in the distance what sounded like heavy locks snapping shut. His ears rang so that he thought he was going to have a stroke; he had a vision of underground dungeons, his family in tears, his pharmacy sold, all his glass jars scattered among strangers; and when the interview was over he had to go to a café and drink a rum and soda to steady his nerves.

Gradually the memory of this warning faded, and he continued as before to give innocuous consultations in his back room. But his relations with the mayor were not good; he had competitors who would rejoice in his ruin: he had to watch his step. By being polite to Monsieur Bovary he could win his gratitude and insure his looking the other way should he notice anything. So every morning Homais brought him "the paper," and often left the pharmacy in the afternoon to call on him for a moment's conversation.

Charles was in a gloomy state: he had no patients. He sat silent for hours on end, took naps in his consulting room, or watched his wife as she sewed. To keep occupied he acted as handyman around the house, even attempt-

ing to paint the attic with what the painters had
left behind. But he was worried about money. He had
spent so much for repairs at Tostes, for dresses for Madame, for the move, that the entire dowry and three thousand écus besides had been swallowed up in two years. Besides, so many things had been broken or lost between
Tostes and Yonville! The plaster priest was one of them: a
particularly violent bump had thrown it out of the van,
and it had been smashed into a thousand pieces on the
cobblestones of Quincampoix.

He had another, happier concern—his wife's pregnancy.
As her term drew near she became ever dearer to him.
Another bond of the flesh was being forged between them,
one which gave him an all-pervasive feeling that their
union was now closer. The indolence of her gait, the gentle sway of her uncorseted body, her tired way of sitting
in a chair, all filled him with uncontrollable happiness: he
would go up to her and kiss her, stroke her face, call her
"little mother," try to dance with her; and half laughing,
half weeping, he would think of a thousand playful endearments to shower her with. The idea of having begotten
a child enchanted him. Now he had everything he could
ever hope for. He had been granted all that human life had
to offer, and he was serenely ready to enjoy it.

Emma's first reaction to her condition was one of great
surprise; and then she was eager to be delivered and know
what it was like to be a mother. But since she couldn't
spend the money she would have liked and buy embroidered baby bonnets and a boat-shaped cradle with pink silk
curtains, she resentfully gave up her own ideas about the
layette and ordered the whole thing from a seamstress in
the village without indicating any preferences or discussing any details. Thus she had none of the pleasure she
might have had in the preparations that whet the appetite
of mother love; and this perhaps did something to blunt

her affection from the beginning. But Charles spoke of the baby every time they sat down to a meal, and gradually she became accustomed to the idea.

She wanted a son. He would be strong and dark; she would call him Georges; and this idea of having a male child was like a promise of compensation for all her past frustrations. A man is free, at least—free to range the passions and the world, to surmount obstacles, to taste the rarest pleasures. Whereas a woman is continually thwarted. Inert, compliant, she has to struggle against her physical weakness and legal subjection. Her will, like the veil tied to her hat, quivers with every breeze: there is always a desire that entices, always a convention that restrains.

The baby was born one Sunday morning, about six o'clock, as the sun was rising.

"It's a girl!" cried Charles.

She turned her head away and fainted.

Almost immediately Madame Homais rushed in and kissed her, followed by Madame Lefrançois of the Lion d'Or. The pharmacist, a man of discretion, confined himself to a few provisional words of congratulation, spoken through the half-open door. He asked to see the child and pronounced it well formed.

During her convalescence she gave a great deal of thought to a name for her daughter. First she went over all she could think of that had Italian endings—Clara, Louisa, Amanda, Atala; she was tempted by Galsuinde, too, and even more by Isolde and Léocadie. Charles wanted the child named for its mother; Emma was opposed. They went through the almanac from end to end and asked everyone for suggestions.

"Monsieur Léon," said the pharmacist, "told me the other day he's surprised you haven't decided on Madeleine: it's so very fashionable just now."

But the older Madame Bovary protested loudly against

a name so associated with sin. Monsieur Homais' predilec-
tion was for names that recalled great men, illustrious
deeds or noble thoughts: such had been his guiding princi-
ple in baptising his own four children. Napoléon stood for
fame, Franklin for liberty; Irma was perhaps a concession to
romanticism; but Athalie was a tribute to the most immortal masterpiece of the French stage. For—mind you!—
his philosophical convictions didn't interfere with his artistic appreciation: in him, the thinker didn't stifle the man
of feeling; he was a man of discrimination, quite capable of
differentiating between imagination and fanaticism. In
the tragedy in question, for example, he condemned the
ideas but admired the style, abhorred the conception but
praised all the details, found the characters impossible but
their speeches marvelous. When he read the famous passages
he was carried away, but the thought that the clergy
made use of it all for their own purposes distressed him
immensely; and so troubling was his confusion of feelings
that he would have liked to place a wreath on Racine's
brow with his own hands and then have a good long argument with him.

In the end, Emma remembered hearing the marquise at
Vaubyessard address a young woman as Berthe, and that
promptly became the chosen name. Since Monsieur Rouault was unable to come, Monsieur Homais was asked
to be godfather. As presents he brought several items from
his pharmaceutical stock, namely, six boxes of jujubes, a full
jar of racahout, three packages of marshmallow paste, and
six sticks of sugar candy that he found in a cupboard and
threw in for good measure. The evening of the ceremony
there was a large dinner party. The priest was present:
words became rather heated, and with the liqueurs Monsieur Homais broke into Béranger's *Le Dieu des bonnes
gens*. Monsieur Léon sang a barcarolle, and the older Madame Bovary (who was godmother) a Napoleonic ballad.

Finally the older Monsieur Bovary insisted that the baby be brought down, and proceeded to baptise it with a glass of champagne, pouring the wine over its head. This mockery of the first sacrament brought indignant words from the Abbé Bournisien; the older Monsieur Bovary replied with a quotation from *La Guerre des dieux;* and the priest started to leave. The ladies implored him to stay; Homais intervened; and after considerable persuasion the abbé sat down again in his chair and calmly took up his saucer and his half-finished demitasse.

The older Monsieur Bovary stayed on for a month at Yonville, dazzling the inhabitants with a magnificent silver-braided policeman's cap that he wore mornings when he smoked his pipe in the square. He was used to drinking large quantities of brandy, and often sent the maid to the Lion d'Or to buy a bottle, which was charged to his son's account; and to perfume his foulards he used up his daughter-in-law's entire supply of eau de Cologne.

Emma didn't in the least dislike his company. He had seen the world: he spoke of Berlin, of Vienna, of Strasbourg, of his years as an army officer, of the mistresses he had had, of the official banquets he had attended. Then he would become gallant; and sometimes, on the stairs or in the garden, he would even seize hold of her waist and cry, "Better watch out, Charles!" The older Madame Bovary was alarmed for her son's happiness, and began to urge her husband to take her home, lest in the long run he corrupt the young woman's mind. Possibly her fears went further: Monsieur Bovary was a man to whom nothing was sacred.

One day Emma suddenly felt that she had to see her little daughter, who had been put out to nurse with the cabinetmaker's wife; and without looking at the almanac to see whether the six weeks of the Virgin had elapsed, she made her way toward the house occupied by Rollet, at the end of the village at the foot of the hills, between the main road and the meadows.

It was noon: the houses had their shutters closed, and under the harsh light of the blue sky the ridges of the glittering slate roofs seemed to be shooting sparks. A sultry wind was blowing. Emma felt weak as she walked; the stones of the footpath hurt her feet, and she wondered whether she shouldn't return home or stop in somewhere to rest.

At that moment Monsieur Léon emerged from a nearby door, a sheaf of papers under his arm. He advanced to greet her and stood in the shade in front of Lheureux's store, under the gray awning.

Madame Bovary said that she was on her way to see her child but was beginning to feel tired.

"If . . ." Léon began, and then dared go no further.

"Have you an appointment somewhere?" she asked him.

And when he replied that he hadn't she asked him to accompany her. By evening the news of this had spread throughout Yonville, and Madame Tuvache, the wife of the mayor, said in her maid's presence that Madame Bovary was risking her reputation.

To reach the wet-nurse's house they had to turn left at the end of the village street, as though going to the cemetery, and follow a narrow path that led them past cottages and yards between privet hedges. These were in bloom; and blooming, too, were veronicas and wild roses and nettles and the wild blackberries that thrust out their slender sprays from the thickets. Through holes in the hedges they could see, in the farmyards, a pig on a manure pile or cows in wooden collars rubbing their horns against tree trunks. The two of them walked on slowly side by side, she leaning on his arm and he shortening his step to match hers; in front of them hovered a swarm of flies, buzzing in the warm air.

They recognized the house by an old walnut tree that shaded it. It was low, roofed with brown tiles, and from the attic window hung a string of onions. Brushwood propped up against a thorn hedge formed a fence around a bit of garden given over to lettuce, a few plants of lavender, and sweet peas trained on poles. A trickle of dirty water ran off into the grass, and all around were odds and ends of rags, knitted stockings, a red calico wrapper, a large coarsely woven sheet spread out on the hedge. At the sound of the gate the wet nurse appeared, carrying an infant at her breast. With her other hand she was pulling along a frail, unhappy-looking little boy, his face covered with scrofulous sores—the son of a Rouen knit-goods dealer whom his parents were too busy in their shop to bother with.

"Come in," she said. "Your little girl's asleep inside."

The ground-floor bedroom—the only bedroom in the house—had a wide uncurtained bed standing against its rear wall; the window wall (one pane was mended with a bit of wrapping paper) was taken up by the kneading-trough. In the corner behind the door was a raised slab for washing, and under it stood a row of heavy boots with shiny hobnails and a bottle of oil with a feather in its mouth. A Mathieu Laensberg almanac lay on the dusty mantelpiece among gun flints, candle ends and bits of tinder. And as a final bit of clutter there was a figure of Fame blowing her trumpets—a picture probably cut out of a perfume advertisement and now fastened to the wall with six shoe tacks.

Emma's baby was asleep in a wicker cradle on the floor, and she took it up in its little blanket and began to sing softly to it and rock it in her arms.

Léon walked around the room: it seemed to him a strange sight, this elegant lady in her nankeen gown here among all this squalor. Madame Bovary blushed; he turned away, fearing that his glance might have been indiscreet; and she put the baby back in its cradle—it had just thrown up over the collar of her dress. The wet nurse quickly wiped off the mess, assuring her it wouldn't show.

"It isn't the first time, you know," she said. "I do nothing but wipe up after her all day long. Would you mind leaving word with Camus the grocer to let me pick up a little soap when I need it? That would be the easiest for you—I wouldn't have to trouble you."

"I will, I will," said Emma. "Good-bye, Madame Rollet."

And she left the house, wiping her feet on the doorsill.

The wet nurse walked with her as far as the gate, talking about how hard it was to have to get up during the night.

"I'm so worn out sometimes I fall asleep in my chair. So couldn't you at least let me have just a pound of ground coffee? It would last me a month; I'd drink it with milk in the morning."

After undergoing a deluge of thanks, Madame Bovary moved on; and then when she had gone a little way down the path there was the sound of sabots and she turned around: it was the wet nurse again.

"What is it now?"

And the peasant woman drew her aside behind an elm and began to talk to her about her husband. He "had only his trade and the six francs a year the captain gave him, so . . ."

"Come to the point!" said Emma brusquely.

"Well, what I mean is," the wet nurse said, sighing after every word, "I'm afraid he wouldn't like it, seeing me sitting there drinking coffee by myself; you know how men are, they . . ."

"But you'll both have coffee!" Emma cried. "I just told you I'd give you some! Leave me alone!"

"Ah, Madame, you see he's had terrible cramps in his

chest ever since he was wounded, and he says cider makes him feel worse, and . . ."

"Won't you please let me go?"

"So," she went on, making a curtsy, "if it isn't too much to ask"—she curtsied again—"if you would"—and she gave a beseeching glance—"just a little jug of brandy," she finally got out, "and I'll rub your little girl's feet with it—they're as tender as your tongue."

When she was finally rid of the wet nurse, Emma once again took Monsieur Léon's arm. She walked rapidly for a little while; then she slowed, and her glance fell on the shoulder of the young man she was with. His brown hair, smooth and neatly combed, touched the black velvet collar of his frock coat. She noticed that his fingernails were longer than those of most other inhabitants of Yonville. The clerk spent a great deal of time caring for them: he kept a special penknife in his desk for the purpose.

They returned to Yonville along the river. The summer weather had reduced its flow and left uncovered the river walls and water steps of the gardens along its bank. It ran silently, swift and cold-looking; long fine grasses bent with the current, like masses of loose green hair streaming in its limpid depths. Here and there on the tip of a reed or on a water-lily pad a spidery-legged insect was poised or crawling. Sunbeams pierced the little blue air bubbles that kept forming and breaking on the ripples; branchless old willows mirrored their gray bark in the water; in the distance the meadows seemed empty all around them. It was dinner time on the farms, and as they walked the young woman and her companion heard only the rhythm of their own steps on the earth of the path, the words they themselves were uttering, and the whisper of Emma's dress as it rustled around her.

The garden walls, their copings bristling with broken

bits of bottles, were as warm as the glass of a greenhouse. Wallflowers had taken root between the bricks; and as she passed, the edge of Madame Bovary's open parasol crumbled some of their faded flowers into yellow dust; or an over-hanging branch of honeysuckle or clematis would catch in the fringe and cling for a moment to the silk.

They talked about a company of Spanish dancers sched-uled soon to appear at the theatre in Rouen.

"Are you going?" she asked.

"If I can," he answered.

Had they nothing more to say to each other? Their eyes, certainly, were full of more meaningful talk; and as they made themselves utter banalities they sensed the same languor invading them both: it was like a murmur of the soul, deep and continuous, more clearly audible than the sound of their words. Surprised by a sweetness that was new to them, it didn't occur to them to tell each other how they felt or to wonder why. Future joys are like tropic shores: out into the immensity that lies before them they waft their native softness, a fragrant breeze that drugs the traveler into drowsiness and makes him careless of what awaits him on the horizon beyond his view.

In one spot the ground was boggy from the trampling of cattle, and they had to walk on large green stones that had been laid in the mud. She kept stopping to see where to place her foot; and teetering on an unsteady stone, her arms lifted, her body bent, a hesitant look in her eye, she laughed, fearing lest she fall into the puddles.

When they reached her garden, Madame Bovary pushed open the little gate, ran up the steps and disappeared.

Léon returned to his office. His employer was out; he glanced at the piles of papers, sharpened a quill pen, and then —took up his hat and went out again.

He climbed to the Pasture, on the hilltop at the edge of the Argueil forest, and there he stretched out on the ground under the firs and looked up at the sky through his fingers.

"God!" he said to himself. "What a boring existence!"

He felt that he was much to be pitied for having to live in this village, with Homais for a friend and Maître Guillaumin for a master. The latter, completely taken up with business, wore gold-framed spectacles, red side whiskers and a white tie; fine feelings were a closed book to him, though the stiff British manner he affected had impressed the clerk at first. As for Madame Homais, she was the best wife in Normandy, placid as a sheep and devoted to her children, her father, her mother and her cousins; she wept at others' misfortunes, let everything in the house go, and hated corsets. But she was so slow-moving, so boring to listen to, so common-looking and limited in conversation, that it never occurred to him—though she was thirty and he twenty, and they slept in adjoining rooms and he spoke to her every day—that anyone could look on her as a woman, that she had any attributes of her sex except the dress she wore.

Who was there besides? Binet, a few shopkeepers, two or three tavern-keepers, the priest, and lastly, Monsieur Tuvache, the mayor, and his two sons—a comfortably-off, surly, dull-witted trio who farmed their own land, ate huge meals with never a guest, faithful churchgoers for all that, and utterly insufferable in company.

But against the background of all these human faces, Emma's stood out—isolated from them and yet further removed than they, for he sensed that some abyss separated him from her.

At first he had gone to her house several times with the pharmacist. Charles had not seemed too eager to have him; and Léon felt helpless, torn as he was between fear of being indiscreet and desire for an intimacy that he considered all but impossible.

IV

WITH THE COMING OF COLD WEATHER EMMA MOVED OUT OF
her bedroom into the parlor, a long low-ceilinged room
where a chunky branch of coral stood on the mantelpiece
in front of the mirror. Sitting in her armchair beside the
window, she could watch the villagers go by on the sidewalk.

Twice a day Léon went from his office to the Lion d'Or.
Emma could hear him coming in the distance; she would
lean forward as she listened, and the young man would slip
past on the other side of the window curtain, always
dressed the same, never turning his head. At twilight,
when she had put down her embroidery and was sitting
there with her chin in her left hand, she often started at
the sudden appearance of this gliding shadow. She would
jump up, order the maid to set the table.

Monsieur Homais often called during dinner. Tasseled cap
in hand, he would tiptoe in so as to disturb no one, and he
always gave the same greeting: "Good evening, everybody!" Then, sitting down at the table between them,
he would ask the doctor for news of his patients, and
Charles would ask him what the chances were of being paid.
Then they would talk about what was "in the paper." By
this time of day Homais knew it almost by heart, and he
would repeat it *in toto*, complete with editorials and the
news of each and every disaster that had occurred in France
and abroad. When these topics ran dry he never failed to
comment on the dishes he saw being served. Sometimes,

half rising, he would even considerately point out to Madame the tenderest piece of meat; or, turning to the maid, he would advise her on the preparation of her stews and the use of seasoning from a health point of view: he was quite dazzling on the subject of aromas, osmazomes, juices and gelatines. Indeed, Homais had more recipes in his head than there were bottles in his pharmacy, and he excelled at making all kinds of jellies, vinegars and cordials. He was acquainted with all the latest fuel-saving stoves, and with the arts of preserving cheeses and treating spoiled wine.

At eight o'clock Justin always called for him: it was time to shut the pharmacy. Monsieur Homais would give him a quizzical glance, especially if Félicité were in the room, for he had noticed that his pupil was partial to the doctor's house. "My young man's beginning to get ideas," he would say. "Something tells me he's after your maid!"

And there was worse: despite all rebukes, the boy persisted in his habit of listening to conversations. On Sundays, for instance, Madame Homais would summon him to the parlor to take away the children, who had fallen asleep in armchairs, dragging down the loose calico slip covers, and there was no way of getting him to leave the room.

These soirées at the pharmacist's were not very well attended, for his slanderous tongue and his political opinions had alienated one respectable person after another. The clerk was invariably present. At the sound of the doorbell he would run down to greet Madame Bovary, take her shawl, and stow away under the desk in the pharmacy the overshoes she wore when it snowed.

First they would play a few rounds of *trente-et-un*; then Monsieur Homais would play écarté with Emma, Léon standing behind her and giving advice. With his hands on the back of her chair, he would look down and see the teeth of her comb piercing her chignon. Each time she threw down a card the right side of her dress gave an upward twist, and he could follow the gradually paling shadow cast down her neck by the knot of her hair, until it was lost in a darker shadow. Then her dress would drop down on both sides of her chair, swelling out in full folds and spreading to the floor. Sometimes Léon would feel himself touching it with the sole of his shoe, and he would quickly move away, as though he had been treading on someone.

When they finished their cards, the apothecary and the doctor played dominoes; and Emma would move to another chair, lean her elbows on the table and leaf through *L'Illustration*, or take up the fashion magazine she usually brought with her. Léon would sit beside her, and together they would look at the pictures and wait for each other before turning a page. Often she would ask him to read a poem aloud, and Léon would recite it in a languid voice that he carefully let die away at the love passages. But the noise of the dominoes annoyed him: Monsieur Homais was an expert, easily outplaying Charles. When the score reached three hundred the two of them would stretch out before the fireplace and quickly fall asleep. The fire smoldered, the teapot was empty; Léon continued to read, and Emma listened, absent-mindedly turning the lampshade, its gauzy surface painted with pierrots in carriages and tightrope dancers balancing with their poles. Léon would stop, indicating with a gesture his sleeping audience; and then they would talk in low voices, their conversation seeming the sweeter for not being overheard.

Thus a kind of intimacy grew up between them, a continual exchange of books and ballads. Monsieur Bovary was not jealous; he found it all quite natural.

For his birthday he received a splendid phrenological head, all marked over with numerals down to the thorax and painted blue. This was an offering from the clerk. He was attentive in many other ways, too, even doing errands for Charles in Rouen. When a new novel launched a craze for exotic plants, Léon bought some for Madame, holding them on his knees in the Hirondelle and pricking his fingers on their spikes.

Emma had a railed shelf installed in her window to hold her flowerpots. The clerk, too, had his hanging garden, and they could look out and see each other tending their blossoms.

There was one person in the village who spent even more time at his window than they: from morning till night on Sunday, and every afternoon in good weather, the lean profile of Monsieur Binet could be seen in a dormer bent over his lathe, its monotonous drone audible as far as the Lion d'Or.

One evening when he returned home Léon found in his room a velvet and wool coverlet, with foliage designs on a pale ground. He showed it to Madame Homais, Monsieur Homais, Justin, the children, and the cook, and spoke about it to his employer. Everybody wanted to see it: why should the doctor's wife give presents to the clerk? The whole thing seemed suspicious, and everyone was sure that they must be having an affair.

By speaking incessantly about Emma's charms and intelligence, Léon gave plenty of grounds for the belief. Binet turned on him one day with a snarl: "What's it to me? She doesn't let *me* hang around her!"

He was in agony trying to think of a way of "declaring himself" to her. He was constantly torn between the fear of offending her and shame at his own cowardice; he shed tears of despair and frustrated desire. Every so often he resolved to take energetic action: he wrote letters, only to tear them up; he gave himself time limits, only to extend them. More than once he started out intending to dare all; but in Emma's presence he quickly lost his courage, and if Charles happened to appear at such a moment and invited him to get into the buggy and go with him to see a patient living somewhere nearby, he would accept at once, bow to Madame and drive off. Her husband, after all, was part of herself, was he not?

As for Emma, she never tried to find out whether she was in love with him. Love, to her, was something that comes suddenly, like a blinding flash of lightning—a heaven-sent storm hurled into life, uprooting it, sweeping every will before it like a leaf, engulfing all feelings. It never occurred to her that if the drainpipes of a house are clogged, the rain may collect in pools on the roof; and she suspected no danger until suddenly she discovered a crack in the wall.

V

IT WAS A SNOWY SUNDAY AFTERNOON IN FEBRUARY.

All of them—Monsieur and Madame Bovary, Homais and Monsieur Léon—had gone to see a new flax mill that was being built in the valley, a mile or so from Yonville. The apothecary had taken Napoléon and Athalie along to give them some exercise, and Justin accompanied them, carrying a supply of umbrellas over his shoulder.

Nothing, however, could have been less interesting than this point of interest. A long rectangular building pierced with innumerable little windows stood in the midst of a large tract of bare land, with a few already rusty gear-wheels lying here and there among piles of sand and gravel. It was still unfinished, and the sky could be seen between the rafters. Attached to the ridgepole at the peak of one of the gables was a bouquet of straw and wheat, tied with red, white and blue ribbons that flapped in the wind.

Homais was holding forth. He expatiated to them all on how important the mill was going to be, estimated the strength of the floors and the thickness of the walls, and keenly regretted not owning a carpenter's rule, such as Monsieur Binet possessed for his personal use.

Emma, who had taken his arm, was leaning slightly against his shoulder and looking up at the far-off disc of the sun that was suffusing the mist with its pale brilliance; then she turned her head, and saw—Charles. His cap was pulled down over his eyes; and the quivering of his thick lips in the cold gave him a stupid look. Even his back, his placid back, was irritating to look at: all his dullness was written right there, on his coat.

As she was looking at him, deriving a kind of perverse enjoyment from her very irritation, Léon moved a step closer. White in the cold, his face was more languorous and appealing than ever; a bit of his bare skin showed through a gap in his shirt collar; she could see the tip of one of his ears below a lock of his hair; and his large blue eyes, lifted toward the clouds, seemed to Emma more limpid and lovely than mountain lakes mirroring the sky.

"Stop that!" the apothecary suddenly cried.

And he rushed over to his son, who had just jumped into a heap of lime to whiten his shoes. To his father's scoldings Napoléon replied with howls; Justin scraped off the shoes with a bit of plaster; but a knife was needed, and Charles offered his.

"Ah!" she cried to herself. "He carries a knife around with him, like a peasant!"

The cold was beginning to pinch, and they turned back toward Yonville.

That evening Madame Bovary did not attend her neighbor's soirée; and when Charles had gone and she felt herself alone, the comparison returned to her mind almost with the sharpness of an actual sensation, and with the increased perspective conferred on things by memory. Watching the brightly burning fire from her bed, she saw once again, as at the scene itself, Léon standing there, leaning with one hand on his slender, flexing cane and with the other holding Athalie, who was placidly sucking a piece of ice. She found him charming; she could not take her mind off him; she remembered how he had looked on other occasions, things he had said, the sound of his voice, everything about him; and she kept saying to herself, protruding her lips as though for a kiss: "Charming, charming! . . . Isn't he in love? Who could it be?" she asked herself. "Why—he's in love with me!"

All the evidence burst on her at once; her heart leapt up. The flames in the fireplace cast a merry, flickering light on the ceilings; she lay on her back and stretched out her arms.

Then began the eternal lament: "Oh, if only fate had willed it so! Why didn't it? What stood in the way?"

When Charles came in at midnight she pretended to wake up. He made some noise as he undressed, and she complained of migraine; then she casually asked what had happened during the evening.

"Monsieur Léon went up to his room early," said Charles.

She couldn't help smiling, and she fell asleep filled with new happiness.

At nightfall the next day she had a visit from Monsieur Lheureux, the proprietor of the local dry-goods store. He was a clever man, this tradesman.

Born a Gascon, but long settled in Normandy, he combined his southern volubility with the cunning of his adopted region. His fat, flabby, clean-shaven face looked as though it had been dyed with a faint tincture of licorice, and his white hair emphasized the piercing boldness of his small black eyes. What he had been in earlier life was a mystery to all: peddler, some said; and others, banker in Routot. What was certain was that he could do in his head intricate feats of calculation that startled Binet himself. Polite to the point of obsequiousness, he was continually in a semi-bent position, like someone making a bow or extending an invitation.

He left his hat with its black mourning band at the door, placed a green case on the table, and began by complaining, with many civilities, at not having been honored up till now with Madame's patronage. A poor shop like his could scarcely be expected to attract so elegant a lady: he emphasized the adjective. But she had only to give him an order and he would undertake to supply anything she wanted, whether accessories, lingerie, hosiery and other knit goods, or notions, for he went to the city four times a month regularly. He was in constant touch with the biggest firms. She could mention his name at the Trois Frères, at the Barbe d'Or or at the Grand Sauvage: everyone in those places knew all about him. Today he would just like to show Madame a few articles he happened to have with him, thanks to a lucky buy; out of his box he took half a dozen embroidered collars.

Madame Bovary looked them over.

"I don't need anything," she said.

Then Monsieur Lheureux daintily held out for her inspection three Algerian scarves, some packages of English needles, a pair of straw slippers, and finally four cocoanut-shell egg cups, carved in an openwork design by convicts. Then, both hands on the table, leaning forward, his neck outstretched, he watched Emma open-mouthed, following her gaze as it wandered uncertainly over the merchandise. From time to time, as though to brush off a bit of dust, he gave a flick of a fingernail to the silk of the scarves, lying there unfolded to their full length; and they quivered and rustled under his touch, their gold sequins gleaming like little stars in the greenish light of the dusk.

"How much are they?"

"They're absurdly cheap," he said. "Besides, there's no hurry. Pay whenever you like—we're not Jews!"

She meditated a few moments, then finally told Monsieur Lheureux once more that she didn't want to buy.

"That's quite all right," he answered impassively. "You and I will do business some other time. I've always known how to get along with the ladies—except my wife."

Emma smiled.

"I just want you to know," he said, dropping his facetious tone and assuming an air of candor, "that I'm not worried about the money. In fact, I could let you have some if you needed it."

Emma made a gesture of surprise.

"Ah," he said quickly, in a low voice. "I wouldn't have to go far to find it, believe me!"

Then he turned the conversation to the subject of Monsieur Tellier, proprietor of the Café Français, whom Monsieur Bovary was treating.

"What's his trouble, anyway? He's got a cough that shakes the house. I'm afraid he may soon need a wooden overcoat more than a flannel undershirt! He was a wild one in his younger days! The kind that doesn't know even the meaning of self-control, Madame! He literally burned his insides out with brandy! Still, it's hard to see an old friend go."

And as he tied up his box he talked on about the doctor's patients.

"It must be the weather," he said, scowling at the windowpanes, "that's causing all this illness. I don't feel right myself: one of these days I'll have to come and talk to Monsieur about a pain I have in my back. Well—au revoir, Madame Bovary; at your service, any time."

And he shut the door softly behind him.

Emma had her dinner brought to her in her bedroom on

a tray, and ate it beside the fire. She lingered over her food: everything tasted good.

"How sensible I was!" she told herself, as she thought of the scarves.

She heard footsteps on the stairs: it was Léon. She jumped up and snatched the topmost dish towel from a pile she had left for hemming on the chest of drawers. She looked very busy when he came in.

Conversation languished: Madame Bovary kept letting his remarks drop unanswered, and he seemed very ill at ease. He sat in a low chair beside the fire, toying with her ivory needlecase; she continued to sew, occasionally creasing the cloth together with her fingernail. She said nothing, and he, too, was quiet, captivated by her silence as he would have been by her words.

"Poor fellow!" she was thinking.

"What does she dislike about me?" he was wondering.

Finally Léon said that he would be going to Rouen some day soon on office business.

"Your subscription at the music library has run out," he said. "Shall I renew it?"

"No," she answered.

"Why not?"

"Because . . ."

And pursing her lips she slowly drew out a new length of gray thread.

Her sewing irritated Léon: the cloth seemed to be roughening the tips of her fingers. A compliment occurred to him, but he hadn't the courage to utter it.

"You're giving it up?"

"What?" she asked quickly. "Oh, my music? Heavens, yes! Haven't I got my house and my husband to look after —a thousand things—all kinds of duties that come first?"

She looked at the clock. Charles was late. She pretended

to be worried. "He's such a good man," she said, two or three times.

The clerk was fond of Monsieur Bovary, but he was unpleasantly surprised to hear her speak so affectionately of him. Nevertheless he continued the praises she had begun, and assured her that he heard them from everyone, especially the pharmacist.

"Ah, Monsieur Homais is a fine man," said Emma.

"He certainly is," said the clerk.

He began to speak of Madame Homais, whose sloppy appearance usually made them laugh.

"What of it?" Emma interrupted. "A good wife and mother doesn't worry about her clothes."

And once again she fell silent.

It was the same the following days: her talk, her manner, everything changed. She immersed herself in household tasks, went regularly to church, and was stricter with the maid.

She took Berthe away from the wet nurse. Félicité brought her in when there was company, and Madame Bovary undressed her to show off her little legs and arms. She adored children, she said: they were her consolation, her joy, her delight; and she accompanied her caresses with gushings that would have reminded anyone except the Yonvillians of Esmeralda's mother in *Notre-Dame de Paris*.

Nowadays when Charles came in, he found his slippers set out to warm by the fire. Now his vests were never without linings, his shirts never without buttons; it was a pleasure to see the piles of cotton nightcaps stacked so neatly in the closet. She no longer frowned at the idea of taking a walk in the garden; she agreed to all his suggestions without trying to understand his reasons. And when Léon saw him beside the fire in the evening, his face flushed from dinner, his hands folded over his stomach, his feet on the andirons, his eyes moist with happiness, the baby crawling on the carpet, and this slender woman leaning over the back of his armchair to kiss him on the forehead—"I must be mad," he told himself. "How can I ever hope to come near her?"

She seemed so virtuous and inaccessible that he lost all hope, even the faintest.

But by thus renouncing her, he transformed her into an extraordinary being. She was divested in his eyes of the earthly attributes that held no promise for him; and in his heart she rose higher and higher, withdrawing further from him in a magnificent, soaring apotheosis. His feeling for her was so pure that it did not interfere with his daily life—it was one of those feelings that are cherished because of their very rarity: the distress caused by their loss would be greater than the happiness given by their possession.

Emma grew thinner: her face became paler, more emaciated. With her smooth black hair, her large eyes, her straight nose, her birdlike movements, her new habit of silence, she seemed all but out of contact with life, bearing on her brow the vague mark of a sublime fate. She was so melancholy and so subdued, so sweet and yet so withdrawn, that in her presence he felt transfixed by a glacial spell— just as in a church the fragrance of flowers and the cold given off by marble will sometimes set us shivering. Even other men were not immune to this seduction. The pharmacist put it this way:

"She's got class! She'd hold her own in Le Havre or Dieppe!"

The village housewives admired her for her thrift; Charles's patients for her politeness; the poor for her charity.

And all this time she was torn by wild desires, by rage, by hatred. The trim folds of her dress hid a heart in turmoil, and her reticent lips told nothing of the storm. She was in love with Léon, and she sought the solitude that allowed her to revel undisturbed in his image. The sight of his person spoiled the voluptuousness of her musings. She trembled at the sound of his footsteps; then, with him before her, the agitation subsided, and she was left with nothing but a vast bewilderment that turned gradually into sadness.

Léon did not know, when he left her house in despair, that she went immediately to the window and watched him disappear down the street. She worried over his every move, watched every expression that crossed his face; she concocted an elaborate story to have a pretext for visiting his room. The pharmacist's wife seemed to her blessed to sleep under the same roof; and her thoughts came continually to rest on that house, like the pigeons from the Lion d'Or that alighted there to soak their pink feet and white wings in the eaves-trough. But the more aware Emma became of her love the more she repressed it in an effort to conceal it and weaken it. She would have been glad had Léon guessed; and she kept imagining accidents and disasters that would open his eyes. It was indolence, probably, or fear, that held her back, and a feeling of shame. She had kept him at too great a distance, she decided: now it was too late; the occasion was lost. Besides, the pride and pleasure she derived from thinking of herself as "virtuous" and from wearing an air of resignation as she looked at herself in the mirror consoled her a little for the sacrifice she thought she was making.

Her carnal desires, her cravings for money, and the fits of depression engendered by her love gradually merged into a single torment; and instead of trying to put it out of her mind she cherished it, spurring herself on to suffer, never missing an opportunity to do so. A dish poorly served or a door left ajar grated on her nerves; she sighed thinking of the velvet gowns she didn't own, the happiness that eluded her, her unattainable dreams, her entire cramped existence.

What exasperated her was Charles's total unawareness of her ordeal. His conviction that he was making her happy she took as a stupid insult: such self-righteousness could only mean that he didn't appreciate her. For whose sake, after all, was she being virtuous? Wasn't he the obstacle to every kind of happiness, the cause of all her wretchedness, the sharp-pointed prong of this many-stranded belt that bound her on all sides?

So he became the sole object of her resentment. Her attempts to conquer this feeling served only to strengthen it, for their failure gave her additional cause for despair and deepened her estrangement from her husband. She had moments of revulsion against her own meekness. She reacted to the drabness of her home by indulging in daydreams of luxury, and to matrimonial caresses by adulterous desires. She wished that Charles would beat her: then she would feel more justified in hating him and betraying him out of revenge. Sometimes she was surprised by the horrible possibilities that she imagined; and yet she had to keep smiling, hear herself say time and again that she was happy, pretend to be so, let everyone believe it!

Still, there were times when she could scarcely stomach the hypocrisy. She would be seized with a longing to run off with Léon, escape to some far-off place where they could begin life anew; but at such moments she would shudder, feeling herself at the brink of a terrifying precipice.

"What's the use—he doesn't love me any more," she would decide. What was to become of her? What help could she hope for? What comfort? What relief?

Such a crisis always left her shattered, gasping, prostrate, sobbing to herself, tears streaming down her face.

"Why in the world don't you tell Monsieur?" the maid would ask her, finding her thus distraught.

"It's nerves," Emma would answer. "Don't mention it to him. It would only upset him."

"Ah, yes," Félicité said, one day. "You're just like the daughter of old Guérin, the fisherman at Le Pollet. I knew her at Dieppe before I came to you. She used to be so sad, so terribly sad, that when she stood in her door she made you think of a funeral pall hanging there. It seems it was some kind of a fog in her head that ailed her. The doctors couldn't do anything for her, or the priest either. When it came over her worst, she'd go off by herself along the beach, and sometimes the customs officer would find her stretched out flat on her face on the pebbles and crying, when he made his rounds. It passed off after she was married, they say."

"With me," said Emma, "it was after I was married that it began."

VI

ONE EVENING WHEN THE WINDOW WAS OPEN AND SHE HAD been sitting beside it watching Lestiboudois the sacristan trim the boxwood, she suddenly heard the tolling of the Angelus.

It was the beginning of April, primrose time, when soft breezes blow over newly spaded flower beds, and gardens, like women, seem to be primping themselves for the gaieties of summer. Through the slats of the arbor, and all around beyond, she could see the stream flowing through the meadows, winding its vagabond course amid the grass.

The evening mist was rising among the bare poplars, blur-ring their outlines with a tinge of purple that was paler and more transparent than the sheerest gauze caught on their branches. In the distance cattle were moving: neither their steps nor their lowing could be heard, and the stead-ily sounding churchbell sent its peaceful lament into the evening air.

As the ringing continued, the young woman's thoughts began to stray among old memories of girlhood and the convent. She remembered the tall altar candlesticks that soared above the vases full of flowers and the columned tabernacle. She wished she could be again what she once had been, one in the long line of white-veiled girls, black-specked here and there by the stiff cowls of the nuns bowed over their *prie-dieus*. Sundays at Mass when she raised her head she used to see the gentle features of the Virgin among the bluish clouds of rising incense. The memory filled her with emotion: she felt limp and passive, like a bit of bird's-down whirling in a storm; and automatically she turned her steps toward the church, ready for any devotion that would enable her to humble her heart and lose herself entirely.

In the square she met Lestiboudois on his way back: in order not to lose pay by cutting his work-day short, he pre-ferred to interrupt his gardening and then go back to it, with the result that he rang the Angelus when it suited him. Besides, early ringing served to remind the village boys that it was time for catechism.

Some of them were already there, playing marbles on the slabs in the cemetery. Others, astride the wall, were swing-ing their legs, their wooden shoes breaking off the tall net-tles that grew between the wall itself and the nearest graves. This was the only spot that was green: all the rest was stones, always covered with a fine dust despite the sacris-tan's sweeping.

Other boys had taken off their sabots and were running about on the stones as though the cemetery were a smooth floor made specially for them. Their shouts could be heard above the dying sounds of the bell; the heavy rope that hung down from the top of the bell tower and trailed on the ground was swaying ever more slowly. Swallows flew past, twittering as they sliced the air with their swift flight, and disappeared into their yellow nests under the eave-tiles. At the far end of the church a lamp was burning—a wick in a hanging glass, whose light seemed from a distance like a whitish spot dancing on the oil. A long shaft of sunlight cutting across the nave deepened the darkness in the side aisles and corners.

"Where is the priest?" Madame Bovary asked a boy who was happily trying to wrench the turnstile loose from its socket.

"He'll be here," he answered.

Just then the door of the rectory creaked open and the abbé Bournisien appeared. The boys fled helter-skelter into the church.

"Won't they ever behave?" he muttered to himself. "No respect for anything." He picked up a tattered catechism that he had almost stepped on. Then he saw Madame Bovary. "Excuse me," he said. "I didn't place you for a minute."

He stuffed the catechism into his pocket and stood swinging the heavy sacristy key between two fingers.

The setting sun was full in his face; and the black cloth of his cassock, shiny at the elbows and frayed at the hem, seemed paler in its glow. Grease spots and snuff stains ran parallel to the row of little buttons on his broad chest; they were thickest below his neckband, which held back the heavy folds of his red skin; this was sprinkled with yellow splotches, half hidden by the bristles of his graying beard. He had just had his dinner, and was breathing heavily.

"How are you?" he went on.

"Poorly," said Emma. "Not well at all."

"Neither am I," the priest answered. "These first hot days take it out of you terribly, don't they? But what can we do? We're born to suffer, as St. Paul says. What does your husband think is the trouble?"

"My husband!" she said, with a scornful gesture.

The country priest looked surprised. "He must have prescribed something for you, hasn't he?"

"Ah!" said Emma. "It isn't earthly remedies that I need."

But the priest kept looking away, into the church, where the boys were kneeling side by side, each shoving his neighbor with his shoulder and all of them falling down like ninepins.

"Could you tell me . . ." she began.

"Just wait, Riboudet!" he shouted furiously. "I'll box your ears when I get hold of you!"

Then, turning to Emma: "That's the son of Boudet the carpenter; his parents don't bother with him, they let him do as he likes. He'd learn fast if he wanted to: he's very bright. Sometimes as a joke I call him Riboudet—you know, from the name of the hill near Maromme; sometimes I say 'mon Riboudet'—Mont Riboudet! Ha! Ha! The other day I told my little joke to the bishop. He laughed. He was good enough to laugh. And Monsieur Bovary—how is he?"

She seemed not to hear him, and he went on: "Always on the move, probably? He and I are certainly the two busiest people in the parish. He takes care of the bodies," he added, with a heavy laugh, "and I look after the souls."

She fastened her imploring eyes upon him. "Yes," she said. "You must be called on to relieve all kinds of suffering."

"Believe me, I am, Madame Bovary! This very morning I had to go to Bas-Diauville for a cow that had the colic:

the peasants thought it was a spell. All their cows, for some reason . . . Excuse me, Madame! Longuemarre! Boudet! Drat you both! Will you cut it out?"

And he rushed into the church.

By now the boys were crowding around the high lectern, climbing up on the cantor's bench and opening the missal; and others, moving stealthily, were about to invade the confessional. But the priest was suddenly upon them, slapping them right and left; seizing them by the coat collar, he lifted them off the ground and then set them on their knees on the stone floor of the choir, pushing them down hard as though he were trying to plant them there.

"Well!" he said, returning to Emma. And then, as he opened his large calico handkerchief, holding a corner of it between his teeth: "As we were saying, farmers have plenty of troubles."

"Other people, too," she answered.

"Of course! Workingmen in the cities, for instance . . ."

"I wasn't thinking of them . . ."

"Ah, but I assure you I've known mothers of families, good women, true saints, who didn't even have a crust of bread."

"I was thinking of women who have bread, Monsieur le curé," Emma said, the corners of her mouth twisting as she spoke, "but who lack . . ."

"Firewood for the winter," the priest anticipated.

"Ah, never mind . . ."

"What do you mean, never mind? It seems to me that to be warm and well fed . . ."

"Oh, my God!" Emma whispered to herself. "My God!"

"Are you feeling ill?" he asked. He looked concerned, and advanced a step. "Something must have disagreed with you. You'd better go home, Madame Bovary, and drink a cup of tea; that will pick you up. Or a glass of water with a little brown sugar."

"What for?"

She looked as though she were emerging from a dream.

"You were holding your hand to your forehead. I thought you must be feeling faint." Then: "But weren't you asking me a question? What was it? I can't recall . . ."

"I? Oh, no, nothing . . . nothing," Emma said.

And her wandering glance came slowly to rest on the old man in his cassock. For a few moments they looked at each other without speaking.

"Well, Madame Bovary," he said, finally, "you'll excuse me, but duty calls. I have to look after my youngsters. First Communion will be here soon: it will be on us before we know it. Time's so short I always keep them an extra hour on Wednesdays after Ascension. Poor things! We can't begin too soon to steer their young souls in the Lord's path—indeed it's what he Himself tells us to do, through the mouth of His divine Son. Keep well, Madame; remember me kindly to your husband!"

And he entered the church, genuflecting just inside the door.

Emma watched him as he disappeared between the double line of pews, treading heavily, his head slightly bent to one side, his half-open hands held with palms outward.

Then she turned stiffly, like a statue on a pivot, and set out for home. Behind her she heard the booming voice of the priest and the lighter voices of the boys.

"Are you a Christian?"

"Yes, I am a Christian."

"What is a Christian?"

"A Christian is one who, after being baptised . . . baptised . . . baptised . . ."

She climbed her stairs holding tight to the rail, and once in her room she sank heavily into a chair.

The whitish light coming through the windowpanes was slowly fading and ebbing away. The various pieces of furniture seemed to be fixed more firmly in their places, lost in shadow as in an ocean of darkness. The fire was out, the clock kept up its tick-tock; and Emma vaguely marveled that all these things should be so quiet while she herself was in such turmoil. Then little Berthe was in front of her, tottering in her knitted shoes between the window and the sewing table, trying to reach her mother and catch hold of the ends of her apron strings.

"Let me alone!" Emma cried, pushing her away.

But a few moments later the little girl was back, this time coming closer. Leaning her arms on her mother's knees she looked up at her with her big blue eyes, and a thread of clear saliva dripped from her lip onto the silk of the apron.

"Let me alone!" Emma cried again, very much annoyed.

The expression on her face frightened the child, who began to scream.

"Won't you let me alone!" she cried, thrusting her off with her elbow.

Berthe fell just at the foot of the chest of drawers, cutting her cheek on one of its brasses. She began to bleed. Madame Bovary rushed to pick her up, broke the bell-rope, called loudly for the maid; and words of self-reproach were on her lips when Charles appeared. It was dinner time; he had just come in.

"Look what's happened, darling," she said, in an even voice. "The baby fell down and hurt herself playing."

Charles reassured her: it was nothing serious, he said, and he went for some adhesive plaster.

Madame Bovary didn't go downstairs for dinner that evening: she insisted on staying alone with her child. As she watched her lying there asleep, her anxiety, such as it was, gradually wore off; and she thought of herself as having been silly and good-hearted indeed to let herself be upset over so small a matter. Berthe had stopped sobbing; and now the cotton coverlet rose and fell imperceptibly with her regular breathing. A few large tears had gathered in the corners of her half-closed eyelids; through the lashes could be seen the pupils, pale and sunken-looking; the adhesive stuck on her cheek pulled the skin to one side.

"It's a strange thing," Emma thought, "what an ugly child she is."

At eleven o'clock, when Charles came back from the pharmacy, where he had gone after dinner to take back the plaster that was left, he found his wife on her feet beside the cradle.

"Really, believe me—it will be all right," he said, kissing her on the forehead. "Don't worry about it, darling: you'll make yourself ill."

He had stayed out a long time. He had not seemed unduly upset, but even so Monsieur Homais had done his best to cheer him up, "raise his morale." The conversation had then turned on the various dangers that beset children because of the absent-mindedness of servants. Madame Homais could speak from experience, bearing as she did to this day on her chest the marks of a panful of burning coals that a cook had dropped inside her pinafore when she was small. No wonder the Homais' went out of their way to be careful with their children! In their house knives were never sharpened, floors never waxed. There were iron grills at the windows and heavy bars across the fireplaces. Though taught to be self-reliant, the Homais children couldn't move a step without someone in attendance; at the slightest sign of a cold their father stuffed them with cough syrups, and well past their fourth birthdays they were all mercilessly made to wear padded caps. This, it must be said, was a pet idea of Madame Homais': her husband was secretly worried about it, fearing lest the intellectual organs suffer as a result of such pressure; and he sometimes went so far as to say:

"Do you want to turn them into Caribs or Botocudos?"

Charles, meanwhile, had tried several times to end the conversation. "I'd like to have a word with you," he whispered in the clerk's ear; and Léon walked downstairs ahead of him.

"Can he be suspecting something?" he wondered. His heart pounded, and he imagined a thousand contingencies.

Charles, after closing the door behind them, asked him to inquire in Rouen as to the price of a good daguerreotype: he was thinking of paying a delicate tribute to his wife by giving her a sentimental surprise—a portrait of himself in his black tail coat. But he wanted to know, first, "what he was letting himself in for." Such inquiries would be no trouble for Monsieur Léon, since he went to the city almost every week.

What was the purpose of these visits? Homais suspected that there was a story there, an intrigue of some kind. But he was mistaken: Léon was not carrying on any amourette. These days his spirits were lower than ever: Madame Lefrançois could tell it from the amount of food he left on his plate. To find out more about it she questioned the tax collector; but Binet rebuffed her, saying that he "wasn't in the pay of the police."

Nevertheless his table companion struck him as exceedingly odd. Léon often lay back in his chair, stretched out his arms and complained vaguely about life.

"That's because you have no hobbies," said the tax collector.

"What would you advise?"

"If I were you I'd buy myself a lathe!"

"But I wouldn't know how to use it," the clerk answered.

"That's so, you wouldn't," said Binet. And he stroked his chin with an air of mingled scorn and satisfaction.

Léon was tired of loving without having anything to show for it, and he was beginning to feel the depression that comes from leading a monotonous life without any guiding interest or buoyant hope. He was so sick of Yonville and the Yonvillians that the sight of certain people and certain buildings irritated him beyond endurance: the pharmacist, worthy soul that he was, he found utterly unbearable. Still, though he longed for a new position, the prospect of change frightened him.

But now timidity gave way to impatience, and Paris beckoned from afar, with the fanfare of its masked balls, the laughter of its grisettes. Since he would have to finish his law studies there sooner or later, why shouldn't he go now? What was preventing him? And he began to make imaginary plans, sketch out his new existence. He furnished a dream apartment. He would lead an artist's life— take guitar lessons, wear a dressing gown, a Basque beret, blue velvet slippers! And in his mind's eye he particularly admired his overmantel arrangement: a pair of crossed fencing-foils, with a skull and the guitar hanging above.

The difficulty lay in obtaining his mother's consent; still, there could scarcely be a more reasonable request. Even his employer was urging him to think of another office, where he could widen his experience. Taking a middle course, therefore, Léon looked for a place as second clerk in Rouen, found nothing, and finally wrote his mother a long detailed letter in which he set forth his reasons for moving to Paris at once. She consented.

He didn't hurry. Every day for a month Hivert transported for him, from Yonville to Rouen and from Rouen to Yonville, trunks, valises and bundles; and after Léon had had his wardrobe restocked and his three armchairs reupholstered and had bought a whole new supply of foulard handkerchiefs—after he had made more preparations than for a trip around the world—he kept putting off his departure from week to week, until he received a second letter from his mother urging him to be on his way, since he wanted to pass his examination before the summer vacation.

When the moment came for farewells, Madame Homais wept and Justin sobbed. Homais hid his emotion as a strong man should, and insisted on carrying his friend's overcoat as far as the notary's. Maître Guillaumin was to drive Léon to Rouen in his carriage.

There was just time to say good-bye to Monsieur Bovary. When Léon reached the top of the stairs he was so breathless that he stood still for a moment. As he entered the room Madame Bovary rose quickly to her feet.

"Here I am again," said Léon.

"I knew you'd come!"

She bit her lip, and the blood rushed under her skin, reddening it from the roots of her hair to the edge of her collar. She remained standing, leaning against the wall paneling.

"Monsieur isn't here?" he said.

"He's out."

He repeated: "He's out."

There was a silence. They looked at each other; and their thoughts clung together in their common anguish like two throbbing hearts.

"I'd love to kiss Berthe," said Léon.

Emma went down a few steps and called Félicité.

He glanced quickly around him, taking in the walls, the tables, the fireplace, as though to record them forever down to their last detail and carry them away in his memory.

Then she was back, and the maid brought in Berthe, who was swinging a pinwheel upside down on a string.

Léon kissed her several times on the neck. "Good-bye, sweetheart! Good-bye!" And he handed her back to her mother.

"You may take her," Emma said to the maid.

They were left alone.

Madame Bovary had turned her back, her face pressed to a windowpane. Léon was holding his cap in his hand and kept brushing it against his thigh.

"It's going to rain," said Emma.

"I have a coat," he answered.

"Ah!"

She half turned to him, her face lowered. The light seemed to glide down her forehead to her arching brows as on a marble statue; and there was no way of knowing what she was gazing at on the horizon or what her deepest thoughts might be.

"Good-bye, then," he said, sighing deeply.

She raised her head with an abrupt movement.

"Yes, good-bye—you must be on your way."

They both stepped forward: he held out his hand; she hesitated.

"A handshake, then—English style," she said, with a forced laugh, putting her hand in his.

Léon felt her moist palm in his grasp, and into it seemed to flow the very essence of his being.

Then he released it; their eyes met again; and he was off.

As he crossed the roofed market he stopped behind a pillar to stare for a last time at the white house with its four green shutters. He thought he saw a shadowy form at the bedroom window; then the curtain, released from its hook as though of its own accord, swung slowly for a moment in long slanting folds and sprang fully out to hang straight and motionless as a plaster wall. Léon set off at a run.

Ahead he saw his employer's gig in the road, and beside it a man in an apron holding the horse. Homais and Maître Guillaumin were talking together, waiting for him.

The apothecary embraced him, tears in his eyes. "Here's your overcoat, my boy: wrap up warm! Look after yourself! Take it easy!"

"Come, Léon—jump in!" said the notary.

Homais leaned over the mudguard, and in a voice broken by sobs gulped the sad, familiar words of parting: "*Bon voyage!*"

"*Bon soir!*" replied Maître Guillaumin. "Anchors aweigh!"

They rolled off, and Homais went home.

Madame Bovary had opened her window that gave on to the garden, and was watching the clouds.

They were gathering in the west, in the direction of Rouen, twisting rapidly in black swirls; out from behind them shot great sun rays, like the golden arrows of a hanging trophy; and the rest of the sky was empty, white as porcelain. Then came a gust of wind; the poplars swayed; and suddenly the rain was pattering on the green leaves. But soon the sun came out again; chickens cackled; sparrows fluttered their wings in the wet bushes; and rivulets flowing along the gravel carried away the pink flowers of an acacia.

"Ah, by now he must be far away!" she thought.

Monsieur Homais dropped in as usual at half-past six, during dinner.

"Well," he said, sitting down, "so we've sent our young man on his way, have we?"

"I guess so," said the doctor. And then, turning in his chair: "What's new at your house?"

"Nothing much. Just that my wife wasn't quite herself this afternoon. You know how women are—anything upsets them, mine especially. We've no right to complain: their nervous system is much more impressionable than ours."

"Poor Léon!" said Charles. "How will he get along in Paris, do you think? Will he get used to it?"

Madame Bovary sighed.

"Never fear!" said the pharmacist, making a clicking noise with his tongue. "Think of the gay parties in restaurants, the masked balls! The champagne! Everything will go at a merry pace, I assure you!"

"I don't think he'll do anything wrong," Bovary objected.

"Nor do I," Monsieur Homais said quickly, "but he'll have to go along with the others if he doesn't want to be taken for a Jesuit. You have no idea of the life those bohemians lead in the Latin Quarter with their actresses! You know, students are very highly thought of in Paris. If they have even the slightest social grace they're admitted to the very best circles. They're even fallen in love with sometimes by ladies of the Faubourg Saint-Germain. Some of them make very good marriages."

"But," said the doctor, "I'm afraid that in the city he may . . ."

"You're right," interrupted the apothecary. "It's the reverse of the medal. In the city you've got to keep your hand in your watch-pocket every minute. Suppose you're sitting in a park. Some fellow comes up to you—well dressed, perhaps even wearing a decoration—somebody you could take for a diplomat. He addresses you, you talk, he ingratiates himself—offers you a pinch of snuff or picks up your hat for you. Then you get friendlier; he takes you to a café, invites you to visit him in the country, introduces you to all kinds of people over your drinks—and three-quarters of the time it's only to get his hands on your purse or lead you into evil ways."

"That's true," said Charles, "but I was thinking chiefly of diseases—typhoid fever, for example: students from the country are susceptible to it."

Emma shuddered.

"Because of the change of diet," agreed the pharmacist, "and the way it upsets the entire system. And don't forget the Paris water! The dishes they serve in restaurants—all those spicy foods—they overheat the blood: don't let anybody tell you they're worth a good stew. I've always said there's nothing like home cooking: it's better for the health. That was why when I was studying pharmacy in Rouen I went to board in a boarding house: I ate where my teachers ate."

And he continued to expound his general opinions and personal preferences until Justin came to fetch him to make an eggnog for a customer.

"Not a moment's peace!" he cried. "It's grind, grind, grind! I can't leave the shop for a minute. I'm like a plough-horse—sweating blood every second. It's a heavy yoke, my friends!"

And when he was at the door: "By the way," he said. "Have you heard the news?"

"What news?"

"It is very likely," Homais announced, raising his eyebrows and looking excessively solemn, "that the annual Agricultural Show of the department of the Seine-Inférieure will be held this year at—Yonville-l'Abbaye. There is, at least, a rumor to that effect. The paper referred to it this morning. An event of the very greatest importance for our district! But we'll talk about it later. I can see, thank you. Justin has the lantern."

VII

THE NEXT DAY WAS A FUNEREAL ONE FOR EMMA. EVERYTHING appeared to her as though shrouded in vague, hovering blackness; and grief swirled into her soul, moaning softly like the winter wind in a deserted castle. She was prey to the brooding brought on by irrevocable partings, to the weariness that follows every consummation, to the pain caused by the breaking off of a confirmed habit or the brusque stopping of a prolonged vibration.

It was like the days following her return from La Vaubyessard, when the dance tunes had kept whirling in her head: she was sunk in the same mournful melancholy, the same torpid despair. Léon seemed taller, handsomer, more charming and less distinct: though he had gone, he had not left her; he was there, and the walls of her house seemed to retain his shadow. She kept staring at the rug he had walked on, the empty chairs he had sat in. The stream at the foot of her garden flowed on as usual, rippling past the slippery bank. They had often strolled there, listening to this same murmur of the water over the moss-covered stones. How they had enjoyed the sun! And the shade, too, afternoons by themselves in the garden! He had read aloud to her, bareheaded on a rustic bench, the cool wind from the meadows ruffling the pages of his book and the nasturtiums on the arbor. . . . And now he was gone, the one bright spot in her life, her one possible hope of happiness! Why hadn't she grasped that good fortune when it had offered itself? And when it had first threatened to slip away—why hadn't she seized it with both hands, implored it on her knees? She cursed herself for not having surrendered to her love for Léon: she thirsted for his lips. She was seized with a longing to run after him, to fling herself into his arms, to cry, "Take me! I'm yours!" But the difficulties of such an enterprise discouraged her in advance; and her longings, increased by regret, became all the more violent.

Thereafter, the image she had of Léon became the center of her distress: it glowed more brightly than a travelers' fire left burning on the snow of a Russian steppe. She ran up to it, crouched beside it, stirred it carefully when it was on the verge of extinction, grasped at everything within reach that might bring it back to life. Distant memories and present-day events, experiences actual and imagined, her starved sensuality, her plans for happiness, blown down like dead branches in the wind, her barren "virtue," the collapse of her hopes, the litter of her domestic life—all these she gathered up and used as fuel for her misery.

Nevertheless the flames did die down—whether exhausted from lack of supplies or choked by excessive feeding. Little by little, love was quenched by absence; regret was smothered by routine; and the fiery glow that had reddened her pale sky grew gray and gradually vanished. In this growing inner twilight she even mistook her recoil from her husband for an aspiration toward her lover, the searing waves of hatred for a rekindling of love. But the storm kept raging, her passion burned itself to ashes, no help was forthcoming, no new sun rose on the horizon. Night closed in completely around her, and she was left alone in a horrible void of piercing cold.

Then the bad days of Tostes began all over again. She considered herself far more unhappy now than she had been then, for now she had experienced grief, and she knew that it would never end.

A woman who had assumed such a burden of sacrifice was certainly entitled to indulge herself a little. She bought herself a Gothic *prie-dieu,* and in a month spent fourteen francs on lemons to blanch her fingernails; she wrote to Rouen for a blue cashmere dress; and at Lheureux's she chose the finest of his scarves. She wound it around her waist over her dressing gown, and thus arrayed she closed the shutters and stretched out on her sofa with a book.

She kept changing her way of wearing her hair: she tried it *à la chinoise,* in soft curls, in braids; she tried parting it on one side and turning it under, like a man's.

She decided to learn Italian: she bought dictionaries, a grammar, a supply of paper. She went in for serious reading—history and philosophy. Sometimes at night Charles would wake up with a start, thinking that someone had come to fetch him to a sickbed. "I'm coming," he would mutter, and it would be the sound of the match that Emma was striking to light her lamp. But her books were like her many pieces of needlepoint: barely begun, they were tossed into the cupboard; she started them, abandoned them, discarded them in favor of new ones.

She had spells in which she would have gone to extremes with very little urging. One day she insisted, Charles to the contrary, that she could drink half a water glass of brandy; and when Charles was foolish enough to dare her, she downed every drop of it.

For all her "flightiness"—that was the Yonville ladies' word for it—Emma did not have a happy look. The corners of her mouth were usually marked with those stiff, pinched lines so often found on the faces of old maids and failures. She was pale, white as a sheet all over; the skin of her nose was drawn down toward the nostrils, and she had a way of staring vacantly at whoever she was talking with. When she discovered two or three gray hairs at her temples she began to talk about growing old.

She often had dizzy spells. One day she even spit blood; and when Charles hovered over her and showed his concern she shrugged. "What of it?" she said.

Charles shut himself in his consulting room, and sitting in his office armchair under the phrenological head he put his elbows on the table and wept.

He wrote his mother asking her to come, and they had long conversations on the subject of Emma.

What course to follow? What could be done, since she refused all treatment?

"Do you know what your wife needs?" said the older Madame Bovary. "She needs to be put to work—hard, manual work. If she had to earn her living like so many other people, she wouldn't have those vapors—they come from all those ideas she stuffs her head with, and the idle life she leads."

"She keeps busy, though," Charles said.

"Busy at what? Reading novels and all kinds of bad books—anti-religious books that quote Voltaire and ridicule the priests. It's a dangerous business, son: anyone who lacks respect for religion comes to a bad end."

So it was decided to prevent Emma from reading novels. The project presented certain difficulties, but the old lady undertook to carry it out: on her way through Rouen she would personally call on the proprietor of the lending library and tell him that Emma was canceling her subscription. If he nevertheless persisted in spreading his poison, they would certainly have the right to report him to the police.

Farewells between mother-in-law and daughter-in-law were curt. During the three weeks they had been together they hadn't exchanged four words apart from the formal greetings and absolute essentials called for at mealtime and bedtime.

The older Madame Bovary left on a Wednesday—market day at Yonville.

From early morning, one side of the square was taken up with a row of carts—all tipped up on end, with their shafts in the air, stretching along the house fronts from the church to the hotel. On the other side were canvas booths for the sale of cotton goods, woolen blankets and stockings, horse halters, and rolls of blue ribbon whose ends fluttered in the wind. Heavy hardware was spread out on the ground between pyramids of eggs and cheese baskets bristling with sticky straw; and close by the harvesting machines were the flat poultry boxes, with clucking hens sticking their necks out between the slats. The crowd always filled the same corner, unwilling to move on: sometimes it seemed on the point of pushing through the glass of the pharmacy window. On Wednesdays the shop was never empty, and everyone elbowed his way in, less to buy pharmaceutical products than to consult the pharmacist, so celebrated was Monsieur Homais' reputation in the villages round about. His hearty self-confidence bewitched the country folk: to them he was a greater doctor than all the doctors.

Emma was leaning out her window (she often did this: in the provinces windows take the place of boulevards and theatres) watching the crowd of yokels, when she caught sight of a gentleman in a green velvet frock coat. His dressy yellow gloves contrasted with his heavy gaiters, and he was approaching the doctor's house. Behind him was a peasant who followed along with lowered head and decidedly pensive expression.

"May I see Monsieur?" he asked Justin, who was chatting in the doorway with Félicité. And assuming that he was one of the house servants, he added: "Give him my name—Monsieur Rodolphe Boulanger, de la Huchette."

The new arrival had added the "de" and the "La Huchette" to his name not out of vanity as a landowner but rather to indicate more clearly who he was. La Huchette was an estate near Yonville, and he had recently bought the chateau and its two dependent farms. The latter he worked himself—not too seriously. He kept a bachelor establishment and was rumored to have "a private income of at least fifteen thousand francs a year."

Charles came into the parlor, and Monsieur Boulanger introduced his man, who wanted to be bled because "he felt prickly all over." There was no arguing with him: he said it would "clear him out."

So Bovary told the maid to bring a bandage, and a basin that he asked Justin to hold. The peasant turned pale at once. "There's nothing to be afraid of," Charles told him.

"I'm all right," the man said. "Go ahead."

He held out his sturdy arm with an air of bravado. At the prick of the scalpel the blood spurted out and spattered against the mirror.

"Hold the basin closer!" Charles cried.

"Look at that!" said the peasant. "Just like a fountain! I've got real red blood: that's a good sign, isn't it?"

"Sometimes," remarked the *officier de santé*, "they don't feel anything at first, and then they keel over—especially the husky ones, like this one here."

At those words the peasant dropped the scalpel case, which he had been twisting in his fingers. The back of the chair creaked under the heavy impact of his shoulders, and his hat fell to the floor.

"Just what I thought," said Bovary, pressing the vein with his finger.

The basin began to shake in Justin's hands; his knees wobbled and he turned pale.

"Where's my wife?" Charles cried, and he called her loudly. She came rushing down the stairs.

"Vinegar!" he cried. "We've got a pair of them, damn it!"

In his excitement he had trouble applying the compress.

"It's nothing," said Monsieur Boulanger, quite calmly; and he lifted Justin in his arms and propped him up on the table with his back against the wall.

Madame Bovary set about loosening Justin's cravat. There was a knot in the strings that fastened his shirt, and when she had undone it she rubbed his boyish neck lightly for a few minutes; then she moistened her batiste handker-chief in vinegar and patted his forehead with it, blowing gently on it as she did so.

The teamster revived; but Justin remained in his faint, the pupils of his eyes sunk into the whites like blue flowers in milk.

"We'd better not let him see this," said Charles.

Madame Bovary took away the basin. As she bent down to put it under the table, her dress—a long-waisted, full-skirted yellow summer dress with four flounces—belled out around her on the tile floor of the parlor; and as she put out her arms to steady herself the material billowed and settled, revealing the lines of her body. Then she brought in a pitcher of water, and was dissolving sugar in it when the pharmacist arrived. The maid had gone after him in the midst of the fracas, and when he found his apprentice with his eyes open he breathed a sigh of relief. Then he stalked back and forth in front of him, staring him up and down.

"Idiot!" he said. "Idiot, with a capital *I!* A terrible thing, a little blood-letting, isn't it! A fine fearless fellow, too. Just look at him! And yet I've seen him go up a tree after nuts like a squirrel—up to the dizziest heights, *Messieurs et Madame!* Say something, can't you? Tell us how good you are! You'll certainly make a fine pharmacist! Don't you know that some day you may be called on to give important evidence in court? The judges may need your expert opinion. You'll have to keep calm at such times, and know what to say! You'll have to show them you're a man, or else be called a fool!"

Justin made no answer, and the apothecary went on:

"Who asked you to come here anyway? You're always bothering Monsieur and Madame! You know perfectly well I always need you Wednesdays! There are twenty people in the shop right now—I left everything out of consideration for you! Go on! Get back there! Keep an eye on things till I come!"

When Justin had put himself to rights and gone, they talked a little about fainting spells. Madame Bovary had never had one.

"That's unusual for a lady," said Monsieur Boulanger. "But there are men who are extraordinarily susceptible, you know. I've seen a second at a duel lose consciousness at the mere sound of the loading of the pistols."

"I don't mind the sight of other people's blood a bit," said the pharmacist. "But the very idea of shedding my own would be enough to turn my stomach if I thought about it too much."

Meanwhile Monsieur Boulanger sent away his man, urging him to stop worrying now that he'd got what he wanted.

"His whim has afforded me the privilege of making your acquaintance," he said; and as he spoke the words he looked at Emma.

Then he put three francs on the corner of the table, bowed casually, and left.

He was soon on the other side of the river (it was the way back to La Huchette); and Emma saw him crossing the meadow under the poplars, occasionally slowing his pace as though he were pondering something.

"She's very nice," he was saying to himself, "very nice, that wife of the doctor's! Lovely teeth, black eyes, a dainty foot—she's like a real Parisian. Where the devil does she come from? How did such a clodhopper ever get hold of her?"

Monsieur Rodolphe Boulanger was thirty-four. He was brutal and shrewd. He was something of a connoisseur: there had been many women in his life. This one seemed pretty, so the thought of her and her husband stayed with him.

"I have an idea he's stupid. I'll bet she's tired of him. His fingernails are dirty and he hasn't shaved in three days. He trots off to see his patients and leaves her home to darn his socks. How bored she must be! Dying to live in town, to dance the polka every night! Poor little thing! She's gasping for love like a carp on a kitchen table gasping for water. A compliment or two and she'd adore me, I'm positive. She'd be sweet! But—how would I get rid of her later?"

And the thought of the troubles inevitable in such an affair brought to his mind by contrast his present mistress, an actress he kept in Rouen. He found he could not evoke her image without a feeling of satiety, and after a time he said to himself:

"Ah, Madame Bovary is much prettier—and what's more, much fresher. Virginie's certainly growing too fat. She's getting on my nerves with all her enthusiasms. And her mania for shrimps . . . !"

The countryside was deserted, and the only sounds were the regular swish of the tall grass against his gaiters and the chirping of crickets hidden in the distant oats. He thought of Emma in the parlor, dressed as he had seen her, and he undressed her.

"I'll have her!" he said aloud, bringing his stick down on a clod of earth in front of him.

And he immediately began to consider the question of strategy.

"Where could we meet? How could we arrange it? The brat would always be around, and the maid, and the neighbors, and the husband—there'd be a lot of headaches. Bah! It would all take too much time."

Then he began all over again:

"Those eyes really bore into you, though! And that pale complexion . . . God! How I love pale women. . . ."

By the time he had reached the top of the hill his mind was made up.

"The only thing to do now is keep my eyes open for opportunities. I'll call on them occasionally and send them presents—game and chickens. I'll have myself bled, if I have to. We'll get to be friends. I'll invite them to the house. . . . And . . . Oh, yes"—it came to him—"we'll soon be having the show. She'll be there. I'll see her. We'll get started. The approach direct: that's the best."

VIII

THE GREAT DAY ARRIVED AT LAST.

The morning of the Agricultural Show all the Yonvillians were standing on their doorsteps discussing the preparations. The pediment of the town hall had been looped with ivy; a marquee had been set up for the banquet in one of the meadows; and in the middle of the square, in front of the church, stood an antiquated fieldpiece that was to be fired as a signal announcing the arrival of the prefect and the proclamation of the prize winners. The Buchy national guard (Yonville had none) had come to join forces with the fire brigade, commanded by Binet. Today he wore a collar even higher than usual; and his bust, tightly encased in his tunic, was so stiff and inflexible that all his animal fluids seemed to be concentrated in his legs, which rose and fell with the music in rhythmic jerks. Since the tax collector and the colonel were rivals, each showed off his talents by drilling his men separately. First the red epaulettes would march up and down, and then the black breastplates. And then it would begin all over again: there was no end to it. Never had there been such a display of pomp! A number of citizens had washed their housefronts the day before; tricolor flags were hanging from half-open windows; all the cafés were full; and in the perfect weather the headdresses of the women seemed whiter than snow, their gold crosses glittered in the bright sun, and their multicolored neckcloths relieved the somber monotony of the men's frock coats and blue smocks. As the farm women dismounted from their horses they undid the big pins that had held their skirts tucked up away from splashing. The men's concern was for their hats: to protect them they had covered them with large pocket handkerchiefs, holding the corners between their teeth as they rode.

The crowd converged on the main street from both ends of the village, from the paths between the houses, from the lanes, and from the houses themselves; knockers could be heard falling against doors as housewives in cotton gloves emerged to watch the festivities. Particularly admired were the two large illumination frames laden with colored glass lamps that flanked the official grandstand; and against the four columns of the town hall stood four poles, each with a little banner bearing a legend in gold letters on a greenish ground. One said "Commerce," another "Agriculture," the third "Industry," and the fourth "Fine Arts."

But the jubilation brightening all faces seemed to cast a gloom over Madame Lefrançois, the hotel-keeper. She was standing on her kitchen steps muttering to herself:

"It's a crime—a crime, that canvas shack! Do they really think the prefect will enjoy eating his dinner in a tent, like a circus performer? They pretend the whole thing's for the good of this village—so why bring a third-class cook over from Neufchâtel? And who's it all for, anyway? A lot of cowherds and riffraff."

The apothecary came by. He was wearing a black tail coat, yellow nankeen trousers, reverse-calf shoes, and—most exceptionally—a hat: a stiff, low-crowned hat.

"Good morning!" he said. "Forgive me for being in such a hurry."

And as the buxom widow asked him where he was going:

"I imagine it must seem funny to you, doesn't it? Considering that most of the time I can't be pried loose from my laboratory any more than the old man's rat from his cheese."

"What cheese is that?" asked the landlady.

"Oh, nothing, nothing," said Homais. "I was merely referring to the fact, Madame Lefrançois, that I usually stay at home, like a recluse. But today things are different. I must absolutely . . ."

"You don't mean you're going *there?*" she said with a scornful look.

"Of course I'm going there," the apothecary replied, surprised. "Don't you know I'm on the advisory committee?"

Madame Lefrançois looked at him for a moment or two and then answered with a smile:

"That's all right, then. But what have you got to do with farming? Do you know anything about it?"

"Certainly I know something about it, being a pharmacist! A pharmacist is a chemist, Madame Lefrançois; and since the aim of chemistry is to discover the laws governing the reciprocal and molecular action of all natural bodies, it follows that agriculture falls within its domain! Take the composition of manures, the fermentation of liquids, the analysis of gasses, the effects of noxious effluvia—what's all that, I ask you, if it isn't chemistry in the strictest sense of the word?"

The landlady made no reply. Homais went on:

"Do you think that to be an agronomist you must till the soil or fatten chickens with your own hands? No: you have to study the composition of various substances—geological strata, atmospheric phenomena, the properties of the various soils, minerals, types of water, the density of different bodies, their capillary attraction. And a hundred other things. You have to be thoroughly versed in all the principles of hygiene—that's an absolute prerequisite if you're going to serve in a supervisory or consultant capacity in anything relating to the construction of farm buildings, the feeding of livestock, the preparation of meals for hired men. And then you've got to know botany, Madame Lefrançois: be able to tell one plant from another—you know what I mean? Which ones are benign and which ones are poisonous, which ones are unproductive and which ones are nutritive; whether it's a good thing to pull them out here and resow them there, propagate some and destroy others. In short, you've got to keep abreast of science by reading pamphlets and publications; you've got to be always on the alert, always on the lookout for possible improvements. . . ."

All this time the landlady never took her eyes off the door of the Café Français. The pharmacist continued:

"Would to God our farmers were chemists, or at least that they listened more carefully to what science has to say. I myself recently wrote a rather considerable little treatise—a monograph of over seventy-two pages, entitled: *Cider: Its Manufacture and Its Effects; Followed by Certain New Observations on This Subject.* I sent it to the Agronomical Society of Rouen, and it even brought me the honor of being admitted to membership in that body—Agricultural Section, Pomology Division. Now if this work of mine had been made available to the public . . ."

The apothecary broke off: Madame Lefrançois' attention was obviously elsewhere.

"Just look at them," she said. "How can they patronize such a filthy place?"

And with shrugs that stretched her sweater tight over her bosom, she pointed with both hands to her competitor's café, out of which came the sound of singing.

"Anyway, it won't be there much longer," she said. "Just a few days more, and then—*finis.*"

Homais drew back in amazement, and she came down her three steps and put her lips to his ear:

"What! Haven't you heard? They're padlocking it this week. It's Lheureux who's forcing the sale; all those notes Tellier signed were murder."

"What an unutterable catastrophe!" The apothecary always had the proper expression ready, whatever the occasion.

The landlady proceeded to tell him the story, which she had from Théodore, Maître Gullaumin's servant; and although she detested Tellier she had nothing but harsh words for Lheureux. He was a wheedler, a cringer.

"Look—there he is now, in the market," she said. "He's greeting Madame Bovary. She's wearing a green hat. In fact, she's on Monsieur Boulanger's arm."

"Madame Bovary!" cried Homais. "I must go and pay her my respects. She might like to have a seat in the enclosure, under the portico."

And ignoring Madame Lefrançois' attempts to detain

him with further details, he hurried off, smiling and with springy step, bestowing innumerable salutations right and left, and taking up a good deal of room with his long black coat tails that streamed in the wind behind him.

Rodolphe had seen him coming and had quickened his pace; but Madame Bovary was out of breath, and he slowed and smiled at her. "I was trying to avoid that bore," he said savagely. "You know, the apothecary."

She nudged him with her elbow.

"What does that mean?" he wondered, glancing at her out of the corner of his eye as they moved on.

Her face, seen in profile, was so calm that it gave him no hint. It stood out against the light, framed in the oval of her bonnet, whose pale ribbons were like streaming reeds. Her eyes with their long curving lashes looked straight ahead: they were fully open, but seemed a little narrowed because of the blood that was pulsing gently under the fine skin of her cheekbones. The rosy flesh between her nostrils was all but transparent in the light. She was inclining her head to one side, and the pearly tips of her white teeth showed between her lips.

"Is she laughing at me?" Rodolphe wondered.

But Emma's nudge had been no more than a warning, for Monsieur Lheureux was walking along beside them, now and then addressing them as though to begin conversation.

"What a marvelous day! Everybody's out! The wind is from the east."

Neither Madame Bovary nor Rodolphe made any reply, though at their slightest movement he edged up to them saying, "Beg your pardon?" and touching his hat.

When they were in front of the blacksmith's, instead of following the road as far as the gate Rodolphe turned abruptly into a side path, drawing Madame Bovary with him.

"Good-bye, Monsieur Lheureux!" he called out. "We'll be seeing you!"

"You certainly got rid of him!" she said, laughing.

"Why should we put up with intruders?" he said. "Today I'm lucky enough to be with you, so . . ."

Emma blushed. He left his sentence unfinished, and talked instead about the fine weather and how pleasant it was to be walking on the grass. A few late daisies were blooming around them.

"They're pretty, aren't they?" he said. "If any of the village girls are in love they can come here for their oracles." And he added: "Maybe I should pick one. What do you think?"

"Are you in love?" she asked, coughing a little.

"Ah, ah! Who knows?" answered Rodolphe.

The meadow was beginning to fill up, and housewives laden with big umbrellas, picnic baskets and babies were bumping into everyone. It was constantly necessary to turn aside, out of the way of long lines of girls—servants from farms, wearing blue stockings, low-heeled shoes and silver rings and smelling of the dairy when they came close. They walked holding hands, forming chains the whole length of the meadow, from the row of aspens to the banquet tent. It was time for the judging, and one after another the farmers were filing into a kind of hippodrome marked off by a long rope hung on stakes.

Here stood the livestock, noses to the rope, rumps of all shapes and sizes forming a ragged line. Lethargic pigs were nuzzling the earth with their snouts; calves were lowing and sheep bleating; cows with their legs folded under them lay on the grass, slowly chewing their cud and blinking their heavy eyelids under the midges buzzing around them. Bare-armed teamsters were holding rearing stallions by the halter: these were neighing loudly in the direction of the mares, who stood there quietly, necks outstretched and manes drooping, as their foals rested in their shadow or came now and again to suck. Above the long undulating line of these massed bodies a white mane would occasionally surge up like a wave in the wind, or a pair of sharp horns would stick out, or men's heads would bob up as they ran. Quite apart, outside the arena, a hundred yards off, was a big black bull with a strap harness and an iron ring through its nose, motionless as a brazen image. A ragged little boy held it by a rope.

Meanwhile a group of gentlemen were solemnly advancing between the two rows, inspecting each animal and then conferring in an undertone. One, who seemed the most important, was writing details in a notebook as he walked. This was the chairman of the jury, Monsieur Derozerays de la Panville. As soon as he recognized Rodolphe he quickly stepped forward and addressed him with a cordial smile: "What's this, Monsieur Boulanger? You've deserted us?"

Rodolphe assured him that he was coming directly. But when the chairman had passed:

"I'll certainly *not* be going," he said to Emma. "I like your company better than his."

And though he kept making fun of the show, Rodolphe displayed his blue pass to the guard so that they could walk about unmolested, and he even stopped from time to time in front of some particularly fine exhibit. It was never anything that Madame Bovary cared about: he noticed this, and began to make jokes about the Yonville ladies and the way they dressed; then he apologized for the carelessness of his own costume. This was a mixture of the casual and the refined—the kind of thing that both fascinates and exasperates the common herd, hinting as it does at an eccentric way of life, indulgence in wild passions and "artistic" affectations, and a contempt for social conventions. His batiste shirt (it had pleated cuffs) puffed out from the opening of his gray twill vest at each gust of wind; and his broad-striped trousers ended at nankeen shoes trimmed with patent leather so shiny that the grass was reflected in it. He tramped unconcernedly through horse dung, one thumb in his vest pocket, his straw hat tilted over one ear.

"Anyway," he said, "when you live in the country . . ."

"Any trouble you take is wasted," said Emma.

"Completely," replied Rodolphe. "Think of it: there isn't a single person here today capable of appreciating the cut of a coat."

And they talked about the mediocrity of provincial life, so suffocating, so fatal to all noble dreams.

"So," said Rodolphe, "I just get more and more engulfed in gloom as time goes on. . . ."

"You do!" she cried, in surprise. "I thought of you as being very jolly."

"Of course—that's the impression I give: I've learned to wear a mask of mockery when I'm with other people. But many's the time I've passed a cemetery in the moonlight and asked myself if I wouldn't be better off lying there with the rest. . . ."

"Oh! And what about your friends?" she asked. "Have you no thought for them?"

"My friends? What friends? Have I any? Who cares anything about me?"

And he accompanied those last words with a kind of desperate whistle.

But they had to draw apart to make way for a tall tower of chairs borne by a man coming up behind them. He was so excessively laden that the only parts of him visible were the tips of his wooden shoes and his two outstretched hands. It was Lestiboudois, the gravedigger, who was renting out church seats to the crowd. He was highly inventive where his own interests were concerned, and had thought up this way of profiting from the show. It was a good idea: everyone was hailing him at once. The villagers were hot; they clamored for the straw-seated chairs that gave off a smell of incense, and they leaned back with a certain veneration against the heavy slats stained with candlewax.

Then once again Madame Bovary took Rodolphe's arm, and he went on as though talking to himself:

"Yes, so many things have passed me by! I've always been so alone! Ah! If I'd had a purpose in life, if I'd met anyone with true affection, if I'd found somebody who . . . Oh! Then I wouldn't have spared any effort; I'd have surmounted every obstacle, let nothing stand in my way . . . !"

"It seems to me, though," said Emma, "that you're scarcely to be pitied."

"Oh? You think that?" said Rodolphe.

"Yes," she answered, "because after all you're free"—she hesitated—"rich . . ."

"Don't make fun of me," he begged.

And she was swearing that she was doing nothing of the kind, when a cannon shot resounded and everyone began to hurry toward the village.

It was a false alarm: the prefect wasn't even in sight, and the members of the jury were in a quandary, not knowing whether to begin the proceedings or wait a while longer.

Finally at the far end of the square appeared a big hired landau drawn by two skinny horses who were being furiously whipped on by a white-hatted coachman. Binet had just time to shout, "Fall in!" and the colonel to echo him; there was a rush for the stacked rifles; and in the confusion some of the men forgot to button their collars. But the official coach-and-pair seemed to sense the difficulty, and the emaciated beasts, dawdling on their chain, drew up at a slow trot in front of the portico of the town hall just at the moment when the national guard and the fire brigade were deploying into line to the beating of the drums.

"Mark time!" cried Binet.

"Halt!" cried the colonel. "Left, turn!"

And after a present-arms during which the rattle of the metal bands as they slid down the stocks and barrels sounded like a copper cauldron rolling down a flight of stairs, all the rifles were lowered.

Then there emerged from the carriage a gentleman clad in a short, silver-embroidered coat, his forehead high and bald, the back of his head tufted, his complexion wan and his expression remarkably benign. His eyes, very large and heavy-lidded, half shut as he peered at the multitude; and at the same time he lifted his sharp nose and curved his sunken mouth into a smile. He recognized the mayor by his sash, and explained that the prefect had been unable to come. He himself was a prefectural councilor, and he added a few words of apology. Tuvache replied with compliments, the emissary declared himself unworthy of them; and the two officials stood there face to face, their foreheads almost touching, all about them the members of the jury, the village council, the local elite, the national guard and the crowd. Holding his little black three-cornered hat against his chest, the prefectural councilor reiterated his greetings; and Tuvache, bent like a bow, returned his smiles, stammered, clutched uncertainly for words, protested his devotion to the monarchy and his awareness of the honor that was being bestowed on Yonville.

Hippolyte, the stable-boy at the hotel, came to take the horses from the coachman; and limping on his clubfoot he led them through the gateway of the Lion d'Or, where a crowd of peasants gathered to stare at the carriage. There was a roll of the drums, the howitzer thundered, and the gentlemen filed up and took their seats on the platform in red plush armchairs loaned by Madame Tuvache.

All in this group looked alike. Their flabby, fair-skinned, slightly sun-tanned faces were the color of new cider, and their bushy side whiskers stuck out over high, stiff collars that were held in place by white cravats tied in wide bows. Every vest was of velvet, with a shawl collar; every watch had an oval carnelian seal at the end of a long ribbon; and every one of the gentlemen sat with his hands planted on his thighs, his legs carefully apart, the hard-finished broadcloth of his trousers shining more brightly than the leather of his heavy shoes.

The invited ladies were seated to the rear, under the portico between the columns, while the ordinary citizens faced the platform, either standing, or sitting on chairs. Lestiboudois had retransported to this new location all those that he had previously taken to the meadow; now he kept bringing still more from the church; and he was crowding the place so with his chair-rental business that it was almost impossible for anyone to reach the few steps leading to the platform.

"In my opinion," said Monsieur Lheureux, addressing the pharmacist, who was passing by on his way to take his seat, "they should have set up a pair of Venetian flagstaffs: trimmed with something rich and not too showy they'd have made a very pretty sight."

"Certainly," said Homais. "But what can you expect! The mayor took everything into his own hands. He hasn't much taste, poor Tuvache: in fact, he's completely devoid of what is known as the artistic sense."

Meanwhile Rodolphe, with Madame Bovary, had gone up to the second floor of the town hall, into the "council chamber": it was quite empty—a perfect place, he said, from which to have a comfortable view of the ceremonies. He took three of the stools that stood around the oval table under the king's bust and moved them over to one of the windows; and there they sat down close together.

There was a certain agitation on the platform—prolonged whisperings and consultations. Finally the prefectural councilor rose to his feet. It had become known that he was called Lieuvain, and his name was repeated from one to another in the crowd. He made sure that his sheets of paper were in proper order, peered at them closely, and began:

"Gentlemen: I should like, with your permission (before speaking to you about the object of today's meeting—and this sentiment, I am sure, will be shared by all of you), I should like, with your permission, to pay tribute to the national administration, to the government, to the monarch, gentlemen, to our sovereign, to the beloved king to whom no branch of public or private prosperity is indifferent, and who, with so firm and yet so wise a hand, guides the chariot of state amidst the constant perils of a stormy sea, maintaining at the same time public respect for peace as well as for war—for industry, for commerce, for agriculture, for the fine arts."

"I ought to move a little further back," said Rodolphe.

"Why?" said Emma.

But at that moment the councilor's voice rose to an extraordinary pitch. He was declaiming:

"Gone forever, gentlemen, are the days when civil discord drenched our streets with blood; when the landlord, the business man, nay, the worker, sank at night into a peaceful slumber trembling lest they be brutally awakened by the sound of inflammatory tocsins; when the most subversive principles were audaciously undermining the foundations . . ."

"It's just that I might be caught sight of from below," said Rodolphe. "If I were, I'd have to spend the next two

weeks apologizing; and what with my bad reputation . . ."

"Oh! You're slandering yourself," said Emma.

"No, no, my reputation's execrable, I assure you."

"But, gentlemen," continued the councilor, "if I dis-
miss those depressing evocations and turn my eyes to the
present situation of our cherished fatherland, what do I
see before me? Commerce and the arts are thriving everywhere; everywhere new channels of communication, like so
many new arteries in the body politic, are multiplying contacts between its various parts; our great manufacturing
centers have resumed their activity; religion, its foundations strengthened, appeals to every heart; shipping fills
our ports; confidence returns; at long last, France breathes
again!"

"Moreover, from the point of view of society it's probably deserved," Rodolphe said.

"What do you mean?" she asked.

"Do you really not know," he said, "that there exist
souls that are ceaselessly in torment? That are driven now
to dreams, now to action, driven from the purest passions to
the most orgiastic pleasures? No wonder we fling ourselves
into all kinds of fantasies and follies!"

She stared at him as if he were a traveler from mythical
lands. "We poor women," she said, "don't have even that
escape."

"A poor escape," he said, "since it doesn't bring happiness."

"But do we ever find happiness?" she asked.

"Yes, it comes along one day," he answered.

"And the point has not been lost on you," the councilor was saying. "Not on you, farmers and workers in the
fields! Not on you, champions of progress and morality!
The point has not been lost on you, I say, that the storms

of political strife are truly more to be dreaded than the disorders of the elements!"

"Yes, it comes along one day," Rodolphe repeated. "All of a sudden, just when we've given up hope. Then new horizons open before us: it's like a voice crying, 'Look! It's here!' We feel the need to pour out our hearts to a given person, to surrender, to sacrifice everything. In such a meeting no words are necessary: each senses the other's thoughts. Each is the answer to the other's dreams." He kept staring at her. "There it is, the treasure so long sought for—there before us: it gleams, it sparkles. But still we doubt; we daren't believe; we stand there dazzled, as though we'd come from darkness into light."

As he ended, Rodolphe enhanced his words with pantomime. He passed his hand over his face, like someone dazed; then he let it fall on Emma's hand. She withdrew hers. The councilor read on:

"And who is there who would wonder at such a statement, gentlemen? Only one so blind, so sunk (I use the word advisedly), so sunk in the prejudices of another age as to persist in his misconceptions concerning the spirit of our farming population. Where, I ask you, is there to be found greater patriotism than in rural areas, greater devotion to the common weal, greater—in one word—intelligence? And by intelligence, gentlemen, I do not mean that superficial intelligence that is a futile ornament of idle minds, but rather that profound and moderate intelligence that applies itself above all to useful ends, contributing in this manner to the good of all, to public improvement and the upholding of the state—that intelligence that is the fruit of respect for law and the performance of duty!"

"Ah, there they go again!" said Rodolphe. "Duty, duty, always duty—I'm sick of that word. Listen to them! They're a bunch of doddering old morons and bigoted old church mice with foot warmers and rosaries, always squeaking, 'Duty! Duty!' at us. I have my own idea of duty. Our duty is to feel what is great and love what is beautiful —not to accept all the social conventions and the infamies they impose on us."

"Still . . . still . . ." objected Madame Bovary.

"No! Why preach against the passions? Aren't they the only beautiful thing in this world, the source of heroism, enthusiasm, poetry, music, the arts, everything?"

"But still," said Emma, "we have to be guided a little by society's opinions; we have to follow its standards of morality."

"Ah! But there are two moralities," he replied. "The petty one, the conventional one, the one invented by man, the one that keeps changing and screaming its head off—that one's noisy and vulgar, like that crowd of fools you see out there. But the other one, the eternal one . . . Ah! This one's all around us and above us, like the landscape that surrounds us and the blue sky that gives us light."

Monsieur Lieuvain had just wiped his mouth with his pocket handkerchief. He resumed:

"Why should I presume, gentlemen, to prove to you who are here today the usefulness of agriculture? Who is it that supplies our needs, who is it that provisions us, if not the farmer? The farmer, gentlemen, sowing with laborious hand the fertile furrows of our countryside, brings forth the wheat which, having been ground and reduced to powder by means of ingenious machinery, emerges in the form of flour, and from thence, transported to our cities, is presently delivered to the baker, who fashions from it a food for the poor man as well as for the rich. Is it not the farmer, once again, who fattens his plentiful flocks in the pastures to provide us with our clothing? For how would we be clothed, for how would we be nourished, without agriculture? Indeed, gentlemen—is there need to seek so far afield for examples? Who among you has not often given thought to the immense benefit we derive from that modest creature—adornment of our kitchen yards—which provides at one and the same time a downy pillow for our beds, its succulent meat for our tables, and eggs? But I should never end, had I to enumerate one after another the different products which properly cultivated soil lavishes on its children like a generous mother. Here, the grape; there, the cider apple; yonder, the colza; elsewhere, a thousand kinds of cheese. And flax, gentlemen, do not forget flax!—an area in which within the past few years there has been considerable development, and one to which I particularly call your attention."

There was no need for him to "call their attention": every mouth in the crowd was open, as though to drink in his words. Tuvache, sitting beside him, listened wide-eyed; Monsieur Derozerays' lids now and again gently shut; and further along the pharmacist, holding his son Napoléon between his knees, cupped his hand to his ear lest he miss a single syllable. The other members of the jury kept slowly nodding their chins against their vests to express their approval. The fire brigade, at the foot of the platform, leaned on their bayonets; and Binet stood motionless, elbow bent, the tip of his sword in the air. He could hear, perhaps, but he certainly could not see, for the visor of his helmet had fallen forward onto his nose. His lieutenant, who was Monsieur Tuvache's younger son, had gone him one better: the helmet he was wearing was far too big for him and kept teetering on his head and showing a corner of the calico nightcap he had on under it. He was smiling from beneath his headgear as sweetly as a baby; and his small pale face, dripping with sweat, wore an expression of enjoyment, exhaustion and drowsiness.

The square was packed solidly with people as far as the houses. Spectators were leaning out of every window and standing on every doorstep; and Justin, in front of the pharmacy show window, seemed nailed to the spot in contemplation of the spectacle. Despite the crowd's silence, Monsieur Lieuvain's voice didn't carry too well in the open air. What came was fragmentary bits of sentences interrupted here and there by the scraping of chairs; then all at once from behind there would resound the prolonged lowing of an ox, and lambs bleated to one another on the street corners. For the cowherds and shepherds had driven their animals in that close, and from time to time a cow would bellow as her tongue tore off some bit of foliage hanging down over her muzzle.

Rodolphe had come close to Emma and was speaking rapidly in a low voice:

"Don't you think it's disgusting, the way they conspire to ruin everything? Is there a single sentiment that society doesn't condemn? The noblest instincts, the purest sympathies are persecuted and dragged in the mud; and if two poor souls do find one another, everything is organized to keep them apart. They'll try, just the same; they'll beat their wings, they'll call to each other. Oh! Never fear! Sooner or later, in six months or ten years, they'll come together and love one another, because they can't go against fate and because they were born for each other."

He was leaning forward with his arms crossed on his knees, and lifting his face to Emma's he looked at her fixedly from very near. In his eyes she could see tiny golden lines radiating out all around his black pupils, and she could even smell the perfume of the pomade that lent a gloss to his hair. Then a languor came over her; she remembered the vicomte who had waltzed with her at La Vaubyessard and whose beard had given off this same odor of vanilla and lemon; and automatically she half closed her eyes to breathe it more deeply. But as she did this, sitting up straight in her chair, she saw in the distance, on the farthest horizon, the old stagecoach, the Hirondelle, slowly descending the hill of Les Leux, trailing a long plume of dust behind it. It was in this yellow carriage that Léon had so often returned to her; and that was the road he had taken when he had left forever. For a moment she thought she saw him across the square, at his window; then everything became confused, and clouds passed before her eyes; it seemed to her that she was still whirling in the waltz, under the blaze of the chandeliers, in the vicomte's arms, and that Léon was not far off, that he was coming. . . . And yet all the while she was smelling the perfume of Rodolphe's hair beside her. The sweetness of this sensation permeated her earlier desires, and like grains of sand in the wind these whirled about in the subtle fragrance that was filling her soul. She opened her nostrils wide to breathe in the freshness of the ivy festooning the capitals outside the window. She took off her gloves and wiped her hands; then she fanned herself with her handkerchief, hearing above the beating of the pulse in her temples the murmur of the crowd and the councilor's voice as he intoned his periods.

"Persist!" he was saying. "Persevere! Follow neither the beaten tracks of routine nor the rash counsels of reckless empiricism. Apply yourselves above all to the improvement of the soil, to rich fertilizers, to the development of fine breeds—equine, bovine, ovine and porcine. May this exhibition be for you a peaceful arena where the winner, as he leaves, will stretch out his hand to the loser and fraternize with him, wishing him better luck another time! And you, venerable servants, humblest members of the household, whose painful labors have by no government up until today been given the slightest consideration: present yourselves now, and receive the reward of your silent heroism! And rest assured that the state henceforth has its eyes upon you, that it encourages you, that it protects you, that it will honor your just demands, and lighten, to the best of its ability, the burden of your painful sacrifices!"

Monsieur Lieuvain sat down.

Monsieur Derozerays stood up, and began another speech. His was perhaps not quite so flowery as the councilor's; but it had the advantage of being characterized by a more positive style—by a more specialized knowledge, that is, and more pertinent arguments. There was less praise of the government, and more mention of religion and agriculture. He showed the relation between the two and how they had always worked together for the good of civilization. Rodolphe was talking to Madame Bovary about dreams, forebodings, magnetism. Going back to the cradle of human society, the orator depicted the savage ages when men lived off acorns in the depths of the forest. Then they had cast off their animal skins, garbed themselves in cloth, dug the ground and planted the vine. Was this an advance? Didn't this discovery entail more disadvantages than benefits? That was the problem Monsieur Derozerays set himself. From magnetism Rodolphe gradually moved on to affinities; and as the chairman cited Cincinnatus and his plow, Diogenes planting his cabbages and the Chinese emperors celebrating the New Year by sowing seed, the young man was explaining to the young woman that these irresistible attractions had their roots in some earlier existence.

"Take us, for example," he said. "Why should we have met? How did it happen? It can only be that something in our particular inclinations made us come closer and closer across the distance that separated us, the way two rivers flow together."

He took her hand, and this time she did not withdraw it.

"First prize for all-round farming!" cried the chairman.

"Just this morning, for example, when I came to your house . . ."

"To Monsieur Bizet, of Quincampoix."

"Did I have any idea that I'd be coming with you to the show?"

"Seventy francs!"

"A hundred times I was on the point of leaving, and yet I followed you and stayed with you . . ."

"For the best manures."

". . . as I'd stay with you tonight, tomorrow, every day, all my life!"

"To Monsieur Caron, of Argueil, a gold medal!"

"Never have I been so utterly charmed by anyone . . ."

"To Monsieur Bain, of Givry-Saint-Martin!"

". . . so that I'll carry the memory of you with me. . . ."

"For a merino ram . . ."

"Whereas you'll forget me: I'll vanish like a shadow."

"To Monsieur Belot, of Notre-Dame . . ."

"No, though! Tell me it isn't so! Tell me I'll have a place in your thoughts, in your life!"

"Hogs: a tie! To Messieurs Lehérissé and Cullembourg, sixty francs!"

Rodolphe squeezed her hand, and he felt it all warm and trembling in his, like a captive dove that longs to fly away; but then, whether in an effort to free it, or in response to his pressure, she moved her fingers.

"Oh! Thank God! You don't repulse me! How sweet, how kind! I'm yours: you know that now! Let me see you! Let me look at you!"

A gust of wind coming in the windows ruffled the cloth on the table; and down in the square all the tall head-dresses of the peasant women rose up like fluttering white butterfly wings.

"Use of oil-cakes!" continued the chairman.

He was going faster now.

"Flemish fertilizer . . . flax-raising . . . drainage, long-term leases . . . domestic service!"

Rodolphe had stopped speaking. They were staring at each other. As their desire rose to a peak their dry lips quivered; and, languidly, of their own accord, their fingers intertwined.

"Catherine-Nicaise-Elizabeth Leroux, of Sassetot-la-Guerrière, for fifty-four years of service on the same farm, a silver medal, value twenty-five francs!"

"Where is Catherine Leroux?" repeated the councilor.

There was no sign of her, but there was the sound of whispering voices:

"Go ahead!"

"No!"

"To the left!"

"Don't be scared!"

"Stupid old thing!"

"Is she there or isn't she?" cried Tuvache.

"Yes! Here she is!"

"Then send her up!"

Everyone watched her as she climbed to the platform: a frightened-looking little old woman who seemed to have shriveled inside her shabby clothes. On her feet were heavy wooden clogs, and she wore a long blue apron. Her thin face, framed in a simple coif, was more wrinkled than a withered russet, and out of the sleeves of her red blouse hung her large, gnarled hands. Years of barn dust, washing soda and wool grease had left them so crusted and rough and hard that they looked dirty despite all the clear water they'd been rinsed in; and from long habit of service they hung half open, as though offering their own humble testimony to the hardships they had endured. A kind of monklike rigidity gave a certain dignity to her face, but her pale stare was softened by no hint of sadness or human kindness.

Living among animals, she had taken on their muteness and placidity. This was the first time she had ever been in the midst of so great a crowd; and inwardly terrified by the flags and the drums, by the gentlemen in tail coats and by the decoration worn by the councilor, she stood still, uncertain whether to move ahead or to turn and run, comprehending neither the urgings of the crowd nor the smiles of the jury. Thus did half a century of servitude stand before these beaming bourgeois.

"Step forward, venerable Catherine-Nicaise-Elizabeth Leroux!" cried the councilor, who had taken the list of prize winners from the chairman.

Looking at the sheet of paper and at the old woman in turn, he kept urging her forward like a father: "Come right here, come ahead!"

"Are you deaf?" cried Tuvache, jumping up from his chair.

And he proceeded to shout into her ear: "Fifty-four years of service! A silver medal! Twenty-five francs! For you!"

She took the medal and stared at it. Then a beatific smile spread over her face, and as she left the platform those nearby could hear her mumble: "I'll give it to our priest and he'll say some Masses for me."

"Such fanaticism!" hissed the pharmacist, bending toward the notary.

The ceremonies were ended; the crowd dispersed; and now that the speeches had been read everyone resumed his rank and everything reverted to normal. Masters bullied their servants, the servants beat their cows and their sheep, and the cows and the sheep—indolent in their triumph—moved slowly back to their sheds, their horns decked with the green wreaths that were their trophies.

Meanwhile the national guard had gone up to the second floor of the town hall: brioches were impaled on their bayonets, and their drummer bore a basketful of bottles. Madame Bovary took Rodolphe's arm; he escorted her home; they said good-bye at her door; and then he went for a stroll in the meadow until it was time for the banquet.

The feast was long, noisy, clumsily served: the guests were so crowded that they could scarcely move their elbows; and the narrow planks that were used for benches threatened to snap under their weight. They ate enormously, each piling his plate high to get full value for his assessment. Sweat poured off every forehead; and over the table, between the hanging lamps, hovered a whitish vapor, like a river mist on an autumn morning. Rodolphe, his back against the cloth side of the tent, was thinking so much about Emma that he was aware of nothing going on around him. Out on the grass behind him servants were stacking dirty plates; his tablemates spoke to him and he didn't answer; someone kept filling his glass, and his mind was filled with stillness despite the growing noise. He was thinking of the things she had said and of the shape of her lips; her face shone out from the plaques on the shakos as from so many magic mirrors; the folds of her dress hung down the walls; and days of love-making stretched endlessly ahead in the vistas of the future.

He saw her again that evening, during the fireworks, but she was with her husband and Madame Homais and the pharmacist. The latter was very worried about stray rockets, and constantly left the others to give Binet a word of advice.

Through overprecaution, the fireworks, which had been delivered in care of Monsieur Tuvache, had been stored in his cellar, with the result that the damp powder could scarcely be got to light; and the culminating number, which was to have depicted a dragon swallowing its own tail, was a complete fiasco. Now and then some pathetic little Roman candle would go off and bring a roar from the gaping crowd—a roar amidst which could be heard the screams of women, fair game for ticklers in the darkness. Emma nestled silently against Charles's shoulder, raising her head to follow the bright trail of the rockets in the black sky. Rodolphe watched her in the glow of the colored lamps.

Gradually these went out, the stars gleamed; then came a few drops of rain, and she tied a scarf over her hair.

Just then the councilor's landau drove out of the hotel yard. The drunken coachman chose that moment to collapse; and high above the hood, between the two lamps, everyone could see the mass of his body swaying right and left with the pitching of the springs.

"There ought to be strong measures taken against drunkenness," said the apothecary. "If I had my way, there'd be a special bulletin board put up on the door of the town hall, and every week there'd be a list posted of all who had intoxicated themselves with alcoholic liquors during that period. Such a thing would be very valuable statistically, a public record that might . . . Excuse me!"

And once again he hurried off toward the captain.

The latter was homeward bound. He was looking forward to rejoining his lathe.

"It might not do any harm," said Homais, "to send one of your men, or go yourself, to . . ."

"Get away and leave me alone," replied the tax collector. "Everything's taken care of."

"You can all stop worrying," the apothecary announced when he was back with his friends. "Monsieur Binet guarantees that all necessary measures have been taken. Not a spark has fallen. The pumps are full. We can safely retire to our beds."

"I can certainly do with some sleep," said Madame Homais, with a vast yawn. "Never mind—we had a wonderfully beautiful day for the show."

Rodolphe echoed her words in a low voice, his eyes soft: "Yes, it was: wonderfully beautiful."

They exchanged good-byes and went their respective ways.

Two days later, in the *Fanal de Rouen*, there was a great article about the Agricultural Show. Homais had written it in a burst of inspiration the very next day.

"Why these festoons, these flowers, these garlands? Whither was it bound, this crowd rushing like the billows of a raging sea under a torrential tropic sun that poured its torrid rays upon our fertile meadows?"

Then he went on to speak of the condition of the peasants. The government was doing something, certainly, but not enough. "Be bold!" he cried, addressing the administration. "A thousand reforms are indispensable: let us accomplish them." Then, describing the arrival of the councilor, he didn't forget "the warlike air of our militia," or "our sprightliest village maidens," or the bald-headed old men, veritable patriarchs, "some of whom, survivors of our immortal phalanxes, felt their hearts throb once again to the manly sound of the drums." His own name came quite early in his listing of the members of the jury, and he even reminded his readers in a footnote that Monsieur Homais, the pharmacist, had sent a monograph concerning cider to the Agricultural Society. When he came to the distribution of the prizes, he depicted the joy of the winners in dithyrambic terms. Father embraced son, brother embraced brother, husband embraced wife. More than one worthy rustic proudly displayed his humble medal to the assemblage; and, returning home to his helpmeet, doubtless wept tears of joy as he hung it on the modest wall of his cot.

"About six o'clock the leading participants in the festivities forgathered at a banquet in the pasture belonging to Monsieur Liégeard. The utmost cordiality reigned throughout. A number of toasts were proposed. By Monsieur Lieuvain: 'To the king!' By Monsieur Tuvache: 'To the prefect!' By Monsieur Derozerays: 'To agriculture!' By Monsieur Homais: 'To those twin sisters, industry and the fine arts!' By Monsieur Leplichey: 'To progress!' After nightfall a brilliant display of fireworks all at once illumined the heavens. It was a veritable kaleidescope, a true stage-set for an opera, and for a moment our modest village imagined itself transported into the midst of an Arabian Nights dream.

"We may mention that no untoward incidents arose to disturb this family gathering."

And he added:

"Only the clergy was conspicuous by its absence. Doubtless a totally different idea of progress obtains in the sacristies. Suit yourselves, *messieurs de Loyola!*"

IX

SIX WEEKS WENT BY WITHOUT FURTHER VISIT FROM RODOLPHE. Then one evening he came.

The day after the Show he had admonished himself: "I mustn't go back right away. That would be a mistake." And at the end of the week he had left for a hunting trip.

After his hunting was over he thought he had waited too long. But then: "If she loved me from the first, she must be impatient to see me again," he reasoned. "And this means she must love me all the more by now. So—back to the attack!"

And when he saw Emma turn pale as he entered the parlor he knew he was right.

She was alone. Daylight was fading. The muslin sash curtains deepened the twilight; and the gilt barometer had just caught a ray of sun and was blazing in the mirror between the lacy edges of the coral.

Rodolphe remained standing, and Emma scarcely replied to his first conventionally polite phrases.

"I've been having all kinds of things happen," he said. "I was ill."

"Anything serious?" she cried.

"Well, not really," he said, sitting beside her on a stool. "It was just that I didn't want to come here again."

"Why?"

"Can't you guess?"

He stared at her—this time so intently that she blushed and lowered her head.

"Emma . . ." he said.

"Monsieur!" she exclaimed, drawing away a little.

"Ah, you can see for yourself," he said, in a resigned voice, "that I was right not to want to come here again. Your name—my heart's full of it—I spoke it without meaning to, and you stopped me. 'Madame Bovary'! Everyone calls you that, and it's not your name at all. It's somebody else's. Somebody else's," he said a second time; and he buried his face in his hands. "I think of you every minute! The thought of you drives me crazy! Forgive me—I won't stay with you. I'll go away—far away—so far that you'll never hear of me again. But today . . . I don't know what power it was that made me come. We can't fight against fate. There's no resisting when an angel smiles. Once something lovely and charming and adorable has wound itself around your heart . . ."

It was the first time that Emma had had such things

said to her; and her pride, like someone relaxing in a steam bath, stretched luxuriously in the warmth of his words.

"No," he continued. "I didn't come, these past few weeks. I haven't seen you. But everything close to you I've looked at and looked at. At night—night after night—I got up and came here and stared at your house—the roof shining in the moonlight, the trees in the garden swaying at your window, and a little lamp, just a gleam, shining through the windowpanes in the dark. Ah! You little knew that a poor wretch was standing there, so near you and yet so far. . . ."

She turned to him with a sob. "How kind you are . . . !"

"I'm not kind! I love you, that's all! You must know it. Tell me you do: one word! Just one word!"

And Rodolphe was sliding imperceptibly from the stool to his knees when there was a sound of sabots in the kitchen and he saw that the door of the room was ajar.

"You'd be doing me a favor," he said, resuming his position on the stool, "if you'd gratify a whim I have."

The whim was to be taken through her house: he wanted to see it. Madame Bovary saw nothing out of the way in the request, and they were both just rising to their feet when Charles appeared.

"*Bonjour, docteur*," Rodolphe greeted him.

Flattered to be so addressed, the *officier de santé* was profusely obsequious, and Rodolphe profited from those few moments to regain some of his composure.

"Madame was talking to me about her health," he began, "and . . ."

Charles interrupted him. He was very worried indeed; his wife was having difficulty breathing again. Rodolphe asked whether horseback riding might not be good for her.

"Certainly it would! Just the thing! An excellent suggestion, darling! You ought to follow it."

She pointed out that she had no horse; Monsieur

Rodolphe offered her one of his; she declined; he did not insist; and finally, to explain the purpose of his visit, he told Charles that his teamster, the man who had been bled, was still having dizzy spells.

"I'll stop by and see him," said Bovary.

"No, no, I'll send him to you. We'll come here; that will be easier for you."

"Very good; thank you."

As soon as they were alone:

"Why don't you accept Monsieur Boulanger's suggestions? He's being so gracious."

She pouted, made one excuse after another, and finally said that "it might look strange."

"A lot I care about that!" said Charles, turning on his heel. "Health comes first! You're wrong!"

"But how do you expect me to ride a horse if I have no habit?"

"You must order one," he replied.

It was the riding habit that decided her.

When it was ready, Charles wrote to Monsieur Boulanger that his wife was at his disposition, and that they thanked him in advance for his kindness.

The next day at noon Rodolphe presented himself at Charles's door with two riding horses. One of them had pink pompons decorating its ears and bore a lady's buckskin saddle.

Rodolphe had put on a pair of high soft boots, telling himself that she had probably never seen anything like them; and Emma was indeed charmed with his appearance when he came up to the landing in his velvet frock coat and white tricot riding breeches. She was ready and waiting for him.

Justin ran out of the pharmacy to take a look at her, and the apothecary himself left his work for a few moments. He gave Monsieur Boulanger several bits of advice:

"Accidents happen so quickly! Take care! Your horses may be more spirited than you know!"

She heard a sound above her head: it was Félicité drumming on the windowpanes to amuse little Berthe. The child blew her a kiss, and Emma made a sign with her riding crop in answer.

"Have a good ride!" cried Monsieur Homais. "Be careful! That's the main thing! Careful!"

And he waved his newspaper after them as he watched them ride away.

As soon as it felt soft ground, Emma's horse broke into a gallop. Rodolphe galloped at her side. Now and again they exchanged a word. With her head slightly lowered, her hand raised and her right arm outstretched, she let herself go to the rhythmic rocking motion.

At the foot of the hill Rodolphe gave his horse its head: both horses leapt forward as one, and then at the top they as suddenly stopped, and Emma's large blue veil settled and hung still.

It was early October. There was a mist over the countryside. Wisps of vapor lay along the horizon, following the contours of the hills, and elsewhere they were drifting and rising and evaporating. Now and then as the clouds shifted, a ray of sun would light up the roofs of Yonville in the distance, with its riverside gardens, its yards and its church steeple. Emma half closed her eyes trying to pick out her house, and never had the wretched village she lived in looked so very small. From the height on which they were standing the whole valley was like an immense pale lake, dissolving into thin air: clumps of trees stood out here and there like dark rocks, and the tall lines of poplars piercing the fog were like its leafy banks, swaying in the wind.

To one side, over the turf between the firs, the light was dim and the air mild. The reddish earth, the color of snuff, deadened the sound of the hoofs; and the horses kicked fir cones before them as they walked.

For a time Rodolphe and Emma continued to follow the edge of the wood. Now and then she turned her head away to avoid his eyes, and at such moments she saw only the regularly spaced trunks of the firs, almost dizzying in their unbroken succession. The horses were blowing, and the leather creaked in the saddles.

Then they turned into the forest, and at that moment the sun came out.

"God's watching over us," said Rodolphe.

"You think so?" she said.

"Let's go on!" he said.

He clicked his tongue, and both horses broke into a trot.

Tall ferns growing along the path kept catching in Emma's stirrup, and Rodolphe bent over as he rode and pulled them out. At other times he came close to her to push aside overhanging branches, and she felt his knee brush against her leg. Now the sky was blue, and the leaves were still. There were clearings full of heather in bloom, and the sheets of purple alternated with the multicolored tangle of the trees, gray, fawn and gold. Often a faint rustling and fluttering of wings would come from under the bushes; or there would be the cry, at once raucous and sweet, of crows flying off among the oaks.

They dismounted. Rodolphe tethered the horses. She walked ahead of him on the moss between the cart tracks.

But the long skirt of her habit impeded her, even though she held it up by the end; and Rodolphe, walking behind her, kept staring at her sheer white stocking that showed between the black broadcloth and the black shoe as though it were a bit of her naked flesh.

She stopped.

"I'm tired," she said.

"Just a little further," he said. "Come along, try."

Then a hundred yards further on she stopped again; and the veil that slanted down from her man's hat to below her waist covered her face with a translucent blue film, as though she were swimming under limpid water.

"Where are we going?"

He didn't answer. She was breathing quickly. Rodolphe looked this way and that, biting his mustache.

They came to a larger open space, one that had recently been cleared of saplings. They sat down on a log, and Rodolphe spoke to her of his love.

He was careful not to frighten her, at first, by saying anything overbold: he was calm, serious, melancholy.

She listened to him with lowered head, stirring the wood chips on the ground with the toe of her shoe.

But when he said, "Our lives are bound up together now, aren't they?" she answered, "No—you know they can't be."

She rose to leave. He grasped her wrist. She stood still and gave him a long look, her eyes moist and tender. Then she said hastily:

"Please—let's not talk about it any more. Where are the horses? Let's go back."

A movement of angry displeasure escaped him.

"Where are the horses?" she asked again. "Where are the horses?"

Then, smiling a strange smile, staring fixedly, his teeth clenched, he advanced toward her with arms outstretched. She drew back trembling.

"You're frightening me!" she stammered. "What are you doing? Take me back!"

His expression changed. "Since you insist," he said.

And abruptly he was once more considerate, tender, timid. She took his arm and they turned back.

"What was the matter?" he asked. "What came over you? I don't understand. You must have some mistaken idea. I have you in my heart like a Madonna on a pedestal—in an exalted place, secure, immaculate. But I need you if I'm to go on living! I need your eyes, your voice, your thoughts. I beseech you: be my friend, my sister, my angel!"

And he reached out his arm and put it around her waist. She made a half-hearted effort to free herself, but he kept it there, holding her as they walked.

Now they were so close to the horses that they heard them munching leaves.

"Just a little longer," begged Rodolphe. "Let's not go yet. Wait."

He drew her further on, to the edge of a little pond whose surface was green with duck weed and where faded water lilies lay still among the rushes. At the sound of their steps in the grass, frogs leaped to hiding.

"It's wrong of me," she said. "Wrong. I must be out of my mind to listen to you."

"Why? Emma! Emma!"

"Oh! Rodolphe!" The syllables came out slowly, and she pressed against his shoulder.

The broadcloth of her habit clung to the velvet of his coat. She leaned back her head, her white throat swelled in a sigh, and, her resistance gone, weeping, hiding her face, with a long shudder she gave herself to him.

Evening shadows were falling, and the level rays of the sun streamed through the branches and dazzled her eyes. Here and there, all about her, among the leaves and on the ground, were shimmering patches of light, as though hummingbirds winging by had scattered their feathers. All was silent; a soft sweetness seemed to be seeping from the trees; she felt her heart beating again, and her blood flowing in her flesh like a river of milk. Then from far off, beyond the woods in distant hills, she heard a vague, long, drawn-out cry—a sound that lingered; and she listened silently as it mingled like a strain of music with the last vibrations of her quivering nerves. Rodolphe, a cigar between his teeth, was mending a broken bridle with his penknife.

They returned to Yonville by the same route. In the mud they saw, side by side, the hoof prints left there by their own two horses; they saw the same bushes, the same stones in the grass. Nothing around them had changed: and yet to her something had happened that was more momentous than if mountains had moved. Rodolphe reached over, now and then, and raised her hand to his lips.

She was charming on horseback—erect and slender, her knee bent against the animal's mane, her face flushed a little by the air in the red glow of evening.

As she entered the village she made her horse prance on the stone pavement, and people stared at her from their windows.

Her husband, at dinner, found that she looked well; but she seemed not to hear him when he asked about her ride; and she leaned her elbow on the table beside her plate, between the two lighted candles.

"Emma!" he said.

"What?"

"Well, I called on Monsieur Alexandre this afternoon. He bought a filly a few years ago and she's still in fine shape, just a little broken in the knees; I'm sure I could get her for a hundred écus. . . ."

And he went on:

"I thought you might like to have her, so I reserved her. . . . I bought her. . . . Did I do right? Tell me."

She nodded her head in assent. Then, a quarter of an hour later:

"Are you going out tonight?" she asked.

"Yes, why?"

"Oh, nothing—nothing, dear."

And as soon as she was rid of Charles she went upstairs and shut herself in her room.

At first it was as though she were in a daze: she saw the trees, the paths, the ditches, Rodolphe; once again she felt his arms tighten around her as the leaves were all a-tremble and the reeds whistled in the wind.

Then she caught sight of herself in the mirror, and was amazed by the way she looked. Never had her eyes been so enormous, so dark, so deep: her whole being was transfigured by some subtle emanation.

"I have a lover! I have a lover!" she kept repeating to herself, reveling in the thought as though she were beginning a second puberty. At last she was going to know the joys of love, the fever of the happiness she had despaired of. She was entering a marvelous realm where all would be passion, ecstasy, rapture: she was in the midst of an endless blue expanse, scaling the glittering heights of passion; everyday life had receded, and lay far below, in the shadows between those peaks.

She remembered the heroines of novels she had read, and the lyrical legion of those adulterous women began to sing in her memory with sisterly voices that enchanted her. Now she saw herself as one of those *amoureuses* whom she had so envied: she was becoming, in reality, one of that gallery of fictional figures; the long dream of her youth was coming true. She was full of a delicious sense of vengeance. How she had suffered! But now her hour of triumph had come; and love, so long repressed, was gushing forth in joyful effervescence. She savored it without remorse, without anxiety, without distress.

The next day brought a new delight. They exchanged vows. She told him her sorrows. Rodolphe interrupted her with kisses; and she begged him, gazing at him with half-shut eyes, to say her name again and tell her once more that he loved her. They were in the forest, like the day before, this time in a hut used by sabot-makers. The walls were of straw, and the roof was so low that they could not stand erect. They sat side by side on a bed of dry leaves.

From that day on they wrote each other regularly every night. Emma took her letter out into the garden and slipped it into a crack in the terrace wall beside the river; Rodolphe came, took it, and left one for her—one that was always, she complained, too short.

One morning when Charles had gone out before sunrise she was seized with a longing to see Rodolphe at once. She could go quickly to La Huchette, stay there an hour, and be back in Yonville before anyone was up. The thought made her pant with desire, and soon she was halfway across the meadow, walking fast and not looking back.

Day was just breaking. From far off Emma recognized her lover's farm, with its two swallow-tailed weathervanes silhouetted in black against the pale twilight.

Beyond the farmyard was a building that could only be the chateau. She entered it as though the walls opened of themselves at her approach. A long straight staircase led to an upper hall. Emma turned the latch of a door, and there at the far end of a room she saw a man asleep. It was Rodolphe. She uttered a cry.

"It's you!" he cried. "You, here! How did you come? Ah! Your dress is wet!"

"I love you!" was her answer; and she flung her arms around his neck.

She had dared and won; and from then on, each time that Charles went out early she quickly dressed and stole down the river stairs.

If the cow plank had been raised she had to follow the garden walls that bordered the stream; the bank was slippery, and to keep from falling she would clutch at tufts of faded wallflowers. Then she would strike out across the ploughed fields, sinking in, stumbling, her light shoes getting continually stuck in the soft soil. The scarf she had tied over her head fluttered in the wind as she crossed the meadows; she was afraid of the oxen, and would begin to run; and she would arrive breathless, rosy-cheeked, everything about her smelling of sap and verdure and fresh air. Rodolphe would still be asleep. She was like a spring morning entering his room.

The yellow curtains masking the windows let through a soft, dull golden light. Emma would grope her way, squinting, dewdrops clinging to her hair like a halo of topazes around her face. And Rodolphe would laugh and draw her to him and strain her to his heart.

Afterwards she would explore the room, opening drawers, combing her hair with his comb, looking at herself in his shaving mirror. Often she took the stem of his pipe in her teeth—a large pipe that he kept on his night table, beside the lemons and lumps of sugar that were there with his water jug.

It always took them a good quarter of an hour to say good-bye. Emma invariably wept: she wished that she never had to leave him. Some irresistible force kept driving her time and again to his side, until one day when she arrived unexpectedly he frowned as though displeased.

"What's wrong?" she cried. "Are you ill? Tell me!"

After some urging, he declared gravely that her visits were becoming foolhardy and that she was risking her reputation.

X

AS TIME WENT ON SHE CAME TO SHARE RODOLPHE'S FEARS. LOVE
had intoxicated her at first, and she had had no thought
beyond it. But now that life was inconceivable without it
she was terrified lest she be deprived of any portion of this
love, or even that it be in any way interfered with. Each
time she returned from one of her visits she cast uneasy
glances about her, peering at every figure moving on the
horizon, at every dormer in the village from which she
might be seen. Her ears picked up the sound of every footstep, every voice, every plough; and she would stand still,
paler and more trembling than the leaves of the swaying
poplars overhead.

One morning on her way back she suddenly thought she
saw a rifle pointing at her. It was slanting out over the
edge of a small barrel half hidden in the grass beside a ditch.
She felt faint with fright, but continued to walk ahead,
and a man emerged from the barrel like a jack-in-the-box.
He wore gaiters buckled up to his knees, and his cap was
pulled down over his eyes; his lips were trembling with cold
and his nose was red. It was Captain Binet, out after wild
duck.

"You should have called!" he cried. "When you see a gun
you must always give warning."

That reproach was actually the tax collector's attempt
to cover up the fright that Emma had given *him*. There
was a police ordinance prohibiting duck-shooting except
from boats, and for all his respect for the law, Monsieur

Binet was in the process of committing a violation. He had been expecting the game warden to appear any minute. But fear had added spice to his enjoyment, and in the solitude of his barrel he had been congratulating himself on his luck and his deviltry.

At the sight of Emma he felt relieved of a great weight, and he opened conversation:

"Chilly, isn't it! Really nippy!"

Emma made no answer.

"You're certainly out bright and early," he went on.

"Yes," she stammered. "I've been to see my baby at the nurse's."

"Ah, I see! I see! As for me, I've been right here where I am now ever since daybreak, but it's such dirty weather that unless you have the bird at the very end of your gun . . ."

"Good-bye, Monsieur Binet," she interrupted, turning away.

"Good-bye, Madame," he answered dryly.

And he went back into his barrel.

Emma regretted having taken such brusque leave of the tax collector. Whatever surmises he made would certainly be to her discredit. What she had said about the wet nurse was the worst possible story she could have invented: everyone in Yonville knew perfectly well that little Berthe had been back with her parents for a year. Besides, no one lived out in that direction; that particular path led only to La Huchette. Binet must certainly have guessed where she was coming from: he wouldn't keep his mouth shut, either; he would gossip, unquestionably. All day she racked her brains, trying to dream up all possible lies; and she brooded incessantly about that fool with his game bag.

After dinner Charles, seeing that she looked worried about something, had the idea of distracting her from whatever it was by taking her to call on the pharmacist; and the first person she saw in the pharmacy was, once again, the tax collector! He was standing at the counter in the glow of the red jar, saying, "Give me a half-ounce of vitriol."

"Justin," called the pharmacist, "bring the sulphuric acid."

Then, to Emma, who was about to go up to Madame Homais' quarters:

"No, don't bother to climb the stairs: she'll be coming down directly. Warm yourself at the stove while you wait. Excuse me . . . *Bonjour, docteur*." (The pharmacist greatly enjoyed uttering the word *docteur*, as though by applying it to someone else he caused some of the glory it held for him to be reflected on himself.) "But be careful not to knock over the mortars," he called to Justin. "No, no! Go get some of the chairs from the little room! You know perfectly well we never move the parlor armchairs."

And Homais was just bustling out from behind the counter to put his armchair back where it belonged when Binet asked him for a half-ounce of sugar acid.

"Sugar acid?" said the pharmacist scornfully. "I don't know what that is. I never heard of it. You want oxalic acid, perhaps? Oxalic is what you mean, isn't it?"

Binet explained that he needed a corrosive: he wanted to make some metal polish to clean the rust off parts of his hunting gear. Emma stood rigid.

"Yes, the weather is certainly unpropitious," said the pharmacist, "what with all this dampness."

"Still," said the tax collector slyly, "there are people who don't mind it."

She was choking.

"Now give me . . ."

"He'll never go!" she thought.

". . . a half-ounce of rosin and turpentine, four ounces

of beeswax, and an ounce and a half of boneblack to clean the patent leather on my outfit."

As the apothecary began cutting the wax, Madame Homais appeared with Irma in her arms, Napoléon beside her and Athalie bringing up the rear. She sat down on the plush-covered bench by the window, while the boy took a stool and his elder sister kept close to the jujube jar, near her dear papa. The latter was pouring things into funnels, corking bottles, gluing labels and wrapping parcels. Everyone watched him in silence: the only sound was an occasional clink of weights in the scales, and a few low-voiced words of advice from the pharmacist to his apprentice.

"How is your little girl?" Madame Homais suddenly asked.

"Quiet!" cried her husband, who was jotting figures on a scratch-pad.

"Why didn't you bring her?" she went on, in an undertone.

"Sh! Sh!" said Emma, pointing to the apothecary.

But Binet, absorbed in checking the pharmacist's arithmetic, seemed to have heard nothing. Then at last he left. Emma gave a deep sigh of relief.

"How heavily you're breathing!" said Madame Homais.

"Don't you find it rather warm?" she answered.

The next day, therefore, Emma and Rodolphe discussed the best way of arranging their meetings. Emma was for bribing her maid with a present, but it would be better if they could find some other, safer place in Yonville. Rodolphe promised to look for one.

From then on, three or four times a week throughout the winter, he came to the garden in the dark of the night. Emma had removed the key from the gate, letting Charles think it was lost.

To announce himself, Rodolphe threw a handful of gravel against the shutters. She always started up; but sometimes she had to wait, for Charles loved to chat beside the fire, and went on and on. She would grow wild with impatience: if she could have accomplished it with a look, she would have flung him out a window. Finally she would begin to get ready for bed, and then she would take up a book and sit quietly reading, as though absorbed. Charles, in bed by this time, would call her.

"Come, Emma," he would say. "It's time."

"Yes, I'm coming," she would answer.

But the candles shone in his eyes, and he would turn to the wall and fall asleep. Then she slipped out, holding her breath, smiling, palpitating, half undressed.

Rodolphe would enfold her in the large full cape he wore and, with his arm around her waist, lead her without a word to the foot of the garden.

It was in the arbor that they spent their time together, on the same dilapidated rustic bench from which Léon used to stare at her so amorously on summer evenings. She scarcely thought of him now.

The stars glittered through the bare branches of the jasmine. Behind them they heard the flowing of the river, and now and again the crackle of dry reeds on the bank. Here and there in the darkness loomed patches of deeper shadow; and sometimes these would suddenly seem to shudder, rear up and then curve downward, like huge black waves threatening to engulf them. In the cold of the night they clasped each other the more tightly, the sighs that came from their lips seemed deeper, their half-seen eyes looked larger; and amidst the silence their soft-spoken words had a crystalline ring that echoed and reechoed in their hearts.

If the night was rainy they sought shelter in the consulting room, between the shed and the stable. She would light a kitchen lamp that she kept hidden behind the books. Rodolphe made himself at home here, as though the place belonged to him. The sight of the bookcase and the desk—indeed the whole room—aroused his hilarity: he couldn't keep from joking about Charles in a way that made Emma uncomfortable. She would have liked him to be more serious—or even more dramatic sometimes, like the night she thought she heard the sound of approaching footsteps in the lane.

"Someone's coming," she whispered.

He blew out the light.

"Have you got your pistols?"

"What for?"

"Why—to defend yourself," said Emma.

"You mean against your husband? That poor . . . ?" And Rodolphe ended his sentence with a gesture that meant that he could annihilate Charles with a flick of his finger.

This display of fearlessness dazzled her, even though she sensed in it a crudity and bland vulgarity that shocked her.

Rodolphe thought a good deal about that episode of the pistols. If she had spoken in earnest, it was absurd of her, he thought, really an odious thing, for he had no cause to hate poor Charles. He was by no means "devoured by jealousy," as the saying went: and indeed, in this connection, Emma had made him a tremendous vow that he, for his part, thought in rather poor taste.

Besides, she was becoming frightfully sentimental. They had had to exchange miniatures and cut handfuls of each other's hair; and now she was asking for a ring—a real wedding band, as a sign of eternal union. She often talked to him about the "bells of evening," or the "voices of nature"; and then she would go on about her mother and his. Rodolphe's mother had been dead for twenty years, but Emma kept consoling him in the kind of affected language one uses to a bereaved child; and sometimes she would even look at the moon and say to him, "Somewhere up there I'm sure they're both looking down at us and approving of our love."

But she was so pretty! He couldn't remember ever having had so unspoiled a mistress. The purity of her love was something entirely new to him. It was a change from his usual loose habits, and it both flattered his pride and inflamed his senses. Emma's continual raptures, which his bourgeois common sense despised, seemed to him in his heart of hearts charming, since it was he who inspired them.

As time went on he stopped making any effort, secure in the knowledge that he was loved; and imperceptibly his manner changed. No longer did he speak to her, as before, in words so sweet that they made her weep; nor were there any more of those fervid embraces that frenzied her. Their great love, in which she lived completely immersed, seemed to be ebbing away, like the water of a river that was sinking into its own bed; and she saw the mud at the bottom. She refused to believe it; she redoubled her caresses; and Rodolphe hid his indifference less and less.

She didn't know whether she regretted having yielded to him or whether she didn't rather long to love him more dearly. Her humiliating feeling of weakness was turning into resentment: but this melted away in the heat of his embraces. It was not an attachment; it was a kind of permanent seduction. She was in his bondage. It almost frightened her.

Nevertheless, from the outside everything looked more serene than ever, Rodolphe having succeeded in conducting the affair as he pleased; and at the end of six months, when spring came, they were like a married couple peacefully tending a domestic flame.

It was the time of the year when Monsieur Rouault always sent his turkey, in commemoration of his mended leg. As usual, the present was accompanied by a letter. Emma

cut the string tying it to the basket, and read the following:

> Dear Children:
> I hope these lines find you well and that this one
> will be up to the others: it seems to me a little
> tenderer, if I may say so, and meatier. But next time
> I'll send you a cock for a change, unless you'd rather
> stick to gobblers, and please send me back the basket
> along with the last two. I had an accident with the
> cart shed, one night a heavy wind blew the roof off
> into the trees. Crops haven't been too good either. I
> can't tell when I'll come to see you. It's so hard for
> me to leave the place now that I'm alone.

Here there was a space between the lines, as though the
old man had put down his pen to think a while.

> As for me, I'm all right, except for a cold I caught
> the other day at the fair in Yvetot, where I went to
> hire a shepherd, having got rid of the one I had be-
> cause he was too particular about his food. All these
> good-for-nothings give you more trouble than
> they're worth. This one was disrespectful besides.
> I heard from a peddler who stopped in your town
> to have a tooth drawn that Bovary keeps busy. It
> doesn't surprise me, and he showed me his tooth; we
> took a cup of coffee together. I asked if he'd seen
> you, Emma, he said no, but he'd seen two horses in
> the stable from which I assume that business is
> prospering. I'm glad of it, dear children, may the
> good Lord send you every possible happiness.
> It grieves me that I've never seen my beloved
> granddaughter Berthe Bovary. I've planted a tree of

September plums for her under the window of your room and I won't let anybody touch it except to make some jam for her later that I'll keep in the cupboard for her when she comes.

Good-bye, dear children. I kiss you on both cheeks, all three of you.

I am, with all good wishes,
Your loving father,
Théodore Rouault

She sat for a few minutes with the sheet of coarse paper in her hand. The letter was thick with spelling mistakes, and Emma brooded on the affectionate thought that cackled through them like a hen half hidden in a thorn hedge. Her father had dried his writing with ash from the fireplace, for a bit of gray dust drifted out of the letter onto her dress, and she could almost see the old man bending down toward the hearth to take up the tongs. How long it was since she had sat there beside him, on the fireseat, burning the end of a stick in the flame of the crackling furze! She remembered summer evenings, full of sunshine. The foals would whinny when anyone came near, and gallop and gallop to their hearts' content. There had been a beehive under her window, and sometimes the bees, wheeling in the light, would strike against the panes like bouncing golden balls. How happy she had been in those days! How free! How full of hope! How rich in illusions! There were no illusions left now! She had had to part with some each time she had ventured on a new path, in each of her successive conditions—as virgin, as wife, as mistress; all along the course of her life she had been losing them, like a traveler leaving a bit of his fortune in every inn along the road.

But what was making her so unhappy? Where was the extraordinary disaster that had wrought havoc with her life? And she lifted her head and looked about her, as though trying to discover the cause of her suffering.

An April sunbeam was dancing on the china in the what-not; the fire was burning; she felt the rug soft beneath her slippers; the day was cloudless, the air mild, and she could hear her child shouting with laughter.

The little girl was rolling on the lawn, in the cut grass that Lestiboudois was raking. She was lying on her stomach on a pile that he had got together; Félicité was holding her by the skirt; the gardener was working nearby, and whenever he came close she leaned over toward him, waving her arms in the air.

"Bring her in to me!" her mother cried. And she rushed over and kissed her. "How I love you, darling! How I love you!"

Then, noticing that the tips of the child's ears were a little dirty, she quickly rang for hot water; and she washed her, changed her underclothes, stockings and shoes, asked a thousand questions about how she felt, as though she were just back from a trip, and finally, giving her more and more kisses, and weeping a little, she handed her back to the maid, who stood gaping at this overflow of affection.

That night Rodolphe found her more reserved than usual.

"It will pass," he thought. "It's some whim."

And on three successive evenings he didn't appear for their rendezvous. When he finally came she was cold, almost disdainful.

"Ah! You'll get nowhere playing that game . . . !" And he pretended not to notice her melancholy sighs or the handkerchief she kept bringing out.

Then Emma's repentance knew no bounds.

She even wondered why she detested Charles, and whether it mightn't be better to try to love him. But there was so little about him to which her resurgent feeling could attach itself that she was at a loss as to how to put her noble resolution into effect. And then one day the apothecary provided the desired opportunity.

XI

HOMAIS HAD LATELY READ AN ARTICLE EXTOLLING A NEW method of curing clubfoot; and since he was on the side of progress he conceived the patriotic idea that Yonville, to keep abreast of the times, should have its own operation for talipes, as he learnedly called the deformity.

"After all," he said to Emma, "what's the risk? Look." And he enumerated on his fingers the advantages that would accrue from the attempt. "Almost sure success, relief and improved appearance for the patient, and for the surgeon a rapid rise to fame. Why shouldn't your husband fix up poor Hippolyte, at the Lion d'Or? The boy would unquestionably talk about his cure to every traveler at the inn, and then"—here Homais lowered his voice and cast a glance about him—"what is there to keep me from sending a little piece about it to the paper? Ah! An article gets around—people talk about it—a thing like that really snowballs. Who can tell? Who can tell?"

He was right: Bovary might very well succeed. Emma had never had any reason to think that he wasn't skillful in his work; and what satisfaction *she* would derive from persuading him to take a step that would increase his fame and fortune! Something more solid than love to lean on would be only too welcome.

Egged on by her and by the apothecary, Charles consented. He sent to Rouen for Doctor's Duval's treatise; and every night, his head in his hands, he buried himself in its pages.

He studied talipes in its various forms—equinus, varus and valgus: in other words, the varying malformations of the foot downwards, inwards, or outwards, sometimes scientifically called *strephocatopodia, strephendopodia* and *strephexopodia;* and he studied *strephypopodia* and *strephanopodia*—downward or upward torsion. And meanwhile Monsieur Homais tried to persuade the stable-boy to agree to be operated. He used every possible argument.

"You'll scarcely feel it—there'll be the very slightest pain if any. It's just a prick, like the tiniest blood-letting. Not nearly as bad as cutting out certain kinds of corns."

Hippolyte rolled his eyes stupidly as he thought it over.

"Besides," the pharmacist went on, "it's not for my sake that I'm urging you, but for yours—out of pure humanity. I'd like to see you rid of that ugly limp, my boy, and that swaying in the lumbar region that must interfere seriously with your work, whatever you say."

Then Homais painted a picture of how much more lively and nimble he would feel, and even intimated that he'd be much more successful with women. The stable-boy grinned sheepishly at that. Then Homais played on his vanity:

"Are you a man or aren't you? Think what it would have been like if you'd had to serve in the army and go into combat! Ah, Hippolyte!"

And Homais moved off, declaring that such stubbornness, such blindness in refusing the benefits of science were beyond his understanding.

In the end the poor wretch yielded, unable to stand up against what was a veritable conspiracy. Binet, who never meddled in other people's affairs, Madame Lefrançois, Artémise, the neighbors, even the mayor, Monsieur Tuvache—everybody urged him, lectured him, shamed him; but what finally decided him was that it wouldn't cost him anything. Bovary even offered to supply the apparatus that would be used after the operation. Emma had thought up that bit of generosity, and Charles had agreed, inwardly marveling at what an angel his wife was.

Guided by the pharmacist's advice, he finally succeeded on the third try in having the cabinetmaker and the locksmith construct a sort of box weighing about eight pounds —a complicated mass of iron, wood, tin, leather, screws and nuts.

Meanwhile, in order to know which of Hippolyte's tendons had to be cut, he first had to find out what variety of clubfoot his was.

The foot made almost a straight line with the leg, and at the same time was twisted inward, so that it was an equinus with certain characteristics of a varus, or else a varus with strong equinus features. But with his equinus—which actually was as wide across as an equine hoof, with rough skin, stringy tendons, oversized toes, and black nails that were like the nails of a horseshoe—the taliped ran about fleet as a deer from morning to night. He was constantly to be seen in the square, hopping about among the carts, thrusting his clubfoot ahead of him. Actually, the affected leg seemed to be stronger than the other. From its long years of service it had taken on moral qualities, as it were —qualities of patience and energy; and whenever Hippolyte was given a particularly heavy task to do, it was that leg that he threw his weight on.

Since it was an equinus, the Achilles tendon would have to be cut, and then later, perhaps, the anterior tibial muscle, to take care of the varus. Charles didn't dare risk two operations at once, and indeed he was trembling already lest he interfere with some important part of the foot he knew nothing about.

Neither Ambroise Paré, applying an immediate ligature

to an artery for the first time since Celsus had done it fifteen centuries before; nor Dupuytren cutting open an abscess through a thick layer of the brain; nor Gensoul, when he performed the first removal of an upper maxillary— none of them, certainly, felt such a beating of the heart, such a quivering of the hand, such a tenseness of the mind, as Monsieur Bovary when he approached Hippolyte with his tenotomy knife. On a table nearby, just as in a hospital, lay a pile of lint, waxed thread and a quantity of bandages—a veritable pyramid of bandages, the apothecary's entire stock. It was Monsieur Homais who had been making these preparations ever since early morning, as much to dazzle the multitude as to inflate his self-importance. Charles pierced the skin: there was a sharp snap. The tendon was cut; the operation was over. Hippolyte couldn't stop marveling: he bent over Bovary's hands and covered them with kisses.

"Don't get excited," said the apothecary. "You'll have plenty of occasion to express your gratitude to your benefactor."

And he went out to announce the result to five or six sensation-seekers who were waiting in the yard expecting Hippolyte to make his appearance walking normally. Then Charles strapped his patient into the apparatus and went home, where Emma was anxiously awaiting him at the door. She flung her arms around his neck; they sat down at table; he ate heartily, and even asked for a cup of coffee with his dessert—a bit of intemperance he ordinarily allowed himself only on Sunday when there was company.

Their evening together was charming: they spoke of their future, the improvement they expected in their fortunes, changes they would make in their house. He saw himself a man of renown and riches, adored by his wife; and she felt herself pleasantly revived by this new sensation—this noble, wholesome experience of returning at least some of

poor Charles's love. For a moment the thought of Rodolphe crossed her mind; but then her eyes swung back to
Charles, and she noticed with surprise that his teeth
weren't bad at all.

They were in bed when Monsieur Homais suddenly entered their room: he had brushed aside the cook's attempts to announce him, and was holding a newly written
sheet of paper. It was the publicity article he had prepared
for the *Fanal de Rouen*: he had brought it for them to
read.

"You read it to us," said Bovary.

He began:

" 'Despite the network of prejudices that still extends
across part of the face of Europe, our country districts are
beginning to see the light. Just this Tuesday our small community of Yonville was the scene of a surgical experiment
that was also an act of pure philanthropy. Monsieur
Bovary, one of our most distinguished practitioners . . .'

"That's going too far! Too far!" cried Charles, choked
with emotion.

"Not at all! Certainly not! '. . . performed an operation
on a clubfoot. . . .' I didn't use the scientific term—in a
newspaper, you know . . . not everybody would understand; the masses have to be . . ."

"You're right," said Bovary. "Go ahead."

"Where was I?" said the pharmacist. "Oh, yes. 'Monsieur
Bovary, one of our most distinguished practitioners, performed an operation on a clubfoot. The patient was one
Hippolyte Tautain, stable-boy for the past twenty-five years
at the Lion d'Or hotel, owned by Madame Lefrançois, on
the Place d'Armes. The novelty of the enterprise and the
interest felt in the patient had attracted such a large throng
of our local citizenry that there was a veritable crush outside the establishment. The operation went off like magic,
and only a few drops of blood appeared on the skin, as

though to announce that the rebellious tendon had finally surrendered to the surgeon's art. The patient, strange though it may seem (we report this fact *de visu*), experienced not the slightest pain. Up to the moment of the present writing, his condition is entirely satisfactory. Everything gives us reason to expect that his convalescence will be rapid. Who knows? At the next village festival we may well see our good friend Hippolyte tripping Bacchic measures amidst a chorus of joyous companions, thus demonstrating to all, by his high spirits and his capers, the completeness of his cure. All honor to our generous men of science! All honor to those tireless benefactors who go without sleep to work for the improvement or the relief of mankind! All honor to them! Now indeed we can proclaim that the blind shall see, the deaf shall hear and the lame shall walk! But what fanaticism promised in times past to the elect, science is now achieving for all men! We shall keep our readers informed concerning the subsequent stages of this remarkable cure.' "

But all that eloquence did not alter the course of events. Five days later Madame Lefrançois rushed into the doctor's house frightened out of her wits, crying: "Help! He's dying! It's driving me mad!"

Charles made a dash for the Lion d'Or; and the pharmacist, catching sight of him as he rushed bareheaded across the square, hurriedly left his pharmacy. He, too, arrived at the hotel breathless, flushed and worried. "What has happened," he inquired of the numerous people climbing the stairs, "to our interesting taliped?"

The taliped was writhing—writhing in frightful convulsions, so severe that the apparatus locked around his leg was beating against the wall, threatening to demolish it.

Taking every precaution not to disturb the position of the leg, Charles and Monsieur Homais removed the box— and a terrible sight met their eyes. The foot was completely formless, so immensely swollen that the skin seemed ready to burst; and the entire surface was covered with black and blue spots caused by the much-vaunted apparatus. Hippolyte had been complaining of pain for some time, but no one had paid any attention; now it was clear that he hadn't entirely imagined it, and he was allowed to keep his foot out of the box for several hours. But hardly had the swelling subsided a little than the two experts decided that the treatment should be resumed; and they screwed the apparatus on more tightly than before, to hasten results. Finally, three days later, when Hippolyte could bear it no longer, they removed the box again and were amazed by what they saw. A livid tumescence now extended up the leg, and a dark liquid was oozing from a number of blood blisters. Things were taking a serious turn. Hippolyte had no courage left; and Madame Lefrançois moved him into the small room, just off the kitchen, so that he might at least have some distraction.

But the tax collector, who took his dinner there every evening, complained bitterly of such company, so Hippolyte was moved again, this time into the billiard room.

He lay there, groaning under his heavy blankets, pale, unshaven, hollow-eyed, turning and twisting his sweaty head on the dirty, fly-covered pillow. Madame Bovary came to see him. She brought him linen for his poultices, comforted him, tried to cheer him. He had no lack of company, especially on market days, when the peasants crowded around him, playing billiards, dueling with the cues, smoking, drinking, singing, shouting.

"How're you getting along?" they would say, giving him a poke in the shoulder. "You don't look too good. But it's your own fault. You should have . . ." And they would give their advice, telling him about people who had all been cured by methods quite different from the one that had been used on him. Then they would add, by way of comfort: "You fuss too much! Why don't you get up, instead of having everybody wait on you? Well, never mind, old boy—you certainly stink!"

And indeed the gangrene was climbing higher and higher. Bovary was sick about it. He kept coming in every hour, every few minutes. Hippolyte would look at him with terror-filled eyes, and sob and stammer:

"When will I be cured? Help me! Help me! Oh, God, it's terrible!"

And each time the doctor could only go away again, advising him to eat lightly.

"Don't listen to him," Madame Lefrançois would say, when Bovary had left. "They've made you suffer enough already. You'll lose still more of your strength. Here, swallow this!"

And she would give him some tasty soup, or a slice from a leg of mutton, or a bit of bacon, and now and again a little glass of brandy that he hardly dared drink.

The abbé Bournisien, learning that he was getting worse, came to the hotel and asked to see him. He began by condoling with him on his suffering—declaring, however, that he should rejoice in it, since it was the Lord's will, and lose no time taking advantage of this occasion to become reconciled with heaven.

"You've been a little neglectful of your religious duties," he pointed out in a paternal tone. "I've seldom seen you at Mass. How many years is it since you've been to Communion? It's understandable that your work and other distractions should have made you careless about your eternal salvation. But now is the time to think about it. Don't give way to despair: I've known grievous sinners who implored God's mercy when they were about to appear before Him—I know you haven't reached that point yet—and who certainly made better deaths as a result. Be an example to us, as they were! What's to prevent you from saying a Hail

Mary and an Our Father every night and morning just as a precaution? Do it! Do it for me, to oblige me! It doesn't amount to much. Will you promise?"

The poor devil promised. The priest came again the following days. He chatted with the hotel-keeper, told stories, made jokes and puns that were over Hippolyte's head. Then, at the first possible opening, he would return to religious matters, his face taking on an appropriate expression as he did so.

His zeal seemed to have some effect, for soon the taliped expressed a wish to make a pilgrimage to Bon-Secours if he was cured—to which the abbé replied that he could see nothing against it: two precautions were better than one. What—as he put it—was the risk?

The apothecary railed against what he called the priest's "manoeuvers": they were interfering, he claimed, with Hippolyte's convalescence; and he kept saying to Madame Lefrançois, "Leave him alone! Leave him alone! You're confusing him with all your mysticism!"

But the lady wouldn't listen to him. He was "to blame for everything." And on a nail in the wall at the head of the sickbed she defiantly hung a brimming holy-water font with a sprig of boxwood in it.

However, religion seemed to be of no greater help than surgery, and the gangrenous process continued to extend inexorably upward toward the groin. In vain did they change medications and poultices: each day the muscles rotted a little more, and finally Charles replied with an affirmative nod when Madame Lefrançois asked him whether as a last resort she couldn't call in Monsieur Canivet, a celebrated surgeon in Neufchâtel.

This fellow practitioner, a fifty-year-old M.D. of considerable standing and equal self-assurance, laughed with unconcealed scorn when he saw Hippolyte's leg, by now gangrenous to the knee. Then, after declaring flatly that he would have to amputate, he visited the pharmacist and inveighed against the jackasses capable of reducing an unfortunate man to such a plight. He grasped Monsieur Homais by one of his coat buttons and shook him, shouting:

"New-fangled ideas from Paris! It's like strabismus and chloroform and lithotrity—the government ought to forbid such tomfoolery! But everybody wants to be smart nowadays, and they stuff you full of remedies without caring about the consequences! We don't pretend to be so clever, here in the country. We're not such know-it-alls, such la-di-das! We're practitioners, healers! It doesn't occur to us to operate on somebody who's perfectly well! Straighten a clubfoot! Who ever heard of straightening a clubfoot? It's like wanting to iron out a hunchback!"

Those words were a whiplash to Homais, but he hid his discomfiture under an obsequious smile: it was important to humor Canivet, whose prescriptions were sometimes brought into the pharmacy by Yonvillians, and so he made no defense of Bovary and expressed no opinion; he cast principles to the winds, and sacrificed his dignity to the weightier interests of his business.

It was quite an event in the village, that mid-thigh amputation by Doctor Canivet! All the citizens rose early that morning; and the Grande-Rue, thronged though it was, had something sinister about it, as though it were execution day. At the grocer's, Hippolyte's case was discussed from every angle; none of the stores did any business; and Madame Tuvache, the mayor's wife, didn't budge from her window, so eager was she not to miss the surgeon's arrival.

He drove up in his gig, holding the reins himself. Over the years the right-hand spring had given way under the weight of his corpulence, so that the carriage sagged a little to one side as it rolled along. Beside him, on the higher half of the seat cushion, could be seen a huge red leather case, its three brass clasps gleaming magisterially.

The doctor drew up in the hotel yard with a flourish and called loudly for someone to unharness his mare; and then he went to the stable to see whether she was really being given oats as he had ordered. His first concern, whenever he arrived at a patient's, was always for his mare and his gig. "That Canivet—he's a character!" people said of him; and they thought the more of him for his unshakable self-assurance. The universe might have perished to the last man, and he wouldn't have altered his habits a jot.

Homais made his appearance.

"I'm counting on you," said the doctor. "Are we ready? Let's go!"

But the apothecary blushingly confessed that he was too sensitive to be present at such an operation.

"When you just stand there watching," he said, "your imagination begins to play tricks on you, you know. And I'm of such a nervous temperament anyway that . . ."

"Bah!" interrupted Canivet. "You look more like the apoplectic type to me. It doesn't surprise me, either: you pharmacists are always cooped up in your kitchens—it can't help undermining your constitutions in the long run. Look at me: I'm up every day at four, shave in cold water every season of the year; I'm never chilly, never wear flannel underwear, never catch cold—I'm sound as a bell. I eat well one day, badly the next, however it comes. I take it philosophically. That's why I'm not a bit squeamish, like you. And that's why it's all the same to me whether I carve up a Christian or any old chicken they put in front of me. It's all a question of habit."

Thereupon, with no consideration whatever for Hippolyte, who was sweating with pain and terror under his bedclothes in the billiard room, the two gentlemen proceeded there in the kitchen to engage in a conversation in which the apothecary likened the coolness of a surgeon to that of a general. The comparison pleased Canivet, who expatiated on the demands made by his profession. He looked on it as a kind of sacred charge, even though dishonored nowadays by the activities of the *officiers de santé*. Then, finally giving thought to his patient, he inspected the bandages Homais had brought—the same ones he had furnished the day of the earlier operation—and asked for someone to hold the leg for him while he worked. Lestiboudois was sent for, and Canivet rolled up his sleeves and went into the billiard room. The apothecary stayed outside with Artémise and the landlady, both of the latter whiter than their aprons and all three of them with their ears to the door.

Bovary, meanwhile, didn't dare show himself outside his house. He sat downstairs in the parlor beside the empty fireplace, his chin on his chest, his hands folded, his eyes set. What a misfortune! he was thinking. What a disappointment! Certainly he had taken all conceivable precautions. Fate had played a hand in it. Be that as it may, if Hippolyte were later to die it would be he who would have murdered him. And then—how was he to answer the questions his patients were sure to ask him? What reason could he give for his failure? Perhaps he *had* made some mistake? He sought for what it might be, and failed to find it. The greatest surgeons made mistakes, didn't they? That was something no one would ever believe. Everyone would laugh at him, talk about him. The news would spread to Forges, to Neufchâtel, to Rouen—everywhere! Who knew —other doctors might write letters and articles attacking him! There would be a controversy: he would have to send replies to the newspapers. Hippolyte himself might sue him. He saw himself dishonored, ruined, lost! And his imagination, engendering countless fears, was tossed about like an empty barrel carried out to sea and bobbing on the waves.

Emma, sitting opposite, was watching him. She was not participating in his humiliation. She was experiencing a humiliation of a different sort: the humiliation of having imagined that such a man might be worth something—as though she hadn't twenty times already had full proof of his mediocrity.

Charles began to stride up and down the room. The floor creaked under his heavy boots.

"Sit down!" she said. "You're getting on my nerves!"

He sat down.

How in the world had she managed (she who was so intelligent) to commit yet another blunder? What deplorable mania was it that had made her wreck her life by constant self-sacrifice? She recalled all her desires for luxury, all her spiritual privations, the sordid details of marriage and housekeeping, her dreams mired like wounded swallows, everything she had ever craved for, everything she had denied herself, all the things she might have had. And for whose sake had she given up so much?

The silence that hung over the village was suddenly rent by a scream. Bovary went deathly pale. For an instant her brows contracted in a nervous frown; then she resumed her brooding. It was for him that she had done it—for this creature here, this man who understood nothing, who felt nothing. He was sitting quite calmly, utterly oblivious of the fact that the ridicule henceforth inseparable from his name would disgrace her as well. And she had tried to love him! She had wept tears of repentance at having given herself to another!

"I wonder—could it perhaps have been a valgus?" The question came abruptly from the musing Charles.

At the sudden impact of those words, crashing into her mind like a leaden bullet into a silver dish, Emma felt herself shudder; and she raised her head, straining to understand what he had meant by them. They looked at each other in silence, almost wonderstruck, each of them, to see that the other was there, so far apart had their thoughts carried them. Charles stared at her with the clouded gaze of a drunken man; motionless in his chair, he was listening to the screams that continued to come from the hotel. One followed after another; each was a long, drawn-out succession of tones, and they were interspersed with short, shrill shrieks; it was all like the howling of some animal being butchered far away. Emma bit her pale lips; and twisting and turning in her fingers a sliver she had broken off the coral, she stared fixedly at Charles with blazing eyes that were like twin fiery arrows. Everything, everything about him exasperated her now—his face, his clothes, what he didn't say, his entire person, his very existence. She repented her virtue of days past as though it had been a crime; and what virtue she had left now crumbled under the furious assault of her pride. Adultery was triumphant; and she reveled in the prospect of its sordid ironies. The thought of her lover made her reel with desire; heart and soul she flung herself into her longing, borne toward him on waves of new rapture; and Charles seemed to her as detached from her life, as irrevocably gone, as impossible and done for, as though he were a dying man, gasping his last before her eyes.

There was a sound of footsteps on the sidewalk. Charles looked through the lowered blind: in the hot sun near the market Doctor Canivet was mopping his forehead with his handkerchief. Behind him was Homais, carrying a large red box, and they were both heading for the pharmacy.

Flooded with sudden tenderness and despondency, Charles turned to his wife. "Kiss me!" he cried. "Kiss me, darling!"

"Don't touch me!" she flared, scarlet with fury.

"What . . . what is it?" he stammered, bewildered. "What's wrong? You're not yourself! You know how I love you! I need you!"

"Stop!" she cried in a terrible voice.

And rushing from the room she slammed the door so violently that the barometer was flung from the wall and broke to pieces on the floor.

Charles sank into his chair, crushed, wondering what her trouble was, fearing some nervous illness, weeping, and vaguely aware that the air about him was heavy with something baleful and incomprehensible.

When Rodolphe came to the garden that night he found his mistress waiting for him on the lowest step of the river stairs. They fell into each other's arms: and all their accumulated resentments melted like snow in the heat of this embrace.

XII

ONCE AGAIN THEIR LOVE WAS AT HIGH TIDE.

Now Emma would often take it into her head to write him during the day. Through her window she would signal to Justin, and he would whip off his apron and fly to La Huchette. And when Rodolphe arrived in response to her summons, it was to hear that she was miserable, that her husband was odious, that her life was a torment.

"Can I do anything about it?" he snapped at her one day.

"Ah, if you only would. . . ."

She was sitting at his feet staring at nothing, her head between his knees, her hair streaming.

"What could I do?" Rodolphe demanded.

She sighed. "We could go live somewhere else, away from here. . . ."

"You're really crazy!" he said, laughing. "You know it's impossible!"

She tried to pursue the subject, but he pretended not to understand, and spoke of other things.

He saw no reason why there should be all this to-do about so simple a thing as love-making.

But for her there was a reason: there was a motive force that gave an additional impetus to her passion. Every day her love for Rodolphe was fanned by her aversion for her husband. The more completely she surrendered to the one, the more intensely she loathed the other: never did Charles seem to her so repulsive, so thick-fingered, so heavy-witted, so common, as when she was alone with him after her meetings with Rodolphe. Acting, at such times, the role of wife, of virtuous woman, she thought feverishly of her lover—of his black hair curling over his tanned forehead, of his body so powerful and yet so elegant, of the cool judgment that went hand in hand with his fiery passion. It was for him that she filed her fingernails with the care of the most exquisite artist, that she kept massaging her skin with cold cream, scenting her handkerchiefs with patchouli. She decked herself with bracelets, rings and necklaces. Whenever he was expected she filled her two big blue glass vases with roses; both her room and herself were made ready for him, as though she were a courtesan awaiting a prince. Félicité was perpetually bleaching lingerie: all day long she was in the kitchen, and Justin often sat there with her, watching her work.

His elbows on the ironing board, he would stare hungrily at all the feminine garments strewn about him—the dimity petticoats, the fichus, the collars, the drawstring pantaloons enormously wide at the waist and narrowing below.

"What is this for?" the boy would ask, touching a crinoline lining or a set of fastenings.

"Don't tell me you've never seen anything!" Félicité would laugh. "As if your Madame Homais didn't wear these same things!"

"Oh, Madame Homais . . ." And he would wonder aloud: "Is she a lady, like Madame?"

But Félicité was getting tired of having him hang around her. She was six years his elder, and Théodore, Maître Guillaumin's servant, was beginning to court her.

"Leave me alone!" she would say, reaching for her starch pot. "Go pound your almonds. You're always fussing around the women. You're a nasty little boy: better wait till you get some hair on your face for that sort of thing."

"Don't be cross. I'll do her shoes for you."

And he would go over to the doorsill and reach for Emma's shoes, all caked with the mud she had brought in from her meetings. It would fall away powdery under his fingers, and he would watch the particles float gently upward in a shaft of sun.

"You act as though you're afraid of spoiling them!" the cook would jeer. She herself wasn't so careful when she cleaned them, for Madame always gave them to her as soon as they looked the least bit worn.

Emma had countless pairs in her wardrobe, and discarded them on the slightest pretext. Charles never said a word.

Nor did he protest at paying three hundred francs for a wooden leg that she felt should be given to Hippolyte. It was cork-trimmed and had spring joints—a complicated mechanism hidden under a black trouser leg that ended in a patent-leather shoe. But Hippolyte didn't dare use such a beautiful leg every day, and he begged Madame Bovary to get him another that would be more suitable. Naturally Charles paid for the new one as well.

The stable-boy gradually resumed his work. He went about the village as before; and whenever Charles heard the sharp tap of his stick on the cobblestones in the distance, he quickly changed his direction.

It was Monsieur Lheureux, the shopkeeper, who had taken charge of the order. It gave him an opportunity to see a good deal of Emma. He chatted with her about the latest novelties from Paris, about a thousand feminine trifles; he was more than obliging, and never pressed for payment. Emma let herself slide into this easy way of gratifying all her whims. When she decided she wanted to give Rodolphe a handsome riding crop she had seen in an umbrella shop in Rouen, she told Lheureux to get it for her, and he set it on her table a week later.

The next day, however, he appeared with his bill—two hundred and seventy francs, not to mention the centimes. Emma didn't know what to do: all the desk drawers were empty, they owed Lestiboudois two weeks' pay and the maid six months' wages, there were a number of other bills, and Bovary was waiting impatiently for a remittance from Monsieur Derozerays, who usually settled with him once a year, toward the end of June.

She was able to put Lheureux off for a time, but eventually he lost patience: he was hard pressed, he said, his capital was tied up, and if she couldn't give him something on account he'd be forced to take back all the items she had chosen.

"All right, take them!" she said.

"I didn't really mean that," he answered. "Except perhaps for the riding crop. I guess I'll have to ask Monsieur for it back."

"No! No!" she cried.

"Ah ha!" Lheureux thought. "I've got you!"

And feeling sure that he had ferreted out her secret, he left her. "We'll see," he murmured to himself, with his customary little whistle. "We'll see!"

She was wondering how to extricate herself when the cook came in and put a little cylindrical parcel on the mantel. "From Monsieur Derozerays," she said. Emma seized it and opened it. It contained fifteen napoleons—full payment. She heard Charles on the stairs, and she flung the gold pieces into one of her drawers and took the key.

Three days later Lheureux came again.

"I have a suggestion," he said. "If instead of paying the amount we agreed on you'd like to take . . ."

"Here!" she said, and she handed him fourteen napoleons.

The shopkeeper was taken aback. To hide his disappointment he overflowed with apologies and offers of service, all of which Emma declined. When he had left she stood a few moments with her hand in her apron, fingering the two five-franc pieces he had given her in change. She resolved to economize, so that eventually she could pay Charles back. . . .

"Bah!" she said to herself. "He'll never give it a thought."

Besides the riding crop with the silver-gilt knob, Rodolphe had been given a signet ring with the motto "*Amor nel cor*"; also a scarf to use as a muffler, and a cigar case very like the vicomte's that Charles had picked up on the road and Emma still kept.

But he found her presents humiliating, and on several occasions refused them. She was insistent, however, and he gave in, grumbling to himself that she was high-handed and interfering.

Then she had such crazy notions.

"When the bell strikes midnight," she would command him, "think of me."

And if he confessed that he hadn't done so, there were strings of reproaches, always ending with the eternal:

"Do you love me?"

"Of course I love you!"

"Very much?"

"Of course."

"You've never loved anybody else, have you?"

That made him laugh: "Do you think you deflowered me?"

When Emma burst into tears he tried to comfort her, protesting his love and saying things to make her smile.

"It's because I love you," she would interrupt. "I love you so much that I can't do without you—you know that, don't you? Sometimes I want so much to see you that it tears me to pieces. 'Where is he?' I wonder. 'Maybe he's with other women. They're smiling at him, he's going up close to them. . . .' Tell me it isn't true! Tell me you don't like any of them! Some of them are prettier than I am, but none of them can love you the way I do. I'm your slave and your concubine! You're my king, my idol! You're good! You're beautiful! You're wise! You're strong!"

He had had such things said to him so many times that none of them had any freshness for him. Emma was like all his other mistresses; and as the charm of novelty gradually slipped from her like a piece of her clothing, he saw revealed in all its nakedness the eternal monotony of passion, which always assumes the same forms and always speaks the same language. He had no perception—this man of such vast experience—of the dissimilarity of feeling that might underlie similarities of expression. Since he had heard those same words uttered by loose women or prostitutes, he had little belief in their sincerity when he heard them now: the more flowery a person's speech, he thought, the more suspect the feelings, or lack of feelings, it concealed. Whereas the truth is that fullness of soul can sometimes overflow in utter vapidity of language, for none of us can ever express the exact measure of his needs or his thoughts or his sorrows; and human speech is like a cracked kettle on which we tap crude rhythms for bears to dance to, while we long to make music that will melt the stars.

But with the superior acumen of those who keep aloof in any relationship, Rodolphe discovered that the affair offered still further possibilities of sensual gratification. He abandoned every last shred of restraint and consideration. He made her into something compliant, something corrupt. Hers was an infatuation to the point of idiocy; the intensity of her admiration for him was matched by the intensity of her own voluptuous feelings; she was in a blissful torpor, a drunkenness in which her very soul lay drowned and shriveled, like the duke of Clarence in his butt of malmsey.

This constant indulgence had its effect on her daily behavior. Her glance grew bolder, her language freer; she went so far as to be seen smoking a cigarette in public, in Rodolphe's company—"as though," people said, "to show her contempt for propriety." Even those who had given her the benefit of the doubt stopped doing so when they saw her step out of the Hirondelle one day wearing a tight-fitting vest, like a man's. The elder Madame Bovary, who had taken refuge with her son following a particularly unpleasant scene with her husband, was as scandalized as any of the Yonville matrons. There were many other things that she disliked, too: first of all, Charles hadn't followed her advice about the ban on novels; and then she disapproved of "the way the house was run." She took the liberty of saying how she felt, and there were quarrels—one, especially, about Félicité.

Going down the hall the previous night the elder Madame Bovary had surprised her with a man—a man of about forty, with dark chin whiskers, who had slipped out through the kitchen when he had heard her coming. When she reported this, Emma burst out laughing; the older woman lost her temper, declaring that unless one cared nothing for morals oneself, one was bound to keep an eye on the morals of one's servants.

"What kind of social circles do *you* frequent?" Emma retorted, with such an impertinent stare that her mother-in-law asked her whether in taking her servant's part it wasn't really herself that she was defending.

"Get out!" the young woman cried, springing from her chair.

"Emma! Mother!" cried Charles, trying to stop the argument. But in their rage they both rushed from the room.

"What manners!" Emma sneered when he came to her. And she stamped with fury: "What a peasant!"

He hurried to his mother and found her close to hysterics. "Such insolence! She's irresponsible! Maybe worse!"

And she declared she would leave the house at once unless her daughter-in-law came to her and apologized. So Charles sought out his wife again and begged her to give in. He implored her on his knees. "Oh, all right, I'll do it," she said finally.

She held out her hand to her mother-in-law with the dignity of a marquise: "*Excusez-moi, Madame.*" And then in her own room she flung herself flat on the bed and wept like a child, her head buried in the pillow.

She and Rodolphe had agreed that in case of an emergency she would fasten a piece of white paper to the blind, so that if he happened to be in Yonville he could go immediately into the lane behind the house. Emma hung out the signal; after waiting three-quarters of an hour she suddenly saw Rodolphe at the corner of the market. She was tempted to open the window and call to him; as she hesitated he disappeared. She sank back hopelessly in her chair.

But after a short time she thought she heard someone on

the sidewalk: it must be he. She went downstairs and across the yard. He was outside the gate. She flung herself into his arms.

"Be careful!" he warned.

"Ah, if you knew what I've been through," she breathed.

And she proceeded to tell him everything—hurriedly, disjointedly, exaggerating some facts and inventing others, and putting in so many parentheses that he lost the thread of her story.

"Come, angel, be brave! Cheer up! Be patient!"

"But I've been patient for four years! I've suffered for four years! A love like ours is something to boast of! I'm on the rack, with those people! I can't stand it any longer! Rescue me, for God's sake!"

She clung to him. Her tear-filled eyes were flashing like undersea fires; her breast rose and fell in quick gasps; never had he found her so desirable. He lost his head. "What must we do?" he said. "What do you want me to do?"

"Oh! Take me away!" she cried. "I implore you: take me away!"

And she crushed her lips to his, as though to catch the consent she hadn't dared hope for—the consent that was now breathed out in a kiss.

"But . . ." Rodolphe began.

"What is it?"

"What about your little girl?"

She pondered a few moments; then: "We'll take her with us—it's the only way."

"What a woman!" he thought as he watched her move off. She had quickly slipped back into the garden: someone was calling her.

The elder Madame Bovary was astonished, the next few days, by her daughter-in-law's transformation. Emma was docility itself, deferential to the point of asking her for a recipe for pickles.

Was it her way of covering her tracks more thoroughly? Or was it a kind of voluptuous stoicism—a deliberate, deeper savoring of the bitterness of everything she was about to abandon? Scarcely the latter, for she noticed nothing around her: she was living as though immersed in advance in her future happiness. With Rodolphe she talked of nothing else. She would lean on his shoulder, and murmur:

"Think of what it will be like when we're in the stage-coach! Can you imagine it? Is it possible? The moment I feel the carriage moving, I think I'll have the sensation we're going up in a balloon, sailing up into the clouds. I'm counting the days. Are you?"

Never had Madame Bovary been as beautiful as now. She had that indefinable beauty that comes from happiness, enthusiasm, success—a beauty that is nothing more or less than a harmony of temperament and circumstances. Her desires, her sorrows, her experience of sensuality, her evergreen illusions, had developed her step by step, like a flower nourished by manure and by the rain, by the wind and the sun; and she was finally blooming in the fullness of her nature. Her eyelids seemed strangely perfect when she half closed them in a long amorous glance; and each of her deep sighs dilated her fine nostrils and raised the fleshy corners of her lips, lightly shadowed by dark down. Some artist skilled in corruption seemed to have designed the knot of her hair: it lay on her neck coiled in a heavy mass, twisted carelessly and always a little differently, for every day it was loosened by embraces. Her voice now took on softer inflections; her body, too; something subtle and penetrating emanated from the very folds of her dress, from the very arch of her foot. Charles found her exquisite and utterly irresistible, as in the first days of their marriage.

When he returned home in the middle of the night he dared not wake her. The porcelain night-light cast a trembling circular glow on the ceiling; and the drawn curtains of the cradle made it look like a tiny white hut swelling out in the darkness beside the bed. Charles looked at both sleepers. He thought he could hear the light breathing of his child. She would be growing rapidly now; every season would bring a change. Already he saw her coming home from school at the end of the day, laughing, her blouse spotted with ink, her basket on her arm. Then they would have to send her away to boarding school: that would cost a good deal—how would they manage? He thought and thought about it. He had the idea of renting a little farm on the outskirts, one that he could supervise himself mornings, as he rode out to see his patients. He would put the profits aside, in the savings bank; later he would buy securities of some kind. Besides, his practice would grow: he was counting on it, for he wanted Berthe to have a good education; he wanted her to be accomplished, to take piano lessions. Ah! How pretty she would be later, at fifteen! She would look just like her mother; and like her, in the summer, she would wear a great straw hat: from a distance they'd be taken for sisters. He pictured her sewing at night beside them in the lamplight; she would embroider slippers for him, and look after the house; she would fill their lives with her sweetness and her gaiety. And then he would think about her marriage. They would find her some fine young man with a good position, who would make her happy. And her happiness would last for ever and ever.

Emma wasn't asleep at such times. She was only pretending to be; and as Charles gradually sank into slumber beside her she lay awake dreaming different dreams.

A team of four horses, galloping every day for a week, had been whirling her and Rodolphe toward a new land from which they would never return. On and on the carriage bore them, and they sat there, arms entwined, saying not a word. Often from a mountain top they would espy some splendid city, with domes, bridges, ships, forests of lemon trees, and white marble cathedrals whose pointed steeples were crowned with storks' nests. Here the horses slowed, picking their way over the great paving-stones, and the ground was strewn with bouquets of flowers tossed at them by women laced in red bodices. The ringing of bells and the braying of mules mingled with the murmur of guitars and the sound of gushing fountains; pyramids of fruit piled at the foot of pale statues were cooled by the flying spray, and the statues themselves seemed to smile through the streaming water. And then one night they arrived in a fishing village, where brown nets were drying in the wind along the cliff and the line of cottages. Here they stopped: this would be their dwelling place. They would live in a low flat-roofed house in the shade of a palm tree, on a bay beside the sea. They would ride in gondolas, swing in hammocks; and their lives would be easy and ample like the silk clothes they wore, warm like the soft nights that enveloped them, starry like the skies they gazed upon. Nothing specific stood out against the vast background of the future that she thus evoked: the days were all of them splendid, and as alike as the waves of the sea; and the whole thing hovered on the horizon, infinite, harmonious, blue and sparkling in the sun. But then the baby would cough in the cradle, or Bovary would give a snore louder than the rest, and Emma wouldn't fall asleep till morning, when dawn was whitening the windowpanes and Justin was already opening the shutters of the pharmacy.

She had sent for Monsieur Lheureux and told him she would be needing a cloak: "A long cloak with a deep collar and a lining."

"You're going on a trip?" he asked.

"No! But . . . Anyway, I can count on you to get it, can't I? Soon?"

He bowed.

"I'll want a trunk, too. Not too heavy, roomy."

"I know the kind you mean. About three feet by a foot and a half, the sort they're making now."

"And an overnight bag."

"A little too much smoke not to mean fire," Lheureux said to himself.

"And here," said Madame Bovary, unfastening her watch from her belt. "Take this: you can pay for the things out of what you get for it."

But the shopkeeper protested. She was wrong to suggest such a thing, he said; they were well acquainted; he trusted her completely. She mustn't be childish. But she insisted that he take at least the chain, and Lheureux had put it in his pocket and was on his way out when she called him back.

"Hold the luggage for me," she said. "As for the cloak" —she pretended to ponder the question—"don't bring that to me, either. But give me the address of the shop and tell them to have it ready for me when I come."

They were to elope the following month. She would leave Yonville as though to go shopping in Rouen. Rodolphe was to arrange for their reservations and their passports, and would write to Paris to make sure that they would have the coach to themselves as far as Marseilles; and there they would buy a barouche and continue straight on toward Genoa. She would send her things to Lheureux's, whence they would be loaded directly onto the Hirondelle, thus arousing no one's suspicions. In all these plans there was never a mention of little Berthe. Rodolphe avoided speaking of her: perhaps Emma had forgotten her.

He said he needed two weeks more, to wind up some affairs; then, at the end of the first of them, he said he would need an additional two; then he said he was sick; then he went on a trip somewhere. The month of August passed. Finally they decided they would leave without fail on the fourth of September, a Monday.

The Saturday night before that Monday, Rodolphe arrived earlier than usual.

"Is everything ready?" she asked him.

"Yes."

They strolled around the flower beds and sat on the terrace wall.

"You seem sad," said Emma.

"No, why?"

But he kept looking at her strangely—with unusual softness and tenderness.

"Is it because you're going away?" she asked. "Leaving everything that's dear to you, everything that makes up your life? I understand that. . . . But I have nothing—nothing in the world. You're my everything. And I'll be yours. I'll be your family, your country; I'll look after you, I'll love you."

"How sweet you are!" he cried, clasping her in his arms.

"Am I really?" she laughed, melting with pleasure. "Do you love me? Swear that you do?"

"Do I love you! Do I! I adore you, darling!"

The moon, a deep red disc, was rising straight out of the earth beyond the meadows. They could see it climb swiftly between the poplar branches that partially screened it like a torn black curtain; and finally, dazzlingly white, it shone high above them in the empty sky illumined by its light. Now, moving more slowly, it poured onto a stretch of the river a great brightness that flashed like a million stars; and this silvery gleam seemed to be writhing in its depths like a headless serpent covered with luminous scales. It looked, too, like a monstrous many-branched candlestick dripping with molten diamonds. The night spread softly around them; patches of shadow hung in the leaves of the trees.

Emma, her eyes half closed, drank in the cool breeze with deep sighs. Lost in their revery, they said not a word. Full and silent as the flowing river, languid as the perfume of the syringas, the sweetness they had known in earlier days once again surged up in their hearts, casting on their memories longer and more melancholy shadows than those of the motionless willows on the grass. Now and again some prowling night animal, hedgehog or weasel, disturbed the leaves; or they heard the sound of a ripe peach as it dropped to the ground.

"What a lovely night!" said Rodolphe.

"We'll have many more," Emma answered.

And as though speaking to herself:

"Yes, it will be good to be traveling. . . . But why should I feel sad? Is it fear of the unknown, or the effect of leaving everything I'm used to? No—it's from too much happiness. How weak of me! Forgive me!"

"There's still time," he cried. "Think carefully—you might be sorry!"

"Never!" she answered impetuously.

And moving close to him:

"What harm can come to me? There's not a desert, not a precipice, not an ocean, that I wouldn't cross with you. Living together will be like an embrace that's tighter and more perfect every day. There'll be nothing to bother us, no cares—nothing in our way. We'll be alone, entirely to ourselves, for ever and ever. Say something, darling! Answer me!"

At regular intervals he answered, "Yes . . . yes . . . " Her fingers were in his hair, and through the great tears that were welling from her eyes she kept repeating his name in a childish voice:

"Rodolphe! Rodolphe! Sweet little Rodolphe!"

Midnight struck.

"Midnight!" she said. "Now it's tomorrow! One more day!"

He stood up to go; and as though his movement were the signal for their flight, Emma suddenly brightened.

"You have the passports?"

"Yes."

"You haven't forgotten anything?"

"No."

"You're sure?"

"Absolutely."

"And you'll be waiting for me at the Hotel de Provence at noon?"

He nodded.

"Till tomorrow, then," said Emma, giving him a last caress.

And she watched him go.

He did not turn around. She ran after him, and leaning out over the water among the bushes:

"Till tomorrow!" she cried.

Already he was on the other side of the river, walking quickly across the meadow.

After several minutes Rodolphe stopped; and when he saw her in her white dress gradually vanishing into the shadows like a wraith, his heart began to pound so violently that he leaned against a tree to keep from falling.

"God, what a fool I am!" he muttered with an obscene curse. "But she certainly made a pretty mistress!"

Emma's beauty and all the joys of their love rushed back into his mind; and for a moment he softened. But then he turned against her.

"After all," he cried, gesticulating and talking aloud to himself to strengthen his resolution, "I can't spend the rest of my life abroad! I can't be saddled with a child! All that trouble! All that expense! No! No! Absolutely not! It would be too stupid!"

XIII

AS SOON AS HE REACHED HOME RODOLPHE SAT DOWN AT HIS desk, under the stag's-head trophy that hung on the wall. But when he took up his pen he couldn't think of what to write, and he leaned on his elbows and pondered. Emma seemed to have receded into a far-off past, as though the resolution he had just made had put a great distance between them.

In order to recapture some feeling of her he went to the wardrobe at the head of his bed and took out an old Rheims cookie box that was his storage place for letters from women. Out of it came a smell of damp dust and withered roses. The first thing his eye fell on was a handkerchief spotted with faint stains. It was one of Emma's: she had had a nosebleed one day when they were out together—he hadn't remembered it till now. Then he took up something that had been knocking against the sides of the box: it was the miniature she had given him; she looked much too fussily dressed, he thought, and her ogling expression was preposterous. He kept staring at the artist's handiwork in an attempt to evoke the model as he remembered her, and this gradually resulted in Emma's features becoming confused in his memory, as though the real face and the painted face had been rubbing against each other and wearing each other away. Finally he read some of her letters. They were as brief, as technical, as urgent as business letters, filled chiefly with details pertaining to their trip. He wanted to reread the longer ones, the earlier ones; they were further down in the box, and to get at them he had to disarrange everything else. He found himself me-chanically going through the pile of letters and other things, turning up a heterogeneous assortment—bouquets, a garter, a black mask, pins, locks of hair. So many locks of hair! Brunette and blond: some of them, catching in the metal hinges of the box, had broken off as he opened it.

He rummaged among his souvenirs, lingering on the differences of handwriting and style in the letters—as marked as the differences of spelling. There were affectionate letters, jolly letters, facetious letters, melancholy letters; there were some that begged for love and others that begged for money. Now and then a word brought back a face, a gesture, the sound of a voice; certain letters brought back nothing at all.

All those women, thronging into his memory, got in each other's way; none of them stood out above the rest, leveled down as they all were by the measure of his love. He took up handfuls of the various letters and for some minutes amused himself by letting them stream from one hand to another. In the end he lost interest in the game and put the box back into the wardrobe. "What a lot of nonsense!" he said to himself.

This accurately summed up his opinion, for his companions in pleasure, like children playing in a schoolyard, had so trampled his heart that nothing green could grow there; indeed they were more casual than children—they hadn't even scribbled their names on the walls.

"Come now," he said to himself. "Get busy."

He began to write:

"You must be courageous, Emma: the last thing I want to do is ruin your life. . . ."

"That's absolutely true, after all," he assured himself "I'm acting in her interest; I'm only being honest."

"Have you given really serious thought to your decision? Do you realize into what abyss I was about to hurl you, poor darling? You don't, I'm sure. You were going ahead blind and confident, full of faith in happiness, in the future. . . . Ah! Poor wretched, insane creatures that we are!"

Here Rodolphe paused, looking for some good excuse.

"I could tell her that I've lost all my money. . . . No—that wouldn't stop her anyway: I'd have to go through the whole thing again later. Is there any way of making such women come to their senses?"

He thought for a while, then added:

"I'll never forget you—believe me—and I'll always feel the deepest devotion to you. But some day sooner or later our passion would have cooled—inevitably—it's the way with everything human. We would have had moments of weariness. Who knows—I might even have had the dreadful anguish of witnessing your remorse—and of sharing in it, since it would have been I who caused it. The very thought of the grief in store for you is a torture to me, Emma! Forget me! Why was it ordained that we should meet? Why were you so beautiful? Is the fault mine? In God's name, no! No! Fate alone is to blame—nothing and no one but fate!"

"That's always an effective word," he remarked to himself.

"Ah! Had you been a shallow-hearted creature like so many others, I could very well have gone ahead and let things happen as they might—purely for what was in it for myself—in that case without danger to you. But that marvelous intensity of feelings you have—such a delight for those who know you, such a source of anguish for yourself! —kept you—adorable woman that you are—from realizing the falsity of the position the future held for us. At first I, too, gave it no thought—I was lying in the shade of that ideal happiness we dreamed of as under a poison tree, without thought for the consequences."

"Maybe she'll think I'm giving her up out of stinginess. . . . What's it to me if she does! Let her. . . . And let's get it over with!"

"The world is cruel, Emma. It would have pursued us everywhere. You'd have been subjected to indiscreet questions—calumny—scorn—even insult, perhaps. You—insulted! Oh, my darling! And I would have been the cause of it—I, who wanted to put you on a throne—I, who shall carry away the thought of you like a talisman! Yes—away—for I am punishing myself for the harm I have done you—I am going into exile! Where? How can I tell? My poor mad brain can give no answer. Adieu, Emma! Continue to be as good as you have always been! Never forget the unfortunate man who lost you! Teach your child my name: tell her to include me in her prayers."

The flames of the two candles were flickering. Rodolphe got up to close the window; and then, back at his desk:

"That's all, I guess," he said to himself. "Oh—just this little bit more, to keep her from coming after me":

"I shall be far away when you read these unhappy lines; I dare not linger—the temptation to see you again is all but irresistible! This is no moment for weakness! I shall come back; and perhaps one day we'll be able to speak of our love with detachment, as a thing of the past. Adieu!"

And he appended one more, last adieu, this time written as two words—"*A Dieu!*": it seemed to him in excellent taste.

"How shall I sign it?" he wondered. " 'Devotedly'? No . . . 'Your friend'? Yes—that's it."

"Your friend."

He read over his letter and thought it was good.

"Poor little thing!" he thought, suddenly sentimental. "She'll think me as unfeeling as a stone. There ought to be a few tears on it, but weeping's beyond me—what can I do?" He poured some water in a glass, wet a finger, and holding it high above the page shook off a large drop. It made a pale blot on the ink. Then, looking around for something to seal the letter with, his eye fell on the signet ring with the motto "*Amor nel cor.*" "Scarcely appropriate under the circumstances, but what the . . ."

Whereupon he smoked three pipes and went to bed.

When he got up the next day (about two in the afternoon—he slept late) Rodolphe had some apricots picked and arranged in a basket. At the bottom, hidden under some vine leaves, he put the letter; and he ordered Girard, his plough-boy, to deliver it carefully to Madame Bovary. This was his usual way of corresponding with her, sending her fruit or game according to the season.

"If she asks you anything about me," he said, "tell her I've left for a trip. Be sure to give the basket to her personally. Get going, now, and do it right!"

Girard put on his new smock, tied his handkerchief over the apricots, and plodding along in his great hobnailed boots, he set out tranquilly for Yonville.

When he reached Madame Bovary's he found her helping Félicité stack linen on the kitchen table.

"Here," said the plough-boy. "My master sent you this."

A feeling of dread came over her, and as she fumbled in her pocket for some change she stared at the peasant with haggard eyes; he in turn looked at her in bewilderment, failing to understand why anyone should be so upset by such a present. Finally he left. Félicité stayed where she was. The suspense was too great for Emma: she ran into the other room as though for the purpose of carrying in the apricots, dumped them out of the basket, tore away the leaves, found the letter and opened it; and as though she were fleeing from a fire she ran panic-stricken up the stairs toward her room.

Charles had come in: she caught sight of him; he spoke to her; whatever he said, she didn't hear it; and she hurried on up the second flight of stairs, breathless, distracted, reeling, clutching the horrible piece of paper that rattled in her hand like a sheet of tin. At the third-floor landing she stopped outside the closed attic door.

She tried to calm herself: only then did she think of the letter. She must finish it—she didn't dare. Besides, where could she read it? How? She'd be seen.

"I'll be all right in here," she thought; and she pushed open the door and went in.

There the roof slates were throwing down a heat that was all but unbearable; it pressed on her so that she could scarcely breathe. She dragged herself over to the dormer, whose shutters were closed; she pulled back the bolt, and the dazzling sunlight poured in.

Out beyond the roof-tops, the open countryside stretched as far as eye could see. Below her the village square was empty; the stone sidewalk glittered; the weathervanes on the houses stood motionless. From the lower floor of a house at the corner came a whirring noise with strident changes of tone: Binet was at his lathe.

Leaning against the window frame she read the letter through, now and then giving an angry sneer. But the more she tried to concentrate, the more confused her thoughts became. She saw Rodolphe, heard his voice, clasped him in her arms; and a series of irregular palpitations, thudding in her breast like great blows from a battering ram, came faster and faster. She cast her eyes about her, longing for the earth to open up. Why not end it all? What was holding her back? She was free to act. And she moved forward. "Do it! Do it!" she ordered herself, peering down at the pavement.

The rays of bright light reflected directly up to her from below were pulling the weight of her body toward the abyss. The surface of the village square seemed to be sliding dizzily up the wall of her house; the floor she was standing on seemed to be tipped up on end, like a pitching ship. Now she was at the very edge, almost hanging out, a great emptiness all around her. The blue of the sky was flooding her; her head felt hollow and filled with the rushing of the wind: all she had to do now was to surrender, yield to the onrush. And the lathe kept whirring, like an angry voice calling her.

But then she heard another voice: "Where are you?" It was Charles.

She listened.

"Where are you? Come down!"

The thought that she had just escaped death almost made her faint from terror; she closed her eyes; then she gave a start as she felt the touch of a hand on her sleeve. It was Félicité.

"Monsieur is waiting, Madame. The soup is on the table."

And she had to go down—had to sit through a meal!

She did her best to eat. Each mouthful choked her. She unfolded her napkin as though to inspect the darns, and began really seriously to devote her attention to it and count the stitches. Suddenly the thought of the letter came back to her. Had she lost it? Where would she lay hands on it? But in her exhaustion of mind she could invent no excuse for leaving the table. Besides, she didn't dare: she was terrified of Charles; he knew everything—she was sure he must! And oddly enough he chose that moment to say:

"I gather we shan't be seeing Monsieur Rodolphe for some time."

She started: "Who told you so?"

"Who told me?" he said, surprised by her abrupt tone. "Girard—I saw him a few minutes ago at the door of the Café Français. He's left for a trip, or he's about to leave."

A sob escaped her.

"What's so surprising about it? He's always going off on

pleasure trips. Why shouldn't he? When you're a bachelor and well off . . . Besides, he knows how to give himself a good time, our friend. He's a real playboy. Monsieur Langlois once told me . . ."

He decorously broke off as the maid came in.

Félicité gathered up the apricots that lay scattered over the sideboard and put them back into the basket. Unaware that his wife had turned scarlet, Charles asked for them, took one, and bit into it.

"Oh, perfect!" he said. "Try one."

He held the basket out toward her, and she gently pushed it away.

"Smell them: such fragrance!" he said, moving it back and forth before her.

"I'm stifling in here!" she cried, leaping to her feet. But she forced herself to conquer her spasm. "It's nothing," she said. "Nothing. Just nerves. Sit down; eat your fruit."

Her great dread was lest he question her, insist on doing something for her, never leave her to herself.

Charles had obediently sat down and was spitting apricot pits into his hand and transferring them to his plate.

Suddenly a blue tilbury crossed the square at a smart trot. Emma gave a cry, fell abruptly backwards and lay on the floor.

Rodolphe had decided, after a good deal of thought, to leave for Rouen. Since the Yonville road was the only route from La Huchette to Buchy, he had to pass through the village; and Emma had recognized him in the glow of his carriage lights as they flashed in the gathering dusk like a streak of lightning.

The commotion at the Bovarys' brought the pharmacist running. The table had been knocked over and all the plates were on the floor; gravy, meat, knives, the salt cellar and the cruet stand littered the room; Charles was calling for help; Berthe was frightened and in tears; and Félicité with trembling hands was unlacing Madame, whose entire body was racked with convulsions.

"I'll run to my laboratory and get a little aromatic vinegar," said the apothecary.

And when he had returned and held the flacon under her nostrils and she opened her eyes:

"I knew it," he said. "This stuff would resuscitate a corpse."

"Speak to us!" cried Charles. "Say something! Can you hear me? It's Charles—Charles, who loves you. Do you recognize me? See—here's your little girl—kiss her, darling."

The child stretched out her arms toward her mother, trying to clasp them around her neck. But Emma turned her head away. "No, no," she said brokenly. "Leave me alone."

She fainted again, and they carried her to her bed.

She lay there on her back, mouth open, eyes closed, hands flat beside her, motionless, white as a wax statue. Two rivulets of tears trickled slowly from her eyes onto the pillow.

Charles stood at the foot of the bed. At his side the pharmacist was observing the thoughtful silence appropriate to life's solemn occasions. Then:

"I think she'll be all right," he said. "The paroxysm seems to be over."

"Yes, she's resting a little now," Charles answered, watching her sleep. "Poor thing! Poor thing! It's a real relapse."

Then Homais asked for details, and Charles told him how she had been stricken suddenly while eating apricots.

"Extraordinary!" said the pharmacist. "Still, the apricots may very well have caused the syncope. Some natures react so strongly to certain odors! It would be an interesting subject to study, in both its pathological and its physiological aspects. The priests are well aware of the importance of this phenomenon—they've always made use of aromatics in their ceremonies. They employ them deliberately, to deaden the understanding and induce ecstatic states—women lend themselves to it easily, they're so much more delicate than the rest of us. Cases are recorded of women fainting from the smell of burnt horn, fresh bread . . ."

"Take care not to wake her!" Bovary warned softly.

"And it's not only humans who are subject to such anomalies," continued the apothecary. "Animals are, too. You are certainly not ignorant of the intensely aphrodisiac effect produced by *nepeta cataria*, vulgarly called catnip, on the feline species; and to mention another example— one whose authenticity I myself can vouch for—Bridoux, one of my old schoolmates, now in business in the Rue Malpalu, has a dog which has convulsions if you show it a snuffbox. Bridoux sometimes makes him perform for his friends, at his suburban residence in Bois-Guillaume. Would you believe that a simple sternutative could work such havoc in the organism of a quadruped? It's extremely curious, don't you find?"

"Yes," said Charles, who wasn't listening.

"This is but another illustration," said the pharmacist, smiling with an air of benign self-satisfaction, "of the innumerable irregularities of the nervous system. As far as Madame is concerned, I confess she has always seemed to me a genuine sensitive. For that reason, my good friend, I advise you not to use any of those so-called remedies which attack the temperament under the guise of attacking the symptoms. No—no futile medication. Just a regimen. Sedatives, emollients, dulcifiers. And then, don't you think it would be a good thing to rouse her imagination—something striking?"

"How? What?"

"Ah, that's the problem. That is indeed the problem.

'*That is the question*,' " he quoted in English, "as I read in the paper recently."

Just then Emma, waking from her sleep, cried: "The letter? Where is the letter?"

They thought her delirious, and from midnight on she was: there could be no doubt that it was brain fever.

For forty-three days Charles did not leave her side. He neglected all his patients; he never lay down; he was constantly feeling her pulse, applying mustard plasters and cold compresses. He sent Justin to Neufchâtel for ice; the ice melted on the way; he sent him back. He called in Doctor Canivet for consultation; he had Doctor Larivière, his old teacher, come from Rouen; he was desperate. What frightened him most was Emma's degree of prostration: she didn't speak, she gave no sign of comprehending or even hearing anything that was said to her; and she seemed to be in no pain. It was as though her body and her soul together had sought rest after all their tribulations. Toward the middle of October she could sit up in bed, propped against pillows. Charles wept when he saw her eat her first slice of bread and jam. Her strength returned; she left her bed for a few hours each afternoon; and one day when she felt better than usual he got her to take his arm and try a walk in the garden. The gravel on the paths was almost hidden under dead leaves; she walked slowly, dragging her slippers; and leaning on Charles's shoulder she smiled continuously.

They made their way to the far end, near the terrace. She drew herself up slowly and held her hand above her eyes: she stared into the distance, the far distance; but on the horizon there were only great grass fires, smoking on the hills.

"You'll tire yourself, darling," said Bovary.

And guiding her gently, trying to induce her to enter the arbor:

"Sit on this bench: you'll be comfortable."

"Oh no! Not there! Not there!" she said in a faltering voice.

Immediately she felt dizzy; and beginning that night there was another onset of her illness. This time it was less clearly identifiable, more complex. Now her heart would pain her, now her chest, now her head, now her limbs. She had vomiting spells, which Charles feared were the first symptoms of cancer.

And as though that were not enough, the poor fellow had money worries!

XIV

TO BEGIN WITH, HE DIDN'T KNOW HOW TO MAKE GOOD TO MONsieur Homais for all the medicaments that had come from the pharmacy: as a doctor he might have been excused from paying for them, but the obligation embarrassed him. Then, what with the cook acting as mistress, the household expenses were getting to be alarming; there was a deluge of bills; the tradespeople were grumbling; Monsieur Lheureux, especially, was harassing him. The drygoods dealer, taking advantage of the circumstances to pad his bill, had chosen a moment at the very height of Emma's illness to deliver the cloak, the overnight bag, two trunks instead of one, and a number of other things as well. Charles protested that he had no use for them, but the shopkeeper arrogantly retorted that all those items had been ordered and that he wouldn't take them back. Besides, he said, it would be upsetting to Madame in her

convalescence. Monsieur should think it over. In short, he
was determined to stand on his rights and carry the matter
to court rather than give in. A little later Charles ordered
that everything be sent back to the shop; but Félicité
forgot; and he had other things on his mind and didn't
think of them. Monsieur Lheureux brought the matter up
again, and by alternating threats and moans got Charles to
sign a six-months' promissory note. No sooner had he
signed than he had a bold idea: he would try to borrow a
thousand francs from Monsieur Lheureux. So he awkwardly
asked whether there was any chance of this, explaining
that it would be for one year and at any rate of interest
Lheureux might specify. Lheureux ran to his shop, brought
back the money, and dictated another promissory note,
whereby Bovary promised to pay to his order, the first of
the following September, the sum of 1,070 francs. Together
with the 180 already stipulated, that came to just 1,250.
In this way, loaning at the rate of six percent, plus his
commission and at least one-third mark-up on the goods,
the whole thing would bring him in a clear 130 francs'
profit in twelve months; and he hoped that it wouldn't
stop there, that the notes wouldn't be met but renewed,
and that his poor little capital, after benefiting from the
doctor's care like a patient in a sanatorium, would eventually come back to him considerably plumper, fat enough to
burst the bag.

Everything Lheureux touched was successful at this moment. His had been the winning bid for the cider-supply
contract at the Neufchâtel public hospital; Maître Guillaumin was promising him some shares in the peatery at
Grumesnil; and he was thinking of setting up a new coach
service between Argueil and Rouen: such a thing would
quickly spell the end of the old rattletrap at the Lion
d'Or, and being faster and cheaper and carrying a bigger
pay load would give him a monopoly of the Yonville trade.

Charles wondered more than once how he was going to be able to pay back so large a sum the following year; and racking his brains he imagined various expedients, such as applying to his father or selling off something. But his father would turn a deaf ear, and he himself owned nothing that could be sold. The difficulties he foresaw were so formidable that he quickly banished the disagreeable subject from his mind. He reproached himself for having let it distract him from Emma—as though his every thought were her property and he were filching something from her if he took his mind off her for a second.

It was a severe winter. Madame's convalescence was slow. On fine days they pushed her armchair to the window—the one overlooking the square, for she had taken an aversion to the garden, and the blind on that side was always down. She asked that her horse be sold: things that had once given her pleasure she now disliked. She seemed to have no thought for anything beyond her own health. She ate her tiny meals in bed, rang for the maid to ask about her tisanes or just to chat. All this while the snow on the roof of the market filled the room with its monotonous white reflection; then came a spell of rain. And every day Emma looked forward, with a kind of anxious expectation, to the same, unfailingly recurring, trivial events, little though they mattered to her. The greatest of these was the nightly arrival of the Hirondelle, when Madame Lefrançois shouted, other voices replied, and Hippolyte's stable lamp, as he looked for luggage under the hood, shone out like a star in the darkness. At noon Charles always returned from his rounds; after lunch he went out again; then she took a cup of bouillon; and toward five, at the close of day, children passed the house on their way home from school, dragging their wooden shoes along the sidewalk, and invariably, one after the other, hitting their rulers against the shutter hooks.

About this time Monsieur Bournisien usually stopped in. He would ask after her health, give her news, and exhort her to prayer in an affectionate, informal way that wasn't without its charm. Just the sight of his cassock she found comforting.

One day at the height of her sickness, when she thought she was dying, she had asked for Communion; and as her room was made ready for the sacrament—the chest of drawers cleared of its medicine bottles and transformed into an altar, the floor strewn with dahlia blossoms by Félicité—Emma felt something powerful pass over her that rid her of all pain, all perception, all feeling. Her flesh had been relieved of its burdens, even the burden of thought; another life was beginning; it seemed to her that her spirit, ascending to God, was about to find annihilation in this love, like burning incense dissolving in smoke. The sheets of her bed were sprinkled with holy water; the priest drew the white host from the sacred pyx; and she was all but swooning with celestial bliss as she advanced her lips to receive the body of the Saviour. The curtains of her alcove swelled out softly around her like clouds; and the beams of the two wax tapers burning on the chest of drawers seemed to her like dazzling emanations of divine light. Then she let her head fall back: through the vastnesses of space seemed to come the music of seraphic harps; and on a golden throne in an azure sky she thought she saw God the Father in all His glory, surrounded by the saints bearing branches of green palm; He was gesturing majestically, and obedient angels with flaming wings were descending to the earth to bear her to Him in their arms.

This splendid vision, the most beautiful of all possible dreams, stayed in her memory—not eclipsing all else as at the time it occurred, but no less intensely sweet; and she kept straining to recapture the original sensation. Her soul, aching with pride, was at last finding rest in Christian humility; and luxuriating in her own weakness she turned her eyes inward and watched the destruction of her will, which was to open wide the way for an onrush of grace. She was filled with wonderment at the discovery that there was a bliss greater than mere happiness—a love different from and transcending all others—a love without break and without end, a love that increased throughout eternity! Among the illusions born of her hope she glimpsed a realm of purity in which she aspired to dwell: it hovered above the earth, merging with the sky. She conceived the idea of becoming a saint. She bought rosaries and festooned herself with holy medals; she wished she had an emerald-studded reliquary within reach at her bed's head, to kiss every night.

The priest was enchanted by her change of heart, though he was of the opinion that her faith might by its very fervor come to border on heresy and even on extravagance. But not being versed in these matters once they went beyond a certain point, he wrote Monsieur Boulard, the bishop's bookseller, and asked him to send him "something particularly good for a lady who had a very fine mind." As casually as though he were shipping trinkets to savages, the bookseller made up a heterogeneous package of everything just then current in the religious book trade —little question-and-answer manuals, pamphlets couched in the contemptuous language made popular by Monsieur de Maistre, so-called novels in pink bindings and sugary style concocted by romantic-minded seminarists or reformed blue-stockings. There were titles such as *Think It Over Carefully; The Man of the World at the Feet of Mary*, by Monsieur de——, *recipient of several decorations; The Errors of Voltaire, for the use of the young;* etc.

Madame Bovary wasn't yet sufficiently recovered in mind to apply herself seriously to anything; and besides, she plunged into all this literature far too precipitately.

The regulations governing worship annoyed her; she disliked the arrogance of the polemical writings because of their relentless attacks on people she had never heard of; and the secular stories flavored with religion seemed to her written out of such ignorance of the world that she was unwittingly led away from the very truths she was longing to have confirmed. Nevertheless she persisted; and when the volume fell from her hands she was convinced that hers was the most exquisite Catholic melancholy that had ever entered an ethereal soul.

As for the memory of Rodolphe, she had buried it in the depths of her heart; and there it remained, as solemn and motionless as the mummy of a pharaoh in an underground chamber. Her great love that lay thus embalmed gave off a fragrance that permeated everything, adding a touch of tenderness to the immaculate atmosphere in which she longed to live. When she knelt at her Gothic *prie-dieu* she addressed the Lord in the same ardent words she had formerly murmured to her lover in the ecstasies of adultery. It was her way of praying for faith; but heaven showered no joy upon her, and she would rise, her limbs aching, with a vague feeling that it was all a vast fraud. This quest she considered meritorious in itself; and in the pride of her piety Emma likened herself to those great ladies of yore whose fame she had dreamed of while gazing at a portrait of La Vallière: how majestically they had trailed the gorgeous trains of their long gowns, as they withdrew into seclusion to shed at the feet of Christ all the tears of their life-wounded hearts!

Now she became wildly charitable. She sewed clothes for the poor, sent firewood to women in childbed; and one day Charles came home to find three tramps sitting at the kitchen table eating soup. She sent for her daughter— during her illness Charles had left the child with the nurse —and she determined to teach her to read. Berthe wept and wept, but she never lost her temper with her. It was a deliberately adopted attitude of resignation, of indulgence toward all. She used a lofty term whenever she could:

"Is your stomach-ache all gone, my angel?" she would say to her daughter.

The elder Madame Bovary found nothing to reproach her for in all this, except perhaps her mania for knitting undershirts for orphans instead of mending her own dish towels. Harassed by the incessant quarrels in her own home, the old lady enjoyed the peaceful atmosphere of this house; and she prolonged her visit through Easter to escape the jibes of her husband, whose invariable habit it was to order pork sausage on Good Friday.

In addition to the company of her mother-in-law, whom she found a steadying influence because of her unswerving principles and solemn demeanor, Emma nearly every day had other visits—from Madame Langlois, Madame Caron, Madame Dubreuil, Madame Tuvache, and, regularly from two to five, from Madame Homais, who—good soul that she was—had always refused to believe any of the gossip that was spread about her neighbor. The Homais children visited her, too; Justin brought them. He came with them up into her bedroom and stood quietly near the door, never saying a word. Often while he was there Madame Bovary would start to dress, oblivious of him. She would begin by taking out her comb and tossing her head; and the first time he saw her mass of black hair fall in ringlets to her knees, it was for the boy like the sudden opening of a door upon something marvelous and new, something whose splendor frightened him.

Emma never noticed his silent eagerness or his timidity. She knew only that love had disappeared from her life: she had no suspicion that it was pulsating there so close to her, beneath that coarse shirt, in that adolescent heart so open to the emanations of her beauty. Moreover, her detachment from everything had become so complete, her language was so sweet and the look in her eye so haughty, her behavior was so mercurial, that there was no longer any way of telling where selfishness and corruption ended and charity and virtue began. One night, for instance, she lost her temper with her servant, who was asking permission to go out and stammering some pretended reason. Then:

"So you love him, do you?" Emma suddenly demanded.

And without waiting for the blushing Félicité to answer, she added, resignedly:

"All right—run along! Enjoy yourself!"

When the weather turned mild she had the garden completely dug up and relandscaped. Bovary objected a little, but he was glad to see her finally caring about things, and she gave more and more evidence of this as her strength returned. She forbade the house to Madame Rollet the nurse, who during her convalescence had formed the habit of coming too often to the kitchen with her own two babes and her little boarder, the latter more ravenous than a cannibal. She cut down on visits from the Homais', discouraged all her other callers, and even went less regularly to church, thus eliciting the apothecary's approval.

"I was afraid you'd been taken in by the mumbo-jumbo," he said amicably.

The abbé Bournisien still came every day, after catechism class. He preferred to sit outdoors in the fresh air—in the "grove," as he called the arbor. This was the hour of Charles's return. Both men would be hot; Félicité would bring them sweet cider, and they would raise their glasses and drink to Madame's complete recovery.

Binet was often there: just below, that is—beside the terrace wall, fishing for crayfish. Bovary would invite him to join them for a drink; he prided himself on being an expert uncorker of cider jugs.

"First," he would say—glancing at his companions complacently and then giving an equally smug look at the landscape—"first you must hold the bottle upright on the table, like this. Then you cut the strings. And then you pry up the cork, a little at a time, gently, gently—the way they open Seltzer water in restaurants."

But during this demonstration the cork would often pop out and the cider would splash one or another of them in the face; and the curé never failed to laugh his thick laugh and make his joke:

"Its excellence is certainly *striking!*"

He was a good-hearted fellow—there was no denying it—and he even expressed no objection one day when the pharmacist advised Charles to give Madame a treat and take her to the opera in Rouen, to hear the famous tenor, Lagardy. Homais was surprised at his silence, and asked him how he felt about it; and the priest declared that he considered music less dangerous to morals than literature.

The pharmacist sprang to the defense of letters. The theatre, he claimed, served to expose prejudice: it taught virtue under the guise of entertainment:

"*Castigat ridendo mores*, Monsieur Bournisien! Take most of Voltaire's tragedies, for example: it's clever the way he's stuck them full of philosophical remarks—they're a complete education in morals and diplomacy for the people."

"I saw a play once, called the *Gamin de Paris*," said Binet. "There's an old general in it that's absolutely first-class. A rich fellow seduces a working girl and the general slaps him down and at the end . . ."

"Of course," Homais went on, "there's bad literature just as there's bad pharmaceutics. But to make a blanket condemnation of the greatest of the fine arts seems to be a yokelism, a medievalism worthy of that abominable age when they imprisoned Galileo."

"I know perfectly well," objected the priest, "that there are good writers who write good things. Still, the fact alone that people of different sexes are brought together in a glamorous auditorium that's the last word in worldly luxury—and then the heathenish disguises, the painted faces, the footlights, the effeminate voices—it all can't help encouraging a certain licentiousness and inducing evil thoughts and impure temptations. Such, at least, is the opinion of all the church fathers. After all," he added, suddenly assuming an unctuous tone and rolling himself a pinch of snuff, "if the church condemns play-going she has good reason for doing so: we must submit to her decrees."

"Why," demanded the apothecary, "does she excommunicate actors? They used to take part openly in ecclesiastical ceremonies, you know. Yes, they used to act right in the middle of the choir—put on farcical plays called mysteries. These often violated the laws of decency, I may say."

The priest's only answer was a groan, and the pharmacist persisted:

"It's the same in the Bible. There's more than one spicy bit in that book, you know—some pret-ty dar-ing things!"

And as Monsieur Bournisien made a gesture of annoyance:

"Ah! You'll agree that it's no book to give a young person! I'd be sorry if my daughter Athalie . . ."

"But *we* don't recommend the reading of the Bible!" cried the abbé impatiently. "It's the Protestants!"

"It makes no difference," said Homais. "I'm astonished that in this day and age—an age of enlightenment—anyone should persist in forbidding a form of intellectual diversion that's harmless, morally uplifting, and sometimes—isn't it true, Doctor?—even good for the health."

"I guess so." Charles made his answer in a vacant tone—

perhaps because he shared Homais' opinion and didn't want to offend the priest, or perhaps because he had no opinion.

The conversation seemed to be at an end, when the pharmacist saw fit to make one last dig.

"I've known priests," he said, "who made a practice of going out in civilian clothes and watching leg shows."

"Come now," said the priest.

"Oh yes, I've known some!"

And once again separating his syllables by way of significant emphasis, Homais repeated:

"I—have—known—some!"

"Well, then, they did wrong," said Bournisien with truly Christian patience.

"I should think so! And that wasn't all they were up to, either!" exclaimed the apothecary.

"*Monsieur!*" The priest jumped to his feet and glared so fiercely that the pharmacist was intimidated.

"All I mean," he said, much more mildly, "is that tolerance is the surest means of bringing souls into the church."

"Quite true, quite true," the curé conceded, sitting down again.

He left a moment or two later, however, and Homais said to the doctor:

"Quite a squabble! How did you like the way I got the better of him? Pretty good, eh? Anyway—follow my advice and take Madame to the opera, if only to give a priest a black eye for once in your life. If I could find a substitute I'd come with you. Don't lose any time getting tickets: Lagardy's giving only one performance—he's scheduled for an English tour at staggering fees. From what they say, he must be quite a lad. He's filthy with money. Everywhere he goes he takes along three mistresses and a cook. All those great artists burn their candles at both ends: they have to lead a wild kind of life—it stimulates their imagination. But they die in the poorhouse, because they haven't the sense to save money when they're young. Well, *bon appétit: à demain!*"

The idea of the opera took rapid root in Bovary's mind. He lost no time suggesting it to his wife. She shook her head, pleading fatigue, trouble and expense; but for once Charles didn't give in, so convinced was he that she would benefit from the excursion. He saw no reason for them not to go: his mother had sent him three hundred francs they had given up hope of getting, their debts of the moment were nothing tremendous, and Lheureux's notes weren't due for so long that there was no use thinking about them. Fancying that Emma was refusing out of consideration for him, Charles insisted the more strongly, and finally she gave in. The next day, at eight in the morning, they bundled themselves into the Hirondelle.

The apothecary, who had nothing in the world to keep him in Yonville, but who was firmly convinced that he couldn't absent himself even briefly, gave a sigh as he watched their departure.

"*Bon voyage!*" he called to them. "Some people have all the luck!"

And to Emma, who was wearing a blue silk dress with four rows of flounces:

"You're pretty as a picture! You'll be the belle of Rouen!"

The coach took them to the Hotel de la Croix-Rouge in the Place Beauvoisine. It was one of those inns such as you find on the edge of every provincial city, with large stables and small bedrooms, and chickens scratching for oats in the coach yard under muddy gigs belonging to traveling salesmen—comfortable, old-fashioned stopovers, with worm-eaten wooden balconies that creak in the wind on winter nights, constantly full of people, bustle and victuals, their blackened table tops sticky with spilled coffee-and-brandies, their thick windowpanes yellowed by flies, their napkins spotted blue by cheap red wine. They always seem a little rustic, like farm hands in Sunday clothes; on the street side they have a café, and in back—on the country side—a vegetable garden. Charles went at once to buy tickets. He got the stage boxes mixed up with the top balconies, and the rest of the boxes with the orchestra; he asked for explanations, didn't understand them, was sent from the box office to the manager, came back to the hotel, went back to the box office again. All in all, between the theatre and the outer boulevard he covered the entire length of the city several times over.

Madame bought herself a hat, gloves and a bouquet. Monsieur was nervous about missing the beginning; and without stopping for as much as a cup of bouillon they arrived at the theatre before the doors were even open.

XV

THERE WAS A CROWD WAITING OUTSIDE, LINED UP BEHIND RAIL-ings on both sides of the entrance. At the adjoining street corners huge posters in fancy lettering announced: *"Lucie de Lammermoor . . . Lagardy . . . Opéra . . .* etc." It was a fine evening; everyone was hot: many a set of curls was drenched in sweat, and handkerchiefs were out, mopping red brows; now and again a soft breeze blowing from the river gently stirred the edges of the canvas awnings over café doors. But just a short distance away there was a coolness, provided by an icy draft smelling of tallow, leather and oil—the effluvia of the Rue des Charettes, with its great, gloomy, barrel-filled warehouses.

Fearing lest they appear ridiculous, Emma insisted that they stroll a bit along the river front before going in; and Bovary, by way of precaution, kept the tickets in his hand and his hand in his trousers pocket, pressed reassuringly against his stomach.

Her heart began to pound as they entered the foyer. A smile of satisfaction rose involuntarily to her lips at seeing the crowd hurry off to the right down the corridor, while she climbed the stairs leading to the first tier. She took pleasure, like a child, in pushing open the wide upholstered doors with one finger; she filled her lungs with the dusty smell of the corridors; and seated in her box she drew herself up with all the airs of a duchess.

The theatre began to fill; opera glasses came out of cases; and subscribers exchanged greetings as they glimpsed one another across the house. The arts, for them, were a relaxation from the worries of buying and selling; that was why they had come; but it was quite impossible for them to forget business even here, and their conversation was about cotton, spirits and indigo. The old men looked blank and placid: with their gray-white hair and gray-white skin they were like silver medals that had been tarnished by lead fumes. The young beaux strutted in the orchestra: the openings of their waistcoats were bright with pink or apple-green cravats; and Madame Bovary looked admiringly down at them as they leaned with tightly yellow-gloved hands on their gold-knobbed walking sticks.

Meanwhile the candles were lighted on the music stands and the chandelier came down from the ceiling, the sparkle of its crystals filling the house with sudden gaiety; then the musicians filed in and there was a long cacophony of booming cellos, scraping violins, blaring horns, and piping flutes and flageolets. Then three heavy blows came from the stage; there was a roll of kettledrums and a series of chords from the brasses; and the curtain rose on an out door scene.

It was a crossroad in a forest, on the right a spring shaded by an oak. A group of country folk and nobles, all with tartans over their shoulders, sang a hunting chorus; then a captain strode in and inveighed against an evil spirit, raising both arms to heaven; another character joined him; they both walked off, and the huntsmen repeated their chorus.

She was back in the books she had read as a girl—deep in Walter Scott. She imagined she could hear the sound of Scottish pipes echoing through the mist across the heather. Her recollection of the novel made it easy for her to grasp the libretto; and she followed the plot line by line, elusive, half-forgotten memories drifting into her thoughts only to be dispelled by the onrush of the music. She let herself be lulled by the melodies, feeling herself vibrate to the very fiber of her being, as though the bows of the violins were playing on her nerve-strings. She couldn't take in enough of the costumes, the sets, the characters, the painted trees that shook at the slightest footstep, the velvet bonnets, the cloaks, the swords—all those fanciful things that fluttered on waves of music as though in another world. Then a young woman came forward, tossing a purse to a squire in green. She was left alone on the stage, and there came the sound of a flute, like the ripple of a spring or the warbling of a bird. Lucie, looking solemn, began her cavatina in G major: she uttered love laments, begged for wings. And at that moment Emma, too, longed that she might leave life behind and take wing in an embrace. Suddenly Edgar Lagardy came on stage.

He was pale to the point of splendor, with that marmoreal majesty sometimes found among the passionate races of the south. His stalwart figure was clad in a tight brown doublet; a small chased dagger swung at his left hip; and he rolled his eyes about him languorously and flashed his white teeth. People said that a Polish princess had heard him sing one night on the beach at Biarritz, where he was a boat-boy, and had fallen in love with him; she had beggared herself for him, and he had left her for other women. This reputation as a ladies' man had done no disservice to his professional career. Shrewd ham actor that he was, he always saw to it that his publicity should include a poetic phrase or two about the charm of his personality and the sensibility of his soul. A fine voice, utter self-possession, more temperament than intelligence, more bombast than feeling—such were the principal attributes of this magnificent charlatan. There was a touch of the hairdresser about him, and a touch of the toreador.

He had the audience in transports from the first. He clasped Lucie in his arms, left her, returned to her, seemed in despair: he would shout with rage, then let his voice expire, plaintive and infinitely sweet; and the notes that poured from his bare throat were full of sobs and kisses. Emma strained forward to watch him, her fingernails scratching the plush of her box. Her heart drank its full of the medodious laments that hung suspended in the air against the sound of the double-basses like the cries of shipwrecked sailors against the tumult of a storm. Here was the same ecstasy, the same anguish that had brought her to the brink of death. The soprano's voice seemed but the echo of her own soul, and this illusion that held her under its spell a part of her own life. But no one on earth had ever loved her with so great a love. That last moonlight night, when they had told each other, "Till tomorrow! Till tomorrow!" *he* had not wept as Edgar was weeping now. The house was bursting with applause. The whole stretto was repeated: the lovers sang about the flowers on their graves, about vows and exile and fate and hope; and when their voices rose in the final farewell, Emma herself uttered a sharp cry that was drowned in the blast of the final chords.

"What's that lord doing, mistreating her like that?" Charles asked.

"No, no," she answered. "That's her lover."

"But he's swearing vengeance on her family, whereas the other one—the one that came on a while ago—said 'I love Lucie and I think she loves me!' Besides, he walked off arm in arm with her father. That is her father, isn't it, the ugly little one with the cock-feather in his hat?"

Despite Emma's explanations, Charles got everything mixed up beginning with the duet in recitative in which Gilbert explains his abominable machinations to his master Ashton. The false engagement ring serving to trick Lucie he took to be a love token sent by Edgar. In fact he couldn't follow the story at all, he said, because of the music: it interfered so with the words.

"What difference does it make?" said Emma. "Be quiet!"

"But I like to know what's going on," he persisted, leaning over her shoulder. "You know I do."

"Be quiet! Be quiet!" she whispered impatiently.

Lucie came on, half borne up by her women; there was a wreath of orange blossoms in her hair, and she was paler than the white satin of her gown. Emma thought of her own wedding day: she saw herself walking toward the church along the little path amid the wheatfields. Why in heaven's name hadn't she resisted and entreated, like Lucie? But no—she had been light-hearted, unaware of the abyss she was rushing toward. Ah! If only in the freshness of her beauty, before defiling herself in marriage, before the disillusionments of adultery, she could have found some great and noble heart to be her life's foundation! Then virtue and affection, sensual joys and duty would all have been one; and she would never have fallen from her high felicity. But that kind of happiness was doubtless a lie, invented to make one despair of any love. Now she well knew the true paltriness of the passions that art painted so large. So she did her best to think of the opera in a different light: she resolved to regard this image of her own griefs as a vivid fantasy, an enjoyable spectacle and nothing more; and she was actually smiling to herself in scornful pity when from behind the velvet curtains at the back of the stage there appeared a man in a black cloak.

A single gesture sent his broad-brimmed Spanish hat to the ground; and the orchestra and the singers abruptly broke into the sextet. Edgar, flashing fury, dominated all the others with his high, clear voice. Ashton flung him his homicidal challenge in solemn tones; Lucie uttered her shrill lament; Arthur sang his asides in middle register; and the chaplain's baritone boomed like an organ while the women, echoing his words, repeated them in delicious chorus. All the characters now formed a single line across the stage; all were gesticulating at once; and rage, vengeance, jealousy, terror, pity and amazement poured simultaneously from their open mouths. The outraged lover brandished his naked sword; his lace collar rose and fell with the heaving of his chest; and he strode up and down, clanking the silver-gilt spurs on his soft, flaring boots. His love, she thought, must be inexhaustible, since he could pour it out in such great quantities on the crowd. Her resolution not to be taken in by the display of false sentiment was swept away by the impact of the singer's eloquence; the fiction that he was embodying drew her to his real life, and she tried to imagine what it was like—that glamorous, fabulous, marvelous life that she, too, might have lived had chance so willed it. They might have met! They might have loved! With him she might have traveled over all the kingdoms of Europe, from capital to capital, sharing his hardships and his triumphs, gathering up the flowers his admirers threw, embroidering his costumes with her own hands; and every night behind the gilded lattice of her box she might have sat open-mouthed, breathing in the outpourings of that divine creature who would be singing for her alone: he would have gazed at her from the stage as he played his role. A mad idea seized her: he was gazing at her now! She was sure of it! She longed to rush into his arms and seek refuge in his strength as in the very incarnation of love; she longed to cry: "Ravish me! Carry me off! Away from here! All my passion and all my dreams are yours—yours alone!"

The curtain fell.

The smell of gas mingled with human exhalations, and the air seemed the more stifling for being stirred up by fans. Emma tried to get out, but there was a crush in the corridors, and she sank back onto a chair, oppressed by palpitations. Charles, fearful lest she fall into a faint, hurried to the bar for a glass of orgeat.

He had a hard time getting back to the box: he held the glass in both hands because his elbows were being jarred at every other step, but even so he spilled three-quarters of it over the shoulders of a Rouen lady in short sleeves, who began to scream like a peacock, as though she were being murdered, when she felt the cold liquid trickling down her spine. While she took her handkerchief to the spots on her beautiful cerise taffeta gown, her mill-owner husband gave poor clumsy Charles a piece of his mind, angrily muttering the words "damages," "cost," and "replacement." Finally Charles made his way to his wife.

"I thought I'd never get out of there," he gasped. "Such a crowd! Such a crowd!"

And he added:

"Guess who I ran into: Monsieur Léon!"

"Léon?"

"Absolutely. He'll be coming along to pay you his respects."

As he uttered the words the former Yonville clerk
entered the box.

He held out his hand with aristocratic casualness; and
Madame Bovary automatically extended hers—yielding,
no doubt, to the attraction of a stronger will. She hadn't
touched it since that spring evening when the rain was
falling on the new green leaves—the evening they had said
farewell as they stood beside the window. But quickly
reminding herself of the social requirements of the situation, she roused herself with an effort from her memories
and began to stammer hurried phrases:

"Ah, good evening! You here? How amazing . . . !"

"Quiet!" cried a voice from the orchestra, for the third
act was beginning.

"So you're living in Rouen?"

"Yes."

"Since when?"

"*Sh! Sh!*"

People were turning around at them indignantly, and
they fell silent.

But from that moment on Emma no longer listened to
the music. The chorus of guests, the scene between Ashton and his attendant, the great duet in D major—for her
it all took place at a distance, as though the instruments
had lost their sound and the characters had moved away.
She recalled the card games at the pharmacist's and the
walk to the wet nurse's, their readings under the arbor,
the tête-à-têtes beside the fire—the whole poor story of
their love, so quiet and so long, so discreet, so tender, and
yet discarded from her memory. Why was he returning like
this? What combination of events was bringing him back
into her life? He sat behind her, leaning a shoulder against

the wall of the box; and from time to time she quivered as she felt his warm breath on her hair.

"Are you enjoying this?" he asked, leaning over so close that the tip of his mustache brushed against her cheek.

"Heavens no," she said carelessly, "not particularly."

And he suggested that they leave the theatre and go somewhere for an ice.

"Oh, not yet! Let's stay!" said Bovary. "Her hair's down: it looks as though it's going to be tragic."

But the mad scene interested Emma not at all: the soprano, she felt, was overdoing her role.

"She's shrieking too loud," she said, turning toward Charles, who was drinking it in.

"Yes . . . perhaps . . . a little," he replied, torn between the fullness of his enjoyment and the respect he had for his wife's opinions.

"It's so hot. . . ." sighed Léon.

"It is. . . . Unbearable."

"Are you uncomfortable?" asked Bovary.

"Yes, I'm stifling; let's go."

Monsieur Léon carefully laid her long lace shawl over her shoulders, and the three of them walked to the river front and sat down on the outdoor terrace of a café. First they spoke of her sickness, Emma interrupting Charles now and then lest, as she said, he bore Monsieur Léon; and Monsieur Léon told them he had just come to Rouen to spend two years in a large office to familiarize himself with the kind of business carried on in Normandy, which was different from anything he had learned about in Paris. Then he asked about Berthe, the Homais', and Madame Lefrançois; and since they had no more to say to each other in front of Charles the conversation soon died.

People coming from the theatre strolled by on the sidewalk, humming or bawling at the top of their voices: "*O bel ange, ma Lucie!*" Léon began to show off his musical knowledge. He had heard Tamburini, Rubini, Persiani, Grisi; and in comparison with them, Lagardy, for all the noise he made, was nothing.

"Still," interrupted Charles, who was eating his rum sherbet a tiny bit at a time, "they say he's wonderful in the last act. I was sorry to leave before the end: I was beginning to like it."

"Don't worry," said the clerk, "he'll be giving another performance soon."

But Charles said they were leaving the next day.

"Unless," he said, turning to his wife, "you'd like to stay on by yourself, sweetheart?"

And changing his tune to suit this unexpected opportunity, the young man sang the praises of Lagardy in the final scenes. He was superb, sublime! Charles insisted:

"You can come home Sunday. Yes, make up your mind to do it. You'd be wrong not to, if you think there's the slightest chance it might do you some good."

Meanwhile the tables around them were emptying; a waiter came and stood discreetly nearby; Charles took the hint and drew out his purse; the clerk put a restraining hand on his arm, paid the bill, and noisily threw down a couple of silver coins for the waiter.

"I'm really embarrassed," murmured Bovary, "at the money that you . . ."

The younger man shrugged him off in a friendly way and took up his hat:

"So it's agreed?" he said. "Tomorrow at six?"

Charles repeated that he couldn't stay away that much longer, but that there was nothing to prevent Emma . . .

"Oh," she murmured, smiling a peculiar smile, "I really don't know whether . . ."

"Well, think it over," said Charles. "Sleep on it and we'll decide in the morning."

Then, to Léon, who was walking with them:

"Now that you're back in our part of the world I hope you'll drop in now and then and let us give you dinner?"

The clerk said that he certainly would, especially since he'd soon be going to Yonville anyway on a business matter. They said good night at the corner of the Passage Saint-Herbland as the cathedral clock was striking half past eleven.

PART THREE

I

BUSY THOUGH HE HAD BEEN WITH HIS LAW STUDIES, MONSIEUR
Léon had nevertheless found time to frequent the Chau-
mière, and in that cabaret he had done very well for
himself with the grisettes, who considered him "distin-
guished-looking." He was the best-behaved student imaginable; his hair was neither too long nor too short, he didn't
spend his entire quarter's allowance the day he got it, and
he kept on good terms with his professors. As for excesses,
he had been too timorous as well as too squeamish to go in
for them.

Often, when he sat reading in his room, or under the
lindens of the Luxembourg in the evening, he let his law
book fall to the ground, and the memory of Emma came
back to him. But gradually his feeling for her faded, and

other sensual appetites supplanted it. Even so, it persisted
in the background, for Léon never gave up all hope: it was
as though a vague promise kept dangling before him in the
future, like a golden fruit hanging from some exotic tree.

Then, seeing her again after three years, his passion
revived. This time, he decided he must make up his mind
to possess her. Much of his shyness had worn off as a result
of the gay company he had kept, and he had returned to
the provinces filled with contempt for the local ladies, so
different from the trim-shod creatures of the boulevards.
Before an elegant Parisienne in the salon of some famous,
rich, be-medaled physician, the poor clerk would doubtless have trembled like a child; but here on the Rouen
river front, in the presence of this wife of an *officier de
santé*, he felt at ease, sure in advance that she would be
dazzled. Self-confidence depends on surroundings: the same
person talks quite differently in the drawing room and in
the garret, and a rich woman's virtue is protected by her
banknotes quite as effectively as by any cuirass worn
under a corset.

After taking leave of Monsieur and Madame Bovary the
previous night, Léon had followed them at a distance in
the street; and when he saw them turn into the Croix-
Rouge, he retraced his steps and spent the rest of the night
working out a plan of action.

The next afternoon about five, pale-faced, with a tight-
ness in his throat and with the blind resolution of the
panic-stricken, he walked into the inn kitchen.

"Monsieur isn't here," a servant told him.

He took that to be a good omen, and went upstairs.

She received him calmly, and even apologized for having
forgotten to mention where they were staying.

"Oh, I guessed!" said Léon.

"How?"

He pretended that he had been led to her by pure

chance, a kind of instinct. That made her smile; and, ashamed of his blunder, he quickly told her that he had spent the morning looking for her all over the city, in one hotel after another.

"So you decided to stay?" he asked.

"Yes," she said, "and I was wrong. One can't afford to be self-indulgent if one has a thousand things to attend to."

"Oh, I can imagine . . ."

"No, you can't! You're not a woman."

But men had their troubles, too; and so the conversation got under way, with philosophical reflections. Emma expatiated on the vanity of earthly attachments and on the eternal isolation of every human heart. Either to impress her, or naturally taking on the color of her melancholy, the young man declared that he had found his studies prodigiously frustrating. The technicalities of law irritated him, he was tempted by other careers, and in her letters his mother never stopped pestering him. Indeed, as they talked on they both became more specific in their complaints, and less reserved in their confidences. Occasionally they shrank from giving full expression to their thought, and groped for phrases that would convey it obliquely. But she never disclosed having had another passion, and he said nothing about having forgotten her.

Perhaps he no longer remembered the suppers following fancy-dress balls, with the girls costumed as stevedores; and doubtless she didn't recall those early-morning meetings when she had run through the fields to her lover's chateau. The sounds of the city reached them only faintly, and the room seemed small, designed with them in mind, to make their solitude the closer. Emma, in a dimity dressing gown, leaned her chignon against the back of the old armchair; the yellow wallpaper was like a gold ground behind her; and her bare head was reflected in the mirror, with the white line of her center part, and the tips of her ears peeping out from under the sweeps of her hair.

"But forgive me," she said. "I shouldn't bore you with all my complaints!"

"How can you say that!" he said reproachfully.

"Ah!" she said, lifting her lovely tear-bright eyes to the ceiling. "If you knew all the dreams I've dreamed!"

"It's the same with me! Oh, I had a terrible time! Very often I dropped everything and went out and wandered along the quays, trying to forget my thoughts in the noise of the crowd. But I could never drive out the obsession that haunted me. In the window of a print shop on the boulevard there's an Italian engraving showing one of the Muses. She's draped in a tunic and looking at the moon—her hair's streaming down, with forget-me-nots in it. Something made me go back there over and over again: I used to stand in front of that window for hours on end."

Then, in a trembling voice:

"She looked like you a little."

Madame Bovary averted her face lest he see the smile that she couldn't suppress.

"I kept writing you letters," he said, "and then tearing them up."

She made no answer. He went on:

"I used to imagine we'd meet by chance. I kept thinking I saw you on street corners, and I even ran after cabs sometimes, if I saw a shawl or a veil at the window that looked like yours. . . ."

She seemed determined to let him speak without interruption. Arms crossed and head lowered, she stared at the rosettes on her slippers, now and again moving her toes a little under the satin.

Finally she gave a sigh. "The worst thing of all, it seems to me, is to go on leading a futile life the way I do. If our unhappiness were of use to someone, we could find consolation in the thought of sacrifice!"

He launched into a eulogy of virtue, duty, silent renunciation: he, too, he said, had a fantastic need for selfless dedication that he was unable to satisfy.

"What I should love to do," she said, "would be to join an order of nursing Sisters."

"Alas!" he answered. "No such sacred missions are open to men. I can't think of any calling . . . except maybe becoming a doctor. . . ."

She gave a slight shrug and interrupted him, expressing regret that her illness had not been fatal. What a pity! By now she would be past all suffering. Léon at once chimed in with a longing for "the peace of the grave." One night he had even written out his will, asking to be buried in the beautiful velvet-striped coverlet she had given him.

That was how they would have liked to be: what they were doing was to dream up ideals and then refashion their past lives to match them. Speech is a rolling-machine that always stretches the feelings it expresses!

But:

"Why?" she asked him, at his made-up tale about the coverlet.

"Why?" He hesitated. "Because—I was terribly in love with you!"

And congratulating himself on having got over the hurdle, Léon watched her face out of the corner of his eye.

It was like the sky when a gust of wind sweeps away the clouds. The mass of sad thoughts that had darkened her blue eyes seemed to lift: her whole face was radiant.

He waited. Finally she answered:

"I always thought so."

They went over, then, the tiny happenings of that far-off time, whose joys and sorrows had been evoked by a single word. He spoke of the clematis bower, of the dresses she had worn, of the furniture in her room—of everything in the house.

"And our poor cactuses—what's become of them?"

"The cold killed them last winter."

"I've thought about them so often, would you believe it? I've pictured them the way they used to look on summer mornings, with the sun on the blinds and your bare arms in among the flowers."

"Poor boy," she said, holding out her hand.

Léon lost no time pressing it to his lips. Then, after taking a deep breath:

"You were a strange, mysterious, captivating force in my life in those days. There was one time, for example, when I came to call on you . . . But you probably don't remember."

"Yes, I do. Go on."

"You were downstairs in the hall, ready to go out, standing on the bottom step. I even remember your hat—it had little blue flowers on it. And without your asking me at all I went with you. I couldn't help it. I felt more and more foolish every minute, though, and I kept on walking near you. I didn't dare really follow you, and yet I couldn't bear to go away. When you went into a shop I stayed in the street, watching you through the window take off your gloves and count the change on the counter. Then you rang Madame Tuvache's bell; you went in; and I stood there like an idiot in front of the big heavy door even after it had closed behind you."

As she listened to him, Madame Bovary marveled at how old she was: all those re-emerging details made her life seem vaster, as though she had endless emotional experiences to look back on. Her voice low, her eyes half closed, she kept saying:

"Yes, I remember! I remember! I remember . . . !"

They heard eight o'clock strike from several belfries near the Place Beauvoisine, a section of Rouen full of boarding schools, churches and great deserted mansions. They were no longer speaking; but as they looked at one another they felt a throbbing in their heads: it was as though their very glances had set off a physical vibration. Now they had clasped hands; and in the sweetness of their ecstasy everything merged—the past, the future, their memories and their dreams. Night was darkening the walls of the room: still gleaming in the dimness were the garish colors of four prints showing four scenes from *La Tour de Nesle*, with captions below in Spanish and French. Through the sash window they could see a patch of dark sky between peaked roofs.

She rose to light two candles on the chest of drawers, and then sat down again.

"Well . . . ?" said Léon.

"Well . . . ?" she echoed.

And as he wondered how to resume the interrupted conversation, she asked:

"Why has no one ever said such things to me before?"

The clerk assured her warmly that idealistic natures were rarely understood. But he had loved her the moment he saw her, and despair filled him whenever he thought of the happiness that might have been theirs. Had fortune been kind, had they met earlier, they would long since have been united indissolubly.

"I've thought about that, sometimes," she said.

"What a dream!" murmured Léon.

And then, gently fingering the blue border of her long white belt:

"What's to prevent us from beginning all over again, now?"

"No, no," she said. "I'm too old . . . you're too young . . . forget me! You'll find other women to love you . . . and to love."

"Not as I do you!" he cried.

"What a child you are! Come, let's be sensible. I want us to be."

And she explained why they couldn't be lovers, why they must continue to be friends—like brother and sister—as in the past.

Did she mean those things she was saying? Doubtless Emma herself couldn't tell, engrossed as she was by the charm of seduction and the need to defend herself. Looking fondly at the young man, she gently repulsed the timid caresses his trembling hands essayed.

"Ah! Forgive me!" he said, drawing back.

And Emma was seized by a vague terror in the face of this timidity, a greater danger for her than Rodolphe's boldness when he had advanced with outstretched arms. Never had any man seemed to her so handsome. There was an exquisite candor about him. His long, fine, curving eyelashes were lowered; the smooth skin of his cheek was flushing with desire for her—so she thought; and she felt an all but invincible longing to touch it with her lips. She leaned away toward the clock, as though to see the time.

"Heavens!" she said. "How late! How we've been chattering!"

He understood, and rose to go.

"I forgot all about the opera! And poor Bovary left me here on purpose to see it! It was all arranged that I was to go with Monsieur and Madame Lormeaux, of the Rue Grand-Pont!"

It was her last chance, too, for she was leaving the next day.

"Really?" said Léon.

"Yes."

"But I must see you again," he said. "I had something to tell you. . . ."

"What?"

"Something . . . something serious, important. No—really: you mustn't go, you mustn't. If you knew . . . Listen . . . You haven't understood me, then? You haven't guessed . . ."

"On the contrary, you have a very clear way of putting things," said Emma.

"Ah! Now you're laughing at me! Please don't! Have pity on me: let me see you again. Once—just once."

"Well . . ."

She paused; then, as though changing her mind:

"Not here, certainly!"

"Wherever you like."

"Will you . . ."

She seemed to ponder; and then, tersely:

"Tomorrow at eleven in the cathedral."

"I'll be there!" he cried. He seized her hands, but she pulled them away.

They were standing close together, he behind and she with lowered head, and he bent over and kissed her long and lingeringly on the nape of the neck.

"You're crazy, crazy!" she cried between short bursts of laughter as he kissed her again and again.

Then, leaning his head over her shoulder, he seemed to be imploring her eyes to say yes, but the gaze he received was icy and aloof.

Léon stepped back; in the doorway he paused, and tremblingly whispered:

"Till tomorrow."

Her only reply was a nod, and like a bird she vanished into the adjoining room.

That night Emma wrote the clerk an endless letter canceling their appointment: everything was over between them, and for the sake of their own happiness they must never meet again. But when she finished the letter she didn't know what to do with it—she hadn't Léon's address.

"I'll give it to him myself," she thought, "when he comes."

Léon, the next morning—humming a tune on his balcony beside his open window—polished his pumps himself, going over them again and again. He donned a pair of white trousers, fine socks, and a green tail coat; he doused his handkerchief with all the perfumes he possessed, had his hair curled, then uncurled it again to make it look more elegantly natural.

"Still too early!" he thought: he was looking at the barber's cuckoo clock, and it pointed to nine.

He read an old fashion magazine, went out, smoked a cigar, walked a few blocks. Finally he decided it was time to go, and set off briskly toward the Parvis Notre-Dame.

It was a fine summer morning. Silver gleamed in jewelers' windows, and the sunlight slanting onto the cathedral flashed on the cut surface of the gray stone; a flock of birds was swirling in the blue sky around the trefoiled turrets; the square, echoing with cries, smelled of the flowers that edged its pavement—roses, jasmine, carnations, narcissus and tuberoses interspersed with well-watered plants of catnip and chickweed. The fountain gurgled in the center; and under great umbrellas, among piles of cantaloups, bareheaded flower-women were twisting paper around bunches of violets.

The young man chose one. It was the first time he had bought flowers for a woman; and his chest swelled with pride as he inhaled their fragrance, as though this homage that he intended for another were being paid, instead, to him.

But he was afraid of being seen, and resolutely entered the church.

The verger was just then standing in the left doorway, under the figure of the dancing Salomé. He was in full regalia, with plumed hat, rapier and staff, more majestic than a cardinal, shining like a pyx.

He advanced toward Léon, and with the smiling, bland benignity of a priest questioning a child, he said:

"Monsieur is from out of town, perhaps? Monsieur would like to visit the church?"

"No," said Léon.

He walked down one of the side aisles and up the other, then stood outside and looked over the square; there was no sign of Emma, and he re-entered the church and strolled as far as the choir.

The nave was mirrored in the holy-water fonts, with the lower portions of the ogives and some of the stained glass; the reflection of the painted windows broke off at the marble rim only to continue beyond, on the pavement, like a many-colored carpet. Brilliant daylight streamed into the church in three enormous shafts through the three open portals. Now and again a sacristan moved across the far end, dipping before the altar in the half-sidewise genuflection practiced by hurried worshippers. The crystal chandeliers hung motionless. A silver lamp was burning in the choir; and from the side chapels and shadowy corners of the church came an occasional sound like a sigh, and the noise of a metal gate clanging shut and echoing under the lofty vaults.

Léon walked meditatively, keeping near the walls. Never had life seemed so good. Any minute now she would appear, charming, all aquiver, turning around to see whether anyone was looking—with her flounced dress, her gold eyeglass, her dainty shoes, all kinds of feminine elegancies he had never had a taste of, and all the ineffable allurement of virtue on the point of yielding. The church was like a gigantic boudoir, suffused by her image: the vaults curved dimly down to breathe in the avowal of her love; the windows were ablaze to cast their splendor on her face; and even the incense burners were lighted, to welcome her like an angel amid clouds of perfume.

But still she didn't come. He took a chair and his eyes rested on a blue stained-glass window showing boatmen carrying baskets. He stared at it fixedly, counting the scales on the fish and the buttonholes in the doublets, his thoughts meanwhile roving in search of Emma.

The verger, standing to one side, was raging inwardly at this person who was taking it upon himself to admire the cathedral on his own. He was behaving monstrously, he considered: he was stealing from him, really—almost committing sacrilege.

Then there was a rustle of silk on the stone pavement, the edge of a hat under a hooded cape. . . . It was she! Léon jumped up and ran to meet her.

She was pale. She walked quickly.

"Read this!" she said, holding out a sheet of paper. "Oh, no!"

And abruptly she drew back her hand and turned into the chapel of the Virgin, where she knelt down against a chair and began to pray.

The young man was irritated by this sanctimonious bit of whimsy; then he felt a certain charm at seeing her, in the midst of a love meeting, plunged into devotions like an Andalusian *marquesa;* but he soon grew impatient, for there seemed to be no end to it.

Emma was praying, or rather forcing herself to pray, in the hope that heaven might miraculously send her strength of will; and to draw down divine aid she filled her eyes with the splendors of the tabernacle, she breathed the fragrance of the sweet rockets, white and lush in their tall vases, and she listened intently to the silence of the church, which only increased the tumult of her heart.

She rose, and they were about to leave when the verger came swiftly over:

"Madame is perhaps from out of town? Madame would like to visit the church?"

"Oh, no!" the clerk cried.

"Why not?" she retorted.

Her desperate attempt to steady her virtue made her clutch at the Virgin, at the sculptures, at the tombs, at anything that came to hand.

Insisting that they must "begin at the beginning," the verger led them outside the entrance door to the edge of the square, and there pointed with his staff to a large circle of black stones in the pavement, devoid of carving or inscription:

"That," he said majestically, "is the circumference of the great Amboise bell. It weighed forty thousand pounds. It was without equal in all Europe. The workman who cast it died of joy. . . ."

"Let's get away from here," said Léon.

The guide moved on; and back in the chapel of the Virgin he extended his arms in a showman's gesture that took in everything, and addressed them more proudly than a gentleman farmer displaying his fruit trees:

"This plain stone marks the resting place of Pierre de Brézé, lord of La Varenne and Brissac, grand marshal of Poitou and governor of Normandy, killed at the battle of Montlhéry, July 16, 1465."

Léon bit his lips in a fury of impatience.

"And on the right the nobleman in full armor on a rearing horse is his grandson Louis de Brézé, lord of Braval and Montchauvet, comte de Maulevrier, baron de Mauny, royal chamberlain, knight of the order and likewise governor of Normandy, who died July 23, 1531, a Sunday, as it says on the inscription; and below, the man about to descend into the tomb represents the same person exactly.

Human mortality has never been more perfectly represented."

Madame Bovary raised her eyeglass. Léon stood still
and stared at her, no longer even trying to utter a word or
make the slightest move, so discouraged was he by this
combination of patter and indifference.

The guide droned on:

"Near him, there, that kneeling weeping woman is his
wife, Diane de Poitiers, comtesse de Brézé, duchesse de
Valentinois, born 1499, died 1566; and on the left, holding
a child, the Holy Virgin. Now face this way: those are the
tombs of the Amboises. They were both cardinals and arch-
bishops of Rouen. That one was one of King Louis XII's
ministers. He was a great benefactor of the cathedral. In
his will he left 30,000 *écus d'or* for the poor."

And immediately, without interrupting his stream of
talk, he pushed them into a chapel cluttered with railings,
some of which he moved aside to reveal a blockish object
that looked like a roughly carved statue.

"This," he said with a deep sigh, "once formed part of the
decoration of the tomb of Richard Coeur-de-Lion, king of
England and duke of Normandy. It was the Calvinists,
Monsieur, who reduced it to the condition in which you see
it now. Out of pure malice they buried it in the earth,
under Monseigneur's episcopal throne. That door, there,
by the way, is the one he uses—Monseigneur, I mean—to
reach his residence. Now we'll move on to the gargoyle
windows."

But Léon hastily took a silver piece from his pocket and
grasped Emma's arm. The verger was taken aback, mystified
by such premature munificence: the visitor still had so
much to see! He called after him:

"Monsieur! The steeple! The steeple!"

"No, thanks," said Léon.

"Monsieur is wrong! It's going to be four hundred forty

feet high, only nine feet lower than the Great Pyramid
of Egypt. It's entirely of cast iron, it . . ."

Léon fled, for it seemed to him that his love, after being
reduced to stonelike immobility in the church for nearly
two hours, was now going to vanish like smoke up that
truncated pipe, that elongated cage, that fretwork chimney, or what you will, that perches so precariously and
grotesquely atop the cathedral like the wild invention of a
crazy metal-worker.

"But where are we going?" she asked.

Making no answer, he continued swiftly on, and Madame
Bovary was already dipping a finger in the holy water when
behind them they heard a sound of heavy panting regularly
punctuated by the tapping of a staff. Léon turned around.

"Monsieur!"

"What?"

It was the verger, holding about twenty thick paper-
bound volumes against his stomach. They were "books
about the cathedral."

"Fool!" muttered Léon, hurrying out of the church.

An urchin was playing in the square:

"Go get me a cab!"

The youngster vanished like a shot up the Rue des
Quatre-Vents, and for a few minutes they were left alone,
face to face and a little constrained.

"Oh, Léon! Really—I don't know whether I should . . . !"

She simpered. Then, in a serious tone:

"Its very improper, you know."

"What's improper about it?" retorted the clerk. "Everybody does it in Paris!"

It was an irresistible and clinching argument.

But there was no sign of a cab. Léon was terrified lest
she retreat into the church. Finally the cab appeared.

"Drive past the north door, at least!" cried the verger,
from the entrance. "Take a look at the Resurrection, the

Last Judgment, Paradise, King David, and the souls of the damned in the flames of hell!"

"Where does Monsieur wish to go?" asked the driver.

"Anywhere!" said Léon, pushing Emma into the carriage.

And the lumbering contraption rolled away.

It went down the Rue Grand-Pont, crossed the Place des Arts, the Quai Napoléon and the Pont Neuf, and stopped in front of the statue of Pierre Corneille.

"Keep going!" called a voice from within.

It started off again, and gathering speed on the downgrade beyond the Carrefour Lafayette it came galloping up to the railway station.

"No! Straight on!" cried the same voice.

Rattling out through the station gates, the cab soon turned into the Boulevard, where it proceeded at a gentle trot between the double row of tall elms. The coachman wiped his brow, stowed his leather hat between his legs, and veered the cab off beyond the side lanes to the grass strip along the river front.

It continued along the river on the cobbled towing path for a long time in the direction of Oyssel, leaving the islands behind.

But suddenly it rushed off through Quatre-Mares, Sotteville, the Grande-Chaussée, the Rue d'Elbeuf, and made its third stop—this time at the Jardin des Plantes.

"Drive on!" cried the voice, more furiously.

And abruptly starting off again it went through Saint-Sever, along the Quai des Curandiers and the Quai aux Meules, recrossed the bridge, crossed the Place du Champ-de-Mars and continued on behind the garden of the hospital, where old men in black jackets were strolling in the sun on a terrace green with ivy. It went up the Boulevard Bouvreuil, along the Boulevard Cauchoise, and traversed Mont-Riboudet as far as the hill at Deville.

There it turned back; and from then on it wandered at random, without apparent goal. It was seen at Saint-Pol, at Lescure, at Mont-Gargan, at Rouge-Mare and the Place du Gaillardbois; in the Rue Maladrerie, the Rue Dinanderie, and in front of one church after another— Saint-Romain, Saint-Vivien, Saint-Maclou, Saint-Nicaise; in front of the customs house, at the Basse Vieille-Tour, at Trois-Pipes, and at the Cimetière Monumental. From his seat the coachman now and again cast a desperate glance at a café. He couldn't conceive what locomotive frenzy was making these people persist in refusing to stop. He tried a few times, only to hear immediate angry exclamations from behind. So he lashed the more furiously at his two sweating nags, and paid no attention whatever to bumps in the road; he hooked into things right and left; he was past caring—demoralized, and almost weeping from thirst, fatigue, and despair.

Along the river front amidst the trucks and the barrels, along the streets from the shelter of the guard posts, the bourgeois stared wide-eyed at this spectacle unheard of in the provinces—a carriage with drawn shades that kept appearing and reappearing, sealed tighter than a tomb and tossing like a ship.

At a certain moment in the early afternoon, when the sun was blazing down most fiercely on the old silver-plated lamps, a bare hand appeared from under the little yellow cloth curtains and threw out some torn scraps of paper. The wind caught them and scattered them, and they alighted at a distance, like white butterflies, on a field of flowering red clover.

Then, about six o'clock, the carriage stopped in a side street near the Place Beauvoisine. A woman alighted from it and walked off, her veil down, without a backward glance.

II

WHEN SHE REACHED THE HOTEL, MADAME BOVARY WAS SUR-
prised to see no sign of the stagecoach. Hivert had waited
for her fifty-three minutes, and then driven off.

Nothing really obliged her to go, even though she had
said that she would be back that evening. But Charles
would be waiting for her: and in advance her heart was
filled with that craven submissiveness with which many
women both redeem their adultery and punish themselves
for it.

She quickly packed her bag, paid her bill, and hired a gig
in the yard. She told the driver to hurry, and kept urging
him on and asking him the time and how many miles they
had gone. They caught up with the Hirondelle on the outskirts of Quincampoix.

She shut her eyes almost before she was seated in her
corner, and opened them at the outskirts of· the village:
ahead she saw Félicité standing watch outside the blacksmith's. Hivert pulled up the horses, and the cook, standing on tiptoe to address her through the window, said
with an air of mystery:

"Madame, you must go straight to Monsieur Homais'.
It's something urgent."

The village was silent as usual. Little pink mounds were
steaming in the gutters: it was jelly-making time, and
everyone in Yonville was putting up the year's supply the
same day. The mound in front of the pharmacy was by far
the largest and most impressive, and quite properly so: a

laboratory must always be superior to home kitchens; a universal demand must always overshadow mere individual tastes!

She went in. The big armchair was overturned, and—what was more shocking—the *Fanal de Rouen* itself had been left lying on the floor between the two pestles. She pushed open the hall door, and in the middle of the kitchen —amid earthenware jars full of stemmed currants, grated sugar, lump sugar, scales on the table and pans on the fire—she found all the Homais', big and little, swathed to the chin in aprons and wielding forks. Justin was standing there hanging his head, and the pharmacist was shouting:

"Who told you to go get it in the Capharnaum?"

"What is it?" Emma asked. "What's the matter?"

"What's the matter?" replied the apothecary. "We're making jelly. It's on the fire. It threatens to boil over. I call for another pan. And this good-for-nothing, out of sheer laziness, goes and takes—goes into my laboratory and takes off the hook—the key to the Capharnaum!"

Such was the apothecary's name for a small room under the eaves, filled with pharmaceutical utensils and supplies. He often spent long hours there alone, labeling, decanting, repackaging. He considered it not a mere storeroom, but a veritable sanctuary, birthplace of all kinds of pills, boluses, tisanes, lotions and potions concocted by himself and destined to spread his renown throughout the countryside. Not another soul ever set foot in it: so fiercely did he respect the place that he even swept it out himself. If the pharmacy, open to all comers, was the arena where he paraded in all his glory, the Capharnaum was the hideaway where he rapturously pursued his favorite occupations in selfish seclusion. No wonder Justin's carelessness seemed to him a monstrous bit of irreverence. His face was redder than the currants as he continued his tirade:

"Yes, the key to the Capharnaum! The key that guards

the acids and the caustic alkalis! And to calmly go and take one of the spare pans! A pan with a lid! One I may never use! Every detail is important in an art as precise as ours! Distinctions must be preserved! Pharmaceutical implements mustn't be used for near-domestic tasks! It's like carving a chicken with a scalpel, as though a judge were to . . ."

"Stop exciting yourself!" Madame Homais kept saying.

And Athalie pulled at his frock coat and cried: "Papa! Papa!"

"No! Leave me alone!" ordered the apothecary. "Leave me alone! God! I might as well be a grocer, I swear! Go ahead—go right ahead—*don't* respect anything! Smash! Crash! Let the leeches loose! Burn the marshmallow! Make pickles in the medicine jars! Slash up the bandages!"

"But you had something to . . ." said Emma.

"One moment, Madame!—Do you know the risk you were running? Didn't you notice anything in the corner, on the left, on the third shelf? Open your mouth! Say something!"

"I . . . don't . . . know . . ." stammered the boy.

"Ah! You don't know! Well, *I* know! You saw a bottle, a blue glass bottle sealed with yellow wax, with white powder in it, and that I myself marked *Dangerous!* Do you know what's in that bottle? Arsenic! And you go meddling with that! You take a pan that's standing right beside it!"

"Right beside it!" cried Madame Homais, clasping her hands. "Arsenic! You might have poisoned us all!"

And the children began to scream, as though they were already prey to the most frightful gastric pains.

"Or you might have poisoned a patient!" the apothecary persisted. "Do you want me to be hauled into court as a common criminal? Do you want to see me dragged to the scaffold? Don't you know how very careful I am about handling anything, no matter how many million times I may have done it before? Sometimes I'm terrified at the thought of my responsibilities! The government positively hounds us! The legal restrictions are absurd—a veritable sword of Damocles hanging over our heads!"

Emma had given up any attempt to ask what was wanted of her, and the pharmacist breathlessly continued:

"That's your way of being grateful for all the kindness you've been shown! That's how you repay me for the father's care I've showered on you! Where would you be if it weren't for me? What would you be doing? Who gives you your food and your lodging, and training, and clothing —everything you need to become a respectable member of society some day? But to achieve that you've got to bend your back to the oar—get some calluses on your hands, as the saying goes. *Fabricando fit faber, age quod agis.*"

His rage had sent him into Latin: he would have spouted Chinese or Greenlandic had he been able to, for he was in the throes of one of those crises in which the soul lays bare its every last corner, just as the ocean, in the travail of storm, splits open to display everything from the seaweed on its shores to the sand of its deepest bottom.

And he went on:

"I'm beginning to repent bitterly that I ever took you into my charge! I'd have done far better to leave you as I found you—let you wallow in the misery and filth you were born in! You'll never be fit to do anything except look after the cows! You haven't the makings of a scientist! You're scarcely capable of sticking on a label! And you live here at my expense, gorging yourself like a priest, like a pig in clover!"

Emma turned to Madame Homais:

"I was told to come . . ."

"I know," the lady said, wringing her hands, "but how can I possibly tell you . . . ? It's a calamity . . ."

She left her words unfinished. The apothecary was thundering on:

"Empty it out! Scour it! Take it back! Be quick about it!"

And as he shook Justin by the collar of his overall a book fell out of one of the pockets.

The boy bent down for it, but Homais was quicker, and he picked up the book and stared at it open-mouthed.

"*Conjugal . . . Love!*" he cried, placing a deliberate pause between the two words. "Ah! Very good! *Very good!* Charming, in fact! And with illustrations . . . Really! This goes beyond everything!"

Madame Homais stepped forward as though to look.

"No! Don't touch it!"

The children clamored to see the pictures.

"Leave the room!" he said imperiously.

They left.

First he strode up and down, holding the volume open, rolling his eyes, choking, puffing, apoplectic. Then he walked straight up to his apprentice and stood in front of him, arms folded.

"So you're going in for *all* the vices, are you, you little wretch? Watch out, you're on the downward path! Did it ever occur to you that this wicked book might fall into my children's hands? It might be just the spark that . . . It might sully the purity of Athalie! It might corrupt Napoléon! Physically, he's a man already! Are you sure, at least, that they haven't read it? Can you swear to me . . ."

"Really, Monsieur," said Emma. "Did you have something to tell me?"

"So I did, Madame. . . . Your father-in-law is dead!"

It was true: the elder Bovary had died two days before, very suddenly, from an apoplectic stroke, as he was leaving the table; and Charles, overanxious to spare Emma's sensibilities, had asked Monsieur Homais to acquaint her tactfully with the horrible news.

The pharmacist had devoted much thought to the wording of his announcement. He had rounded it and polished it and given it cadence. It was a masterpiece of discretion and transition, of subtlety and shading. But anger had swept away rhetoric.

Emma, seeing that it was useless to ask for details, left the pharmacy, for Monsieur Homais had resumed his vituperations. He was quieting down, however, and now was grumbling in a fatherly way as he fanned himself with his cap:

"It's not that I disapprove entirely of the book. The author was a doctor. It deals with certain scientific aspects that it does a man no harm to know about—aspects, if I may say so, that a man *has* to know about. But later, later! Wait till you're a man yourself, at least; wait till your character's formed."

The sound of the knocker told the expectant Charles that Emma had arrived, and he came toward her with open arms. There were tears in his voice:

"*Ah! Ma chère amie . . .*"

And he bent down gently to kiss her. But at the touch of his lips the memory of Léon gripped her, and she passed her hand over her face and shuddered.

Nevertheless she answered him. "Yes," she said. "I know . . . I know . . ."

He showed her the letter in which his mother told what had happened, without any sentimental hypocrisy. Her only regret was that her husband had not received the succor of the church: he had died not at home, but at

Doudeville, in the street, just outside a café, after a patriotic banquet with some ex-army officers.

Emma handed back the letter. At dinner she pretended
a little for the sake of good manners to have no appetite,
but when Charles urged her, she proceeded to eat heartily,
while he sat opposite her motionless, weighed down by
grief.

Now and again he lifted his head and gave her a long,
stricken look.

"I wish I could have seen him again!" he sighed.

She made no answer. And finally, when she knew that
she must say something:

"How old was your father?"

"Fifty-eight."

"Ah!"

And that was all.

A little later:

"My poor mother!" he said. "What's to become of her
now?"

She conveyed with a gesture that she had no idea.

Seeing her so silent, Charles supposed that she, too, was
affected, and he forced himself to say no more lest he
exacerbate her sorrow, which he found touching. But for a
moment he roused himself from his own.

"Did you have a good time yesterday?" he asked.

"Yes."

When the tablecloth was removed, Bovary did not get
up, nor did Emma; and as she continued to look at him the
monotony of the sight gradually banished all compassion
from her heart. He seemed to her insignificant, weak, a
nonentity—contemptible in every way. How could she
rid herself of him? What an endless evening! She felt torpid,
drugged, as though from opium fumes.

From the entry came the sharp tap of a stick on the
wooden floor. It was Hippolyte, bringing Madame's bags.

To set them down, he swung his wooden leg around in an awkward quarter-circle.

"Charles doesn't even think about him any more," she remarked to herself as she watched the poor devil, his mop of red hair dripping sweat.

Bovary fumbled in his purse for a coin; and, apparently unaware of the humiliation implicit in the very presence of the man who was standing there, like a living reproach for his incurable ineptitude:

"Oh, you have a pretty bouquet!" he said, noticing Léon's violets on the mantelpiece.

"Yes," she said carelessly. "I bought it just before I left —from a beggar-woman."

Charles took up the violets, held their coolness against his tear-reddened eyes, and gently sniffed them. She quickly took them from his hand, and went to put them in a glass of water.

The following day the older Madame Bovary arrived. She and her son did a good deal of weeping. Emma, pleading household duties, kept out of the way. The day after that, they had to consult about mourning, and the three of them sat down together, the ladies with their workboxes, under the arbor on the river bank.

Charles thought about his father, and was surprised to feel so much affection for one whom up till then he had thought he loved but little. The older Madame Bovary thought of her husband. The worst of her times with him seemed desirable now. Everything was submerged in grief, so intensely did she miss the life she was used to; and from time to time as she plied her needle a great tear rolled down her nose and hung there for a moment before dropping. Emma was thinking that scarcely forty-eight hours before they had been together, shut away from the world, in ecstasy, devouring each other with their eyes. She tried to recapture the tiniest details of that vanished day. But the presence of her mother-in-law and her husband interfered. She wished she could hear nothing, see nothing: she wanted merely to be left alone to evoke her love, which despite her best efforts was becoming blurred under the impact of external impressions.

She was ripping the lining of a dress, and scraps of the material lay scattered around her; the older Madame Bovary, never raising her eyes, kept squeaking away with her scissors; and Charles, in his cloth slippers and the old brown frock coat that he used as a dressing gown, kept his hand in his pockets and said no more than the others. Near them, Berthe, in a little white apron, was scraping the gravel of the path with her shovel.

Suddenly they saw Monsieur Lheureux, the dry-goods dealer, push open the gate.

He had come to offer his services "on this very sad occasion." Emma answered that she thought she could do without them. But the shopkeeper did not concede defeat.

"If you'll excuse me," he said, "I'd like to speak to you privately."

And in a low voice:

"It's about that little matter . . . you know what I'm referring to?"

Charles blushed to the roots of his hair.

"Oh, yes . . . of course."

And in his embarrassment he turned to his wife:

"Darling, would you take care of . . . ?"

She seemed to understand, for she rose; and Charles said to his mother:

"It's nothing—just some household detail, I imagine."

He didn't want her to learn about the promissory note: he dreaded her comments.

As soon as Emma was alone with Monsieur Lheureux he began to congratulate her rather bluntly on coming into money, and then spoke of indifferent matters—fruit trees, the harvest, and his own health, which was always the same, "so-so, could be worse." He worked like a galley slave, he informed her, and even so, despite what people said about him, he didn't make enough to buy butter for his bread.

Emma let him talk. She had been so prodigiously bored these last two days!

"And you're entirely well again?" he went on. "Your husband was in quite a state, I can tell you! He's a fine fellow, even if we did have a little trouble."

"What trouble?" she asked, for Charles had told her nothing about the dispute over the various items.

"But you know perfectly well!" said Lheureux. "About the little things you wanted—the trunks."

He had pushed his hat forward over his eyes, and with his hands behind his back, smiling, and whistling to himself under his breath, he was staring straight at her in a way she found intolerable. Did he suspect something? She waited in a panic of apprehension. But finally he said:

"We made it up, and I came today to propose another arrangement."

What he proposed was the renewal of the note signed by Bovary. Monsieur should of course do as he pleased: he shouldn't worry, especially now that he was going to have so many other things on his mind.

"He'd really do best to turn it over to somebody else—you, for example. With a power of attorney everything would be very simple, and then you and I could attend to our little affairs together."

She didn't understand. He let the matter drop, and turned the conversation back to dry goods: Madame really couldn't not order something from him. He'd send her a piece of black barège—twelve meters, enough to make a dress.

"The one you have there is all right for the house, but you need another for going out. I saw that the minute I came in. I've got an eye like a Yankee!"

He didn't send the material: he brought it. Then he came again to do the measuring, and again and again on other pretexts, each time putting himself out to be agreeable and helpful—making himself her liegeman, as Homais might have put it—and always slipping in a few words of advice about the power of attorney. He didn't mention the promissory note. It didn't occur to her to think of it: early in her convalescence Charles had, in fact, said something to her about it, but her mind had been so agitated that she had forgotten. Moreover she was careful never to bring up anything about money matters. This surprised her mother-in-law, who attributed her new attitude to the religious sentiments she had acquired during her illness.

But as soon as the older woman left, Emma lost no time in impressing Bovary with her practical good sense. It was up to them, she said, to make inquiries, check on mortgages, see if there were grounds for liquidating the property by auction or otherwise. She used technical terms at random, and impressive words like "order," "the future" and "foresight," and she continually exaggerated the complications attendant on inheritance. Then one day she showed him the draft of a general authorization to "manage and administer his affairs, negotiate all loans, sign and endorse all promissory notes, pay all sums," etc. She had profited from Lheureux's lessons.

Charles naïvely asked her where the document came from.

"From Maître Guillaumin."

And with the greatest coolness imaginable she added:

"I haven't too much confidence in him. You hear such dreadful things about notaries! Perhaps we ought to consult . . . We don't know anyone except . . . We don't know anyone, really."

"Unless Léon . . ." said Charles, who was thinking hard.

But it was difficult to make things clear by letter. So she offered to make the trip. He thanked her but said she mustn't. She insisted. Each outdid the other in consideration. Finally, imitating the pert disobedience of a child, she cried:

"I will, too, go! I will!"

"How good you are!" he said, kissing her on the forehead.

The next morning she set out in the Hirondelle for Rouen to consult Monsieur Léon, and she stayed there three days.

III

THEY WERE THREE FULL, EXQUISITE, GLORIOUS DAYS, A REAL honeymoon.

They stayed at the Hotel de Boulogne on the river front, living there behind drawn shutters and locked doors; their room was strewn with flowers, and iced fruit drinks were brought up to them all day long.

At dusk they hired a covered boat and went to dine on one of the islands.

From the shipyards came the thumping of caulking irons against hulls. Wisps of tar smoke curled up from among the trees, and on the river floated great oily patches, the color of Florentine bronze, undulating unevenly in the purple glow of the sun.

They drifted downstream amidst anchored craft whose long slanting cables grazed the top of their boat.

The sounds of the city gradually receded—the rattle of wagons, the tumult of voices, the barking of dogs on the decks of ships. As they touched the shore of their island she loosened the silk ribbon of her hat.

They sat in the low-ceilinged room of a restaurant with black fishnets hanging at its door, and ate fried smelts, cream and cherries. Then they stretched out on the grass in an out-of-the-way corner and lay in each other's arms under the poplars: they wished they might live forever, like two Robinson Crusoes, in this little spot that seemed to them in their bliss the most magnificent on earth. It wasn't the first time in their lives that they had seen trees, blue sky and lawn, or heard the flowing of water or the rustle of the breeze in the branches, but never before, certainly, had they looked on it all with such wonder: it was as though nature had not existed before, or had only begun to be beautiful with the slaking of their desires.

At nightfall they returned to the city. The boat followed the shoreline of the islands, and they crouched deep in its shadow, not saying a word. The square-tipped oars clicked in the iron oar-locks: it sounded, in the silence, like the beat of a metronome, and the rope trailing behind kept up its gentle splashing in the water.

One night the moon shone out, and of course they rhapsodized about how melancholy and poetical it was. She even sang a little:

> *One night—dost thou remember?—*
> *We were sailing . . .*

Her sweet, small voice died away over the river: borne off on the breeze were the trills that Léon heard flit past him like the fluttering of wings.

She was sitting opposite him, leaning against the wall of the little cabin, the moonlight streaming in on her through an open shutter. In her black dress, its folds spreading out around her like a fan, she looked taller, slimmer. Her head was raised, her hands were clasped, her eyes turned heavenward. One moment she would be hidden by the shadow of some willows; the next, she would suddenly re-emerge in the light of the moon like an apparition.

Léon, sitting on the bottom beside her, picked up a bright red ribbon.

The boatman looked at it.

"Oh," he said, "that's probably from a party I took out the other day. They were a jolly lot, all right, the men *and* the girls: they brought along food and champagne and music—the whole works. There was one of them, especially —a big, good-looking fellow with a little mustache—he was a riot. They all kept after him. 'Come on, tell us a story, Adolphe'—or Dodolphe, or some name like that."

She shuddered.

"Don't you feel well?" asked Léon, moving closer to her.

"Oh, it's nothing. Just a chill."

"He was another one who never had to worry about where his women would come from," the old boatman added softly, as a compliment to his present passenger.

Then he spit on his hands and took up his oars.

But finally they had to part. Their farewells were sad. He was to write her in care of Madame Rollet; and she gave him such detailed instructions about using a double envelope that he marveled greatly at her shrewdness in love matters.

"So I have your word for it that everything's in order?" she said, as they kissed for the last time.

"Absolutely— But why the devil," he wondered, as he walked home alone through the streets, "is she so set on having that power of attorney?"

IV

BEFORE LONG, LÉON BEGAN TO GIVE HIMSELF SUPERIOR AIRS around the office. He kept aloof from his colleagues and totally neglected his work. He waited for Emma's letters, and read them over and over. He wrote to her. He evoked her image with all the strength of his passion and his memories. Far from being lessened by absence, his longing to see her again increased, until finally one Saturday morning he took the road to Yonville.

When he looked down on the valley from the top of the hill and saw the church steeple with its tin flag turning in the wind, he was filled with an exquisite pleasure: smug satisfaction and selfish sentimentality were mingled in it —it was the feeling that a millionaire must experience on revisiting his boyhood village.

He prowled around her house. A light was burning in the kitchen. He watched for her shadow behind the curtains. Not a soul was to be seen.

Madame Lefrançois uttered loud cries at the sight of him, and said that he was "taller and thinner." Artémise, on the other hand, found that he had grown "heavier and darker."

He took his dinner in the small dining room, just as in the old days, but alone, without the tax collector: for Binet, sick of waiting for the Hirondelle, had permanently changed his mealtime to an hour earlier, and now dined on the stroke of five. Even so he never missed a chance to grumble that "the rusty old clock was slow."

Finally Léon got up his courage and knocked on the doctor's door. Madame was in her room: it was a quarter of an hour before she came down. Monsieur seemed delighted to see him again, but didn't stir from the house all evening or all the next day.

Only late Sunday evening did he see her alone, in the lane behind the garden—in the lane, just like Rodolphe. It was during a thunderstorm, and they talked under an umbrella, with lightning flashing around them.

The thought of parting was unbearable.

"I'd rather die!" said Emma.

She clung convulsively to his arm and wept:

"Adieu! Adieu! When will I see you again?"

They separated, then turned back for a last embrace; and it was at that moment that she promised him to find, soon, no matter how, some way in which they would be able to see each other alone and regularly, at least once a week. Emma had no doubt about succeeding. She looked forward to the future with confidence: the inheritance money would shortly be coming in.

On the strength of it she bought, for her bedroom, a pair of wide-striped yellow curtains that Monsieur Lheureux extolled as a bargain. She said she wished she could have a carpet; and Lheureux, assuring her that she wasn't "reaching for the moon," promised very obligingly to find her one. By now she didn't know how she could get along without him. She sent for him twenty times a day, and he always promptly left whatever he was doing and came, without a word of protest. Nor was it clear to anyone why Madame Rollet lunched at her house every day, and even visited with her privately.

It was about this time—the beginning of winter—that she became intensely musical.

One evening while Charles was listening she started the same piece over again four times, each time expressing annoyance with herself. Charles was unaware of anything wrong. "Bravo!" he cried. "Very good! Why stop? Keep going."

"No, I'm playing abominably. My fingers are rusty."

The next day he asked her to "play him something else."

"Very well, if you like."

Charles had to admit that she seemed a little out of practice. She fumbled, struck wrong notes, and finally broke off abruptly:

"That's enough of that! I should take some lessons, but . . ."

She bit her lips and added: "Twenty francs an hour—it's too expensive."

"Yes, it certainly is . . . a little . . ." said Charles, with a silly giggle. "But it seems to me you ought to be able to find somebody for less. There are plenty of musicians without big names who are better than the celebrities."

"Try and find some," said Emma.

When he came in the next day he gave her a sly look, and finally came out with: "You certainly have a way sometimes of thinking you know better than anybody else. I was at Barfeuchères today and Madame Liégeard told me that her three girls—the three at school at the Miséricorde —take lessons at two and a half francs an hour, and from a marvelous teacher!"

She shrugged, and from then on left her instrument unopened.

But whenever she walked by it she would sigh (if Bovary happened to be there): "Ah, my poor piano!"

And she always made a point of telling visitors that she had given up her music and now couldn't possibly go on with it again, for imperative reasons. Everybody pitied her. What a shame! She had so much talent! People even spoke to Bovary about it. They made him feel ashamed, especially the pharmacist.

"You're making a mistake! Natural faculties must never be let lie fallow! Besides, my friend, look at it this way: by encouraging Madame to take lessons now, you'll save money later on your daughter's lessons. In my opinion, mothers should teach their children themselves. It's an idea of Rousseau's—maybe a little new, still, but bound to prevail eventually, I'm sure, like mother's breast feeding and vaccination."

So Charles brought up the question of the piano again. Emma answered tartly that they'd better sell it. Poor old piano! It had so often been a source of pride for him, that to see it go would be like watching Emma commit partial suicide.

"If you really want to go ahead with it," he said, "I suppose a lesson now and then wouldn't ruin us."

"But lessons aren't worth taking," she said, "unless they're taken regularly."

That was how she obtained her husband's permission to go to the city once a week to meet her lover. By the end of the first month everyone found that her playing had improved considerably.

V

AND SO, EVERY THURSDAY, SHE ROSE AND DRESSED WITHOUT A sound, lest she wake Charles, who would have remarked on her getting ready too early. Then she paced up and down, stood at the windows, looked out at the square. The first light of morning was stealing into the pillared market place; and on the pharmacist's house, its shutters still drawn, the pale tints of dawn were picking out the capital letters of the shop sign.

When the clock said quarter past seven she made her way to the Lion d'Or and was let in by the yawning Artémise. The servant paid her the attention of digging out the smoldering coals from under the ashes, and then left her to herself in the kitchen. From time to time she walked out into the yard. Hivert would be harnessing the horses. He went about it very deliberately, listening as he did so to Madame Lefrançois, who had stuck her head, nightcap and all, out of a window and was briefing him on his errands in a way that anyone else would have found bewildering. Emma tapped her foot on the cobbles.

Finally, when he had downed his bowl of soup, put on his overcoat, lighted his pipe and picked up his whip, he unhurriedly climbed onto the seat.

The Hirondelle set off at a gentle trot, and for the first mile or two kept stopping here and there to take on passengers who stood watching for it along the road, outside their gates. Those who had booked seats the day before kept the coach waiting: some, even, were still in their beds, and Hivert would call, shout, curse, and finally get down from his seat and pound on the doors. The wind whistled in through the cracked blinds.

Gradually the four benches filled up, the coach rattled along, row upon row of apple trees flashed by; and the road, lined on each side by a ditch of yellow water, stretched on and on, narrowing toward the horizon.

Emma knew every inch of it: she knew that after a certain meadow came a road sign, then an elm, a barn, or a road-mender's cabin; sometimes she even shut her eyes, trying to give herself a surprise. But she always knew just how much farther there was to go.

Finally the brick houses crowded closer together, the road rang under the wheels, and now the Hirondelle moved smoothly between gardens: through iron fences were glimpses of statues, artificial mounds crowned by arbors, clipped yews, a swing. Then, all at once, the city came into view.

Sloping downward like an amphitheatre, drowned in mist, it sprawled out shapelessly beyond its bridges. Then open fields swept upward again in a monotonous curve, merging at the top with the uncertain line of the pale sky. Thus seen from above, the whole landscape had the static quality of a painting: ships at anchor were crowded into one corner, the river traced its curve along the foot of the green hills, and on the water the oblong-shaped islands looked like great black fish stopped in their course. From the factory chimneys poured endless trails of brown smoke, their tips continually dissolving in the wind. The roar of foundries mingled with the clear peal of chimes that came from the churches looming in the fog. The leafless trees along the boulevards were like purple thickets in amongst the houses; and the roofs, all of them shiny with rain, gleamed with particular brilliance in the upper reaches of the town. Now and again a gust of wind blew the clouds toward the hill of Sainte-Catherine, like aerial waves breaking soundlessly against a cliff.

A kind of intoxication was wafted up to her from those closely packed lives, and her heart swelled as though the 120,000 souls palpitating below had sent up to her as a collective offering the breath of all the passions she supposed them to be feeling. In the face of the vastness her love grew larger, and was filled with a turmoil that echoed the vague ascending hum. All this love she, in turn, poured out—onto the squares, onto the tree-lined avenues, onto the streets; and to her the old Norman city was like some fabulous capital, a Babylon into which she was making her entry. She leaned far out the window and filled her lungs with air; the three horses galloped on, there was a grinding of stones in the mud beneath the wheels; the coach swayed; Hivert shouted warningly ahead to the wagons he was about to overtake, and businessmen leaving their suburban villas in Bois-Guillaume descended the hill at a respectable pace in their little family carriages.

There was a stop at the city gate: Emma took off her overshoes, changed her gloves, arranged her shawl, and twenty paces further on she left the Hirondelle.

The city was coming to life. Clerks in caps were polishing shop windows, and women with baskets on their hips stood on street corners uttering loud, regular cries. She walked on, her eyes lowered, keeping close to the house walls and smiling happily under her lowered black veil.

For fear of being seen, she usually didn't take the shortest way. She would plunge into a maze of dark alleys, and emerge, hot and perspiring, close to the fountain at the lower end of the Rue Nationale. This is the part of town near the theatre, full of bars and prostitutes. Often a van rumbled by, laden with shaky stage-sets. Aproned waiters were sanding the pavement between the tubs of green bushes. There was a smell of absinthe, cigars and oysters.

Then she turned a corner. She recognized him from afar by the way his curly hair hung down below his hat.

He walked ahead on the sidewalk. She followed him to the hotel; he went upstairs, opened the door of the room, went in— What an embrace!

Then, after kisses, came a flood of words. They spoke of the troubles of the week, of their forebodings, their worries about letters; but now they could forget everything, and they looked into each other's eyes, laughing with delight and exchanging loving names.

The bed was a large mahogany one in the form of a boat. Red silk curtains hung from the ceiling and were looped back very low beside the flaring headboard, and there was nothing so lovely in the world as her dark hair and white skin against the deep crimson when she brought her bare arms together in a gesture of modesty, hiding her face in her hands.

The warm room, with its discreet carpet, its pretty knickknacks and its tranquil light, seemed designed for the intimacies of passion. The arrow-tipped curtain rods, the brass ornaments on the furniture and the big knobs on the andirons—all gleamed at once if the sun shone in. Between the candlesticks on the mantelpiece was a pair of those great pink shells that sound like the ocean when you hold them to your ear.

How they loved that sweet, cheerful room, for all its slightly faded splendor! Each piece of furniture was always waiting for them in its place, and sometimes the hairpins she had forgotten the Thursday before were still there, under the pedestal of the clock. They lunched beside the fire, on a little table inlaid with rosewood. Emma carved, murmuring all kinds of endearments as she put the pieces on his plate; and she gave a loud, wanton laugh when the champagne foamed over the fine edge of the glass onto the rings on her fingers. They were so completely lost in their possession of each other that they thought of themselves as being in their own home, destined to live there for the rest of their days, eternal young husband and eternal young wife. They said "our room," "our carpet," "our chairs"; she even said "our slippers," meaning a pair that Léon had given her to gratify a whim. They were of pink satin, trimmed with swansdown. When she sat in his lap her legs swung in the air, not reaching the floor, and the dainty slippers, open all around except at the tip, hung precariously from her bare toes.

He was savoring for the first time the ineffable subtleties of feminine refinement. Never had he encountered this grace of language, this quiet taste in dress, these relaxed, dovelike postures. He marveled at the sublimity of her soul and at the lace on her petticoat. Besides—wasn't she a "lady," and married besides? Everything, in short, that a mistress should be?

With her ever-changing moods, by turns brooding and gay, chattering and silent, fiery and casual, she aroused in him a thousand desires, awakening instincts or memories. She was the *amoureuse* of all the novels, the heroine of all the plays, the vague "she" of all the poetry books. Her shoulders were amber-toned, like the bathing odalisques he had seen in pictures; she was long-waisted like the feudal chatelaines; she resembled Musset's *"pâle femme de Barcelone,"* too: but at all times she was less woman than angel!

Often, as he looked at her, it seemed to him that his soul, leaving him in quest of her, flowed like a wave around the outline of her head, and then was drawn down into the whiteness of her breast.

He would kneel on the floor before her, and with his elbows on her knees gaze at her smilingly, his face lifted.

She would bend toward him and murmur, as though choking with rapture:

"Don't move! Don't say a word! Just look at me! There's something so sweet in your eyes, something that does me so much good!"

She called him "child": "Do you love me, child?"

She never heard his answer, so fast did his lips always rise to meet her mouth.

On the clock there was a little bronze cupid, simpering and curving its arms under a gilded wreath. They often laughed at it, but when it came time to part, everything grew serious.

Motionless, face to face, they would say, over and over: "Till Thursday! Till Thursday!"

Then she would abruptly take his face between her

hands, quickly kiss him on the forehead, cry, "Adieu!" and run out into the hall.

She always went to a hairdresser in the Rue de la Comédie and had her hair brushed and put in order. Darkness would be falling; in the shops they would be lighting the gas.

She could hear the bell in the theatre summoning the actors to the performance, and across the street she would see white-faced men and shabbily dressed women going in through the stage door.

It was hot in this little place with its too-low ceiling and its stove humming in the midst of wigs and pomades. The smell of the curling irons and the touch of the soft hands at work on her head soon made her drowsy, and she dozed off a little in her dressing gown. Often, as he arranged her hair, the coiffeur would ask her to buy tickets for a masked ball.

Then she was off. She retraced her way through the streets, reached the Croix-Rouge, retrieved the overshoes that she had hidden there that morning under a bench, and squeezed herself in among the impatient passengers. To spare the horses, the men got out at the foot of the hill, leaving Emma alone in the coach.

At each bend of the road more and more of the city lights came into view, making a layer of luminous mist that hung over the mass of the houses. Emma would kneel on the cushions and look back, letting her eyes wander over the brilliance. Sobs would burst from her, she would call Léon's name, and send him sweet words, and kisses that were lost in the wind.

On this hill-road was a wretched beggar, who wandered with his stick in the midst of the traffic. His clothes were a mass of rags, and his face was hidden under a battered old felt hat that was turned down all around like a basin; when

he took this off, it was to reveal two gaping, bloody sock-
ets in place of eyelids. The flesh continually shredded off in
red gobbets, and from it oozed a liquid matter, hardening
into greenish scabs that reached down to his nose. His
black nostrils sniffled convulsively. Whenever he began to
talk, he leaned his head far back and gave an idiot laugh;
and at such times his bluish eyeballs, rolling round and
round, pushed up against the edges of the live wound.

As he walked beside the coaches he sang a little song:

> *A clear day's warmth will often move*
> *A lass to stray in dreams of love . . .*

And the rest of it was all about the birds, the sun, and
the leaves on the trees.

Sometimes he would loom up all at once from behind
Emma, bareheaded. She would draw back with a cry.
Hivert always joked with him, urging him to hire a booth
at the Saint-Romain fair, or laughingly asking after the
health of his sweetheart.

Often while the coach was moving slowly up the hill his
hat would suddenly come through the window, and he
would be there, clinging with his other hand to the foot-
board, between the spattering wheels. His voice, at the
outset a mere wail, would grow shrill. It would linger in
the darkness like a plaintive cry of distress; and through the
jingle of the horse bells, the rustle of the trees and the
rumble of the empty coach, there was something eerie
about it that gave Emma a shudder of horror. The sound
spiraled down into the very depths of her soul, like a whirl-
wind in an abyss, and swept her off into the reaches of a
boundless melancholy. But Hivert would become aware
that his vehicle was weighed down on one side, and would
strike out savagely at the blind man with his whip. The
stinging lash would cut into his wounds, and he would drop
off into the mud with a shriek.

One by one the Hirondelle's passengers would fall asleep, some with their mouths open, others with their chins on their chests, leaning on their neighbor's shoulder or with an arm in the strap, all the while rocking steadily with the motion of the coach; and the gleam of the lamp, swaying outside above the rumps of the shaft-horses and shining in through the chocolate-colored calico curtains, cast blood-red shadows on all those motionless travelers. Emma, numb with sadness, would shiver under her coat; her feet would grow colder and colder, and she felt like death.

Charles would be at the house, waiting: the Hirondelle was always late on Thursdays. Then at last Madame would arrive! She would scarcely take time to kiss her little girl. Dinner wasn't ready—no matter! She forgave the cook: Félicité seemed to have everything her own way, these days.

Often her husband would notice her pallor, and ask whether she were ill.

"No," Emma would say.

"But you're acting so strangely tonight!"

"Oh, it's nothing! It's nothing!"

Some Thursdays she went up to her room almost the minute she came in. Justin would be there and would busy himself silently, cleverer at helping her than an experienced ladies' maid. He would arrange matches, candlesticks, a book, lay out her dressing jacket, open her bed.

"Very good," she would tell him. "Now run along."

For he would be standing there, his hands at his sides and his eyes staring, as though a sudden revery had tied him to the spot with a thousand strands.

The next day was always an ordeal, and the days that followed were even more unbearable, so impatient was she to recover her happiness. It was a fierce desire that was kept aflame by the vividness of her memories, and on the seventh day burst forth freely under Léon's caresses. His transports took the form of overflowing wonderment and gratitude. Emma enjoyed this passion in a way that was both deliberate and intense, keeping it alive by every amorous device at her command, and fearing all the while that some day it would come to an end.

Often she would say to him, sweetly and sadly:

"Ah! Sooner or later you'll leave me! You'll marry! You'll be like all the others."

"What others?"

"Why, men—all men."

And, languidly pushing him away, she would add: "You're faithless, every one of you!"

One day when they were having a philosophical discussion about earthly disillusionments, she went so far as to say (whether testing his jealousy, or yielding to an irresistible need to confide) that in the past, before him, she had loved someone else. "Not like you!" she quickly added; and she swore by her daughter that "nothing had happened."

The young man believed her, but nevertheless asked her what kind of man "he" had been.

"He was a sea captain," she told him.

Did she say that, perhaps, to forestall his making any inquiries, and at the same time to exalt herself by making the supposed victim of her charms sound like an imperious kind of man accustomed to having his way?

This impressed upon the clerk the mediocrity of his own status: he longed to have epaulettes, decorations and titles. Such things must be to her liking, he suspected, judging by her spendthrift ways.

There were a number of her wildest ideas, however, that Emma never said a word about, such as her craving to be driven to Rouen in a blue tilbury drawn by an English horse, with a groom in turned-down boots on the seat. It was Justin who had inspired her with this particular fancy, by begging her to take him into her service as footman; and though being deprived of it didn't prevent her from enjoying each weekly arrival in the city, it certainly added to the bitterness of each return to Yonville.

Often, when they spoke of Paris, she would murmur:

"Ah! How happy we'd be, living there!"

"Aren't we happy here?" the young man would softly ask, passing his hand over her hair.

"Of course we are! I'm being foolish. Kiss me!"

With her husband she was more charming than ever; she made him pistachio creams and played waltzes for him after dinner. He considered himself the luckiest of mortals, and Emma had no fear of discovery—until suddenly, one evening:

"It is Mademoiselle Lempereur you take lessons from, isn't it?"

"Yes."

"Well, I just saw her," said Charles, "at Madame Liégeard's. I talked to her about you: she doesn't know you."

It was like a thunderbolt. But she answered in a natural tone.

"Oh, she must have forgotten my name."

"Or else maybe there's more than one Mademoiselle Lempereur in Rouen who teaches piano."

"Maybe so."

Then, quickly:

"Besides, it just occurs to me: I have her receipts. Look!"

And she went to the secretary, rummaged in all the drawers, mixed up all the papers, and finally grew so rattled that Charles begged her not to go to so much trouble for a few wretched receipts.

"Oh, I'll find them," she said.

And indeed, the following Friday, while Charles was putting on one of his shoes in the dark dressing room where his clothes were kept, he felt a piece of paper between the sole and his sock, and pulled it out and read:

"Three months' lessons, plus supplies. Sixty-five francs. Paid. Félicité Lempereur, *Professeur de musique*."

"How the devil did this get in my shoe?"

"It probably fell down from the old bill file on the shelf."

From that moment on, she piled lie upon lie, using them as veils to conceal her love.

Lying became a need, a mania, a positive joy—to such a point that if she said that she had walked down the right-hand side of a street the day before, it meant that she had gone down the left.

One morning just after she had gone, rather lightly clad as usual, there was a sudden snowfall; and Charles, looking out the window at the weather, saw Monsieur Bournisien setting out for Rouen in Monsieur Tuvache's buggy. So he ran down with a heavy shawl and asked the priest to give it to Madame as soon as he got to the Croix-Rouge. The moment he reached the inn, Bournisien asked where the wife of the Yonville doctor was. The hotel-keeper replied that she spent very little time there. That evening, therefore, finding Madame Bovary in the Hirondelle, the curé told her of the *contretemps:* he seemed to attach little importance to it, however, for he launched into praise of a preacher, the sensation at the cathedral, adored by all the ladies.

Still, though he hadn't asked for explanations, others, in the future, might be less discreet. So she thought it practical to take a room each time at the Croix-Rouge, in order that her fellow villagers might see her there and have no suspicion.

One day, however, Monsieur Lheureux ran into her as she was leaving the Hotel de Boulogne on Léon's arm. She was frightened, thinking that he might talk. He was too smart for that.

But three days later he came into her room, closed the door, and said:

"I'd like some money."

She declared that she had none to give him. Lheureux began to moan, and reminded her of how many times he'd gone out of his way to oblige her.

And indeed, of the two notes signed by Charles, Emma had so far paid off only one. As for the second, the shop-keeper had agreed at her request to replace it with two others, which themselves had been renewed for a very long term. Then he drew out of his pocket a list of goods still unpaid for: the curtains, the carpet, upholstery material for armchairs, several dresses and various toilet articles, totaling about two thousand francs.

She hung her head.

"You may not have any cash," he said, "but you do have some property."

And he mentioned a wretched, tumbledown cottage situated at Barneville, near Aumale, which didn't bring in very much. It had once been part of a small farm that the elder Bovary had sold: Lheureux knew everything, down to the acreage and the neighbors' names.

"If I were you I'd get rid of it," he said. "You'd still have a balance after paying me."

She brought up the difficulty of finding a buyer; he was encouraging about the possibility of locating one. But: "What would I have to do to be able to sell?" she asked.

"Haven't you power of attorney?" he countered.

The words came to her like a breath of fresh air.

"Leave your bill with me," said Emma.

"Oh, it's not worth bothering about," replied Lheureux.

He came again the following week, very proud of having unearthed, after a lot of trouble, a certain Monsieur Langlois, who had been eying the property for a long time without ever mentioning the price he was willing to pay.

"The price doesn't matter!" she cried.

On the contrary, he said: they should take their time, sound Langlois out. The affair was worth the bother of a trip, and since she couldn't make it he offered to go himself and talk things over with Langlois on the spot. On his return he announced that the buyer offered 4,000 francs.

Emma beamed at the news.

"Frankly," he said, "it's a good price."

Half the amount was paid her at once, and when she said that now she'd settle his bill, he told her:

"Honestly, it hurts me to see you hand over every bit of all that money right away."

She stared at the banknotes and had a vision of the countless love-meetings those 2,000 francs represented. "What?" she stammered. "What do you mean?"

"Oh," he said, with a jovial laugh, "there's more than one way of making out a bill. Don't you think I know how it is with married couples?"

And he stared at her, running his fingernails up and down two long sheets of paper he had in his hand. After a long moment he opened his billfold and spread out on the table four more promissory notes, each for a thousand francs.

"Sign these," he said, "and keep all the money."

She gave a shocked cry.

"But if I give you the balance," Monsieur Lheureux answered, "don't you see that I'm doing you a service?"

And taking up a pen he wrote at the bottom of the bill: "Received from Madame Bovary the sum of 4,000 francs."

"What's there to worry you? In six months you'll have the rest of the money due on your cottage, and I'll make the last note payable after that date."

She was getting a little mixed up in her arithmetic, and she felt a ringing in her ears as though gold pieces were bursting out of their bags and dropping to the floor all about her. Finally Lheureux explained that he had a friend named Vinçart, a Rouen banker, who would discount these four new notes, following which he himself would pay Madame the balance of what was really owed.

But instead of 2,000 francs, he brought her only 1,800; for his friend Vinçart (as was "only right") had deducted 200, representing commission and discount.

Then he casually asked for a receipt.

"You know . . . in business . . . sometimes . . . And put down the date, please, the date."

A host of things that she could do with the money stretched out before Emma in perspective. She had enough sense to put 3,000 francs aside, and with them she paid, as they came due, the first three notes; but the fourth, as luck would have it, arrived at the house on a Thursday; and Charles, stunned, patiently awaited his wife's return to have it explained to him.

Ah! If she hadn't told him anything about that note it was because she hadn't wanted to bother him with household worries; she sat in his lap, caressed him, cooed at him, and gave a long list of all the indispensables she had bought on credit.

"You'll have to admit," she said, "that considering how many things there were, the bill's not too high."

Charles, at his wits' end, soon had recourse to the inevitable Lheureux, who promised to straighten everything out if Monsieur would sign two more notes, one of them for 700 francs, payable in three months. Charles wrote a pathetic letter to his mother, asking for help. Instead of sending an answer, she came herself; and when Emma asked him if he'd got anything out of her:

"Yes," he answered. "But she insists on seeing the bill."

So early the next morning Emma rushed to Monsieur Lheureux and begged him to make out a different note, for not more than 1,000 francs, for if she were to show the one for 4,000 she would have to say that she had paid off two-thirds of it, and consequently reveal the sale of the cottage. That transaction had been handled very cleverly by the shopkeeper, and never did leak out until later.

Despite the low price of each article, the elder Madame Bovary naturally found such expenditure excessive.

"Couldn't you get along without a carpet? Why re-cover the armchairs? In my day every house had exactly one arm-chair, for elderly persons—at least, that's the way it was at my mother's, and she was a respectable woman, I assure you. Everybody can't be rich! No amount of money will last if you throw it out the window. It would make me blush to pamper myself the way you do—and I'm an old woman and need looking after. . . . Who's ever seen so much finery? What, silk for linings at two francs when you can find jaconet for half a franc and even less that does perfectly well?"

Emma, stretched out on the settee, answered with the greatest calm:

"That's enough, Madame, that's enough."

Her mother-in-law continued to sermonize, prophesying that they'd end in the poorhouse. Besides, it was all Bovary's fault, she said. At least, though, he'd promised her he'd cancel the power of attorney.

"What!"

"Yes, he's given me his word," said the lady.

Emma opened the window and called Charles in, and the poor fellow had to confess the promise his mother had extracted from him.

Emma disappeared, then quickly returned, majestically holding out to her a large sheet of paper.

"I thank you," said the old woman.

And she threw the power of attorney into the fire.

Emma burst out laughing and didn't stop: her laughter was loud and strident—it was an attack of hysterics.

"Ah, my God!" cried Charles. "You're overdoing things, too! You've no right to come here and make scenes."

His mother shrugged her shoulders and said that "it was all put on."

But Charles, rebellious for the first time in his life, took his wife's part, and the older Madame Bovary said she wanted to go. She departed the next day, and on the doorstep, as he was trying to make her change her mind, she answered:

"No! No! You love her more than you do me, and you're right; that's as it should be. There's nothing I can do about it. You'll see, though . . . Take care of yourself . . . I can promise you it will be a long time before I come back here to 'make scenes,' as you put it."

Nevertheless Charles was very hangdog with Emma, and she didn't hide her resentment at having been distrusted. He had to entreat her many times before she would consent to accept power of attorney again, and he even went with her to Maître Guillaumin to have a new one drawn up, identical with the first.

"I well understand your doing this," said the notary. "A man of science can't be expected to burden himself with the practical details of existence."

Charles felt soothed by those oily words: they flattered his weakness, making it look like preoccupation with lofty things.

What exultation there was the next Thursday in their room at the hotel, with Léon! She laughed, cried, sang, danced, sent for water ices, insisted on smoking cigarettes. He found her wild, but adorable, superb.

He had no idea what it was that was driving her more and more to fling herself into a reckless pursuit of pleasure. She grew irritable, greedy, voluptuous; and she walked boldly with him in the street—unafraid, she said, of compromising herself. There were times, though, when Emma trembled at the sudden thought of meeting Rodolphe, for she suspected that even though they had parted forever, he still retained some of his power over her.

One night she didn't return to Yonville at all. Charles lost his head, and little Berthe, unwilling to go to bed without *maman*, sobbed as though her heart would break. Justin had gone off down the road to look for her. Monsieur Homais actually stepped out of his pharmacy.

Finally, at eleven o'clock, unable to stand it any longer, Charles harnessed his buggy, jumped in, whipped the horse on, and reached the Croix-Rouge at two in the morning. No sign of her. It occurred to him that Léon might have seen her: but where did he live? Luckily, Charles remembered the address of his employer, and he hastened there.

The sky was beginning to lighten. He made out some escutcheons over a door, and knocked. Without opening, someone shouted the information he wanted, together with a good deal of abuse about people who disturb other people at night.

The house the clerk lived in boasted neither bell nor knocker nor doorman. Charles pounded with his fists on the shutters, but just then a policeman came along: this frightened him, and he slunk away.

"I'm crazy," he told himself. "The Lormeaux' probably kept her to dinner."

But the Lormeaux' no longer lived in Rouen.

"She must have stayed to look after Madame Dubreuil. Oh, no—Madame Dubreuil died ten months ago. So where can she be?"

He had an idea. In a café he asked for the directory and looked up Mademoiselle Lempereur: 74 Rue de la Renelle-des-Maroquiniers was her address.

Just as he turned into that street, Emma herself appeared at the other end. It would be wrong to say that he embraced her: he flung himself on her, crying:

"What kept you, yesterday?"

"I was ill."

"Ill? How? Where?"

She passed her hand over her forehead:

"At Mademoiselle Lempereur's."

"I knew it! I was on my way there."

"Well, there's no use going there now. She's just gone out. But after this don't get so excited. I won't feel free to do a thing if I know that the slightest delay upsets you like this."

It was a kind of permit that she was giving herself—a permit to feel completely unhampered in her escapades. And she proceeded to make free and frequent use of it. Whenever she felt like seeing Léon, she would go off, using any excuse that came to mind; and since he wouldn't be expecting her that day, she would call for him at his office.

It was all very joyous, the first few times. But before long he stopped hiding the truth from her: his employer was complaining loudly of these incursions.

"Bah!" she said. "Come along."

And he slipped out.

She demanded that he dress entirely in black and grow a little pointed beard, to make himself look like the portraits of Louis XIII. She asked to see his rooms, and found them very so-so; he reddened at that, but she didn't notice, and advised him to buy curtains like hers. When he objected to the expense:

"Ah! So you pinch your pennies!" she said, laughing.

Each time, Léon had to tell her everything he had done since their last rendezvous. She asked for a poem, a poem for herself, a love piece written in her honor: he could never find a rhyme for the second line, and ended up copying a sonnet from a keepsake.

He did that less out of vanity than out of a desire to please her. He never disputed any of her ideas; he fell in with all her tastes: he was becoming her mistress, far more than she was his. Her sweet words and her kisses swept away his soul. Her depravity was so deep and so dissembled as to be almost intangible: where could she have learned it?

VI

ON HIS TRIPS TO SEE HER HE HAD OFTEN TAKEN DINNER AT THE pharmacist's, and he felt obliged out of politeness to invite him in return.

"With pleasure!" Homais answered. "A change will do me good: my life here is such a rut. We'll see a show and eat in a restaurant and really go out on the town."

"Out on the town!" Madame Homais' exclamation was affectionate: she was alarmed by the vague perils he was girding himself to meet.

"Why shouldn't I? Don't you think I ruin my health enough, exposing myself to all those drug fumes? That's women for you! They're jealous of Science, and yet they're up in arms at the mention of even the most legitimate distraction. Never mind, I'll be there. One of these days I'll turn up in Rouen, and we'll turn the town upside down."

In the past, the apothecary would have been careful to avoid such an expression; but now he was going in for a daredevil, Parisian kind of language that he considered very à la mode, and like his neighbor Madame Bovary he asked the clerk many searching questions about life in the big city. He even talked slang in order to show off in front of the "bourgeois," using such terms as *turne, bazar, chicard, chicandard,* the English "Breda Street" for Rue de Bréda and *je me la casse* for *je m'en vais.*

So one Thursday Emma was surprised to find, in the kitchen of the Lion d'Or, none other than Monsieur Homais in traveling garb—that is, wrapped in an old cape that no one had ever seen on him before, with a suitcase in one hand and in the other the foot-warmer from his shop. He hadn't breathed a word about his trip to anyone, fearing lest the public be made nervous by his absence.

The idea of revisiting the scenes of his youth apparently excited him, for he didn't stop talking all the way. The wheels had barely stopped turning when he leapt from the coach in search of Léon; and despite the clerk's struggles he dragged him off to lunch at the Café de Normandie. Here Monsieur Homais made a majestic entrance: he kept his hat on, considering it highly provincial to uncover in a public place.

Emma waited for Léon three-quarters of an hour, then rushed to his office. She was at a loss as to what could have happened: in her mind she heaped him with reproaches for his indifference and herself for her weakness; all afternoon she stood with her forehead glued to the windowpanes of their room.

At two o'clock Léon and Homais were still facing each other across their table. The big dining room was emptying; the stovepipe, designed to resemble a palm tree, spread out in a circle of gilded fronds on the white ceiling; and near them, just inside the window, in full sun, a little fountain gurgled into a marble basin, where among watercress and asparagus three sluggish lobsters stretched their claws toward a heap of quail.

Homais was in heaven. He found the *luxe* even more intoxicating than the fine food and drink; still, the Pomard went to his head a little; and when the rum omelet made its appearance he advanced certain immoral theories concerning women. What particularly captivated him was the quality of *chic*. He adored an elegant *toilette* in a handsome *décor*, and as for physical qualities, he wasn't averse to a "plump little morsel."

Léon desperately watched the clock. The apothecary kept drinking, eating, talking.

"You must feel quite deprived, here in Rouen," he suddenly remarked. "But then, your lady-love doesn't live *too* far away."

And as Léon blushed:

"Come, be frank! You won't deny, will you, that in Yonville . . ."

The young man began to stammer.

". . . at the Bovarys', you did quite some courting of . . ."

"Of whom?"

"Of the maid!"

Homais wasn't joking. But Léon's vanity got the better of his discretion, and despite himself he protested indignantly. Besides, he said, he liked only brunettes.

"I approve your preference," said the pharmacist. "They have more temperament."

And putting his mouth close to his friend's ear, he enumerated the sure signs of temperament in a woman. He even launched into an ethnographical digression: German women were moody, French women licentious, Italian women passionate.

"What about Negro women?" demanded the clerk.

"Much favored by artists," said Homais. "Waiter—two demitasses!"

"Shall we go?" said Léon finally, his patience at an end.

"*Yes*," said Homais, in English.

But before leaving he insisted on seeing the manager, and offered him his congratulations.

Léon, in the hope of being left alone, now pleaded a business appointment.

"Ah! I'll go with you!" said Homais.

And as he accompanied him through the streets he talked about his wife, about his children, about their future, about his pharmacy, told him in what a rundown state he had found it and to what a peak of perfection he had brought it.

When they reached the Hotel de Boulogne, Léon brusquely took leave of him, ran upstairs and found his mistress close to hysterics.

The mention of the pharmacist's name put her into a rage. He pleaded his case persuasively: it wasn't his fault—surely she knew Monsieur Homais. Could she think for a moment that he preferred his company? But she turned away; he caught hold of her, and winding his arms around her waist he sank to his knees, languorous, passionate, imploring.

She stood there, solemn, almost terrible, transfixing him with her great blazing eyes. Then tears came to cloud them, she lowered her reddened eyelids, held out her hands, and Léon was just pressing them to his lips when a servant knocked and said that someone was asking for Monsieur.

"You'll come back?" she said.

"Yes."

"When?"

"Right away."

"How do you like my little trick?" said the pharmacist, when Léon appeared. "I wanted to help you get away from your company: you gave me the impression you didn't expect to enjoy it. Let's go to Bridoux's and have a glass of cordial."

Léon insisted that he had to return to his office. The apothecary made facetious remarks about legal papers and legal flummery.

"Forget about Cujas and Barthole for a bit, for heaven's sake. Who's to stop you? Be a sport. Let's go to Bridoux's. You'll see his dog: it's very interesting."

And when the clerk stubbornly held out:

"I'll come, too. I'll read a newspaper while I wait, or look through a law book."

Overcome by Emma's anger, Monsieur Homais' chatter, and perhaps by the heavy lunch, Léon stood undecided, as though under the pharmacist's spell.

"Let's go to Bridoux's!" the latter kept repeating. "It's only a step from here—Rue Malpalu."

Out of cowardice or stupidity, or perhaps yielding to that indefinable impulse that leads us to do the things we most deplore, he let himself be carried off to Bridoux's. They found him in his little yard, superintending three workmen who were pantingly turning the great wheel of a Seltzer-water machine. Homais offered them several bits of advice and embraced Bridoux; they had their cordial. Twenty times Léon started to leave, but the pharmacist caught him by the arm, saying:

"Just a minute! I'm coming. We'll go to the *Fanal de Rouen* and say hello to everybody. I'll introduce you to Thomassin."

He got rid of him, however, and flew to the hotel. Emma was gone.

She had just left in a fury. She hated him. His failure to keep their appointment seemed to her an insult, and she sought additional reasons for seeing no more of him. He was unheroic, weak, commonplace, spineless as a woman, and stingy and timorous to boot.

Gradually, growing calmer, she came to see that she had been unjust to him. But casting aspersions on those we love always does something to loosen our ties. We shouldn't maltreat our idols: the gilt comes off on our hands.

From then on, matters extraneous to their love occupied

a greater place in their talk. The letters that Emma sent him were all about flowers, poetry, the moon and the stars: she resorted to these naïve expedients as her passion weakened, trying to keep it alive by artificial means. She continually promised herself that the next rendezvous would carry her to the peak of bliss; but when it was over she had to admit that she had felt nothing extraordinary. Each disappointment quickly gave way to new hope; each time, Emma returned to him more feverish, more avid. She could hardly wait to undress: she pulled so savagely at her corset string that it hissed around her hips like a gliding snake. Then she would tiptoe barefoot to see once again that the door was locked, and in a single movement let fall all her clothes; and, pale, silent, solemn, she would fling herself against his body with a long shudder.

There was something mad, though, something strange and sinister, about that cold, sweating forehead, about those stammering lips, those wildly staring eyes, the clasp of those arms—something that seemed to Léon to be creeping between them, subtly, as though to tear them apart.

He didn't dare question her; but realizing how experienced she was, he told himself that she must have known the utmost extremes of suffering and pleasure. What had once charmed him he now found a little frightening. Then, too, he rebelled against the way his personality was increasingly being submerged: he resented her perpetual triumph over him. He even did his best to stop loving her; then at the sound of her footsteps he would feel his will desert him, like a drunkard at the sight of strong liquor.

She made a point, it is true, of showering him with all kinds of attentions—everything from fine foods to coquetries of dress and languorous glances. She brought roses from Yonville in her bosom and tossed them at him; she worried over his health, gave him advice about how to conduct himself; and one day, to bind him the closer, hoping that heaven itself might take a hand in things, she slipped over his head a medal of the Blessed Virgin. Like a virtuous mother, she inquired about his associates:

"Don't see them," she would say. "Don't go out. Just think about us: love me!"

She wished she could keep an eye on him continually, and it occurred to her to have him followed on the street. There was a kind of tramp near the hotel who always accosted travelers and who would certainly be willing to . . . But her pride rebelled.

"What if he does betray me? Do I care?"

One day when they had said farewell earlier than usual, she caught sight of the walls of her convent as she was walking back alone down the boulevard, and she sank onto a bench in the shade of the elms. How peaceful those days had been! How she had longed for that ineffable emotion of love that she had tried to imagine from her books!

The first months of her marriage, her rides in the forest, the vicomte she had waltzed with, Lagardy singing—all passed again before her eyes. And Léon suddenly seemed as far removed as the others.

"I do love him, though!" she told herself.

No matter: she wasn't happy, and never had been. Why was life so unsatisfactory? Why did everything she leaned on crumble instantly to dust? But why, if somewhere there existed a strong and handsome being—a man of valor, sublime in passion and refinement, with a poet's heart and an angel's shape, a man like a lyre with strings of bronze, intoning elegiac epithalamiums to the heavens—why mightn't she have the luck to meet him? Ah, fine chance! Besides, nothing was worth looking for: everything was a lie! Every smile concealed a yawn of boredom; every joy, a curse; every pleasure, its own surfeit; and the sweetest kisses left on one's lips but a vain longing for fuller delight.

Through the air came a hoarse, prolonged metallic

groan, and then the clock of the convent struck four. Only four! And it seemed to her that she had been there on that bench since eternity. But an infinity of passions can be compressed into a minute, like a crowd into a little space. Emma's passions were the sole concern of her life: for money she had no more thought than an archduchess.

One day, however, she was visited by an ill-kempt individual, red-faced and bald, who said he had been sent by Monsieur Vinçart of Rouen. He pulled out the pins fastening the side pocket of his long green frock coat, stuck them in his sleeve, and politely handed her a document.

It was a note for 500 francs, signed by her, which Lheureux, despite all his promises, had endorsed over to Vinçart.

She sent her maid for Lheureux. He couldn't come.

The stranger had remained standing, dissimulating under his thick blond eyebrows the inquisitive glances that he cast left and right. "What answer am I to give Monsieur Vinçart?" he asked, with an innocent air.

"Well," said Emma, "tell him . . . that I haven't got . . . I'll have it next week. . . . He should wait . . . yes, I'll have it next week."

Whereupon the fellow went off without a word.

But the next day, at noon, she received a protest of nonpayment; and the sight of the official document, bearing the words "Maître Hareng, *huissier* at Buchy" several times in large letters, gave her such a fright that she hurried to the dry-goods merchant.

She found him in his shop tying up a parcel.

"At your service!" he said. "What can I do for you?"

He didn't interrupt his task: his clerk, a slightly hunchbacked girl of thirteen or so, who also did his cooking, was helping him.

Finally he clattered across the shop in his wooden shoes, climbed up ahead of Madame to the second floor, and showed her into a small office. Here on a large fir desk lay several ledgers, fastened down by a padlocked metal bar that stretched across them. A safe could be glimpsed against the wall, under some lengths of calico—a safe of such size that it certainly contained something besides cash and promissory notes. And indeed Monsieur Lheureux did some pawnbroking: it was here that he kept Madame Bovary's gold chain, along with some earrings that had belonged to poor Tellier. The latter had finally had to sell the Café Français, and had since bought a little grocery business in Quincampoix, where he was dying of his catarrh, his face yellower than the tallow candles he sold.

Lheureux sat down in his broad, rush-bottomed armchair.

"What's new?" he asked her.

"Look!"

And she showed him the document.

"Well, what can I do about it?"

She flew into a rage, reminding him that he had promised not to endorse her notes. He admitted it.

"But my hand was forced: my creditors had a knife at my throat."

"And what's going to happen now?" she asked.

"Oh, it's very simple: a court warrant, then execution; there's no way out."

Emma had to restrain herself from hitting him. She asked quietly whether there wasn't some way of appeasing Monsieur Vinçart.

"Ha! Appease Vinçart! You don't know him: he's fiercer than an Arab."

But Monsieur Lheureux *had* to do something about it!

"Now listen!" he said. "It seems to me I've been pretty nice to you so far."

And opening one of his ledgers:

"Look!"

He moved his finger up the page:

"Let's see . . . let's see . . . August 3,200 francs . . . June 17, 150 . . . March 23, 46. In April . . ."

He stopped, as though afraid of making a blunder.

"I won't even mention the notes your husband signed, one for seven hundred francs, another for three hundred. And as for your payments on account, and the interest, there's no end to it. It's a mess. I won't have anything more to do with it."

She wept; she even called him her "dear Monsieur Lheureux." But he kept laying the blame on "that scoundrelly Vinçart." Besides, he himself didn't have a centime: no one was paying him at the moment; his creditors were tearing the clothes from his back; a poor shopkeeper like himself couldn't advance money.

Emma stopped speaking; and Monsieur Lheureux, nibbling the quill of his pen, seemed disturbed by her silence.

"Of course," he said, "if I were to have something come in one of these days I might . . ."

"After all," she said, "as soon as the balance on Barneville . . ."

"What's that?"

And when he heard that Langlois hadn't yet paid he seemed very surprised. Then, in an oily voice:

"And our terms will be . . . ?"

"Oh, anything you say!"

Then he shut his eyes to help himself think, wrote down a few figures, and assuring her that he was making things hard for himself, taking a great risk, "bleeding himself white," he made out four notes for 250 francs each, payable a month apart.

"Let's hope that Vinçart's willing to listen to me! Anyway, you have my word: I don't say one thing and mean another; I'm open and aboveboard."

Afterwards he casually showed her a few items, not one of which, in his opinion, was worthy of Madame.

"When I think of dress goods like this selling at seven sous a metre and guaranteed dye-fast! Everybody believes it, too! And they don't get undeceived, I can assure you." The admission that he swindled others was meant as clinching proof of his frankness with herself.

Then he called her back and showed her several yards of point lace that he had come upon recently "in a vendue."

"Isn't it splendid?" he said. "It's being used a good deal now for antimacassars: it's the last word."

And quicker than a juggler he wrapped up the lace and handed it to Emma.

"At least," she said, "let me know how much it . . ."

"Oh, we'll talk about that later," he answered, turning abruptly away.

That very evening she made Bovary write his mother and ask her to send the balance of his inheritance at once. Her mother-in-law replied that there was nothing to send: the estate was settled, and in addition to Barneville they could count on a yearly income of 600 francs, which she would forward punctually.

So Madame sent bills to two or three patients, and before long she was sending them to many more, so successful did the expedient prove. She was always careful to add, in a postscript: "Don't speak of this to my husband—you know how proud he is. With regrets. Your humble servant." There were a few complaints, but she intercepted them.

To raise money she began to sell her old gloves, her old hats, all kinds of household odds and ends. She drove a hard bargain: her peasant blood stood her in good stead. And on her trips to the city she combed the curiosity shops for knickknacks, telling herself that Monsieur Lheureux, if no one else, would take them off her hands. She brought ostrich feathers, Chinese porcelains, old chests; she borrowed from Félicité, from Madame Lefrançois, from the landlady of the Croix-Rouge, from anyone and everyone. With part of the money she finally got from Barneville, she paid off two notes; the rest—1,500 francs—dribbled away. She signed new notes—always new notes.

Occasionally she tried to add up some figures, but the totals were so enormous that she couldn't believe them. Then she'd begin all over again, quickly become confused, and push it all aside and forget it.

The house was a gloomy place these days. Tradesmen called, and left with angry faces. Handkerchiefs lay strewn about on the stoves; and Madame Homais was shocked to see little Berthe with holes in her stockings. If Charles ventured some timid remark, Emma retorted savagely that *she* certainly wasn't to blame.

Why these fits of rage? He laid it all to her old nervous illness; and, penitent at having mistaken her infirmities for faults, he cursed his selfishness and longed to run up to her and take her in his arms.

"Oh, no!" he told himself. "I'd only annoy her."

And he did nothing.

After dinner he would walk alone in the garden. Then, with little Berthe in his lap and his medical journal open, he would try to teach the child to read. But she had never been given the slightest schooling, and after a few moments her eyes would grow round and sad, and the tears would come. He would comfort her: he filled the watering can to help her make rivulets in the paths, or broke privet branches that she could plant as trees in the flower beds. None of this harmed the garden, particularly—it was so choked with high grass anyway: they owed so many days' pay to Lestiboudois! Then the little girl would feel chilly and ask for her mother.

"Call Félicité," Charles would tell her. "You know *maman* doesn't like to be disturbed."

It was the onset of autumn, and already the leaves were falling—like two years before, when she had been so ill. When would there be an end to all this? And he would walk up and down, his hands behind his back.

Madame was in her room. No one else was admitted. She stayed there all day long in a torpor, not bothering to dress, now and again burning incense that she had bought at an Algerian shop in Rouen. She couldn't stand having Charles lying like a log at her side all night, and her repeated complaints finally drove him to sleep in the attic. She would read till morning—lurid novels full of orgies and bloodshed.

Sometimes, in sudden terror, she screamed; but when Charles ran in she dismissed him:

"Oh, get out."

At other times, seared by that hidden fire which her adultery kept feeding, consumed with longing, feverish with desire, she would open her window, inhale the cold air, let the heavy mass of her hair stream out in the wind: as she gazed at the stars she wished she were loved by a prince. Thoughts of Léon filled her. At such moments she would have given anything for a single one of their trysts—the trysts that sated her lust.

Those were her gala days. She was determined that they be glorious; and when he couldn't pay for everything himself she freely made up the difference. This happened almost every time. He tried to convince her that they would be just as well off elsewhere, in a more modest hotel, but she always objected.

One day she opened her bag, produced six little silver-gilt spoons—they had been her father's wedding present— and asked him to run out and pawn them for her. Léon obeyed, though he disliked the errand: he was afraid it might compromise him.

Thinking it over later, he came to the conclusion that

his mistress was certainly beginning to act strangely: maybe the people who were urging him to break with her weren't so mistaken after all.

For indeed someone had sent his mother a long anonymous letter, warning her that he was "ruining himself with a married woman"; and the lady, having visions of the perennial bogey of respectable families—that ill-defined, baleful female, that siren, that fantastic monster forever lurking in the abysses of love—wrote to Maître Bocage, his employer. This gentleman's handling of the matter was flawless. He talked to the young man for three-quarters of an hour, trying to unseal his eyes and warn him of the precipice ahead. Sooner or later, such an affair would harm his career. He begged him to break it off—and if he couldn't make the sacrifice for his own sake, then he should at least do it for his—namely, for the sake of Maître Bocage.

In the end Léon had promised never to see Emma again; and he reproached himself for not having kept his word, especially considering all the trouble and reproaches she still probably held in store for him—not to mention the jokes his fellow clerks cracked every morning around the stove. Besides, he was about to be promoted to head clerk: this was the time to turn over a new leaf. So he gave up playing the flute and said good-bye to exalted sentiments and romantic dreams. There isn't a bourgeois alive who in the ferment of his youth, if only for a day or for a minute, hasn't thought himself capable of boundless passions and noble exploits. The sorriest little woman-chaser has dreamed of Oriental queens; in a corner of every notary's heart lie the moldy remains of a poet.

These days it only bored him when Emma suddenly burst out sobbing on his breast: like people who can stand only a certain amount of music, he was drowsy and apathetic amidst the shrillness of her love; his heart had grown deaf to its subtler overtones.

By now they knew each other too well: no longer did they experience, in their mutual possession, that wonder that multiplies the joy a hundredfold. She was as surfeited with him as he was tired of her. Adultery, Emma was discovering, could be as banal as marriage.

But what way out was there? She felt humiliated by the degradation of such pleasures; but to no avail: she continued to cling to them, out of habit or out of depravity; and every day she pursued them more desperately, destroying all possible happiness by her excessive demands. She blamed Léon for her disappointed hopes, as though he had betrayed her; and she even longed for a catastrophe that would bring about their separation, since she hadn't the courage to bring it about herself.

Still, she continued to write him loving letters, faithful to the idea that a woman must always write her lover.

But as her pen flew over the paper she was aware of the presence of another man, a phantom embodying her most ardent memories, the most beautiful things she had read and her strongest desires. In the end he became so real and accessible that she tingled with excitement, unable though she was to picture him clearly, so hidden was he, godlike, under his manifold attributes. He dwelt in that enchanted realm where silken ladders swing from balconies moon-bright and flower-scented. She felt him near her: he was coming—coming to ravish her entirely in a kiss. And the next moment she would drop back to earth, shattered; for these rapturous love-dreams drained her more than the greatest orgies.

She lived these days in a state of constant and total exhaustion. She was continually receiving writs—official documents that she barely looked at. She wished she were dead, or in a state of continual sleep.

The Thursday night of the mi-carême—the mid-Lenten

festivities—she didn't return to Yonville, but went to a masked ball. She wore velvet knee breeches and red stockings and a peruke, and a cocked hat over one ear. She danced all night to the wild sound of trombones; she was the center of an admiring throng; and morning found her under the portico of the theatre with five or six maskers dressed as stevedores and sailors—friends of Léon's, who were wondering where they might have something to eat.

The nearby cafés were all full. On the river front they found a nondescript restaurant whose owner showed them up to a little room on the fifth floor.

The men whispered in a corner, doubtless consulting about the expense. A clerk, two medical students and a shop assistant: what company she was keeping! As for the women, Emma was quickly aware from their voices that most of them must be of the lowest class. That frightened her, and she drew back her chair and lowered her eyes.

The others began to eat. She did not. Her forehead was afire, her eyelids were smarting, her skin was icy cold. In her head she still felt the quaking of the dance floor under the rhythmic tread of a thousand feet. The smell of punch and cigar smoke made her dizzy. She fainted, and they carried her to the window.

Day was beginning to break, and in the pale sky toward Sainte-Catherine a large streak of red was widening. The leaden river shivered in the wind; the bridges were empty; the street lamps were going out.

Gradually she revived, and somehow she thought of Berthe, asleep out there beyond the horizon, in Félicité's room. But a wagon laden with long strips of iron went by, and the impact of its metallic clang shook the house walls.

Abruptly, she left the place. She took off her costume, told Léon she had to go home, and at last was alone in the Hotel de Boulogne. She loathed everything, including herself. She longed to fly away like a bird, to recapture her youth somewhere far away in the immaculate reaches of space.

She went out, followed the boulevard, crossed the Place Cauchoise and walked through the outskirts of the city to an open street overlooking gardens. She walked swiftly; the fresh air calmed her; and gradually the faces of the crowd, the maskers, the quadrilles, the blazing lights, the supper, and those women she had found herself with all disappeared like mist blown off by the wind. Then she returned to the Croix-Rouge and flung herself down on her bed in the little third-floor room with the prints of the Tour de Nesle. At four that afternoon Hivert woke her.

When she arrived home Félicité showed her a gray sheet of paper stuck behind the clock.

"By virtue of an instrument," she read, "duly setting forth the terms of a judgment to be enforced . . ."

What judgment? The previous day, she found, another paper had arrived; she hadn't seen it; and now she was dumbfounded to read these words:

"To Madame Bovary: You are hereby commanded by order of the king, the law and the courts . . ."

Then, skipping several lines, she saw:

"Within twenty-four hours." What was this? "Pay the total amount of 8,000 francs." And lower down: "There to be subjected to all due processes of law, and notably to execution of distraint upon furniture and effects."

What was to be done? In twenty-four hours: tomorrow! Lheureux, she thought, was probably trying to frighten her again. Suddenly she saw through all his schemes; the reason for his amiability burst upon her. What reassured her was the very enormity of the amount.

Nonetheless, as a result of buying and never paying, borrowing, signing notes and then renewing those same notes, which grew larger and larger each time they came due, she had gradually built up a capital for Monsieur Lheureux that he was impatient to lay his hands on to use in his speculations.

She called on him, assuming a nonchalant air.

"You know what's happened? It's a joke, I suppose?"

"No."

"What do you mean?"

He slowly turned his head away and folded his arms.

"Did you think, my dear lady," he said, "that I was going to go on to the end of time being your supplier and banker just for the love of God? I have to get back what I laid out: let's be fair!"

She was indignant about the size of the amount claimed.

"What can I do about it? The court upheld it. There's a judgment. You were notified. Besides, I have nothing to do with it—it's Vinçart."

"Couldn't you . . . ?"

"Absolutely nothing."

"But . . . still . . . let's talk it over."

And she stammered incoherently that she had known nothing about it, that the whole thing had come as a surprise. . . .

"Whose fault is that?" said Lheureux, with an ironic bow. "I work like a slave, and you go out enjoying yourself."

"Ah! No preaching!"

"It never did anybody any harm," he retorted.

She was craven: she pled with him, she even put her pretty slender white hand on his knee.

"None of that! Are you trying to seduce me, or what?"

"You're contemptible!" she cried.

"Oh! Oh! How you go on!" he said, laughing.

"I'll let everybody know what you're like. I'll tell my husband. . . ."

"Will you? I have something to *show* your husband!"

And out of his safe Lheureux took the receipt for 1,800

francs that she had given him for the note discounted by Vinçart.

"Do you think," he said, "that he won't see through your little swindle, the poor dear man?"

She crumpled, as though hit over the head with a club. He paced back and forth between the window and the desk, saying over and over:

"I'll show it to him! I'll show it to him!"

Then he came close to her and said softly:

"It's no fun, I know; but nobody's ever died of it, after all, and since it's the only way you have left of paying me back my money . . ."

"But where can I find some?" cried Emma, wringing her hands.

"Ah! Bah! A woman like you, with plenty of friends!"

And he transfixed her with a stare so knowing and so terrible that she shuddered to the depths of her being.

"I promise you!" she said. "I'll sign . . ."

"I have enough of your signatures!"

"I'll sell more . . ."

"Face it!" he said, shrugging his shoulders. "You've got nothing left."

And he called through a peephole that communicated with the shop:

"Annette! Don't forget the three cuttings of No. 14."

The servant entered; Emma took the hint, and asked how much money would be required to stop all proceedings.

"It's too late!"

"But if I brought you a few thousand francs—a quarter of the amount, a third, almost all?"

"No—there's no use!"

He pushed her gently toward the stairs.

"I implore you, Monsieur Lheureux—just a few days more!"

She was sobbing.

"Ah! Tears! Very good!"

"You'll drive me to do something desperate!"

"A lot I care!" he said, closing the door behind her.

VII

SHE WAS STOICAL, THE NEXT DAY, WHEN MAÎTRE HARENG, THE *huissier*, arrived with two witnesses to take inventory of the goods and chattels to be sold.

They began with Bovary's consulting room, and didn't include the phrenological head, which was considered a "professional instrument"; but in the kitchen they counted the plates and the pans, the chairs and the candle-sticks, and in the bedroom all the knickknacks on the whatnot. They inspected her dresses, the linen, the *cabinet de toilette;* and her very being, down to its most hidden and intimate details, was laid open, like a dissected corpse, to the stares of those three men.

Maître Hareng, buttoned up in a close-fitting black tail coat, with a white cravat, his shoestraps very tight, kept repeating:

"*Vous permettez, Madame? Vous permettez?*"

And frequently he exclaimed:

"Charming! Very pretty!"

Then he would resume his writing, dipping his pen in the inkhorn he held in his left hand..

When they had finished with the various rooms they went up to the attic.

She kept a desk there, where Rodolphe's letters were locked away. They made her open it.

"Ah! Personal papers!" said Maître Hareng, with a discreet smile. "*Mais permettez!* I have to make sure there's nothing else in the box."

And he held the envelopes upside down, very gently, as though expecting them to disgorge gold pieces. She was put into a fury by the sight of that great red hand, with its soft, sluglike fingers, touching those pages that had caused her so many heartthrobs.

They left at last. Félicité came back: she had sent her out to watch for Bovary and keep him away. They quickly installed the watchman in the attic, and he promised to stay there.

Charles, she thought during the evening, looked careworn. She scrutinized him with an agonized stare, reading accusations in the drawn lines of his face. Then, as her eyes roved over the mantelpiece, gay with Chinese fans, over the full curtains, the armchairs, all the things that had tempered the bitterness of her life, she was overcome with remorse, or rather with immense regret; and this, far from eclipsing her passion, only exasperated it. Charles placidly stirred the fire, lounging in his chair.

At one moment the watchman—bored, no doubt, in his hiding place—made a slight noise.

"Is somebody walking around up there?" said Charles.

"No!" she answered. "It's a dormer that's been left open, blowing in the wind."

The next day, Sunday, she left for Rouen, determined to call on every banker she had heard of. Most of them were away in the country or traveling. She persisted, however, and those whom she succeeded in seeing she asked for money, insisting that she must have it, swearing to repay. Some of them laughed in her face; they all refused.

At two o'clock she hurried to Léon's and knocked on his door. No one came to open. Finally he appeared.

"What brings you here?"

"Are you sorry to see me?"

"No . . . but . . ."

And he confessed that his landlord didn't like the tenants to entertain "women."

"I've got to talk to you," she said.

He reached for his key. She stopped him:

"Oh, no—let's go to our place."

And they went to their room in the Hotel de Boulogne. There she drank a large glass of water. She was very pale.

"Léon," she said to him, "you have to do something for me."

And clutching both his hands tightly in hers, she shook them and said:

"Listen! I've got to have eight thousand francs!"

"But you're out of your mind!"

"Not yet!"

And in a rush she told him all about the execution. She was in desperate straits: Charles had been kept in total ignorance, her mother-in-law hated her, her father could do nothing. He—Léon—must save her. He must go out at once and find her the money that she absolutely had to have.

"How in the world do you expect me . . . ?"

"Don't just stand there, like a spineless fool!"

"You're making things out to be worse than they are," he said stupidly. "You could probably quiet your man with three thousand francs."

All the more reason for trying to do something: it wasn't conceivable that three thousand francs couldn't be found. Besides, Léon's signature could go on the notes instead of hers.

"Go ahead! Try! I've got to have it! Hurry! Oh, try! Try! Then I'll show you how I love you!"

He went out. In an hour he was back.

"I've seen three people," he told her, solemn-faced. "Nothing doing."

They sat face to face across the fire, still and silent. Emma kept shrugging her shoulders, tapping her foot. Then he heard her say, low-voiced:

"If I were in your place I'd know where to find the money!"

"You would? Where?"

"In your office!"

She stared at him.

There was a demonic desperation burning in her eyes, and she narrowed them in a look of lascivious provocation: the young man felt himself giving way before the mute will of this woman who was urging him to crime. He took fright; and to avoid hearing anything further he clapped his hand to his forehead.

"Morel should be back tonight!" he cried. "He won't refuse me, I hope!" (Morel was one of his friends, the son of a wealthy businessman.) "I'll bring it to you tomorrow," he promised.

Emma didn't appear to welcome this hope of relief as joyfully as he had thought. Did she suspect his lie? He blushed as he added:

"But if I'm not back by three, don't wait for me any longer, darling. Now I have to go out. Forgive me! Good-bye!"

He pressed her hand, but it lay inert in his: Emma was drained of all feeling.

Four o'clock struck; and she got up to go back to Yonville, automatic in her obedience to the force of habit.

The day was fine—one of those clear, sharp March days with the sun brilliant in a cloudless sky. Contented-looking Rouennais were strolling in their Sunday best. As she came to the Place du Parvis, vespers in the cathedral had just ended: crowds were pouring out through the three portals, like a river through the three arches of a bridge; and in their midst, immovable as a rock, stood the verger.

She remembered how tremulous she had been, how full of hope, the day she had entered that lofty nave: how it had stretched away before her, on and on—and yet not as infinite as her love! And she kept walking, weeping under her veil, dazed, tottering, almost in a faint.

"Watch out!" The cry came from within a porte-cochère that was swinging open; she stopped, and out came a black horse, prancing between the shafts of a tilbury. A gentleman in sables was holding the reins. Who was he? She knew him. . . . The carriage leapt forward and was gone.

The vicomte! It was the vicomte! She turned to stare: the street was empty. And the encounter left her so crushed, so immeasurably sad, that she leaned against a wall to keep from falling.

Then she thought that she might be mistaken. How could she tell? She had no way of knowing. Everything—everything within her, everything without—was abandoning her. She felt lost, rolling dizzily down into some dark abyss; and she was almost glad, when she reached the Croix-Rouge, to see good old Monsieur Homais. He was watching a case of pharmaceutical supplies being loaded onto the Hirondelle, and in his hand he carried a present for his wife—six *cheminots* wrapped in a foulard handkerchief.

Madame Homais was particularly fond of those heavy turban-shaped rolls, which the Rouennais eat in Lent with salted butter—a last relic of Gothic fare, going back perhaps to the times of the Crusades. The lusty Normans of those days gorged themselves on *cheminots*, picturing them as the heads of Saracens, to be devoured by the light of yellow torches along with flacons of spiced wine and giant slabs of meat. Like those ancients, the apothecary's wife crunched them heroically, despite her wretched teeth; and every time Monsieur Homais made a trip to the city he faithfully brought some back to her, buying them always at the best baker's, in the Rue Massacre.

"Delighted to see you!" he said, offering Emma a hand to help her into the Hirondelle.

Then he put the *cheminots* in the baggage net and sat there hatless, his arms folded, in a pose that was pensive and Napoleonic.

But when the blind beggar made his appearance as usual at the foot of the hill, he exclaimed in indignation:

"I cannot understand why the authorities continue to tolerate such dishonest occupations! All these unfortunates should be put away—and put to work! Progress moves at a snail's pace, no doubt about it: we're still wallowing in the midst of barbarism!"

The blind man held out his hat, and it swung to and fro at the window like a loose piece of upholstery.

"That," pronounced the pharmacist, "is a scrofulous disease."

And though he had often seen the poor devil before, he pretended now to be looking at him for the first time, and he murmured the words "cornea," "opaque cornea," "sclerotic," "facies." Then, in a paternal tone:

"Have you had that frightful affliction long, my friend? You'd do well to follow a diet, instead of getting drunk in cafés."

He urged him to take only good wine and good beer, and to eat good roast meat. The blind man kept singing his song: actually, he seemed fairly close to idiocy. Finally Monsieur Homais took out his purse:

"Here—here's a sou: change it for me and keep half of it for yourself. And don't forget my suggestions—you'll find they help."

Hivert presumed to express certain doubts about their efficacy. But the apothecary swore that he could cure the fellow himself, with an antiphlogistic salve of his own invention, and he gave him his address:

"Monsieur Homais, near the market—ask anyone."

"Come now," said Hivert. "Show the gentleman you're grateful by doing your act."

The blind man squatted on his haunches and threw back his head, and rolling his greenish eyes and sticking out his tongue he rubbed his stomach with both hands, meanwhile uttering a kind of muffled howl, like a famished dog. Emma, shuddering with disgust, flung him a five-franc piece over her shoulder. It was all the money she had in the world: there was something grand, she thought, in thus throwing it away.

The coach was again in motion, when suddenly Monsieur Homais leaned out the window.

"Nothing farinaceous!" he shouted. "No dairy products! Wear woolens next to your skin! Fumigate the diseased areas with the smoke of juniper berries!"

The sight of all the familiar things they passed gradually took Emma's mind off her misery. She was oppressed, crushed with fatigue, and she reached home numb and spiritless, almost asleep.

"Let come what may!" she told herself.

Besides—who knew? Something extraordinary might happen any moment. Lheureux himself might die.

She was awakened the next morning at nine by the sound of voices in the square. People were crowding around the market to read a large notice posted on one of the pillars, and she saw Justin climb on a guard post and deface the notice. Just then the village policeman seized him by the collar. Monsieur Homais came out of his pharmacy, and Madame Lefrançois seemed to be holding forth in the midst of the crowd.

"Madame! Madame!" cried Félicité, rushing in. "It's an outrage!"

And the poor girl, much agitated, showed her a yellow paper she had just torn off the front door. Emma read in a glance that all the contents of her house were subject to sale.

They looked at each other in silence. There were no secrets between mistress and maid. Finally Félicité murmured:

"If I were you, Madame, I'd go see Maître Guillaumin."

"Do you think so?"

"You know all about the Guillaumins from their manservant," the question meant; "does the master mention me, sometimes?"

"Yes, go ahead: it's worth trying."

She put on her black dress and her bonnet with jade beads; and to keep from being seen (there was still quite a crowd in the square) she avoided the village and took the river path.

She was breathless when she reached the notary's gate. The sky was dark; it was snowing a little.

At the sound of her ring Théodore, in a red vest, emerged from the front door; and he opened the gate for her with an air of familiarity, as though she were someone he knew well, and showed her into the dining room.

A large procelain stove was purring; the niche above it was filled with a cactus plant; and against the oak-grained wallpaper hung Steuben's "Esmeralda" and Schopin's "Potiphar," both in black wood frames. The table set for breakfast, the two silver dishwarmers, the crystal doorknobs, the parquet floor and the furniture—all gleamed with a meticulous English spotlessness; in the corners of each of the windows were panes of colored glass.

"This," thought Emma, "is the kind of dining room I should have "

The notary came in. He was wearing a dressing gown with palm designs, which he clutched about him with his left hand; and with his right he doffed and then quickly replaced his brown velvet skullcap. This he wore rakishly tilted to the right, and out from under it emerged the ends of three strands of fair hair that were combed up from the back and drawn carefully over his bald cranium.

After offering her a chair he sat down to his breakfast, apologizing profusely for his discourtesy.

"Monsieur," she said, "I want to ask you . . ."

"What, Madame? I'm listening."

She told him of her predicament.

It was no news to Maître Guillaumin: he was secretly associated with the dry-goods merchant, who could always be counted on to supply him with capital for the mortgage loans he arranged for his clients.

Thus he knew—far better than she—the long story of the notes, small at first, carrying the names of various endorsers, made out for long terms and continually renewed; he knew how the shopkeeper had gradually accumulated the various protests of nonpayment, and how he had finally had his friend Vinçart institute the necessary legal proceedings in his name, wishing to avoid acquiring a reputation for bloodthirstiness among his fellow villagers.

She interspersed her story with recriminations against Lheureux, and to these the notary returned occasional, empty answers. He ate his chop and drank his tea; his chin kept rubbing against his sky-blue cravat, whose two diamond stickpins were linked by a fine gold chain; and he smiled a strange, sugary, ambiguous smile. Then he noticed that her feet were wet.

"Move closer to the stove! Put them up—higher—against the porcelain."

She was afraid of dirtying it, but his retort was gallant:

"Pretty things never do any harm."

Then she tried to appeal to his emotions: growing emotional herself, she told him about her cramped household budget, her harassments, her needs. He was very sympathetic—an elegant woman like herself!—and without interrupting his meal he gradually turned so that he faced her and his knee brushed against her shoe, whose sole was beginning to curl a little as it steamed in the heat of the stove.

But when she asked him for 3,000 francs he tightened his lips and said that he was very sorry not to have had charge of her capital in the past, for there were a hundred easy ways in which even a lady could invest her money profitably. The Grumesnil peatery, building lots in Le Havre—such speculations were excellent, almost risk-proof; and he let her consume herself with rage at the thought of the fantastic sums she could certainly have made.

"How come," he asked her, "that you never called on me?"

"I really don't know," she said.

"Why didn't you? Did I seem so very frightening to you? But I'm the one who has cause for complaint: we barely know each other! I feel very warmly toward you, though; you realize that now, I hope?"

He reached out his hand, took hers, pressed it to his lips in a greedy kiss, and then kept it on his knee; and he gently fondled her fingers, murmuring a thousand compliments.

His monotonous voice rustled on like a running brook; his eyes were gleaming through the glitter of his glasses; and his hands crept up inside Emma's sleeve and stroked her arm. She felt a panting breath on her cheek. This man was more than she could stand.

She leapt to her feet.

"Monsieur! I'm waiting!"

"What for?" cried the notary, suddenly extremely pale.

"The money."

"But . . ."

Then, yielding to an irresistible surge of desire:

"Yes! Yes!"

He dragged himself toward her on his knees, careless of his dressing gown.

"Please! Don't go! I love you!"

He seized her by the waist.

A flood of crimson rushed to Madame Bovary's face. She shrank back, and with a terrible look she cried:

"It's shameless of you to take advantage of my distress! I'm to be pitied, but I'm not for sale!"

And she walked out.

The notary sat there dumfounded, his eyes fixed on his beautiful embroidered slippers. They were a gift from a mistress, and the sight of them gradually comforted him. Anyway, he told himself, such an affair would have involved too many risks.

"What a contemptible, lowdown cad!" she said to herself, as she fled tremulously under the aspens lining the road. Disappointment at having failed made her all the more indignant at the insult offered her honor: it seemed to her that Providence was hounding her relentlessly. She was filled with pride at the way she had acted: never before had she esteemed herself so highly; never had she felt such contempt for everyone else. She was at war with the world, and the thought transported her. She longed to lash out at all men, to spit in their faces, grind them all to dust; and she hurried straight on, pale, trembling, furious, scanning the empty horizon with weeping eyes, almost gloating in the hatred that was choking her.

When she caught sight of her house she felt suddenly paralyzed. She couldn't go on, and yet she had to: what escape was there?

Félicité was waiting for her at the door.

"Well?"

"No," said Emma.

And for a quarter of an hour they discussed who in Yonville might be willing to help her. But every time Félicité mentioned someone, Emma answered:

"Out of the question! They'd refuse!"

"And Monsieur will soon be home!"

"I know. . . . Go away and leave me alone."

She had tried everything. Now there was nothing more to be done; so when Charles appeared there would be only one thing to tell him:

"Don't stay here! The very rug you're walking on isn't ours. Not a piece of all this furniture belongs to you—not a pin, not a wisp of straw; and I'm the one who has ruined you!"

Then he would utter a great sob, and then weep floods of tears; and in the end, once the shock was over, he would forgive her.

"Yes," she muttered, through clenched teeth, "*he*'ll forgive *me*—the man *I* wouldn't forgive for setting eyes on me if he offered me a million. . . . Never! Never!"

This thought of Bovary in a position to be condescending put her beside herself. But whether she confessed or not, he would inevitably—sooner or later, today or tomorrow—learn of the disaster; so she could only look forward to that horrible scene and to being subjected to the weight of his magnanimity. Suddenly she felt an urge to try Lheureux once more: but what was the use? Or to write to her father: but it was too late. And perhaps she was regretting, now, not having yielded to the notary, when she heard a horse's trot in the lane. It was Charles: he was opening the gate, his face more ashen than the plaster on the wall. Rushing downstairs, she slipped quickly out into the square; and the mayor's wife, who was chatting in front of the church with Lestiboudois, saw her enter the house of the tax collector.

Madame Tuvache ran to tell Madame Caron. The two ladies climbed up to the latter's attic; and there, hidden behind some laundry that was hanging up to dry, they stood so that they could easily see into Binet's.

He was alone in his garret, busily copying, in wood, one of those ivory ornaments that beggar description, a conglomeration of half-moons and of spheres carved one inside the other, the whole thing standing erect like an obelisk and perfectly useless. He was just beginning on the last section: the end was in sight! In the chiaroscuro of his workshop the golden sawdust flew from his lathe like a spray of sparks under the hooves of a galloping horse; the two wheels spun and whirred; Binet was smiling, chin down and nostrils wide: he looked absorbed, in one of those states of utter bliss such as men seem to find only in humble activities, which divert the mind with easy challenges and gratify it with the most utter and complete success.

"Ah! There she is!" said Madame Tuvache.

But the sound of the lathe made it impossible to know what she was saying.

Finally the two ladies thought they heard the word "francs," and Madame Tuvache whispered:

"She's asking him for a postponement of her taxes."

"Looks like it," said the other.

They saw her pacing up and down the room, looking at the shelves along the wall laden with napkin rings, candlesticks and finials, while Binet contentedly stroked his beard.

"Would she be coming to order something from him?" suggested Madame Tuvache.

"But he never sells anything!" the other reminded her.

The tax collector seemed to be listening, staring as though he didn't understand. She continued to talk, her manner gentle and supplicating. She came close to him; her breast was heaving; now they seemed not to be speaking.

"Is she making advances to him?" said Madame Tuvache.

Binet had gone red to the roots of his hair. She grasped his hands.

"Ah! Just look at that . . . !"

And she must have been suggesting something abominable, for the tax collector—and he was a man of courage: he had fought at Bautzen and Lützen, and taken part in the French campaign, and even been proposed for the Legion of Honor—suddenly recoiled as though he had seen a snake.

"Madame!" he cried. "You must be dreaming!"

"Women like that should be horsewhipped," said Madame Tuvache.

"Where has she gone to?" said Madame Caron.

For even as he was speaking she had vanished. Then they saw her darting down the Grande Rue and turning to the right, as though to reach the cemetery, and they didn't know what to make of it.

"Madame Rollet!" she cried, when she reached the wet-nurse's. "I can't breathe! Unlace me!"

She fell sobbing onto the bed. Madame Rollet covered her with a petticoat and stood beside her. Then, when she didn't speak, the peasant woman moved away, took up her wheel and began spinning flax.

"Don't do that!" she murmured: she thought it was Binet's lathe.

"What's the matter with her?" wondered the nurse. "Why did she come here?"

She had come because a kind of terror had sent her—a terror that made her flee her home. Lying on her back, motionless, her eyes vacant, she saw things only in a blur, though she focused her attention on them with idiotic persistence. She stared at the flaking plaster on the wall, at two half-burned sticks smoking end to end in the fire-place, at a large spider crawling overhead in a crack in the rafter. Gradually she collected her thoughts. She remem-bered . . . one day with Léon . . . Oh, how far away it was . . . ! The sun was shining on the river, and the air was full of the scent of clematis. . . . Then, swept along in her memories as in a raging torrent, she quickly recalled the previous day.

"What time is it?" she asked.

Madame Rollet went out, held up the fingers of her right hand against the brightest part of the sky, and came slowly back, saying:

"Almost three."

"Ah! Thank you! Thank you!"

For he would be coming. There could be no question about it: by now he had found the money. But probably he would go to her house, having no idea that she was here; and she ordered the nurse to run and fetch him.

"Hurry!"

"I'm on my way, dear lady! I'm on my way!"

She marveled, now, at not having thought of him in the first place: yesterday he had given his word; he wouldn't fail her; and already she saw herself at Lheureux's, laying the three banknotes on his desk. Then she'd have to in-vent some story that would satisfy Bovary. What would it be?

But the nurse was a long time returning. Still, since there was no clock in the cottage, Emma feared that she might be exaggerating the duration of her absence, and she walked slowly around and around the garden, and down the path by the hedge and quickly back, hoping that the nurse might have returned some other way. Finally, weary of waiting, a prey to suspicions that she resolutely put out of her mind, no longer sure whether she had been there a hundred years or a minute, she sat down in a corner and closed her eyes and put her hands to her ears. The gate squeaked: she leapt up. Before she could speak Madame Rollet said:

"He's not there!"

"What?"

"No, he's not! And Monsieur's crying. He keeps calling your name. Everybody's looking for you."

Emma made no answer. She was gasping and staring wildly about her; the peasant woman, frightened by the expression on her face, instinctively shrank back, thinking her crazed. All at once she clapped her hand to her forehead and gave a cry, for into her mind had come the memory of Rodolphe, like a great lightning-flash in a black night. He was so kind, so sensitive, so generous! And if he should hesitate to help her she'd know how to persuade him: one glance from her eyes would remind him of their lost love. So she set out for La Huchette, unaware that now she was eager to yield to the very thing that had made her so indignant only a short while ago, and totally unconscious that she was prostituting herself.

VIII

AS SHE WALKED SHE WONDERED: "WHAT AM I GOING TO SAY? What shall I tell him first?" Drawing nearer, she recognized the thickets, the trees, the furze on the hill, the chateau in the distance. She was reliving the sensations of her first love, and at the memory her poor anguished heart swelled tenderly. A warm wind was blowing in her face; melting snow dripped from the leaf-buds onto the grass.

She entered, as she always had, by the little park gate, and then came to the main courtyard, planted round with a double row of thick-crowned lindens, their long branches rustling and swaying. All the dogs in the kennel barked, but though their outcry echoed and re-echoed, no one came.

She climbed the wide, straight, wooden-banistered stairs that led up to the hall with its paving of dusty flagstones. A row of doors opened onto it, as in a monastery or an inn. His room was at the far end, the last on the left. When her fingers touched the latch her strength suddenly left her: she was afraid that he would not be there—she almost wished that he wouldn't be, and yet he was her only hope, her last chance of salvation. For a minute she collected her thoughts; then, steeling her courage to the present necessity, she entered.

He was smoking a pipe before the fire, his feet against the mantelpiece.

"Oh, it's you! he said, rising quickly.

"Yes, here I am. . . . Rodolphe, I want . . . I need some advice. . . ."

Despite her best efforts she couldn't go on.

"You haven't changed—you're as charming as ever!"

"Oh, my charms!" she answered bitterly. "They can't amount to much, since you scorned them."

He launched into apology, justifying his conduct in terms that were vague but the best he could muster.

She let herself be taken in—not so much by what he said, as by the sound of his voice and the very sight of him; and she pretended to believe—or perhaps she actually did believe—the reason he gave for their break. It was a secret, he said, involving the honor—the life, even—of a third person.

She looked at him sadly. "Whatever it was," she said, "I suffered a great deal."

He answered philosophically:

"That's how life is!"

"Has it been kind to you, at least," asked Emma, "since we parted?"

"Oh, neither kind nor unkind, particularly."

"Perhaps it would have been better had we stayed together."

"Yes . . . perhaps!"

"Do you really think so?" she said, coming closer. And she sighed:

"Oh, Rodolphe! If you knew! I loved you very much!"

She took his hand; and for a few moments their fingers were intertwined—like that first day, at the Agricultural Show! Pride made him struggle against giving in to his feelings. But she leaned heavily against him, and said:

"How did you ever think that I could live without you? Happiness is a habit that's hard to break! I was desperate! I thought I'd die! I'll tell you all about it. And you . . . you stayed away from me . . . !"

It was true: for the past three years he had carefully avoided her, out of the natural cowardice that characterizes the stronger sex; and now Emma went on, twisting and turning her head in coaxing little movements that were loving and catlike.

"You have other women—admit it. Oh, I sympathize with them: I don't blame them. You seduced them, the way you seduced me. You're a man! You have everything to make us love you. But you and I'll begin all over again, won't we? We'll love each other! Look—I'm laughing, I'm happy! Speak to me!"

And indeed she was ravishing to see, with a tear trembling in her eye like a raindrop in a blue flower-cup after a storm.

He drew her onto his lap, and with the back of his hand caressed her sleek hair: in the twilight a last sunbeam was gleaming on it like a golden arrow. She lowered her head, and soon he was kissing her on the eyelids, very gently, just brushing them with his lips.

"But you've been crying!" he said. "Why?"

She burst into sobs: Rodolphe thought it was from the violence of her love; when she didn't answer him he interpreted her silence as the ultimate refuge of her womanly modesty, and exclaimed:

"Ah! Forgive me! You're the only one I really care about! I've been stupid and heartless! I love you—I'll always love you. . . . What is it? Tell me!"

He was on his knees.

"Well, then . . . I'm ruined, Rodolphe! You've got to lend me three thousand francs!"

"But . . . but . . . ?" he said, slowly rising, a worried expression coming over his face.

"You know," she went on quickly, "my husband gave his money to a notary to invest, and the notary absconded. We've borrowed, patients haven't paid. . . . The estate isn't settled yet: we'll be getting something later. But to-day—just for three thousand francs—they're going to sell us out: now, this very instant. I counted on your friendship. I came to you."

"Ah," thought Rodolphe, suddenly pale. "So that's why she came!"

And after a moment he said, calmly:

"I haven't got it, dear lady."

He wasn't lying. If he had had it he would probably have given it to her, unpleasant though it usually is to make such generous gifts: of all the icy blasts that blow on love, a request for money is the most chilling and havoc-wreaking.

For a long moment she stared at him. Then:

"You haven't got it!"

She said it again, several times:

"You haven't got it! I might have spared myself this

final humiliation. You never loved me! You're no better
than the rest!"

She was giving herself away; she no longer knew what
she was saying.

Rodolphe broke in, assuring her that he was "hard up"
himself.

"Ah, I pity you!" said Emma. "How I pity you!"

And as her eyes fell on a damascened rifle that glittered
in a trophy on the wall:

"When you're as poor as all that you don't put silver on
the stock of your gun! You don't buy things with tortoise-
shell inlay!" she went on, pointing to the Boulle clock. "Or
silver-gilt whistles for your whip!"—she touched them—
"or charms for your watch chain! Oh, he has everything!
Even a liqueur case in his bedroom! You pamper yourself,
you live well, you have a chateau, farms, woods; you hunt,
you make trips to Paris. . . . Why, even things like this,"
she cried, snatching up his cuff links from the mantelpiece,
"the tiniest trifles, you can raise money on . . . ! Oh, I
don't want them! Keep them."

And she hurled the two buttons so violently that their
gold chain snapped as they struck the wall.

"But I—I'd have given you everything, I'd have sold
everything, worked my fingers to the bone, begged in the
streets, just for a smile from you, for a look, just to hear
you say 'Thank you.' And you sit there calmly in your
chair, as though you hadn't made me suffer enough already! If it hadn't been for you I could have been happy!
What made you do it? Was it a bet? You loved me, though:
you used to say so. . . . And you said so again just now.
Ah, you'd have done better to throw me out! My hands
are still hot from your kisses; and right there on the rug
you swore on your knees that you'd love me forever. You
made me believe it: for two years you led me on in a
wonderful, marvelous dream. . . . Our plans for going

away—you remember? Oh! That letter you wrote me! It tore my heart in two! And now when I come back to him —and find him rich and happy and free—to implore him for help that anybody would give me—come in distress, bringing him all my love—he refuses me, because it would cost him three thousand francs!"

"I haven't got it," answered Rodolphe, with that perfect calm that resigned anger employs as a shield.

She walked out. The walls were quaking, the ceiling was threatening to crush her; and she went back down the long avenue of trees, stumbling against piles of dead leaves that were scattering in the wind. At last she reached the ditch before the gate: she broke her nails on the latch, so frantically did she open it. Then, a hundred yards further on, out of breath, ready to drop, she paused. She turned: and once again she saw the impassive chateau, with its park, its gardens, its three courtyards, its many-windowed façade.

She stood there in a daze. Only the pulsing of her veins told her that she was alive: she thought she heard it outside herself, like some deafening music filling the countryside. The earth beneath her feet was as yielding as water, and the furrows seemed to her like immense, dark, breaking waves. All the memories and thoughts in her mind poured out at once, like a thousand fireworks. She saw her father, Lheureux's office, their room in Rouen, another landscape. Madness began to take hold of her; she was frightened, but managed to control herself—without, however, emerging from her confusion, for the cause of her horrible state—the question of money—had faded from her mind. It was only her love that was making her suffer, and she felt her soul leave her at the thought—just as a wounded man, as he lies dying, feels his life flowing out with his blood through the gaping hole.

Night was falling; crows flew overhead.

It suddenly seemed to her that fiery particles were bursting in the air, like bullets exploding as they fell, and spinning and spinning and finally melting in the snow among the tree branches. In the center of each of them appeared Rodolphe's face. They multiplied; they came together; they penetrated her; everything vanished. She recognized the lights of houses, shining far off in the mist.

Suddenly her plight loomed before her, like an abyss. She panted as though her lungs would burst. Then, with a heroic resolve that made her almost happy, she ran down the hill and across the cow plank, ran down the river path and the lane, crossed the square, and came to the pharmacy.

It was empty. She was about to go in, when it occurred to her that the sound of the bell might bring someone; and slipping through the side gate, holding her breath, feeling her way along the walls, she came to the kitchen door. A lighted tallow candle was standing on the stove, and Justin, in shirt sleeves, was just leaving the room carrying a dish.

"Ah, they're at dinner," she said to herself. "Better wait."

Justin returned to the kitchen. She tapped on the window. He came out.

"The key! The one for upstairs, where the . . ."

"What?"

And he stared at her, astounded by the pallor of her face, which stood out white against the blackness of the night. She seemed to him extraordinarily beautiful, majestic as an apparition from another world; without understanding what she wanted, he had a foreboding of something terrible.

But she went on quickly, in a low voice, a voice that was gentle and melting:

"I want it! Give it to me."

The wall was thin, and they could hear the clinking of forks on plates in the dining room.

She pretended she had to kill some rats that were keeping her awake nights.

"I must go ask Monsieur."

"No! Stay here!"

Then, with a casual air:

"There's no use bothering him: I'll tell him later. Come along, give me a light."

She passed into the hall off which opened the laboratory door. There against the wall hung a key marked "capharnaum."

"Justin!" called the apothecary impatiently.

"Let's go up!"

He followed her.

The key turned in the lock, and she went straight to the third shelf—so well did her memory serve her as guide— seized the blue jar, tore out the cork, plunged in her hand, withdrew it full of white powder, and ate greedily.

"Stop!" he cried, flinging himself on her.

"Be quiet! Someone might come. . . ."

He was frantic, wanted to call out.

"Don't say a word about it: all the blame would fall on your master!"

Then she went home, suddenly at peace—almost as serene as though she had done her duty.

When Charles reached home, overwhelmed by the news of the execution, Emma had just left. He called her name, wept, fainted away, but she didn't come back. Where could she be? He sent Félicité to the pharmacist's, to the mayor's, to the dry-goods shop, to the Lion d'Or—everywhere; and whenever his anguish about her momentarily subsided he saw his reputation ruined, all their money gone, Berthe's future wrecked! What was the cause of it all . . . ? Not a word! He waited until six that evening. Finally, unable to bear it any longer, and imagining that she must have gone to Rouen, he went out to the highway, followed it for a mile or so, met no one, waited a while, and returned.

She was back.

"What happened? . . . Why? . . . Tell me!"

She sat down at her desk and wrote a letter, sealed it slowly, and added the date and the hour. Then she said in a solemn tone:

"Read it tomorrow. Till then, please don't ask me a single question—not one!"

"But . . . "

"Oh, leave me alone!"

And she stretched out on her bed.

An acrid taste in her mouth woke her. She caught sight of Charles and reclosed her eyes.

She observed herself with interest, to see whether there was any pain. No—nothing yet. She heard the ticking of the clock, the sound of the fire, and Charles breathing, standing there beside her bed.

"Dying doesn't amount to much!" she thought. "I'll fall asleep, and everything will be over."

She swallowed a mouthful of water and turned to the wall.

There was still that dreadful taste of ink.

"I'm thirsty! I'm so thirsty!" she whispered.

"What's wrong with you, anyway?" said Charles, handing her a glass.

"Nothing! Open the window . . . I'm choking!"

She was seized by an attack of nausea so sudden that she scarcely had time to snatch her handkerchief from under the pillow.

"Get rid of it!" she said quickly. "Throw it out!"

He questioned her, but she made no answer. She lay very still, fearing that the slightest disturbance would make her vomit. Now she felt an icy coldness creeping up from her feet toward her heart.

"Ah! It's beginning!" she murmured.

"What did you say?"

She twisted her head from side to side in a gentle movement expressive of anguish, and kept opening her jaws as though she had something very heavy on her tongue. At eight o'clock the vomiting resumed.

Charles noticed that there was a gritty white deposit on the bottom of the basin, clinging to the porcelain.

"That's extraordinary! That's peculiar!" he kept saying.

"No!" she said loudly. "You're mistaken."

Very gently, almost caressingly, he passed his hand over her stomach. She gave a sharp scream. He drew back in fright.

She began to moan, softly at first. Her shoulders heaved in a great shudder, and she grew whiter than the sheet her clenched fingers were digging into. Her irregular pulse was almost imperceptible now.

Beads of sweat stood out on her face, which had turned blue and rigid, as though from the breath of some metallic vapor. Her teeth chattered, her dilated eyes stared about her vaguely, and her sole answer to questions was a shake of her head; two or three times she even smiled. Gradually her groans grew louder. A muffled scream escaped her; she pretended that she was feeling better and that she'd soon be getting up. But she was seized with convulsions.

"God!" she cried. "It's horrible!"

He flung himself on his knees beside her bed.

"Speak to me! What did you eat? Answer, for heaven's sake!"

And in his eyes she read a love such as she had never known.

"There . . . over there . . ." she said in a faltering voice.

He darted to the secretary, broke open the seal and read aloud: "No one is to blame . . ." He stopped, passed his hand over his eyes, read it again.

"What . . . ! Help! Help!"

He could only repeat the word: "Poisoned! Poisoned!" Félicité ran to Homais, who spoke loudly as he crossed the square; Madame Lefrançois heard him at the Lion d'Or, other citizens left their beds to tell their neighbors, and all night long the village was awake.

Distracted, stammering, close to collapse, Charles walked in circles around the room. He stumbled against the furniture, tore his hair: never had the pharmacist dreamed there could be so frightful a sight.

He went back to his own house and wrote letters to Monsieur Canivet and Doctor Larivière. He couldn't concentrate, had to begin them over fifteen times. Hippolyte left for Neufchâtel, and Justin spurred Bovary's horse so hard that he left it on the hill at Bois-Guillaume, foundered and all but done for.

Charles tried to consult his medical dictionary: he couldn't see; the lines danced before his eyes.

"Don't lose your head!" said the apothecary. "It's just a question of administering some powerful antidote. What poison is it?"

Charles showed him the letter. It was arsenic.

"Well then!" said Homais. "We must make an analysis."

For he knew that an analysis always had to be made in cases of poisoning.

Charles, who hadn't understood, answered with a groan: "Do it! Do it! Save her . . . !"

And returning to her side, he sank down on the carpet and leaned his head on the edge of her bed, sobbing.

"Don't cry!" she said. "I shan't be tormenting you much longer."

"Why did you do it? What made you?"

"It was the only thing," she answered.

"Weren't you happy? Am I to blame? But I did everything I could . . . !"

"Yes . . . I know . . . You're good, you're different. . . ."

She slowly passed her hand through his hair. The sweetness of her touch was more than his grief could bear. He felt his entire being give way to despair at the thought of having to lose her just when she was showing him more love than ever in the past; and he could think of nothing to do—he knew nothing, dared nothing: the need for immediate action took away the last of his presence of mind.

Emma was thinking that now she was through with all the betrayals, the infamies, the countless fierce desires that had racked her. She hated no one, now; a twilight confusion was falling over her thoughts, and of all the world's sounds she heard only the intermittent lament of this poor man beside her, gentle and indistinct, like the last echo of an ever-fainter symphony.

"Bring me my little girl," she said, raising herself on her elbow.

"You're not feeling worse, are you?" Charles asked.

"No! No!"

Berthe was carried in by the maid. Her bare feet peeped out from beneath her long nightdress; she looked serious, still half dreaming. She stared in surprise to see the room in such disorder, and she blinked her eyes, dazzled by the candles that were standing here and there on the furniture. They probably reminded her of other mornings—New Year's day or mi-carême, when she was wakened early in just this same way by candlelight and carried to her mother's bed to be given a shoeful of presents; for she asked:

"Where is it, *maman?*"

And when no one answered:

"I don't see my little shoe!"

Félicité held her over the bed, but she kept looking toward the fireplace.

"Did nurse take it away?" she asked.

At the word "nurse," which brought back her adulteries and her calamities, Madame Bovary averted her head, as though another, stronger, poison had risen to her mouth and filled her with revulsion.

"Oh, how big your eyes are, *maman!*" cried Berthe, whom the maid had put on the bed. "How pale you are! You're sweating . . . !"

Her mother looked at her.

"I'm afraid!" cried the little girl, shrinking back.

Emma took her hand to kiss it; she struggled.

"Enough! Take her away!" cried Charles, sobbing at the foot of the bed.

The symptoms momentarily stopped; she seemed calmer; and at each insignificant word she said, each time she breathed a little more easily, his hope gained ground. When Canivet finally arrived he threw himself in his arms, weeping.

"Ah! You've come! Thank you! You're kind! But she's doing better. Here: look at her!"

His colleague was not at all of this opinion. There was no use—as he himself put it—"beating around the bush," and he prescribed an emetic, to empty the stomach completely.

Soon she was vomiting blood. Her lips pressed together more tightly. Her limbs were contorted, her body was covered with brown blotches, her pulse quivered under the doctor's fingers like a taut thread, like a harpstring about to snap.

Then she began to scream, horribly. She cursed the poison, railed against it, begged it to be quick; and with her stiffened arms she pushed away everything that Charles, in greater agony than herself, tried to make her drink. He was standing, his handkerchief to his mouth, moaning, weeping, choked by sobs and shaking all over; Félicité rushed about the room; Homais, motionless, kept sighing heavily; and Monsieur Canivet, for all his air of self-assurance, began to manifest some uneasiness:

"What the devil . . . ! But she's purged, and since the cause is removed . . ."

"The effect should subside," said Homais. "It's self-evident."

"Do something to save her!" cried Bovary.

Paying no attention to the pharmacist, who was venturing the hypothesis that "this paroxysm may mark the beginning of improvement," Canivet was about to give her theriaca when there came the crack of a whip, all the windows rattled, and a post chaise drawn at breakneck speed by three mud-covered horses flashed around the corner of the market place. It was Doctor Larivière.

The sudden appearance of a god wouldn't have caused greater excitement. Bovary raised both hands, Canivet broke off his preparations, and Homais doffed his cap well before the doctor entered.

He belonged to that great surgical school created by Bichat—that generation, now vanished, of philosopher-practitioners, who cherished their art with fanatical love and applied it with enthusiasm and sagacity. Everyone in his hospital trembled when he was angry; and his students so revered him that the moment they set up for themselves they imitated him as much as they could. There was scarcely a town in the district where one of them couldn't be found, wearing a long merino overcoat and a full black tail coat, exactly like his. Doctor Larivière's unbuttoned cuffs partly covered his fleshy hands—extraordinary hands, always ungloved, as though to be the readier to grapple with suffering. Disdainful of decorations, titles and academies, hospitable, generous, a father to the poor, practicing Christian virtues although an unbeliever, he might have been thought of as a saint if he hadn't been feared as a devil because of the keenness of his mind. His scalpel-sharp glance cut deep into your soul, exposing any lie buried under excuses and reticences. His manner was majestic and genial, conscious as he was of his great gifts and his wealth and the forty years of hard work and blameless living he had behind him.

While he was still in the doorway he frowned, catching sight of Emma's cadaverous face as she lay on her back, her mouth open. Then, seeming to listen to Canivet, he passed his forefinger back and forth beneath his nostrils, repeating:

"Yes, yes."

But his shoulders lifted in a slow shrug. Bovary noticed it; their eyes met. The sight of a grieving face was no novelty to the doctor, yet he couldn't keep a tear from dropping onto his shirt front.

He asked Canivet to step into the next room. Charles followed him.

"She's very low, isn't she? How about poultices? What else? Can't you think of something? You've saved so many lives!"

Charles put his arms around him, sagged against his chest, and looked at him anxiously and beseechingly.

"Come, my poor boy, be brave! There's nothing to be done."

And Doctor Larivière turned away.

"You're leaving?"

"I'll be back."

He pretended he had something to say to the coachman, and went out with Canivet, who was no more eager than he to watch Emma die.

The pharmacist joined them in the square. He was temperamentally incapable of staying away from celebrities, and he begged Monsieur Larivière to do him the signal honor of being his guest at lunch.

Somone was quickly sent to the Lion d'Or for pigeons, the butcher was stripped of all his chops, Tuvache supplied cream and Lestiboudois eggs. The apothecary himself helped with the preparations, while Madame Homais pulled at her wrapper-strings and said:

"I hope you'll forgive us, Monsieur. In this wretched village, if we don't have a full day's warning . . ."

"The stemmed glasses!!!" whispered Homais.

"If we lived in the city we'd at least have stuffed pigs' feet to fall back on."

"Don't talk so much . . . ! Sit down, Doctor!"

After the first few mouthfuls he considered it appropriate to supply a few details concerning the catastrophe.

"First we had a sensation of siccity in the pharynx, then intolerable pain in the epigastrium, superpurgation, coma."

"How did she poison herself?"

"I have no idea, Doctor, and I can't even imagine where she managed to procure that arsenous oxide."

Justin, who was just then carrying in a pile of plates, was seized with a fit of trembling.

"What's the matter with you?" asked the pharmacist.

At the question the young man dropped everything with a great crash.

"Imbecile!" cried Homais. "Clumsy lout! Damned idiot!"

Then, quickly regaining his self-control:

"I wanted to try an analysis, Doctor, and, *primo*, I carefully inserted into a tube . . ."

"It would have been better," said the surgeon, "if you'd inserted your fingers into her throat."

Canivet said nothing, having just a few minutes before been given, in private, a severe rebuke concerning his emetic. Today he was as meek as he had been arrogant and verbose the day he had operated on Hippolyte: his face was fixed in a continual, approving smile.

Homais blossomed in his role of proud host, and the thought of Bovary's distress added something to his pleasure as he selfishly contrasted their lots. Moreover, the doctor's presence excited him. He displayed all his erudition, dragging in, pell-mell, mention of cantharides, the upas, the manchineel, the bite of the adder.

"I've even read about people being poisoned, Doctor—positively struck down—by blood sausages that had been subjected to excessive fumigation! At least, so it says in a very fine report, written by one of our leading pharmaceutical lights, one of our masters, the illustrious Cadet de Gassicourt!"

Madame Homais reappeared, bearing one of those rickety contraptions that are heated with alcohol, for Homais insisted on brewing his coffee at table—having, needless to say, previously done his own roasting, his own grinding and his own blending.

"*Saccharum*, Doctor?" he said, passing the sugar.

Then he called in all his children, eager to have the surgeon's opinion on their constitutions.

Finally, when Monsieur Larivière was about to leave, Madame Homais asked him to advise her about her husband. His "blood was getting thicker" because of his habit of falling asleep every evening after dinner.

"Oh, he's not thick-*blooded!*"

And smiling a little at his joke, which passed unnoticed,

the doctor opened the door. But the pharmacy was thronged, and he had a hard time getting rid of Monsieur Tuvache, was was afraid that his wife would get pneumonia because of her habit of spitting into the fire; then Monsieur Binet complained of often feeling ravenous; Madame Caron had prickling sensations; Lheureux suffered from dizzy spells; Lestiboudois was rheumatic; and Madame Lefrançois had heartburn. Finally the three horses bore him away, and the general verdict was that he had been far from obliging.

Then the attention of the public was distracted by the appearance of Monsieur Bournisien, crossing the market with the holy oils.

Homais paid his debt to his principles by likening priests to ravens: both are attracted by the odor of the dead. Actually, he had a more personal reason for disliking the sight of a priest: a cassock made him think of a shroud, and his execration of the one owed something to his fear of the other.

Nevertheless, not flinching in the face of what he called his "mission," he returned to the Bovary house along with Canivet, whom Monsieur Larivière had urged to stay on to the end. But for his wife's protests, the pharmacist would have taken his two sons along, to inure them to life's great moments, to provide them with a lesson, an example, a momentous spectacle that they would remember later.

The bedroom, as they entered, was mournful and solemn. On the sewing table, now covered with a white napkin, were five or six small wads of cotton in a silver dish, and nearby a large crucifix between two lighted candelabra. Emma lay with her chin sunk on her breast, her eyelids unnaturally wide apart; and her poor hands picked at the sheets in the ghastly and poignant way of the dying, who seem impatient to cover themselves with their shrouds. Pale as a statue, his eyes red as coals, but no longer weeping, Charles stood facing her at the foot of the bed; the priest, on one knee, mumbled under his breath.

She slowly turned her face, and seemed overjoyed at suddenly seeing the purple stole—doubtless recognizing, in this interval of extraordinary peace, the lost ecstasy of her first mystical flights and the first visions of eternal bliss.

The priest stood up and took the crucifix; she stretched out her head like someone thirsting; and pressing her lips to the body of the God-Man, she imprinted on it, with every ounce of her failing strength, the most passionate love-kiss she had ever given. Then he recited the *Misereatur* and the *Indulgentiam*, dipped his right thumb in the oil, and began the unctions. First he anointed her eyes, once so covetous of all earthly luxuries; then her nostrils, so gluttonous of caressing breezes and amorous scents; then her mouth, so prompt to lie, so defiant in pride, so loud in lust; then her hands, that had thrilled to voluptuous contacts; and finally the soles of her feet, once so swift when she had hastened to slake her desires, and now never to walk again.

The curé wiped his fingers, threw the oil-soaked bits of cotton into the fire, and returned to the dying woman, sitting beside her and telling her that now she must unite her sufferings with Christ's and throw herself on the divine mercy.

As he ended his exhortations he tried to have her grasp a blessed candle, symbol of the celestial glories soon to surround her. Emma was too weak, and couldn't close her fingers: but for Monsieur Bournisien the candle would have fallen to the floor.

Yet she was no longer so pale, and her face was serene, as though the sacrament had cured her.

The priest didn't fail to point this out: he even explained to Bovary that the Lord sometimes prolonged people's lives when He judged it expedient for their salvation; and

Charles remembered another day, when, similarly close to death, she had received communion.

"Perhaps there's hope after all," he thought.

And indeed, she looked all about her, slowly, like someone waking from a dream; then, in a distinct voice, she asked for her mirror, and she remained bowed over it for some time, until great tears flowed from her eyes. Then she threw back her head with a sigh, and sank onto the pillow.

At once her breast began to heave rapidly. Her tongue hung at full length from her mouth; her rolling eyes grew dim like the globes of two lamps about to go out; and one might have thought her dead already but for the terrifying, ever-faster movement of her ribs, which were shaken by furious gasps, as though her soul were straining violently to break its fetters. Félicité knelt before the crucifix, and even the pharmacist flexed his knees a little. Monsieur Canivet stared vaguely out into the square. Bournisien had resumed his praying, his face bowed over the edge of the bed and his long black cassock trailing out behind him into the room. Charles was on the other side, on his knees, his arms stretched out toward Emma. He had taken her hands, and was pressing them, shuddering at every beat of her heart, as at the tremors of a falling ruin. As the death-rattle grew louder, the priest speeded his prayers: they mingled with Bovary's stifled sobs, and at moments everything seemed drowned by the monotonous flow of Latin syllables that sounded like the tolling of a bell.

Suddenly from out on the sidewalk came a noise of heavy wooden shoes and the scraping of a stick, and a voice rose up, a raucous voice singing:

> *A clear day's warmth will often move*
> *A lass to stray in dreams of love.*

Emma sat up like a galvanized corpse, her hair streaming, her eyes fixed and gaping.

> *To gather up the stalks of wheat*
> *The swinging scythe keeps laying by,*
> *Nanette goes stooping in the heat*
> *Along the furrow where they lie.*

"The blind man!" she cried.

Emma began to laugh—a horrible, frantic, desperate laugh—fancying that she saw the beggar's hideous face, a figure of terror looming up in the darkness of eternity.

> *The wind blew very hard that day*
> *And snatched her petticoat away!*

A spasm flung her down on the mattress. Everyone drew close. She had ceased to exist.

IX

ANYONE'S DEATH ALWAYS RELEASES SOMETHING LIKE AN AURA of stupefaction, so difficult is it to grasp this irruption of nothingness and to believe that it has actually taken place. But when Charles realized how still she was, he threw himself on her, crying:

"*Adieu! Adieu!*"

Homais and Canivet led him from the room.

"Control yourself!"

"Let me stay!" he said, struggling. "I'll be reasonable; I won't do anything I shouldn't. But I want to be near her— she's my wife!"

And he wept.

"Weep, weep," said the pharmacist. "Let yourself go: you'll feel the better for it."

Helpless as a child, Charles let himself be taken downstairs to the parlor. Monsieur Homais soon went home.

In the square he was accosted by the blind beggar. Lured by the hope of the antiphlogistic salve, he had dragged himself all the way to Yonville, and now was asking every passer-by where the apothecary lived.

"Good Lord! As though I didn't have other things on my mind! Too bad! Come back later."

He hurried into the pharmacy.

He had to write two letters, prepare a sedative for Bovary, and invent a plausible lie that would cover up the suicide for an article in the *Fanal* and for the crowd that was awaiting him in order to learn the news. When all the Yonvillians had heard his story about the arsenic that Emma had mistaken for sugar while making a custard, Homais returned once more to Bovary.

He found him alone (Canivet had just left), sitting in the armchair beside the window, staring vacantly at the parlor floor.

"Now," said the pharmacist, "what you've got to do is decide on a time for the ceremony."

"Why? What ceremony?"

Then, in a frightened stammer:

"Oh no! I don't have to, do I? I want to keep her!"

To hide his embarrassment Homais took a carafe from the whatnot and began to water the geraniums.

"Ah, thank you!" said Charles. "You're so good!"

He broke off, choked by the flood of memories the pharmacist's action evoked.

To distract him, Homais thought it well to talk about horticulture: plants, he ventured, had to be kept moist. Charles nodded in agreement.

"Anyway, we'll soon be having fine spring weather."

"Ah!" said Bovary.

Not knowing what to say next, the apothecary twitched the sash curtain.

"Ah—there's Monsieur Tuvache going by."

Charles repeated mechanically:

"Monsieur Tuvache going by."

Homais didn't dare broach the subject of funeral arrangements again: it was the priest who eventually made Charles see reason.

He locked himself in his consulting room, took a pen, and after sobbing awhile he wrote:

"I want her buried in her bridal dress, with white shoes and a wreath and her hair spread over her shoulders. Three coffins—one oak, one mahogany, one lead. No one has to say anything to me: I'll have the strength to go through with it. Cover her with a large piece of green velvet. I want this done. Do it."

The priest and the pharmacist were much taken aback by Bovary's romantic ideas. Homais expostulated:

"The velvet seems to be supererogatory. Not to mention the expense . . ."

"Is it any concern of yours?" cried Charles. "Leave me alone! You didn't love her! Go away!"

The priest took him by the arm and walked him around the garden, discoursing on the vanity of earthly things. God is all-great, all-good; we must submit to His decrees without complaint; more than that, we must be grateful.

Charles burst into a stream of blasphemy.

"I detest your God!"

"The spirit of rebellion is still in you," sighed the priest.

Bovary had strode away from him and was pacing up and down beside the wall of espaliered fruit trees, grinding his teeth and looking curses at heaven: but not even a leaf stirred in answer.

A fine rain was falling. Charles's shirt was open, and soon he began to shiver. He went back into the house and sat in the kitchen.

At six o'clock there was a clanking in the square. It was

the Hirondelle arriving, and he stood with his head against the windowpanes, watching all the passengers get out, one after the other. Félicité put down a mattress for him in the parlor, and he threw himself on it and fell asleep.

Rationalist though he was, Monsieur Homais respected the dead. So, bearing no grudge against poor Charles, he returned that night to watch beside the body. He brought three books with him, and a writing-pad for making notes.

He found Monsieur Bournisien already there. Two tall candles were burning at the head of the bed, which had been moved out of the alcove.

The apothecary, oppressed by the silence, soon made a few elegiac remarks concerning "this hapless young woman"; and the priest replied that now there was nothing left to do but pray for her.

"Still," said Homais, "it's one thing or the other: either she died in a state of grace (as the church puts it), and therefore had no need of our prayers; or else she died unrepentant (I believe that is the ecclesiastical term) and in that case . . ."

Bournisien interrupted him, replying testily that prayer was called for nonetheless.

"But," objected the pharmacist, "since God knows all our needs, what purpose can be served by prayer?"

"What?" said the priest. "Prayer? Aren't you a Christian, then?"

"I beg your pardon!" said Homais. "I admire Christianity. It freed the slaves, for one thing; it introduced into the world a moral code that . . ."

"That's not the point! All the texts . . ."

"Oh! Oh! The texts! Look in any history book: everybody knows they were falsified by the Jesuits."

Charles came in, walked up to the bed and slowly parted the curtains.

Emma's head was turned toward her right shoulder. The corner of her open mouth was like a black hole in the lower part of her face; her two thumbs were bent inward toward the palms of her hands; a kind of white dust powdered her lashes; and the outline of her eyes was beginning to disappear in a viscous pallor, as though spiders had been spinning cobwebs over her face. From her breasts to her knees the sheet sagged, rising again at her toes; and it seemed to Charles that some infinite mass, some enormous weight, was pressing on her.

The church clock struck two. The flowing river murmured deeply in the darkness at the foot of the terrace. Now and again Monsieur Bournisien blew his nose loudly, and Homais' pen was scratching on his paper.

"Go back to bed, my friend," he said. "Stop torturing yourself."

When Charles had gone, the pharmacist and the curé resumed their arguments.

"Read Voltaire!" said the one. "Read Holbach! Read the Encyclopedia!"

"Read the *Letters of Some Portuguese Jews!*" said the other. "Read the *Proof of Christianity*, by ex-magistrate Nicolas!"

They grew excited and flushed; both spoke at once, neither listening to the other; Bournisien was shocked by such audacity; Homais marveled at such stupidity; and they were on the point of exchanging insults when Charles suddenly reappeared. He couldn't keep away: it was as though a spell kept drawing him upstairs.

He stood at the foot of the bed to see her better, absorbed in contemplation so intense that he no longer felt any pain.

He recalled stories about catalepsy and the miracles of

magnetism; and he told himself that by straining his will to the utmost he might resuscitate her. Once he even leaned over toward her and cried very softly "Emma! Emma!" The force of his breath blew the flickering candle flames against the wall.

At daybreak the older Madame Bovary arrived, and as Charles embraced her he had another fit of weeping. Like the pharmacist, she ventured a few remarks about the funeral expenses, but he flew into such a rage that she said no more, and he sent her straight to the city to buy what was needed.

Charles spent all afternoon alone. Berthe had been taken to Madame Homais'; Félicité stayed upstairs in the bedroom with Madame Lefrançois.

That evening, people called. He rose and shook hands with them, unable to speak; each then took a seat alongside the others, gradually forming a wide semicircle in front of the fireplace. Eyes lowered and legs crossed, they dangled their feet, sighing deeply from time to time. Everyone was bored beyond measure, but no one was willing to be the first to leave.

When Homais returned at nine o'clock (during the past two days he had seemed to spend all his time crossing the square) he brought with him a supply of camphor, benzoin and aromatic herbs. He also had a vase full of chlorine water, to "drive out the miasmas." At that moment the maid, Madame Lefrançois and the older Madame Bovary were clustered around Emma, putting the finishing touches to her toilette: they drew down the long, stiff veil, covering her even to her satin shoes.

Félicité sobbed:

"Ah! Poor mistress! Poor mistress!"

"Look at her," said the hotel-keeper, with a sigh. "How pretty she still is! You'd swear she'd be getting up any minute."

Then they bent over to put on her wreath.

They had to lift her head a little, and as they did so a black liquid poured out of her mouth like vomit.

"Heavens! Watch out for her dress!" cried Madame Lefrançois. "Help us, won't you?" she said to the pharmacist. "You wouldn't be afraid, would you?"

"I, afraid?" he answered, shrugging his shoulders. "Take it from me: I saw plenty of things like this at the hospital, when I was studying pharmacy. We used to make punch in the dissecting room while we worked. Death holds no terrors for a philosopher. In fact, as I often say, I intend to leave my body to the hospitals, so that it can eventually be of service to science."

When the curé arrived he asked how Monsieur was; and at the apothecary's reply he said:

"Of course: he still hasn't got over the shock."

Homais went on to congratulate him on not being exposed, like other men, to the risk of losing a beloved wife; and there followed a discussion on the celibacy of the clergy.

"After all," said the pharmacist, "it's against nature for a man to do without women. We've all heard of crimes . . ."

"But drat it all!" cried the priest. "How would you expect anyone who was married to be able to keep the secrets of the confessional, for example?"

Homais attacked confession. Bournisien defended it: he dilated on the acts of restitution it was constantly responsible for, told stories about thieves suddenly turning honest. Soldiers, approaching the tribunal of repentance, had felt the scales drop from their eyes. There was a minister at Fribourg . . .

His fellow watcher had fallen asleep. Bournisien found it somewhat hard to breathe, the air of the room was so heavy, and he opened a window. This woke the pharmacist.

"Here," the priest said. "Take a pinch of snuff. Do—it clears the head."

There was a continual barking somewhere in the distance.

"Do you hear a dog howling?" said the pharmacist.

"People say that they scent the dead," answered the priest. "It's like bees: they leave the hive when someone dies."

Homais didn't challenge those superstitions, for once again he had fallen asleep.

Monsieur Bournisien, more resistant, continued for some time to move his lips in a murmur, then his chin sank gradually lower, his thick black book slipped from his hand, and he began to snore.

They sat opposite one another, stomachs out, faces swollen, both of them scowling—united, after so much dissension, in the same human weakness; and they stirred no more than the corpse that was like another sleeper beside them.

Charles's coming didn't wake them. This was the last time. He had come to bid her farewell.

The aromatic herbs were still smoking, and at the window their swirls of bluish vapor mingled with the mist that was blowing in.

There were a few stars. The night was mild.

Great drops of wax were falling onto the bedsheets from the candles. Charles watched them burn, tiring his eyes in the gleam of their yellow flames.

The watered satin of her dress was shimmering with the whiteness of moonbeams. Emma was invisible under it; and it seemed to him as though she were spreading out beyond herself, melting confusedly into the surroundings—

the silence, the night, the passing wind, the damp fragrance that rose from the earth.

Then, suddenly, he saw her in the garden at Tostes, on the seat, against the thorn hedge—or in Rouen, in the street—or on the doorstep of their house, in the farmyard at Les Bertaux. Once again he heard the laughter of the merry lads dancing under the apple trees; the wedding chamber was full of the perfume of her hair, and her dress rustled in his arms with a sound of flying sparks. And now she was wearing that very dress!

He stood there a long time thus recalling all his past happiness—her poses, her gestures, the sound of her voice. Wave of despair followed upon wave, endlessly, like the waters of an overflowing tide.

A terrible curiosity came over him: slowly, with the tips of his fingers, his heart pounding, he lifted her veil. He gave a scream of horror that woke the sleepers. They took him downstairs to the parlor.

Then Félicité came up, to say that he was asking for a lock of her hair.

"Cut some!" answered the apothecary.

She didn't dare, and he stepped forward himself, scissors in hand. He trembled so violently that he nicked the skin on the temples in several places. Finally, steeling himself, Homais slashed blindly two or three times, leaving white marks in the beautiful black tresses.

The pharmacist and the curé resumed their respective occupations—not without dozing off now and again and reproaching each other for doing so each time they awoke. Then Monsieur Bournisien would sprinkle the room with holy water and Homais would pour a little chlorine water on the floor.

Félicité had thought to leave a bottle of brandy for them on the chest of drawers, along with a cheese and a big brioche. Finally, about four in the morning, the apothecary could hold out no longer.

"I confess," he sighed, "that I'd gladly partake of some nourishment."

The priest didn't have to be asked twice. He went out, said his Mass, came back; and they proceeded to eat and clink their glasses, chuckling a little without knowing why, prey to that indefinable gaiety that often succeeds periods of gloom. With the last drink of brandy the priest slapped the pharmacist on the back:

"We'll be good friends yet!" he said.

Downstairs in the hall they met the workmen arriving, and for two hours Charles had to suffer the torture of the sound of the hammer on the planks. Then they brought her down in her oaken coffin, which they fitted inside the two others. The outermost was too wide, and they had to stuff the space between with wool from a mattress. Finally, when the three lids had been planed, nailed on and soldered, the bier was exposed at the door. The house was thrown open, and the Yonvillians began to flock in.

Monsieur Rouault arrived. He fell in a faint in the square at the sight of the black cloth.

X

THE PHARMACIST'S LETTER HADN'T REACHED HIM UNTIL thirty-six hours after the event; and to spare his feelings Monsieur Hamais had worded it in such a way that it was impossible for him to know what to think.

On reading it he fell to the ground, as though stricken

by apoplexy. Then he gathered that she was *not* dead. But she might be . . . He put on his smock and his hat, fastened a spur to his boot, and set off at a gallop; and during the entire length of his breathless ride he was frantic with anguish. At one point he had to stop and dismount: he couldn't see, he heard voices, he thought he was losing his mind.

At daybreak he caught sight of three black hens asleep in a tree, and he shuddered, terrified by the omen. He promised the Holy Virgin three chasubles for the church, and vowed to walk barefoot from the cemetery at Les Bertaux to the chapel at Vassonville.

He rode into Maromme, shouting ahead to the people at the inn, burst open the gate with his shoulder, dashed up to the oats bag, poured a bottle of sweet cider into the manger; then he remounted his nag, and it was off again, striking sparks from all four shoes.

He kept telling himself that she would certainly live: the doctors would find a remedy—there was no question. He reminded himself of all the miraculous recoveries people had told him of.

Then he had a vision of her dead. She was there, before him, stretched on her back in the middle of the road. He pulled at the reins, and the hallucination vanished.

At Quincampoix he drank three coffees in a row to fortify himself.

It occurred to him that they might have put the wrong name on the letter. He rummaged for it in his pocket, felt it there, but didn't dare open it.

He even began to imagine that it might be a practical joke, an attempt to get even with him for something, or a wag's idea of a prank. Besides—if she was dead, he'd know it! But no—the countryside was as always: the sky was blue, the trees were swaying; a flock of sheep crossed the road. He caught sight of the village; people saw him racing by, hunched over his horse, beating it furiously, its saddle girths dripping blood.

Then, when he had regained consciousness, he fell weeping into Bovary's arms:

"My daughter! Emma! My baby! Tell me . . ."

Charles answered, sobbing:

"I don't know, I don't know! It's a curse . . ."

The apothecary drew them apart.

"There's no use going into the horrible details. I'll tell Monsieur all about it later. People are coming. Have some dignity, for heaven's sake! Take it like a philosopher!"

Poor Charles made an effort, and repeated several times: "Yes! . . . Be brave!"

"All right, then, I'll be brave, God damn it to hell!" the old man cried. "I'll stay with her to the end."

The bell was tolling. Everything was ready. It was time to set out.

Sitting side by side in one of the choir stalls, they watched the three cantors continually crossing back and forth in front of them, intoning. The serpent player blew with all his might. Monsieur Bournisien, in full regalia, sang in a shrill voice: he bowed to the tabernacle, raised his hands, stretched out his arms, Lestiboudois moved about the church with his verger's staff; near the lectern stood the coffin, between four rows of candles. Charles had to restrain himself from getting up and putting them out.

He did his best, however, to work himself up into a religious frame of mind, to seize on the hope of a future life in which he would see her again. He tried to imagine that she had gone on a trip—far off—a long time ago. But when he remembered that she was right there, in the coffin, and that everything was over, and that now she was going to be buried, he was filled with a rage that was fierce and black and desperate. At moments he thought he was beyond feeling; and he relished this ebbing of grief, cursing himself in the same breath for a scoundrel.

A sharp, regular noise, like the tapping of a metal-tipped walking stick, was heard on the stone floor. It came from the far end of the church and stopped abruptly in the side aisle. A man in a coarse brown jacket sank painfully to his knees. It was Hippolyte, the stable-boy at the Lion d'Or. He had put on his new leg.

One of the cantors came through the nave, taking up the collection, and one after another the heavy coins clattered onto the silver plate.

"Get it over with! I can't stand much more of this!" cried Bovary, angrily throwing him a five-franc piece.

The cantor thanked him with a ceremonious bow.

The singing and the kneeling and the rising went on and on. He remembered that once, early in their marriage, they had attended Mass together, and that they had sat on the other side, at the right, against the wall. The bell began to toll again. There was a great scraping of chairs. The pallbearers slipped their three poles under the bier, and everyone left the church.

At that moment Justin appeared in the doorway of the pharmacy and abruptly retreated, white-faced and trembling.

People stood at their windows to watch the procession. Charles, at the head, held himself very straight. He put on a brave front and nodded to those who came out from the lanes and the doorways to join the crowd.

The six men, three on each side, walked with short steps, panting a little. The priests, the cantors and the two choirboys recited the De profundis; and their voices carried over the fields, rising and falling in waves. Sometimes they disappeared from view at a twist of the path; but the great silver cross was always visible, high up among the trees.

At the rear were the women, in their black cloaks with

turned-down hoods; each of them carried a thick lighted candle; and Charles felt himself overcome amidst this endless succession of prayers and lights, these cloying odors of wax and cassocks. A cool breeze was blowing, the rye and the colza were sprouting green; dewdrops shimmered on the thorn hedges along the road. All kinds of joyous sounds filled the air—the rattle of a jolting cart in distant ruts, the repeated crowing of a cock, the thudding of a colt as it bolted off under the apple trees. The pure sky was dappled with rosy clouds; wisps of bluish smoke trailed down over the thatched cottages, their roofs abloom with iris. Charles recognized each farmyard as he passed. He remembered leaving them on mornings like this after making sick-calls, on his way back home to where she was.

The black pall, embroidered with white tears, flapped up now and again, exposing the coffin beneath. The tired pallbearers were slowing down, and the bier moved forward in a series of jerks, like a boat pitching at every wave.

They reached the cemetery.

The pallbearers continued on to where the grave had been dug in the turf.

Everyone stood around it; and as the priest spoke, the reddish earth, heaped up on the edges, kept sliding down at the corners, noiselessly and continuously.

Then, when the four ropes were in position, the coffin was pushed onto them. He watched it go down. It went down and down.

Finally there was a thud, and the ropes creaked as they came back up. Then Bournisien took the shovel that Lestiboudois held out to him. With his left hand—all the while sprinkling holy water with his right—he vigorously pushed in a large spadeful of earth; and the stones striking the wood of the coffin made that awesome sound that seems to us like the very voice of eternity.

The priest passed his sprinkler to the person beside him.

It was Homais. He shook it gravely, then handed it to Charles, who sank on his knees in the pile of earth and threw it into the grave in handfuls, crying, "*Adieu!*" He blew her kisses, and dragged himself toward the grave as though to be swallowed up in it with her.

They led him away, and he soon grew calmer—vaguely relieved, perhaps, like everyone else, that it was all over.

On the way back Monsieur Rouault calmly lit his pipe—a gesture that Homais silently condemned as improper. He noticed, too, that Monsieur Binet had stayed away, that Tuvache had "sneaked off" after the Mass, and that Théodore, the notary's servant, was wearing a blue coat—"as if he couldn't find a black coat, since it's the custom, for heaven's sake!" And he went from group to group communicating his sentiments. Everyone was deploring Emma's death, especially Lheureux, who hadn't failed to attend the funeral.

"Poor little lady! How terrible for her husband!"

"If it hadn't been for me, let me tell you," the apothecary assured him, "he would have tried to do away with himself!"

"Such a good woman! To think that just last Saturday I saw her in my shop!"

"I didn't have the leisure," said Homais, "to prepare a little speech. I'd have liked to say a few words at the grave."

Back home, Charles took off his funeral clothes and Monsieur Rouault got back into his blue smock. It was a new one: all the way from Les Bertaux he had kept wiping his eyes with the sleeve, and the dye had come off on his face, which was still dusty and tear-streaked.

The older Madame Bovary was with them. All three were silent. Finally the old man sighed:

"You remember, my friend, I came to Tostes once, when

you had just lost your first wife. That time I tried to comfort you. I could think of something to say; but now . . ."

Then, his chest heaving in a long groan:

"Ah! Everything's over for me! I've seen my wife go . . . then my son . . . and now today my daughter!"

He insisted on leaving immediately for Les Bertaux, saying that he couldn't sleep in that house. He even refused to see his granddaughter.

"No! No! It would be too hard on me. . . . But give her a big kiss for me! Good-bye! . . . You're a good man! And—I'll never forget this!" he said, slapping his thigh. "Don't worry—you'll always get your turkey."

But when he reached the top of the hill he turned around as he had turned around once before, after parting from her on the road to Saint-Victor. The windows of the village were all ablaze in the slanting rays of the sun that was setting beyond the meadow. He shaded his eyes with his hand; and on the horizon he made out a walled enclosure where trees stood in dark clumps here and there among white stones; then he continued on his way at a gentle trot, for his nag was limping.

Weary though they were, Charles and his mother sat up very late that night talking. They spoke of days gone by and of the future: she would come and live in Yonville, she would keep house for him; never again would they be apart. She was astute and ingratiating with him, rejoicing inwardly at the thought of recapturing his affection, which had eluded her for so many years. Midnight struck. The village was silent as usual; and Charles lay awake, thinking ceaselessly of *her.*

Rodolphe, who had spent all day roaming the woods to keep his mind off things, was peacefully asleep in his chateau; and Léon was sleeping, too, in the distant city.

But there was someone else—someone who was not asleep at that late hour.

On the grave among the firs knelt a young boy, weeping and sobbing in the darkness, his heart overflowing with an immense grief that was tender as the moon and unfathomable as night. Suddenly the gate creaked. It was Lestiboudois, come to fetch his spade, which he had forgotten a while before. He recognized Justin clambering over the wall: at last he knew who was stealing his potatoes!

XI

THE NEXT DAY CHARLES SENT FOR BERTHE. SHE ASKED FOR *maman:* she was away on a trip, she was told, and would bring her back some toys. She mentioned her again several times, then gradually forgot her. Charles found the little girl's cheerfulness depressing. The pharmacist's consolations, too, were an ordeal.

Before long the question of money came up again. Monsieur Lheureux egged on his friend Vinçart as before, and Charles signed notes for enormous sums: he refused absolutely to consider selling the slightest bit of furniture that had belonged to her. His mother fumed; he flew into an even greater rage. He was a completely changed man. She packed up and left.

Then everyone began to snatch what he could. Mademoiselle Lempereur demanded her fees for six months' lessons. Emma had never taken a single one, despite the receipted bills that she had shown Bovary: the two ladies had concocted this device between them. The lending-library proprietor demanded three years' subscription fees. Madame Rollet demanded postage fees for twenty or so letters, and when Charles asked for an explanation she was tactful enough to answer:

"Oh, I don't know anything about them—some personal matters."

Each debt he paid, Charles thought was the last. Then more came—a continual stream.

He dunned patients for back bills, but they showed him the letters his wife had sent and he had to apologize.

Félicité now wore Madame's dresses. Not all, for he had kept a few and used to shut himself up in her dressing room and look at them. The maid was just about her size, and often when Charles caught sight of her from behind he thought it was Emma, and cried out:

"Oh! Don't go! Don't go!"

But at Pentecost she left Yonville without warning, eloping with Théodore and stealing everything that was left of the wardrobe.

It was about this time that "Madame *veuve* Dupuis" had the honor of announcing to him the "marriage of M. Léon Dupuis, her son, notary at Yvetot, and Mlle. Léocadie Leboeuf, of Bondeville." Charles's letter of congratulation contained the sentence: "How happy this would have made my poor wife!"

One day, wandering aimlessly about the house, he went up to the attic; and through the sole of his slipper he felt a wad of thin paper. He opened it. "You must be courageous, Emma," he read. "The last thing I want to do is ruin your life." It was Rodolphe's letter. It had fallen to the floor in among some boxes and had remained there, and now the draught from the dormer had blown it toward the door. Charles stood there motionless and open-mouthed— in the very spot where Emma, desperate and even paler than he was now, had longed to die. Finally he discovered a small "R" at the bottom of the second page. Who was it? He remembered Rodolphe's attentiveness, his sudden disappearance, and his air of constraint the two or three times they had met since. But the respectful tone of the letter deceived him.

"Perhaps they loved each other platonically," he told himself.

In any case, Charles wasn't one to go to the root of things: he closed his eyes to the evidence, and his hesitant jealousy was drowned in the immensity of his grief.

Everyone must have adored her, he thought. Every man who saw her must certainly have coveted her. This made her the lovelier in his mind; and he conceived a furious desire for her that never stopped; it fed the flames of his despair, and it grew stronger and stronger because now it could never be satisfied.

To please her, as though she were still alive, he adopted her tastes, her ideas: he bought himself patent leather shoes, took to wearing white cravats. He waxed his mustache, and signed—just as she had—more promissory notes. She was corrupting him from beyond the grave.

He was forced to sell the silver piece by piece, then he sold the parlor furniture. But though all the other rooms grew bare, the bedroom—her bedroom—remained as before. Charles went there every day after dinner. He pushed the round table up to the fire, pulled her armchair close to it. He sat opposite. A tallow candle burned in one of the gilded sconces. Berthe, at his side, colored pictures.

It pained him, poor fellow, to see her so shabbily dressed, with her shoes unlaced and the armholes of her smock torn and gaping to below her waist—for the cleaning woman completely neglected her. But she was so sweet and gentle, and she bent her little head so gracefully, letting her fair hair fall against her rosy cheek, that he was flooded with infinite pleasure—an enjoyment that was mixed with bitterness, like an inferior wine tasting of resin. He mended her toys, made puppets for her out of cardboard, sewed up the torn stomachs of her dolls. But the sight of the sewing-box, or a bit of loose ribbon, or even a pin caught in a crack in the table, would send him brooding; and then he looked so gloomy that she, too, grew sad.

No one came to see them now, for Justin had run off to Rouen, where he found work as a grocery clerk, and the apothecary's children saw less and less of Berthe. Monsieur Homais was not eager to prolong the intimacy, considering the difference in their social status.

The blind man, whom his salve had not cured, had resumed his beat on the hill at Bois-Guillaume, where he told everyone about the pharmacist's failure—to such a point that Homais, whenever he went to the city, hid behind the Hirondelle's curtains to avoid meeting him face to face. He hated him. He must get rid of him at all costs, he decided, for the sake of his own reputation; and he launched an underhand campaign against him in which he revealed his deep cunning and his criminal vanity. During the next six months paragraphs like the following would appear in the *Fanal de Rouen:*

> Anyone who has ever wended his way toward the fertile fields of Picardy cannot help but have noticed, on the hill at Bois-Guillaume, an unfortunate afflicted with a horrible facial deformity. He pesters travelers, persecutes them, levies a veritable tax upon them. Are we back in the monstrous days of the Middle Ages, when vagabonds were permitted to display, in our public squares, the leprous ulcers and scrofulous sores they brought back from the Crusades?

Or:

> Despite the laws against vagrancy, the approaches to our large cities continue to be infested by bands of

beggars. There are some who operate single-handed; and these, perhaps, are not the least dangerous of the lot. What are our Municipal Authorities waiting for?

Sometimes Homais invented ancedotes:

Yesterday, on the hill at Bois-Guillaume, a skittish horse . . .

And there would follow the story of an accident caused by the blind man.

This went on until the begger was locked up. But he was released. He took up where he had left off. So did Homais. It was a fight to the finish. Homais was victorious: his enemy was committed to an asylum for the rest of his days.

This success emboldened him; and from then on whenever a dog was run over in the district, or a barn set on fire, or a woman beaten, Homais hastened to publicize the event, inspired always by love of progress and hatred of the clergy. He instituted comparisons between public and religious schools, to the detriment of the latter; he referred to Saint Bartholomew's Eve apropos of every hundred-franc subsidy the government granted the church; he denounced abuses, he flashed the rapier of satire. Such, at least, was the way he put it. In short, Homais was "undermining the foundations": he was becoming a dangerous man.

He found the narrow limitations of journalism stifling, however, and soon he felt the need to produce a book, a "work." So he composed his *General Statistics Concerning the Canton of Yonville, Followed by Climatological Observations;* and statistics led him into philosophy. He dealt with burning issues: the social problem, raising the moral standards of the poor, pisciculture, rubber, railroads, etc. In the end, he felt it a disgrace to be a bourgeois. He affected bohemian ways, he even smoked! He bought two rococo statuettes, very *chic*, to decorate his parlor.

Not that he gave up pharmacy. Far from it! He kept up with all the latest discoveries. He followed every stage in the great development of chocolates. He was the first to introduce into the department of the Seine-Inférieure those two great chocolate health foods, Cho-ca and Reva-lentia. He became an enthusiastic partisan of Pulver-macher electric health belts; he wore one himself, and at night when he took off his flannel undershirt Madame Ho-mais never failed to be dazzled by the golden spiral that almost hid him from view, and her passion redoubled for this man she saw before her swaddled like a Scythian and splendid as a Magian priest.

He had brilliant ideas for Emma's tombstone. First he suggested a broken column with a drapery; then a pyra-mid, then a Temple of Vesta, a kind of rotunda, or per-haps a romantic pile of ruins. One element was constant in all his plans—a weeping willow, which he considered the obligatory symbol of grief.

Charles and he made a trip to Rouen together to look at tombstones at a burial specialist's, accompanied by an artist named Vaufrilard, a friend of Bridoux's, who never stopped making puns. Finally, after examining a hundred designs, getting an estimate, and making a second trip to Rouen, Charles decided in favor of a mausoleum whose two principal sides were to be adorned with "a spirit bear-ing an extinguished torch."

As for the inscription, Homais could think of nothing as eloquent as *Sta viator*. He couldn't get beyond it, rack his brains as he might: he kept repeating "*Sta viator*" to himself over and over again. Finally he had an inspiration —*amabilem conjugem calcas;* and this was adopted.

The strange thing was that Bovary, even though he thought of Emma continually, was forgetting her; and he felt desperate realizing that her image was fading from his memory, struggle as he might to keep it alive. Each night, however, he dreamed of her. It was always the same dream: he approached her, but just when he was about to embrace her she fell into decay in his arms.

The first week, he went to church every evening. Monsieur Bournisien called on him two or three times, then left him alone. The fact is that the priest was becoming decidedly less tolerant—sinking into real fanaticism, as Homais put it. He thundered against the spirit of the modern age, and regularly once a fortnight included in his sermon an account of the last agony of Voltaire—who died eating his own excrement, as everyone knows.

Despite Bovary's frugality, he was quite unable to pay off his old debts. Lheureux refused to renew a single note. Execution was imminent. He had recourse to his mother, who agreed to let him mortgage her house; but she seized the occasion to write him many harsh things about Emma, and in return for her sacrifice she demanded a shawl that had escaped Félicité's depredations. Charles refused to let her have it, and they quarreled.

She made the first overtures toward a reconciliation by offering to take the little girl to live with her: the child could help her in the house. Charles consented. But when the time came for her to leave he couldn't face it, and there was a new break between mother and son, this time irrevocable.

As his bonds with others weakened, his love for his child grew ever stronger. She worried him, however, for occasionally she coughed and had red patches on her cheekbones.

Across the square, in constant view, thriving and jovial, was the family of the pharmacist. He had every reason to be satisfied with his lot. Napoléon helped him in the laboratory, Athalie embroidered him a smoking cap, Irma cut paper circles to cover the jelly jars, and Franklin could recite the multiplication table without stumbling. Homais was the happiest of fathers, the luckiest of men.

Not quite, though! He was eaten with a secret ambition: he wanted the cross of the Legion of Honor. He had plenty of qualifications:

"*First:* during the cholera epidemic, was conspicuous for devotion above and beyond the call of professional duty. *Second:* have published at my own expense various works of public usefulness, such as . . ." (And he cited his treatise on *Cider: Its Manufacture and Its Effects:* also, some observations on the wooly aphis that he had sent to the Academy; his volume of statistics, and even his pharmacist's thesis.) "Not to mention that I am a member of several learned societies." (He belonged to only one.)

"And even suppose," he said with a caper, "that the only thing I had to my credit was my perfect record as a volunteer fireman!"

Homais proceeded to ingratiate himself with the powers that be; he secretly rendered great services to Monsieur le Préfet during an electoral campaign. In short he sold himself; he prostituted himself. He went so far as to address a petition to the sovereign in which he begged him to "do him justice": he called him "our good king" and compared him to Henri IV.

Every morning the apothecary rushed to the newspaper, hoping to find the news of his nomination, but it didn't come. Finally, in his impatience, he had a star-shaped grass plot designed for his garden, to represent the decoration, with two little tufts of greenery as the ribbon. He would walk around it, his arms folded, pondering on governmental stupidity and human ingratitude.

Out of respect, or to prolong the almost sensual pleasure he took in his investigations, Charles had not yet opened the secret compartment of the rosewood desk that Emma had always used. At last, one day, he sat down at it, turned the key and pressed the spring. All Léon's letters were there. No possible doubt, this time! He devoured every last one of them. Then he rummaged in every corner, every piece of furniture, every drawer, looked for hiding places in the walls: he was sobbing, screaming with rage, beside himself, stark mad. He came upon a box, kicked it open. Rodolphe's picture jumped out at him, and all the love letters spilled out with it.

Everyone was amazed at the depth of his depression. He no longer went out, had no visitors, refused even to call on his patients. Everyone said that he "locked himself up to get drunk."

Now and again someone more curious than the rest would peer over the garden hedge and would be startled at the sight of him, wild-eyed, long-bearded, clad in sordid rags, walking and weeping aloud.

Summer evenings he would take his daughter with him and go to the cemetery. They always came back after dark, when the only light in the square was in Binet's dormer.

Still, he was unable to savor his grief to the full, since he had no one with whom he could share it. From time to time he called on Madame Lefrançois, for the sole purpose of talking about "her." But the innkeeper listened to him with only one ear, having her troubles just as he had his: Monsieur Lheureux had finally established his transportation service, *Les Favorites du commerce,* and Hivert, who enjoyed a considerable reputation for his dependability as doer of errands, was demanding an increase in wages and threatening to go to work for her competitor.

One day, at the market in Argueuil, where he had gone to sell his horse—his last asset—he met Rodolphe.

Both men turned pale when they caught sight of each other. Rodolphe, who had merely sent his card with a message of condolence, began by stammering a few excuses; then he grew bolder, and even had the cheek (it was a very hot August day) to invite him to take a bottle of beer in a café.

Sitting opposite him, his elbows on the table, he chewed his cigar as he talked; and Charles was lost in revery as he looked into the face that she had loved. In it, he felt, he was seeing something of her. It was a revelation. He would have liked to be that man.

Rodolphe talked farming, livestock, fertilizers—making use of banalities to stop up all the gaps through which any compromising reference might creep in. Charles wasn't listening. Rodolphe became aware of this; and in the play of expression on Charles's face he could read the sequence of his thoughts. Gradually it grew crimson; Charles's nostrils fluttered, his lips quivered; at one point, filled with somber fury, he stared fixedly at Rodolphe, who in his fright stopped speaking. But almost at once the other man's features reassumed their habitual expression of mournful weariness.

"I don't hold it against you," he said.

Rodolphe sat speechless. And Charles, his head in his hands, repeated, in a dull voice, with all the resignation of a grief that can never be assuaged:

"No, I don't hold it against you, any more."

And he added a bit of rhetoric, the only such utterance that had ever escaped him:

"No one is to blame. It was decreed by fate."

Rodolphe, who had been the instrument of that fate, thought him very meek indeed for a man in his situation—comical, even, and a little contemptible.

The next day Charles sat down on the bench in the arbor. Rays of light came through the trellis, grape leaves traced their shadow on the gravel, the jasmine was fragrant under the blue sky, beetles buzzed about the flowering lilies. A vaporous flood of love-memories swelled in his sorrowing heart, and he was overcome with emotion, like an adolescent.

At seven o'clock little Berthe, who hadn't seen him all afternoon, came to call him to dinner.

She found him with his head leaning back against the wall, his eyes closed, his mouth open; and there was a long lock of black hair in his hands.

"Papa! Come along!" she said.

She thought that he was playing, and gave him a little push. He fell to the ground. He was dead.

Thirty-six hours later Monsieur Canivet arrived, summoned by the apothecary. He performed an autopsy, but found nothing.

When everything was sold, there remained twelve francs and fifteen centimes—enough to pay Mademoiselle Bovary's coach fare to her grandmother's. The old lady died the same year; and since Monsieur Rouault was now paralyzed, it was an aunt who took charge of her. She is poor, and sends her to work for her living in a cotton mill.

Since Bovary's death, three doctors have succeeded one another in Yonville, and not one of them has gained a foothold, so rapidly and so utterly has Homais routed them. The devil himself doesn't have a greater following than the pharmacist: the authorities treat him considerately, and public opinion is on his side.

He has just been awarded the cross of the Legion of Honor.